Mike Brooks was born in Ipswich, England, and moved to Nottingham to study at Nottingham Trent University and never left.

He started to write stories and novels in childhood, has worked for a homeless charity since 2004, and when not working or writing he goes walking in the Peak District, sings and plays guitar in a punk band, and DJs wherever anyone will tolerate him.

He is married, and has two cats and two snakes.

MIKE BROOKS

DARK RUN

DEL REY

1 3 5 7 9 10 8 6 4 2

Del Rey, an imprint of Ebury Publishing
20 Vauxhall Bridge Road,
London SW1V 2SA

Penguin
Random House
UK

Del Rey is part of the Penguin Random House group of companies
whose addresses can be found at global.penguinrandomhouse.com

First published in the UK in 2015 by Del Rey

www.eburypublishing.co.uk

A CIP catalogue record for this book is available from the British Library

ISBN 9780091956646

Typeset in 11.25/13.25pt Sabon LT Std by
Palimpsest Book Production Limited, Falkirk, Stirlingshire

Printed and bound by Clays Ltd, St Ives plc

Penguin Random House is committed to a sustainable future for our
business, our readers and our planet. This book is made from Forest
Stewardship Council® certified paper.

MIX
Paper from
responsible sources
FSC
www.fsc.org   FSC® C018179

To Spike the cat, my dedicated writing buddy.
Thanks for the cuddles, the purring, and for not
trying to eat the laptop's power cable *that* often.

DROWNING BEND

Randall's Bar was at least a mile beneath the rocky surface of Carmella II and had all the inviting ambience of an open sewer. The sign over the door was simple neon tubes rather than a holo projection, the lightpool table inside was glitching and the air had the thin, sour quality which suggested it had already passed through too many lungs. It was populated by a dozen men and half as many women sharing little but the lean, dangerous look of overworked and underfed Undersiders, in various stages of inebriation but all seemingly determined to get deeper into their cups. He'd known better than to even think of asking Randall for a beer, and so was instead nursing a smeared glass tumbler containing a clear liquid which could have passed for paint stripper had its taste been a little more refined.

He had been in less inviting premises of his own

volition, but right now he was struggling to recall more than one or two.

'Hey!'

The thin, reedy voice was that of a kid.

'Hey, mister!'

There was no indication he was being addressed. He didn't turn around, just kept his head low and his concentration on the glass of spirits in his hand. Then, inevitably, there was a tugging on the back of his armavest.

'Hey, mister! Are you Ichabod Drift?'

Drift sighed and looked up at his reflection in the mirror behind the bar: sharp-boned features, shoulder-length hair dyed a shocking violet and kept out of his eyes with a black bandana, skin a golden brown which had everything to do with parentage and nothing to do with the minimal amount of time it had ever been exposed to a star's ultraviolet radiation. He rotated on his stool and absent-mindedly reached up a hand to scratch at the skin around his mechanical right eye as it focused on the kid with a whirring of lenses.

Overlarge mining goggles stared blankly back at him over a dirty face topped by blondish stubble which, combined with the pitch of the voice and a near-shapeless one-piece overall – probably a cast-off from an older sibling – meant Drift wasn't entirely sure whether it was male or female. He essayed a grin, the same winning smile which had worked him into beds and out of trouble more times than he could count (and when money was as large a part of your life as it was for Ichabod Drift, you had to be able to count pretty damn high).

'*Sí, soy yo,*' he said agreeably, 'but who might you be? Kind of young for a Justice, aren't you?' Not that the Justices would be looking for him right now; apart from anything else, Ichabod Drift wasn't an outlaw . . . exactly. He was, as old Kelsier used to say, 'of interest'. Exactly how much interest, and to whom, rather depended on what had happened recently and if he had a suitable alibi for where he'd been at the time.

'You the guy what killed Gideon Xanth?' the kid asked. Drift felt the gloom of the bar take on a sudden watchful flavour. Xanth's Wild Spiders gang had been a menace for the last eighteen standard months over three sectors of the semi-lawless honeycomb of underground passages, caverns and former mineshafts which made up the so-called Underside of the moon named Carmella II by the United States of North America. Drift had personally heard three different variants of the tale of how he and his partner had taken the Spiders down, then dragged Gideon's corpse back to the Justices' office in High Under to collect the handsome bounty posted on his scarred (and partially missing) head.

'That was a way from here,' he said, casually adjusting his weight so he was facing not only his youthful interrogator but the door as well, and letting his right hand idly drop into the general region of the holstered pistol at his hip. 'I'm amazed word has spread so far, so soon. Where'd you hear that piece of news from?'

'There's a gang o' men just come into town,' the kid piped, 'and they was asking about if anyone had seen Ichabod Drift, the Mexican what killed

Gideon Xanth. Said they'd give ten bucks for whoever told 'em where he was.'

'I see,' Drift said, a grim sense of unease stirring in his gut. Not that he hadn't been expecting this, but nonetheless . . . Something must have shown on his face, because the kid suddenly darted back out of arm's length and scuttled for the door, as though worried that he (or possibly she) was about to be forcibly restrained from collecting the promised reward.

'Hey!' Drift shouted after the retreating shape. 'Did you get a name from any of 'em?'

'Only from the big guy,' came the reply, nothing but a begoggled head now visible poking back around the door jamb. Drift raised his eyebrows and motioned with his hand to suggest that maybe the kid should quit stalling.

'He said his name was Gideon Xanth.'

Then the head disappeared, leaving nothing behind but the swinging saloon door and a sudden atmosphere of expectation so tense Drift could practically taste it. Unless that was the bile.

'Well, shit,' he remarked to no one in particular, and slid off his stool to land his booted feet on the dusty floor. With the entire bar's eyes on him he ostentatiously straightened his armavest, adjusted his bandana, checked his pistols and then strode towards the door. Bruiser, the ageing but still massive bouncer, nodded to him on his way past.

'You sure you wanna go out there, Drifty?'

'Just a simple misunderstanding, I'm sure,' Drift replied with a confidence he didn't feel. Bruiser's forehead added some wrinkles to the lines already weathered into it as he regarded the scene outside.

'Don't look too simple from where I'm standing.'

'Oh, I don't know,' the Weasel piped up from next to him. Weasel was short and scrawny, and his job at Randall's Bar was to look after anything Bruiser confiscated from customers – which basically boiled down to any firearm larger than a pistol, as only a fool would enter a Carmellan drinking den completely unarmed – and then return it to them as they left, guided by his perfect memory. 'I'd say Gideon not actually being dead is pretty simple, really.'

'Depends on your point of view,' Drift replied, and sauntered out into what passed for Drowning Bend's town square. The chemical tang of the leak in the nearby industrial outflow lingered in the air, burrowing into his nasal passages again now he was what passed for outside once more, while far above in the solid rock of the curved habdome roof the lights were churning out steady, reliable illumination. Which was a little unfortunate in some respects; a few shadows to hide in would be rather convenient right about now.

The Wild Spiders were in the square. And sitting in his personal, custom-made, six-legged mechanical walker, the padded seat upholstered in what was rumoured to be genuine cowhide, was the imposing shape of Gideon Xanth.

Ichabod Drift had a momentary thought that maybe he'd just turn and head the other way, but then a shout went up. He'd been seen.

'*Drift!*' Xanth bellowed, his voice a basso roar. He flicked something large and shiny off his thumb, and Drift caught sight of the juvie diving to catch the promised ten-buck piece before fleeing into a side alley.

'*Hola*, Gideon!' Drift called back, settling his hands just over his guns. Two of them, at least; his backup was tucked in the small of his back under his belt. 'You're looking well!'

'Looking well for a dead man, you mean?' the gang leader snarled. 'Boys, cover Mister Drift for me, would you?'

At least a dozen weapons of varying calibre and roughly equal deadliness snapped up to point straight at Drift, which did nothing positive for his levels of either calmness or perspiration.

'That's better,' Xanth said, doing something with the controls in front of him and sending his walker clanking forwards while the Wild Spiders advanced on either side, their guns still trained and disappointingly steady. 'Boys, we all know that Mister Drift is a fast draw and a fine shot, so if he starts looking twitchy then feel free to ventilate him for me before he gets any ideas into his head.

'Now, Drift.' The big gang leader's scarred visage frowned as he looked down from his elevated seat. 'I'm sitting there in a bar in Low Under, minding my own business, when I hear me some surprising news. Seems that I'm dead, and that you're to blame.'

'Opinions vary on whether it was me who pulled the trigger on you,' Drift replied, trying not to let his eyes stray around too much.

'Ah yes,' Xanth nodded. 'Your partner. It must have taken some balls to front up to the lawmen in High and claim you'd killed me, knowing that if your lie were found out then they'd string you up. Even *bigger* balls actually, given that you surely knew I'd hear and would want to disabuse people of the notion o' my demise. And given I know that deep down you're a cowardly lickspittle, Drift, it must've been your partner what came up with the plan.'

The theatrically conversational tone in his voice, pitched to carry to the observers behind door jambs and peeking out through curtains all around, abruptly disappeared. What was left was the verbal equivalent of a knife, bare and sharp and about as friendly. 'Where's the bitch, Drift?'

'That's no way to talk about a lady,' Drift shrugged.

He didn't even see the blow coming. He was simply aware of Xanth doing something with his hand, and then one of the spider-walker's metal legs lashed up and knocked him backwards some six feet, leaving him sprawling in the dirt.

'Not talking about a lady, Drift,' Xanth growled. 'I know ladies. I've met 'em, dined 'em and bedded 'em. Even loved one, once upon a time. I'm talking about that bitch you run with, who ain't no more of a lady than I am. Where's Tamara Rourke?'

There were a few seconds of uneasy silence, while Drift tried to get his breath back and disguise the fact that, by propping himself up on one elbow his right hand was once more straying close to the butt of a pistol. However, he was saved having to answer by the appearance of a small red dot on Xanth's left temple.

'Here.'

Drift risked a look to his right. There, Crusader 920 rifle raised to her shoulder and trained on Gideon Xanth as she walked steadily forwards, was Rourke. She was short and slight, dressed in a dark green bodysuit which would have merely emphasised the boyish nature of her figure had it not been drowned in the billowing depths of a long coat. Her hat was pulled low, and her eyes glinted in her dark-skinned face as she flicked her gaze along the length of the Wild Spiders' line. Half of them switched their aim to cover her, but they weren't fool enough to start firing when she had a bead on their boss. Tamara Rourke's reputation as a deadshot was well-earned.

'Rourke, you shouldn't be as loyal as you are,' Xanth snarled. The gang leader wasn't even pretending to be conversational now there was a weapon pointing at his head, which Drift couldn't really fault him for. 'Might be you could've got outta this hole while we were busy with this worm, but you had to come sticking your nose in again.'

'You'd only have chased me down anyway,' Rourke retorted, somehow managing to shrug without losing her aim. 'Could say the same about you, though. You were reported as dead to the authorities. You could have given up terrorising war widows and extorting merchants and crawled off to a retirement somewhere with the money you stole. You wouldn't have been the first.'

'And maybe I woulda done that,' Xanth growled, 'gone off and laughed up my sleeve at the Justices while I was spending my money, but there's some things you don't let lie. One thing would be the two of *you* claiming that you killed *me*.' His scarred face set into an expression of murderous hatred. 'The other is that you needed a body to claim that bounty, and there was only one man this side of the surface who was as big as me. You bastards killed my boy Abe, and dragged his corpse to those scum-suckers in High Under.'

'Told you we should've shaved a dead bear and put it in a coat,' Drift remarked, looking sidelong at his partner.

'The import costs would've swallowed the bounty,' Rourke replied evenly.

'Shut up, you!' one of the Spiders snapped at her, trying to aim his shotgun even more emphatically. Drift attempted to match him against the descriptions circulated of Xanth's known associates, and failed. Either a relatively new recruit, then, or simply someone no one had ever bothered to identify.

'Or you'll do what?' Rourke demanded. 'One of you so much as sneezes, Gideon here's missing his head.'

'You think I care about that?' Xanth roared. '*You killed my boy!* You can shoot me, but the two of you ain't leaving here alive!'

Had it been Ichabod Drift on the other end of that firearm, he would have said something snappy. Something memorable. Something that anyone who'd heard it would have been forced to repeat so the story would have grown in the telling, and listeners would have been astounded at his wit in a dangerous situation.

Of course, that would have given the Spiders a second or so of warning, and Tamara Rourke had never been a gambler. As a result, the moment the last syllable signing their death warrant had left Gideon Xanth's lips, the Crusader barked once and half of the big man's skull exploded sideways in a shower of blood, bone and displaced neurones.

The Wild Spiders, crucially, hesitated for half a second. They were gang fighters and used to bullying barkeeps, extorting tolls from travellers or engaging in piecemeal shootouts with others like themselves, preferably when they had a numerical advantage. The notion of a lone woman casually shooting their leader dead was completely alien to them.

As a result, none of them reacted in time.

Drift hauled his pistols out and started blazing away; he saw two Spiders drop from hits of some sort, but then he had to roll desperately aside as Xanth's bulk slumped forwards onto the controls of his walker and sent the gyroscopically stabilised machine stamping forwards, directly towards him. His weren't the only shots to ring out, however; a hailstorm of fire exploded from the buildings around them, with the suddenly exposed Spiders at its centre. Several of the gang started shooting back, but their misguided attempt at making a stand came to an abrupt end when a whistling noise heralded the arrival of a shell which detonated on the back of one of their number. Virulent orange flames licked up instantly, and the splash from the blast set alight the clothing and flesh of two more.

Some spatters of volatile gel landed mere inches from Drift and he scrambled away from them, cursing Micah as he did so. The immolation cannon carried by the former soldier was far from a precise weapon; it was, however, a devastatingly effective one. As the howling, burning gang member's futile attempt at flight was cut short by a merciful bullet to the head from someone somewhere, the surviving gang members not currently flailing at flames on their own bodies hurriedly threw down their guns and thrust their hands determinedly into the air.

The shooting stopped. Drift got back to his feet, holstered his guns and dusted himself down. He caught sight of one of the Spiders glowering at him.

'What?'

'Everyone said your crew'd left you!' the man accused, his tone one of a six-year-old being told that there was no pudding after all. 'You was meant to have stiffed them on a share of the bounty!' Figures were emerging from the buildings around them; Micah still covering the cowed gangers with the intimidating mouth of his weapon, Apirana's rifle looking like a toy in his huge hands, the Chang siblings carrying pistols like they might even know how to use them and, alongside them, the half-dozen black-clad and mirror-visored Justices with whom they'd planned this whole sting.

'Well,' Drift sighed, 'I guess that's what you get for listening to rumours.'

The Velvet Lounge was a somewhat more upmarket affair than Randall's. For one thing, the spirits came out of branded bottles and didn't taste like more than two glasses would send you blind for a week. For another, it had actual upholstery instead of bare boards, although you'd need a thing for velvet to consider it tasteful. And for a third, instead of being buried deep in the warren of tunnels beneath the crust of Carmella II, it was on the surface, actual stars visible in the sky alongside the winking lights of the atmo-scrapers which towered around them like some sort of glittering fungal growths. Jenna McIlroy kept finding her eyes drawn to them as they flashed in her peripheral vision, occasionally mixed with the running lights of some cargo freighter or passenger liner. She tried to stop herself from wondering what the ships were, where they came from, what their purpose was. There was too much galaxy for her guesses to be anything but wild, and it was a good way to make herself paranoid.

'You'd have thought they'd have made the atmo safe by now,' Apirana Wahawaha opined in his curiously soft-mouthed, lilting Maori accent, nursing his solitary beer and scratching the dark whorls of the *tā moko* on his cheek. 'Big A' was without doubt the most immediately intimidating member of the crew of the *Keiko*, the jack-of-all-trades interstellar freighter which had been Jenna's home for the last four standard months; he was huge in many ways, from build to voice to personality, and the tribal tattoos which covered much of his skin lent him an alien air to Jenna's eyes, even out in this galaxy of wonders. However, he rarely drank alcohol and never had more than one even when he did, so he sipped quietly and slowly. 'Seeing the stars is all well an' good, but I like to take a walk outside every now an' then, know what I mean?'

'Last I heard, they're still working on it,' Ichabod Drift replied. In stark contrast to the virtually teetotal Maori, the *Keiko*'s whip-thin captain was a third of the way down a bottle of whisky and showing little sign of slowing. 'There are plants out there now, or something. Stars only know how long it will take to get it so we can breathe, though.'

'They won't be trying too hard,' Micah van Schaken put in, taking a pull from the tall glass containing the Dutch lager which he swore was the finest in the galaxy, despite the rest of the crew's repeated assertions that it tasted like thin piss. 'Once a person gets outside he gets all these ideas of being free, and that plays merry hell for a government.' He nodded firmly.

'Keep a man inside behind steel walls and thick windows, tell him that what you do, it's for his own protection. Make him think he relies on you, let him think the prison is his home, and he'll thank you for it.'

'You're a fountain of light and cheer, d'you know that?' Drift grinned at him, his silver tooth shining in the white of his smile.

The former soldier just clucked his tongue. 'You can laugh, but I've seen what freedom does to a man. Kills him, like as not.' He trailed off and stared at his drink, seemingly fascinated by the rising bubbles.

What does he see there? Jenna wondered. *Antiaircraft fire? Blood spatters?* Humanity's expansion across the galaxy had not been the expansion into a peaceful utopia the idealists might have hoped. Once away from the First Solar System there were few laws to constrain people, and those rare planets or planet-sized moons which boasted atmospheres habitable to Earth-raised organisms without extensive terra-forming were valuable in the extreme.

It was small wonder unofficial wars over viable agriworlds or mineral-rich moons had been bloody, with all sides sending in troops, under blanket declarations of *protecting our interests*. Micah had once been part of the Europan Commonwealth Frontier Defence Unit but had apparently grown weary of spilling blood to make anyone richer but himself. He was far from the only former soldier to have come to that conclusion, and Jenna couldn't blame any of them.

'You think freedom's so bad? Try the alternative sometime,' Jia Chang said pointedly. The Red Star

Confederate was one of the more heavily authoritarian interstellar governmental conglomerates, and Jia and her brother Kuai made no secret of their desire to earn enough money to move their parents out of Chengdu on Old Earth. The *Keiko* apparently hadn't been to that many Red Star systems, since Drift's Mandarin was poor and his Russian not much better, but by all accounts legitimate shipping was so heavily regulated it was virtually impossible to get work as an independent contractor. And the shadier types of employment were, if anything, even more tightly controlled by the gang bosses.

'They'll green this world if they can,' Tamara Rourke said firmly. She nodded at the looming shadow of Carmella Prime, the mighty gas giant visible as a blue-green crescent through a couple of the higher windows. 'Most of this place would get enough light for crops to grow even with the orbit cycle, and the chance of an agriworld is too good to pass up.'

Micah just grunted. The dour Dutchman had a tendency to do that, Jenna had noticed; give his opinion, then refuse to engage in subsequent debate. Then again, military service was unlikely to install much in the way of back-and-forth reasoning in a person, preferring instead the approach of 'Is it still moving? Shoot it again, then.' Which, to be fair, was what Micah was on the team for.

'So what's the plan now?' Jenna asked. She was the youngest and newest of the crew, and still keenly felt her junior status even if the others didn't really treat her like it.

She'd been in a bar on Franklin Major, desperately

trying to find a way off-planet despite having nowhere near enough money for a fare, but her fruitless search for a ship prepared to take her on had turned into an apparent attempt to drown herself in alcohol instead with what little cash she had.

She didn't remember the evening well, but it seemed that at some point she'd ended up talking to Tamara Rourke and had dragged the older woman outside to demonstrate her ability to hack her way through an electronic lock while apparently blind drunk. That trick had got her a berth with them (as well as nearly bringing down the local law enforcement on their heads, but it seemed that Drift was willing to put that down to teething troubles), and so far she'd proved adept at accessing information they had no right to, patching them a new broadcast ident on the fly when they'd suddenly needed their ship to be something else, and finally fixing the bug which had been causing the holo-display to wobble like an shivering epileptic whenever anyone wasn't leaning on one side of the board. She couldn't shoot straight for love nor money, however, which was why she'd been left on board the planet-going skiff called the *Jonah* during the crew's most recent escapade.

'The plan,' Drift said, sipping his whisky and pausing a moment to roll the smoky flavours around his mouth with what looked to be something approaching genuine pleasure, 'is to head back to the Justice offices tomorrow and see if there are any more tasty-looking bounties posted.'

'The same trick won't work twice,' Rourke warned. She'd removed her hat to reveal her close-cropped hair, a solid mass of black unbroken by any grey. No one seemed to know exactly how old Tamara Rourke was; not even Drift, who'd been running with her for the best part of eight years. Jenna suspected that she was well into her fifth decade, probably a few years older than the Captain, but her face could have belonged to someone twenty years either side of that depending on what sort of life they'd had, not to mention if they'd taken Boost to slow the ageing processes. That, combined with features which were more slightly delicate than overtly feminine, her boyish figure and a surprisingly deep voice, meant that if needed to she had a fairly good chance of passing for a male. Although Rourke had never said anything, Jenna had the faint ghost of a memory and a rather stronger sense of worry that she'd actually made her first contact with the *Keiko*'s crew by drunkenly trying to chat 'him' up.

'Don't be negative,' Drift chided his partner with a clucking noise of his tongue and a wagging finger. 'Think of what we could earn here! I mean, take the money we made today.' He checked items off. 'We made enough to fix the grav-plate on the cargo bay Heim generator, redo the heat shields on the *Jonah*, refuel, and still have some left over for a few drinks. For one day's work!'

'A day's work which could have got us both killed,' Rourke said flatly. Jenna was still learning the minute variations in the older woman's expressions, which were the only indication whether she was being dryly deadpan or deadly serious. Usually, as now, she played it safe and assumed serious. Apirana said he'd seen Rourke laugh once, but Jenna wasn't sure she believed him.

'Everything was completely under control,' Drift insisted, raising a glass with one of his dazzling grins. He was the natural showman of the pair, the carnival barker to Rourke's quartermaster. By the time people realised that they should have been paying attention to the slight, dark figure in the background they'd usually been scammed, bluffed or violently inconvenienced. 'Here's to doing the law's work for them!'

'I reckon we're about done here,' Apirana disagreed. 'Grabbing a few small fry an' then taking Xanth down, that's one thing. Ain't no one gonna be welcoming us now our names are known, though. Xanth was easy to find. Smaller marks won't be; anyone who knows anythin'll clam up, an' then we're no better off than the Justices. Worse, because they've got authority and we've got nothing except guns.'

'Guns can work,' Micah said.

'Only if we wanna break the law ourselves,' Apirana pointed out acidly. Micah just shrugged and returned his attention to his lager: so far as the mercenary was concerned, violence was a language everyone understood.

'I'm enjoying being on the *right* side of the law,' Kuai put in, fingering the dragon talisman which hung around his throat. He didn't add 'for once', but then he barely needed to. Drift and Rourke's approach to the laws of the various governments across the galaxy had always been one of convenience over obedience.

'Because you do so much dangerous work in that engine room,' Jia snorted. She tapped herself firmly on the chest. '*I* judge the radar shadows, dodge security craft, hug a freighter's drive cone to mask our emission trail, risk frying us all in the backwash, plot the jumps between systems—'

'And if *you* get it wrong *I* still get arrested or killed,' Kuai pointed out.

'Whiner.'

'Just saying, I prefer when there's less risk of death or prison, I don't think that's—'

'*Cállate*,' Drift sighed, and the Chang siblings obediently fell silent. He tipped another two fingers of whisky into his glass, sniffed, sipped, then set it down on the table again. 'Tomorrow morning I'll go back to the Justices' office and see if there's anything which looks feasible and worth our time. If there is, we Do Some Good and get paid for it. If not . . .' He shrugged. 'We'll see what our options are.'

There was a definite social strata on many of the mining and ex-mining worlds Drift had been to, and indeed 'strata' was the most accurate word for it. The government offices and the rich, well-to-do and well-connected lived on the surface. Even when the surface didn't yet have a breathable atmosphere, like on Carmella II, hermetically sealed mansions, atmo-scrapers and government office buildings with their faux-Gothic cladding still sprawled in a mess of money and authority, interconnected by a web of elevated pedestrian walkways. Meanwhile, airtight buggies and crawlers drove between ground-level airlocks, tracks and tyres kicking up clouds of dust and dirt into the . . . carbon dioxide, or nitrogen, or whatever the air outside was currently composed of. Drift wasn't sure and didn't really care; if he tried to breathe it then he'd suffocate and that was all he really needed to know.

Below ground, though, people got poorer. Once a mineshaft had been stripped of whatever the locally available mineral was, the company could make a second income by opening it, widening it and selling it on to a developer, who would put in basic prefab living quarters. In somewhere like Carmella II, where the crust had been plundered widely and deeply, there was a veritable honeycomb of passageways and chambers, and no shortage of people to fill them. This was despite the claustrophobic conditions and the dependence on electricity not just for luxuries but for simple survival: the Air Rent scandals of fifty years ago might have been a thing of the past, but if the atmospheric seals failed or the pumps died then the whole shaft could still be at risk of asphyxiation.

'Why would anyone choose to live down there?' Jenna asked, fiddling absent-mindedly with the chunky metal bracelet she always wore on her right forearm and nodding towards one of the maglift platforms which led down into the Underside. They were standing in the brightly lit access hall – a cavernous building almost the size of an aircraft hangar – and watching people bustling to and fro: miners, Justices, cleaners, office personnel and others with less obvious roles and purposes.

'There's not many that do,' Drift replied easily. He was slightly hung-over, but the afterbuzz of yesterday's successful job was keeping him from feeling too sorry for himself. That and the sizeable bounty they'd netted: Gideon Xanth on his own had been worth fifty thousand USNA dollars, although their cut had been reduced since they'd been working with the Justices. Even so, he winced slightly as a growling six-wheeler headed towards one of the larger, vehicle-only shafts with a throbbing roar which seemed to reverberate off the inside of his skull. 'But mining doesn't pay that well, and if you want to save up enough to get off this rock then you need to keep your living costs down. It's cheap down there, and that's the truth.'

'Cheap and grim,' Jenna muttered. Drift allowed himself a smile. Jenna had been guarded about her history but he was fairly certain she'd originally come from either Franklin Major, where they'd taken her on, or its sister planet Franklin Minor. Both had needed little in the way of terraforming to be surface habitable and so were occupied almost exclusively by the middle classes or higher, barring the service staff such well-offs always needed. The odds were good that Jenna came from a monied background, and Drift couldn't help wondering if it was high-level tutoring or teenage rebelliousness which had led her to becoming quite so expert with tech.

'You should see it lower down,' he told her. 'There's less lights and the air's even worse. Down there, you get the shadow communities.'

Jenna looked sideways at him. 'The *what*?'

Drift grinned. He was quite enjoying showing Jenna the galaxy, but couldn't help taking some amusement from her lack of knowledge of some parts of it; it seemed the news holos on the United States of North America's more affluent planets glossed over a lot of the more insalubrious details.

'You know, the people who scratch out a living

from the spoil heaps, or the little bits of mineral vein the mining companies didn't think were worth their time.' He tucked his thumbs into his gunbelt, warming to his theme. 'Yup, that's a place where names aren't given and histories aren't questioned, and you might be lucky to even wake up tomorrow morning, depended on how careful you've been about where you went to sleep. That's where the worst sort of criminal hides out, you know. Of course, if you *do* wake up then you could decide to be someone else entirely.' He stole a sideways glance at her. 'It's not entirely different to the *Keiko*, in that respect.'

'You think we have the worst sort of criminal on board?' Jenna asked, affecting a shocked expression.

'That's not what I meant, and you know it,' Drift grinned. 'Although if you define "worst" as "very bad at it" then Micah might qualify.' He sighed contentedly. 'No, that's one of the great things about being alive now. There's always room to be someone else, and there's always somewhere people will be willing to let the past slide.'

He waited, but Jenna merely nodded soberly and didn't suddenly volunteer any backstory to her life, which disappointed Drift a little. The *Keiko*'s rule that you didn't ask about another crew member's history was only unwritten because he was certain no one would bother to read it, but he at least had an idea of what had brought most of the others together.

Rourke was the same enigma she'd always been, of course, despite running with him for the longest time. It had only been a year or so after joining forces that the pair of them had bailed a then-teenaged Jia out of a Shanghai jail on Old Earth. She'd been on a charge of joyriding a shuttle, and he and Rourke had felt strongly that someone with such obvious natural talent shouldn't be left to rot. The fact that they'd used false identities to do so was by-the-by, as was the fact that they'd jumped her bail the very next day with her brother hired as mechanic.

Apirana had been an ex-con and former gang member looking to go straight: Drift sometimes felt guilty about hiring him as muscle on their ship of questionable repute, but the big Maori had always been grateful so he figured it wasn't that much of a problem. Micah was a more recent addition and had only been with them for about two years. He hadn't talked much about his past in the FDU, but Drift would have put good money on the mercenary's face being on desertion papers somewhere. Jenna, however, was a puzzle. What would make a rich girl who might have just about hit twenty get blind drunk and leave her comfortable home with its breathable atmosphere to enlist with a bunch of ne'er-do-wells?

Normally, Drift would have idly seduced her to get her to talk about it, but to his surprise he'd realised over the last couple of months that although Jenna was pretty he wasn't attracted to her. Even more shockingly, *she* didn't seem attracted to *him*. Instead he'd found himself playing a combined role of tour guide and teacher, and feeling . . . protective.

He must be getting old.

'Well,' he said, when it became clear that the girl

wasn't going to confide exactly why she'd joined them, 'I'd best get on. Don't let Kuai spend all our money on parts, you hear me? I don't want him going to town, we just need what's essential.'

'He says it's *all* essential,' Jenna replied, rolling her eyes. 'Don't worry; if he gets uppity I'll just beat him up.'

'Atta girl,' Drift laughed. He fought down an urge to ruffle her hair, and clapped her on the shoulder instead. 'I'll be back at the *Jonah* in an hour or so. See you then.'

'Have fun,' Jenna grinned, and turned to make her way towards where their engineer was waiting with what might have been impatience. Not that Drift was particularly bothered; for all of Micah's abrasiveness and Jia's arrogance, Kuai's needling passive-aggressiveness was the most tiresome personal trait of any crew member. Still, the man was good enough at his job to make it a price worth paying.

Drift took a deep breath to try to clear his head of the hangover fuzziness and walked over to the nearest pedestrian maglift platform with an undeniable spring in his step. He might not be rich at this precise moment but he was at least well-resourced, and that would make it easier to *get* rich.

The fact that he'd been trying to get rich without much notable long-term success for the last twenty years wasn't really anything he felt like worrying about right now.

The platform, a rectangle of scuffed metal plates, started its smooth descent into the shaft; a far quicker and more direct route than the meandering tunnels dug by the miners as they chased down seams.

Sliding doors flowed together above, but the many small lights in the walls threw illumination over Drift and his fellow passengers: two Justices, rifles slung so they could be accessed quickly but leaving a hand free for the shock sticks at their sides, perhaps going to take up shift at the station below; a small woman in a niqab, her left thumb dancing over the remote operating the datalens which obscured her left eye, brows occasionally lowering into view as she tutted quietly and frowned at whatever she was seeing; a gaggle of teenagers, loudly dressed in clothes which flashed corporation logos brightly enough to challenge the lights around them, the images and slogans crawling across their shoulders on the microweaves just beneath the transparent surface layer; half a dozen miners, destined for some far-off tunnel where the machines still roared and chewed; over in the corner, three hard-looking men who tried to watch the Justices without making it obvious, while radiating an aura even the teenagers seemed to recognise and respect.

Drift kept his eyes fixed somewhere on the floor and listened as hard as he could. The maglift was virtually silent in operation, and he wanted to hear any cough, mutter, whisper or rustle of movement which might indicate that the trio had figured him to be the man who'd taken Gideon Xanth down in Drowning Bend, but he didn't want to look at them for exactly the same reason as they weren't looking at the Justices. Thankfully, it seemed they were concentrating too hard on looking innocent to pay much attention to him.

The maglift glided to a halt in High Under and

the security doors slid back, allowing them to exit the shaft. Everyone except the miners and the trio Drift had pegged as dangerous disembarked, the light from behind them casting their own shadows forwards as they emerged into the comparative gloom. Drift sniffed and grimaced slightly; the air 'upstairs' had the faint tang of purification after-effects but it still tasted cleaner than down here. He sucked down a lungful to get used to it again, then headed off after the receding shapes of the Justices who'd ridden the platform with him.

High Under was relatively affluent as Carmella II went, despite being below ground, but it was still one of the deepest Justice stations on this part of the moon; once you got much further from the surface the patrols started to thin and the response times were measured in days rather than minutes. Still, the pockets of deep shadow were rarer than the pools of illumination here, the stores sold virtually fresh produce shipped in from systems with agriworlds, and the locals gave the Justices he was following no more than a glance instead of challenging stares, or disappearing like cockroaches on a bathroom floor when the light was flicked on.

The two lawmen cut right into a side street, then as he rounded the corner after them they walked through the mirrored double doors which looked almost like a giant representation of a Justice's visor (Drift had never worked out if that was intentional or not, but either way it reminded him of a ghost train he'd ridden on as a kid where you went through the mouth of a skull at the start). He slowed his step slightly to let the doors stop swinging – Ichabod Drift didn't follow Justices like a puppy, he was his own man and would be seen to enter in his own time – then strode boldly up to them and pushed the right-hand one open without a break in his stride.

That was the plan, anyway. As it turned out the door was stiffer than he remembered, so he had to slow to avoid walking his face right into it. Still, he didn't trip over and fall on said face or just end up pushing a 'pull' door, so he counted it as a sort-of win.

'Captain Drift,' Officer Morley greeted him from behind the counter, looking up. 'Brought in another menace to society already?' The mocking tone in her voice was playful, and totally negated by the slight grin; the Justices had, in general, been fairly impressed by Drift's willingness to play bait and with his crew's contribution to the efforts, and the bounty settlement had taken place without the usual twist of resentment as the clerk tried to work out whether he was paying one criminal for bringing in another.

'Am I not allowed a little time off?' Drift replied, spreading his hands in a gesture of faux apology and giving her his best smile. She was pretty, after all, even with a scar which cut down her left temple, and some Justices seemed to have a need for mindless sexual release which bordered on the pathological; what better candidate for such a liaison than a star-ship captain who would be in the next system by next week? No strings, little chance of anyone knowing and even less of him being revealed as a criminal, which would make such pastimes tricky among the terrestrial population. So long as he remained good at distinguishing the ones who wanted practicality above romance there was no reason why he and the law shouldn't scratch each other's backs in more ways than one, so to speak . . .

'Well, since it's you,' she grinned back at him. 'So, what brings you in here today then, if you're not after our money?'

He restrained himself from making some comment about the view; the last thing he wanted was to ruin a good working relationship with the Justices by putting someone's back up with some overambitious flirting. Instead he leaned casually on the counter and lowered his voice mock-conspiratorially.

'In all honesty, I am. I just need to see the other mark sheets so I know who to bring in.'

'Well, let's see what we can rustle up for you then, shall we?' Morley smiled. She tapped the inch-thick perspex to indicate that Drift should place his datapad in the docking port, then skated her fingers over the desktop interface in front of her when he obliged. A faint *ping* noise indicated the data transfer was complete, and Drift retrieved his pad to start cycling through the options.

'Anything juicy?' he asked, flicking through a few. Bail jumper, bail jumper, assault with a deadly weapon, extortion . . . He hadn't necessarily been expecting another payday on the level of Xanth, but these were looking like they'd be more trouble than they were worth, even if they weren't much trouble. No shortage of names, though; the space-time-compressing Alcubierre drive allowed starships to slip through a loophole in physics and travel faster than light but couldn't do anything to speed up radio signals, so news could only travel as fast as a person.

That meant a man could easily leave a system which had become too hot for him without finding an unwelcome reception at his destination, and the law was reduced to chasing people after the fact. Something Drift had taken advantage of on more than one occasion, as it happened.

'Are you a religious man, Captain Drift?'

He paused, and looked down at Officer Morley. Her smile was gone, and she was watching him carefully. He took refuge in honesty.

'Only when I think I'm about to die. Is that relevant?'

'Just wondered,' she replied, tapping a finger beside her right eye. 'In that case, try looking up Javier Morita.'

Puzzled, Drift tapped in the name, and blinked his one natural eye in surprise as a holo flickered up out of his datapad and began rotating. Rather than the flat, two-dimensional images representing the other profiles he'd been browsing through, this sort of detail was only available for someone well known and well documented. Quite apart from a list of offences which seemed to be based around getting other people to commit crimes for him, Morita appeared to have been the victim of a significant accident, judging by the amount of him which had been replaced by mechanical prosthetics. Either that, or . . .

'He's a circuithead,' Drift muttered, then his eyes caught up with the floating text and he inhaled sharply. 'Wait, a circuithead *Logicator*?'

Morley shrugged slightly, her expression largely non-committal with a side order of uneasy. 'Being a priest doesn't mean you can tell people to rise up against the government or burn someone else's church. Even when your god is made of metal and has flashing lights on it.'

'They don't think God is a machine, just that humanity should strive to be like one,' Drift muttered absently. Many people wouldn't replace a body part unless necessary. Others flaunted their 'upgrades' as status symbols, or viewed it as a form of body modification in a similar vein to tattooing and piercing. In the last few decades, however, the Universal Access Movement had appeared, and what had started as a campaign to get cheap, reliable prosthetics to the disabled or accident victims in poverty had morphed into an organisation which championed cybernetic replacements over the flesh and blood they viewed as inherently flawed. They'd been popularly relabelled as the Circuit Cult, despite their secular nature.

Something Morley had said clicked, and he looked up at her again. 'Oh, the eye? No, I'm not Circuit Cult; I lost that to a C-beam at the Tannhäuser Gate.'

Her face registered polite incomprehension.

'No one appreciates the classics anymore,' Drift muttered, half-embarrassed, and rallied with a smile. 'Thanks for the sheets, Officer; hopefully I'll be walking a few of them through your door before long.'

'My doors are always open for you, Captain,' she replied cheerfully, but there was a glint in her eye he was sure he recognised, and it didn't take a Carmellan miner to recognise there was something else beneath the surface.

He was poring over the mark sheets with half his brain, while the other half was wondering exactly how he could broach the possibility of a discreet adventure with Officer Morley and whether she'd bring her own cuffs, and as a result he didn't realise someone had fallen in beside him until they cleared their throat. He automatically shut the pad down with a reflexive stab of his thumb and turned to face the newcomer, becoming aware as he did so that someone had got behind him. No, some *two*, both of them large enough to loom into his peripheral vision.

'Captain Drift?'

He found himself staring down into the face of the small woman in the niqab from the maglift. The datalens was still in place over one eye, the display too tiny for him to see on the translucent screen, never mind that it was reversed. Both that eye and the uncovered one were studying him intently, however.

'Yes?' *Stupid, stupid, stupid. Mind on your surroundings, moron, not on getting laid.*

'I wonder if you would care to join my employer and I for a drink?' the woman asked. Drift cast a casual look over one shoulder and saw the unmistakeable gleam of cybernetics adorning the two sizeable humans arranged behind him. Circuitheads then, or augmented goons. Either way, given the mark sheets he'd just been handed, the omens weren't good. He could shoot her of course, but he'd have to drop his datapad before going for his other gun, and her thugs were close enough to shiv him before he could even turn to face them. He sighed.

'Can I just clarify something? Was that *actually* an invitation?'

He couldn't see the movement of the woman's mouth beneath her niqab, but he got the definite impression that it had pursed in mild annoyance.

'You're supposed to be a reasonably intelligent man, Captain. What do *you* think?'

THE OLD MAN

According to the letters scratched above the door, the bar was called 'The Hole'. Entry was through one of the rock walls which threaded between the streets of High Under, and then down a steep and poorly lit staircase. The woman led the way, one of her goons between her and Drift and the other bringing up the rear to ensure he didn't try to back out. All in all, Drift felt about as well trapped as he'd been for a long, long time.

The name proved to be appropriate. The interior looked to have been converted from some sort of communal washroom for miners, and combined the inhospitable, impersonal air of such a facility with a lack of anything approaching actual cleanliness. A row of showers had been ripped out and replaced with the bottles of spirits which must have been the source of the coarse tang in the air that clawed at his throat, the basic structure of the 'bar' itself looked to be surgical tables looted from some form of medical facility and lashed together, and the once-white tiles were darkened by smoke and a few suspicious stains.

In short, it was exactly the sort of place Drift made a habit of staying out of unless he had Apirana with him.

No one looked up as he entered which, given he had just followed a woman dressed in traditional Muslim clothing into a place where breathing practically constituted imbibing alcohol, told him everything he needed to know about how well practised the regulars were at ignoring anything which might surprise or inconvenience them. The barkeep looked up, of course, but no sooner had his eyes lit on the diminutive woman Drift was following than his gaze took on a sort of studious blankness. The woman herself glanced neither right nor left, instead making straight for the back of the bar to where there were a series of cubbyholes which could be cordoned off from the rest of the bar with something that could only be called a curtain because tea cloths weren't usually manufactured that large. She pulled one aside and ducked through without turning to see if he was following; Drift did, because he was very conscious of the two large, partially metal men at his back, but he was also conscious of the fact that no one had taken his weapons away yet.

As a result, it came as something of a disappointment to him to find a gun levelled between his eyes as he stepped through.

His moment of frozen uncertainty resolved itself into the woman calmly removing his pistols from their holsters, so he decided to put the best face on it he could and look like he'd expected nothing less. The weapon pointing at him was a stargun, a device which used a massive surge of electromagnetism to fire a razor-sharp disc perfectly capable of slicing through flesh and even bone. It had the advantage of being virtually silent barring a pulsing hum as it fired, which made it favoured by assassins and other stealthy operators.

This particular stargun was being held rock-steady by dark-skinned fingers, which his eyes followed up an arm to a nondescript male face; early thirties perhaps, dark hair, one gold ring in the left ear. A couple of minor keloids caught the light at the corner of one eye and faintly across the jawline, but there was nothing which would make this man stand out of most crowds on most worlds.

'You know, some time ago I swore an oath to myself that I would kill anyone who pointed a gun at me,' Drift said conversationally.

The man's expression didn't change. Drift felt his vest being hoicked up and his third pistol was removed from the small of his back, and his spirits sank a little further.

'Then I lost count of who'd done it, so I figured I'd just kill the ones I could remember,' Drift continued. How fast was this man? Holding a gun on someone at point-blank range was a mixed blessing, because they could potentially twist aside and reach you before you could correct your aim and pull the trigger. He looked into the man's eyes, and swallowed.

He looked like the sort of person who'd be quite fast.

'Ichabod, stop posturing,' a crackling voice reprimanded from behind the gunman. 'Marcus, he appears to be disarmed now. Feel free to let him sit, although if he takes leave of his senses and attacks me then by all means hurt him until he stops.'

Drift's mind was racing. That voice was familiar . . . but he also saw the faint narrowing of the gunman's eyes. Something about the instruction he'd just been given didn't sit well with him.

'I don't hurt people,' the man apparently called Marcus said, in a startlingly deep voice spiced with an accent Drift couldn't quite place. 'I kill people. You know that.'

'Well, consider it an opportunity to add to your résumé,' the voice said irritably, and with that second sentence the pieces suddenly dropped into place. Even as the man called Marcus moved to one side and lowered himself smoothly into a seat, Drift knew what he'd see.

He was older, of course; it had been over a decade, and new lines had appeared on his pale face while extant ones had deepened. The hair was thinner, and had faded to more grey than blond, but still fell in an untidy scraggle to his collar, which was a dark blue and as stiffly starched as ever. Other things had changed: one of his hands was mechanical now, perhaps as a result of arthritis. It was an expensive model, the chrome-and-brass fingers and slick servos marking it not as a cheap stainless steel fit for someone who couldn't afford a near-lifelike replacement, but chosen by a man who'd decided that if he was going to have his hand replaced by a machine then it was damn well going to be an aesthetically pleasing machine.

The voice was still largely the same, though; the faint rasp which hinted at a never-witnessed tobacco habit, a drawl dryer than a desert creek bed and the effortless, slightly weary ring of authority. And while the skin around the eyes might have become slightly more weathered, the eyes themselves hadn't changed; they were still an icy blue, lighter than any of the skies of Old Earth, and unwavering in their stare.

Drift suddenly felt naked, and not just because he'd been disarmed.

'Sit down, Ichabod,' the man said perfunctorily, gesturing with his mechanical hand. 'I apologise for the theatrics and the cloak-and-dagger bullshittery, but I've always been a cautious man, and I'm on something of a schedule. I needed to speak to you, here, now, and with no risk that you might respond to my unexpected appearance with panic and gunfire.' Drift hadn't moved, and a pale eyebrow quirked upwards. 'Have you developed some sort of sudden-onset paralysis, or are you deaf? Sit down, I can't be bothered to crane my neck up to look at you.'

Drift sank slowly onto a stool. 'Kelsier.'

The man's lips narrowed slightly, in what might have been the ghost of a smile. 'I seem to remember that during the years of our previous association I always had to remind you to call me "Mr Kelsier", not "Nicolas". You were younger; possibly more arrogant, although I'm not entirely sure of that. Certainly stupider.' He lifted a cup, and the unmistakeable aroma of tea wafted across the table. Tea. In a dingy bar underground on Carmella II, sitting on a bench seat upholstered in fabric mainly constructed of patches, Nicolas Kelsier was drinking tea. Drift found he was almost completely unsurprised. 'So now you've at least moved on to using my second name instead of the first, although the honorific appears to have slipped your attention,' the old man continued. 'No matter.'

'Why . . .' Drift found there were at least a dozen possible ways he could end this question, so went with '. . . are you *here*?'

'Because *you* are here,' Kelsier replied, taking a sip of his beverage and replacing the cup in its saucer with a faint *clink*. 'I need to employ you. Again.'

Drift felt a pit open up in his stomach. This had been on the cards from the moment he realised that Nicolas Kelsier was in front of him, but he'd been clinging to the faint possibility that . . . what? The old man had come here for a chat and a catch-up? No, he'd been deluding himself. *Self-delusion is the worst trait I can think of*, the man in front of him had said once, *because if you can fool yourself then every other bastard has the easiest job in the world.*

'I don't do that work anymore,' he said, proud of how level his voice was. He picked up a very faint tensing in the posture of the man called Marcus. Yes, he was on a hair trigger, there was no doubt about it. If anything, Kelsier's associates had gotten deadlier.

'I heard,' Kelsier said, a small smile tugging at one corner of his mouth. 'Death does tend to limit one's employability somewhat. And yet here you are! Nowhere near as dead as everyone thought and hoped.

Well,' he corrected himself, 'nearly everyone.' He took another sip of tea, set the cup down once more and waved a hand dismissively at Drift's stubborn expression. 'Oh, do relax and stop looking so constipated. *I* don't do that work anymore, either.'

'You don't?' Drift had always prided himself on his poker face in tense situations, but he couldn't stop the surprise from showing. The momentary relief which surged through him was almost instantly stabbed in the back by sudden doubts, however.

'You don't follow the news, do you?' Kelsier asked, somewhat rhetorically. 'Well, why should you? There's an awful lot of galaxy to cover, after all, and the departure of one old Europan politician is hardly going to get much airtime. Even when it was due to "corruption".' He made fingerquotes as he said the last word, burnished metal fingers moving in time with the slightly swollen-looking joints of his natural hand.

'"Corruption"?' Drift asked, mimicking his movement. Kelsier's smile turned wolfish.

'Well, they had to give some reason for me disappearing out of sight, didn't they?' He coughed, frowned, and took another sip of tea. 'Anyway, I *am* on a schedule. I'd ask how you've been, but you and I both know that's just meaningless window dressing when it comes to business, and if you've got any sense you'll realise that I knew enough about how you've been to track you down.' The icy blue eyes flickered up and speared Drift with their gaze.

'I need a smuggler.'

'Right . . .'

'More specifically,' Kelsier continued when it

became clear that Drift wasn't going to offer anything else, 'I need *you* to smuggle something for me.'

'Why me?'

'Because the word on, under, over and around the street is that you're damn good at it,' Kelsier replied simply. The grin returned for a second, fast as a shooting star, as he saw Drift's expression. 'I said, I'm in a different line of work now. I have different contacts in different areas. These people think that you're reliable, insofar as a thief-cum-smuggler-cum-merchant-cum-bounty-hunter-cum-goodness-knows-what-else can *be* reliable. Personally I'd be more inclined to wonder how many different hats your head can support, but then again this is *your* head we're talking about.' He sniffed. 'I need a cargo de-livered to an address in Amsterdam on Old Earth, at a certain time, on a certain day.'

'And you don't trust the mail service?' Drift asked dryly.

'You must evade all customs checks,' Kelsier continued, as though Drift hadn't spoken, 'and I mean *all*. It goes to the address at the right time on the right day, and no one so much as sees it apart from your crew until you hand it over.' He tutted. 'Don't look at me like that, Ichabod; yes, I'm smuggling something into Europa. I'm not a minister any longer, and while I do have some rather interesting new resources I don't have some of the ones I used to. If I could stick this cargo in a diplomatic vessel and get it taken to its destination I would, but I can't, so I need to do this the hard way. You'll need—'

'Don't you think you're jumping the gun a little bit here, Nicolas?' Drift interrupted him. The look on Kelsier's face was almost worth the indignity of his abduction off the street and being disarmed at gunpoint.

The old man's lips pursed. 'How so?'

'You said you wanted to employ me,' Drift said quietly. 'In fact, you said you *needed* to employ me.'

'You did good work for me before, at least until that unfortunate incident in the Ngwena System after which you apparently decided to quit,' Kelsier rasped, 'and my sources say that your ship and crew are capable of pulling this job off. What's the problem?'

'The problem is that I haven't agreed to it,' Drift replied, watching the man called Marcus carefully out of the corner of his eye. '*Employment* isn't the same as *slavery*, you know.'

Kelsier set his teacup down and steepled his fingers, metal digits interlocking with flesh, then looked at Drift over the top. Drift forced himself to return the stare.

'I know it's not the same,' Kelsier said, and his voice was suddenly ice-cold without even the dry humour remaining. 'I'll thank you not to try lecturing *me*. There are many ways I could persuade you of why you might *want* this job, Ichabod. First of all, and let's not ignore what we might call the elephant in the room, there's the fact that sitting on my left is a man whom I could tell to kill you and you'd be dead before you hit the ground. Even from a stool.'

The man called Marcus's lips twitched. Drift eyed him for half a second, then turned his attention back to Kelsier. Never watch the gun; watch the man holding the gun.

'Better men have tried and failed.'

'Better? I doubt it,' Kelsier replied crisply. He looked at Drift for a second, then sighed. 'Very well. Marcus?'

Marcus didn't move a muscle, but his face was abruptly replaced by a blaze of colour; a warped vision of a skull painted in a palette of violent, bilious neons by a tortured mind, dominated by a deranged, lopsided grin of blunt fangs. It lasted for perhaps half a second before fading, but it had succeeded in causing Drift's heart rate to rocket. It was an electat, a neurally activated sub-dermal tattoo: some gangs used them as membership badges, some governments used them as identity badges, some people used them to achieve the kind of body art which would be impractical or unwise to display all the time. This particular electat, however, was famous. Or notorious.

'The Laughing Man,' he muttered. Marcus Hall, the Laughing Man, gave a very slight nod. Ichabod Drift was looking at the most infamous hitman in the galaxy, a man wanted by every government conglomerate and with several personal bounties set on him by various corporations besides. Yet even with all that money hanging over his head, Hall remained alive and free, presumably because if you knew who and where the Laughing Man was, he probably knew who and where *you* were, and that was a gamble no one wanted to take. Besides which, Drift had long since decided that, despite the rewards, no government actually wanted to take this most notoriously skilled of assassins permanently out of the picture just in case they needed to employ him one day.

He swallowed, and turned back to Kelsier. 'If he kills me, I can't do the job for you.'

'If you aren't going to do the job anyway, what do I lose?' Kelsier shrugged. 'But let's dispense with that notion. I'm not going to lie and say you're like a son to me, Ichabod, but you were a solid if somewhat . . . aggravating . . . contractor in the past, for whom I developed something of a fondness. I'd prefer not to leave you in a pool of your own blood in a gin-soaked dive on a Carmellan moon, even to make a point. Shall we perhaps move on to more pleasant matters, like the opportunities I gave you?'

Drift eyed the old man warily. 'You're trying to guilt-trip *me*?'

'Far from it,' Kelsier sighed, 'but I don't think it's remiss of me to point out that without my intervention you would have gone to prison, and quite possibly still be rotting there to this day.'

'And that was such a selfless move on your part,' Drift snorted.

'Do you really want to sit here and squabble about motives?' Kelsier asked. 'You were stupid enough to commit a violent mutiny and then breeze into port without even taking the trouble to cover your tracks—'

'That's not how it happened,' Drift bit out, 'and you know it.'

'I know nothing of the sort,' Kelsier retorted, 'and it doesn't matter anyway. You had no evidence for your defence and were guilty in the eyes of the law. I made you an offer which would keep you free and flying, not to mention keeping you in charge of the ship you'd taken by force, and you accepted it.'

Drift grimaced. 'It's not like I had—'

'*You accepted it*,' Kelsier snapped. He sat back in his seat. 'I must admit, I never thought I'd see you without that ship, given how attached to it you proved to be. It must have killed you to abandon it like you did . . . although not literally, obviously,' he conceded, gesturing lazily with his mechanical hand.

Drift felt his teeth grinding together as Kelsier's smile turned slightly wicked. The man *knew* and he made *jokes* about it!

'I see that this isn't a line of persuasion which is going to work,' Kelsier acknowledged. 'You're a proud man and not that easily cowed, and I've been too long out of the public face of politics to talk bullshit and smile convincingly at the same time. So, where does that leave us?' He rubbed idly at a faint smear on the back of his metal hand. 'Money, I suppose. The job is, as I've mentioned, quite specific, and has a very narrow delivery window. It will take considerable expertise to get to the First System with enough time to get around all the security checks, but without lingering so long that someone catches up with you as you dawdle. It needs to be a swift in-and-out job; your speciality, or so I've heard.'

'If that's a slur on—'

'It's a slur on nothing unless you wish to take it as such,' Kelsier interrupted before he could finished his sentence. 'Don't be so protective about your cock, it's nowhere near as important as you think. You and your crew can do fast, time-critical shipping work where, shall we say, discretion is of the utmost import-ance. Is that correct?'

'Well, yes,' Drift found himself agreeing.

'Then you're the perfect fit for this job,' Kelsier said flatly, 'and since my deadline is fast approaching and trying to find someone else to fit the bill would not be easy, I will make this decision simple for you and appeal directly to your well-developed sense of greed. One hundred thousand USNA, up front, from me, today. You'll have expenses to cover: fuel, possibly repairs, maybe bribes. I know well enough how this game is played.' He sat back and watched those sentences sink in for a moment, then leaned forwards again. 'Another one hundred thousand, Europan, upon delivery.'

Drift forced himself to concentrate as those numbers danced inside his head. 'And your cut from the delivery fee is . . . ?'

'No cut,' Kelsier said, shaking his head. 'I'm not moving contraband to a buyer and expecting you to come back with the sale fee, I'm paying you to deliver something. The two hundred thousand is all yours.'

'Right,' Drift nodded, watching the old man carefully. 'And the catch . . . ?'

'You're smuggling something diplomatically sensitive on a tight timescale onto the most heavily regulated planet in the galaxy,' Kelsier drawled. 'I'd have thought the catch would be fairly bloody obvious. The money up front is to show I'm good for it, the money at the other end is to make sure your crew don't decide to bugger off with my hundred thousand and my cargo between here and there.'

'My crew?' Drift repeated. 'So you trust *me*, then?'

'Should I not?' Kelsier asked airily. 'What do you say, Ichabod? One more contract, for old times' sake?

I suspect two hundred thousand would be of great use to you, even in mixed currencies.'

Drift turned the deal this way and that in his head. The hundred grand up front would be easy to verify, and since the Xanth bounty had taken care of their immediate needs, Kelsier's money could be put to use preparing for the possibility of a double-cross at the other end. His crew *could* do smuggling jobs well; they'd had some close shaves on occasions, but they'd sneaked cargos in and out of systems and on and off planets most other runners had sworn were sewn up tight by the authorities. If anything played to their strengths, this was it. The Changs could even call their parents from in-system, which would please them.

Then there was the Laughing Man to consider. The notion of someone hiring the galaxy's most feared hitman just to use as a *threat* made Drift slightly uneasy in his bones, and he had no doubt it had been planned as such. Whatever Kelsier was doing these days his resources had to be considerable, and that meant he could afford for his patience to be finite. For all that his former employer had claimed to have 'dispensed' with the notion of having the Laughing Man kill him here and now, Drift wasn't prepared to ignore it. If he tried to turn this job down, he didn't fancy his chances of getting out of this booth alive.

Finally, Kelsier had always played him straight before. Harsh, yes. Uncompromising, certainly. But the old man had always laid his terms down clearly and stuck to his side of the deal. Honour among thieves was ten-a-penny compared to honour among politicians, but whatever Kelsier had been or whatever new shadowy game he was playing now, he'd always had that honour.

And yet . . .

'Sorry, Mr Kelsier,' he said carefully, keeping one eye on the Laughing Man, 'I don't think I can help you.'

Kelsier's expression didn't change. 'If this is an attempt to push the price even higher, Ichabod—'

'It isn't,' Drift cut him off. 'I'm not interested. I appreciate you coming to offer me this job, but it's not for me. For us. My crew and I try to stay out of politics as much as possible, and this . . .' He grimaced, shaking his head. 'I think you're further in than you ever were. I can give you some names of other captains who might be able to assist you, but I don't think it's a good move for us.'

'How about getting shot in the head?' Kelsier asked, his tone matter of fact. 'Would that be a good move for you?'

'Not particularly,' Drift conceded, stomach churning, 'but it might be less painful in the long run.' He eyed the Laughing Man. Maybe if he grabbed Kelsier's tea and threw it into the assassin's eyes he'd have enough time to get clear . . . well, if it hadn't been for the two cybernetic thugs. And assuming that the woman in the niqab didn't pull one of his own confiscated guns on him.

'You know,' Kelsier said conversationally, 'when I first realised you were still alive, I must admit I wondered how on Old Earth you'd escaped unnoticed when the Federation of African States massacred your entire former crew. But then again, even at the time it seemed strange to me that they would have done that. Surely at least some would have been captured to face charges, be made an example of, answer interrogations and so forth?'

Drift stared at the old man, trying to swallow back the bile rising in his throat.

'Unless, of course,' Kelsier continued, 'they were actually already dead by the time the FAS found them, and everything after that was the best PR exercise the Africans could spin on it. They wouldn't have known you by sight, I suppose, and must have assumed that you were present among the corpses. I wonder who or what might have killed so many people but left one man alive?' He raised an eyebrow. 'You've worked *very* hard to build yourself a new life, Ichabod. Got yourself a new crew who you seem quite attached to. How do you suppose they would react if I make public who you used to be? Not to mention the interest the FAS would have in the whole affair. I'd wager it would be a toss-up over what did you in first: your crew stabbing you in the back or some African hit squad dispatched to . . . well, dispatch *you*. And you might not find a way out a second time.'

Drift glared at him, impotent rage warring with a chill in his gut, and didn't trust himself to speak.

'So here's what I propose,' Kelsier continued in his rasping voice. 'You do this job, and do it to schedule. You get paid rather handsomely for it and we say no more about any of this or who you might have been, once upon a time. Refuse me, and I'll bring your little world crashing down. Do the job wrong or miss my deadline and the same thing happens, plus I might just send Marcus here to make certain you come to a very sticky end.'

He smiled pleasantly. 'So I'll ask again: what do you say, Ichabod? One more contract, for old times' sake?'

Drift inhaled and exhaled again, trying to banish thoughts of putting his fist right through Kelsier's face, then stopped and seriously considered the notion for a moment. He'd be killed by Kelsier's goons, but would it be better to die instantly at the hands of an expert assassin than to give up the freedom he'd sacrificed so much to obtain?

No. No, probably not.

'One job,' he said, fighting to keep his voice level. 'I'll have your word on this, you slippery bastard. This is the only job you will have me do for you.'

Kelsier smiled easily. 'My word, my promise and my bond. Successful or failed, this will be the very last time I call upon your services.'

There was no hint of deceit that Drift could detect, and the last decade of his work had of necessity seen him become an expert in spotting the telltale signs. Of course, Kelsier's background in the shadier side of politics had made him an expert at this game too, but Drift's gut was telling him that the old man was being entirely truthful.

'What's the cargo?'

'Four standard small shipping containers,' Kelsier replied instantly, 'the contents of which are classified. Don't let your curiosity get the better of you, Ichabod; my factors in Amsterdam will be checking for signs of tampering or opening before they hand over your second payment, and if they're not happy then you will be unpopular in a thoroughly terminal way.'

Drift grimaced. 'It's going to be hard enough to convince my crew to take on a job from an employer they'll never meet, let alone a mystery cargo.'

'Your *crew*?' Kelsier snorted in what seemed to be genuine amusement. 'I'm sorry; are you a captain or a butler? Do you or do you not have final say in what your ship does?' He waved his mechanical hand as though to brush his own question from the air. 'No matter, that's your concern rather than mine. Tell them whatever lies or misdirections you need to tell them. You said you don't want to involve them in politics; don't ask for more details than you need, then. Do the job and have done.'

The sinking feeling in Drift's stomach was growing stronger but his brain was whirring away, judging the angles, rehearsing the conversations. Sometimes the only way out was through. There was one more question he had to ask, though.

'What's the timescale?'

'Three weeks, Old Earth standard,' Kelsier replied. 'One p.m. on the twenty-first of June local time, to be precise.'

Drift checked his wrist chrono – each system tended to adopt the time frame of its principal occupied planet, but everyone used Old Earth as a universal measurement – and winced inwardly. It would be tight, but it was definitely possible, and that meant his last potential objection had fallen. Now it was down to his choices. Refuse the old man and watch his crew turn their backs on him when they found out about his past, and swap his cherished freedom for a life on the run hunted by the FAS? Go out ingloriously in a stinking shithole of a Carmellan bar, one of the Laughing Man's stardiscs lodged in his vertebrae or brainpan? Or take the job, with all the dangers that involved?

There was only one option which held a possibility of everything working out. He gritted his teeth and met the old man's icy gaze.

'Where's your cargo?'

'A dark run? To Old Earth?'

Jia Chang rubbed her index finger thoughtfully across her chin, the minute rubber studs on her flying gloves raising a slight whisper as she did so. Drift tried to ignore the sound and smiled easily. The crew were assembled in the *Jonah*'s canteen, the only space other than the cargo bay which was large enough for them to all come together comfortably, and which had the additional bonus of seats. Jenna, Jia, Kuai and Micah were sitting around the bench-like table, Apirana was in one corner, sunk into the massive armchair he'd bought himself, while Rourke had – probably unconsciously – taken up guard position against the wall next to the door. Drift was leaning back against the food prep bar and trying to look considerably more at ease than he felt.

'That's the shape of it,' he nodded to the Chineseborn pilot. 'You up to it?'

Jia snorted. 'Only reason I'm working for you instead of pulling down squadron leader wages with the Red Starfighters is because I'd have broken mother's heart if I'd gone into the military.'

'That and you hate authority,' her brother put in, not looking up from where he was cleaning under his nails with a small screwdriver. 'You haven't kept a clean licence since you were busted for buzzing a control tower on the moon the day after you passed—'

'Kuai,' Jia said, warning in her tone. Her brother shrugged, but still didn't look at her.

'Just saying, we could be working for a respectable shipping company instead of dodging customs officials if you weren't such a thrusterhead—'

'Enough!' Drift barked, pushing the angrily rising Jia back into her chair with one hand while pointing the other at Kuai. The Changs were hard-working and generally undemanding as crew members, but he regularly had to fight the urge to bang their heads together when they started bickering, and his conversation with Nicolas Kelsier had left him decidedly on edge. 'I'm not after family history or sibling rivalry—'

'Not much rivalry to be had with a *grease monkey*!' Jia cut in acidly.

'*Me cago en la puta,* just tell me if you can do the *fucking* job!' Drift snapped. The canteen went quiet for a moment. Drift felt Tamara Rourke's eyes on him, and he did his best to bite back the anxiety which had momentarily taken hold of his tongue. 'Dark run,' he continued, more levelly. 'We get there and get in without even being *seen* by customs flights or security checks.'

'And the way out?' Jia asked, her expression slightly

sullen but her tone level, possibly because she was studiously ignoring her brother's very existence. 'Have to ghost out too, or we get difficult questions about why we're not on their flight logs.'

'I can probably steal another ship's ID off the central database and we can use that as a patch,' Jenna spoke up. 'So long as the real one doesn't try to leave while we're still nearby, we should be fine.'

'"Probably"? "Should be"?' Jia grimaced. 'Not encouraging. A dark run's doable, sure, but it'll be tough. Not saying it's impossible, even on Old Earth, but we need to be prepared. If we try some fancy ID trick, it fails and we need to go full burn out of there, First System is the last place we want to be.'

'Have you ever sliced a system that big before?' Drift asked Jenna dubiously. The girl was good, no doubt about it, but she was still relatively new and he hadn't yet seen her react to real adversity. If she lost the plot at a bad time then this whole venture could take a rapid nosedive. *And that just isn't an option* . . .

'No, but the bigger a system is, the more holes in it there are.' Jenna shrugged. 'When you've got that many people with access authority there's always a way in, if you know your way around the tech.'

'If you're that good with tech, how come you're riding with us instead of skimming yourself a wage out of someone's bank funds?' Micah asked, reaching across her to pour himself a cup of coffee from the steaming flagon on the table. 'Hell of a lot less dangerous than smuggling.'

Jenna flushed, but it was Tamara Rourke who spoke up, her low voice cutting across the room.

'You're forgetting the rules, Micah. You don't ask about someone's history.'

The mercenary snorted. 'That's not "history", that's—'

'It's close enough,' Drift cut him off, backing his partner up. Micah rolled his eyes but said nothing, so Drift turned back to the slicer. 'Jenna: how long will it take you to get us a new ident ready to use?'

'This is just for the way out, right?' the girl asked. Drift nodded, and Jenna's blue eyes lost their focus slightly, as they usually did when she was thinking about tech. 'Okay. I can do the initial connection as soon as we're out of the comms blackout when we hit atmo on the way in, so ninety seconds tops to hit their system, thirty seconds to make sure I know what program it's running. Call it a minute to send the ping and find any tracer echo—'

'I don't need the details,' Drift said, not unkindly. He'd let Jenna go off thinking out loud before, and everyone else had been lost by the third sentence. 'Just give me an estimate.'

'I'm *giving* you an estimate,' Jenna replied patiently, eyes refocusing on his face. 'It all depends. Two minutes, and I can tell you whether or not I'll be able to get in at all. If I get a tracer echo then someone's been careless and I've got an open line to the system after three. If not I'll have to slice it, so,' she pulled a face to indicate a skilled professional straying into the dreaded realm of guesswork, 'unless they've got anything seriously hardcore going on, I'll have access to the ident logs in five. From there, I can pull a basic name-and-number patch in thirty seconds, or spend two minutes to tidy it up and fool anything but them pulling our complete data logs. Well,' she added, 'or them coming aboard and reading the paperwork. Can't do shit about that.' She looked at his blank expression and sighed. 'I can give you a yes or no before we get into the lower atmosphere. After that, I can have a full ident patch for a logged ship five minutes tops after you give me the green light.'

Drift whistled. 'That's fast work.' He threw a glance at Jia, who nodded. 'Okay, we go in dark, we plan to come out as someone else with nothing to hide. If Jenna can't give us what we need for that, we have plenty of warning to plan sneaking out instead.' He looked around at the rest of them. 'Any questions?'

'What're we moving, bro?' Apirana rumbled. Drift felt his stomach shift uneasily. He'd debated making something up, but skilled liar though he was he'd decided to stick as close to the truth as possible. He didn't want to have to pull the wool over his crew's eyes, even though it was in everyone's best interests.

'Something worth two hundred grand for us not to ask about or look at.'

'Sheeit,' the Maori grunted. 'Gotta be worth a helluva lot more to your contact if he's willing to pay that much for us to shift it.'

'I wonder how much?' Micah said, his expression brightening.

'Don't even think about it!' Drift snapped, turning to the mercenary. 'We're making a small fortune off this job already. Let's say the cargo's worth half a mil, Europan; where would we even fence something that valuable? We don't know anyone who'd touch it.'

'*I* don't,' Micah agreed, 'but it's *my* job to shoot

a gun. It's *your* job to know things like that.' He raised his eyebrows expectantly, but Drift just glared at him. It wasn't like he hadn't been thinking about what might be in Kelsier's crates, but he'd decided that he didn't want to know. Sometimes ignorance really was bliss. Do the job, get paid, move on: the old man had the right of that, if nothing else.

'It's also my job to know when we should just stick to a contract and do a job,' he said flatly, 'and this is one of those times. We're not going to make life any easier for ourselves if we get a rep for breaking deals and running off with cargoes.' He saw Micah's mouth opening again, and sighed. 'Fine, think of it like this: if my contact is willing to pay two hundred grand for us to move this cargo, how much *more* will he be willing to pay for us to be hunted down if we decide to stiff him?'

There was a general chorus of muttering and nods from around the galley, but Micah still wasn't convinced. 'Hey, accidents happen,' the Dutch mercenary said, spreading his hands innocently, 'maybe we all tragically died. You're telling me Jenna here can't rustle us up some new names and histories?'

Something unpleasant clawed at Drift's stomach. He shook his head. 'That wouldn't work.' *Not again.*

'But—'

'I'm through with the discussion here,' Drift told him bluntly. 'Are you in or out?'

He still grumbled, but there was no question of Micah turning down a cut of two hundred grand. Which was just as well; Drift didn't want to have to find another gun hand on short notice, and for all his abrasive nature Micah was at least a known quantity. On a run like this, where so much was going to be unknown, the last thing Drift wanted was an unfamiliar face with untested merits. *It's going to be bad enough hoping that Jenna pulls through in the clinch . . .*

'Ichabod.'

The crew had separated, going to their stations as they prepared the *Jonah* for take-off, ready to fly as unobtrusively as possible to where Kelsier's cargo awaited them. Rourke, however, had apparently followed Drift back towards his cabin.

'Jesus!' He jumped and turned to face her. 'I've told you not to sneak up on me!' He tried to make it sound joking, but it came out harder than he'd intended. Stars, but the woman could move quietly when she wanted to! He took in Rourke's solemn expression and composed himself with an effort. 'Problem?'

'Maybe,' Rourke nodded soberly. She nodded at his cabin door. 'In there?'

Drift palmed the door open and stepped through as it moved aside with the slightest of hisses. Rourke followed him, then leaned back against the green-painted metal surface as it slid shut behind her, and regarded him with folded arms.

'So, what's up?' Drift asked, absent-mindedly pulling a stopper from a bottle of whisky he kept by his bunk.

'We're about to get paid an awful lot of money,' Rourke said flatly. Drift blinked at her, bottle paused halfway to a fingerprint-smeared tumbler.

'And that strikes you as a *problem*?'

'On general principle?' She shook her head. 'No.

But when I don't know the cargo *and* I don't know the employer, I start to get a little . . . twitchy.'

'A long time ago, when we first started working together, you said the only thing you wouldn't 'port is slaves,' Drift reminded her. 'The cargo isn't alive, so . . .' He shrugged, trying to hide the sudden uncomfortable realisation that actually he had no idea if that was true. He'd have assumed that Kelsier would have said, but . . .

'I also don't like not knowing who I'm working for,' Rourke sighed, eyes drifting along the ceiling, from ventilation unit to light fitting. Her gaze had a tendency to wander upwards no matter where she was, Drift had noticed. It had confused him until he'd realised it was probably an old reflex; looking for bugging devices indoors, searching for snipers on rooftops outside. 'And I've got to say, given that, I think you should have gotten my opinion before you committed to this.' Her eyes snapped back to his. 'Or did you forget the last time we took on a job without knowing our employer?'

Drift grimaced. They hadn't even been doing anything *that* illegal: the booze they'd been moving wasn't contraband in and of itself, they'd just been asked to slip it past customs to avoid tax. Unfortunately it had transpired that the warehouse they were delivering to belonged to the gang Apirana had run with in his younger days, and they didn't take kindly to 'deserters'. The sight of the big Maori's distinctive *tā moko* when he appeared with a crate over each shoulder had sparked off a fight which had left Rourke with a bullet in her shoulder, two of the warehousemen bleeding and one probably dead, and

Apirana in a blistering rage which had seen him destroy most of the galley before Kuai had been able to calm him down. The only mercy was that the incident had flown completely under the radar of the local Justices, since neither side had been eager to attract their attention.

'There won't be anything like that,' Drift assured her.

'Then why are *you* so twitchy?'

Drift adopted an expression of puzzlement. 'What?'

'I've flown with you longer than anyone else,' Rourke said levelly, 'and I know you better than anyone on this boat does. You haven't been yourself since you came back from High Under.'

'I . . .' Drift's usual carefree grin didn't seem to want to materialise. He was so used to Rourke's emotions being virtually unreadable that he'd almost forgotten she could still pick up on other people's. 'No, that's . . .'

'The way you yelled at the Changs,' Rourke said, 'the way you fronted up to Micah; you've never given him an ultimatum like that before.'

'Maybe I should have,' Drift muttered.

'I'm not necessarily disagreeing,' Rourke allowed, 'but it's not like *you*. You can't even string a sentence together to try to convince me you're fine. The only time your silver tongue usually stops is when you're asleep, and I'm not even certain about that.'

Drift affected an affronted glare. 'When have you watched me sleeping?'

'Don't try to change the subject.' Rourke's dark eyes were steady, but there was something odd in the lines of her face. *Sweet Jesu, I've kept her in the dark about this job and she's* worried *about me!* His stomach twisted again. He'd always tried to be careful about developing attachments to his crew, because if someone wasn't pulling their weight then sentimentality could endanger everyone, but he couldn't even pretend to himself that Rourke hadn't become a friend. A taciturn and reserved friend, certainly, and not exactly a shoulder to cry on, but a friend nonetheless. For a moment he had an impulse to tell her everything, to explain about the barrel Kelsier had him over and the threats which had been made.

But for someone to understand all of the threats, they need to understand what's at stake for me. And that's what I have to avoid in the first place.

He took a deep breath. He didn't want to lie to Rourke. But he would, if he needed to. However, maybe he could ease by with just enough of the truth to placate her . . . 'Okay, look, *I* know who we're working for. It's just not something I'm in a position to share.'

A lot of people would have grown angry with their business partner at this point. Tamara Rourke, however, was not prone to emotional outbursts of any sort without severe provocation, and her face adopted the look which Drift had privately dubbed her 'holding pattern': a blank poker mask while she waited for more information on which to base an eventual decision.

'Why not?'

Drift took a sip of whisky, in the hope it would help him navigate his way through this mess. 'It's . . . someone I used to work for. A *long* time ago. Different life.'

Rourke's face didn't move. 'That doesn't sound massively reassuring. I'm guessing there's a reason you haven't done business with them for so long?'

'A few,' Drift nodded levelly, feeling the burn of the liquor in the back of his throat. 'But . . . things have changed. I never had a problem with him as an employer, it was just the work I was doing.' *True enough.* 'Now he's simply asking me to take something from one place to another. He never saw me wrong before.' *Also true. Mainly.*

Rourke nodded slowly. 'And you don't want to tell me his name?'

'Not particularly,' Drift acknowledged, watching her face. 'There're things in my past I'd rather not bring up. Same as everyone on this boat.' *The same as you*, he nearly added, but that would have been needlessly antagonistic. So far as Tamara Rourke's history was concerned, she'd apparently sprung into being fully formed, fully clothed and fully armed eight years ago, like Athena from the brow of Zeus, and any mention of her life before that simply got you a blank stare.

Rourke's expression didn't really change, but her second nod had a sense of finality to it. 'Okay then. Because I trust you. Don't make me regret it.'

Drift raised his glass to her in silent salute, and she turned and left his cabin without another word. Once the door had hissed shut behind her again he let out a breath and slumped back into his chair in wordless relief. The crew mostly took his word as captain, but of course a job like this would throw up extra doubts and questions. Similarly, Rourke usually accepted his lead on finding and executing jobs, in the same way as he automatically deferred to her on anything to do with fighting. They each had their own strengths, and they recognised and respected that. Still, you didn't make a living in business by not looking closely at an offer which might be too good to be true, especially if your business was routinely conducted on the edges of the law.

Drift grimaced. If his intuition was any judge, they'd earn their two hundred grand before this run was out. 'Tighter than Old Earth' was in smuggler parlance for a reason, and he couldn't shake the feeling that he was placing all their fates in the hands of a cocky thrusterhead and a rookie slicer.

'Well,' he muttered, gulping down the rest of the whisky, 'at least life is never dull.'

HANDLE WITH CARE

'There.'

Jia pointed through the *Jonah*'s viewshield at a distant, blinking light, almost indistinguishable against the inky, star-studded backdrop of space. She looked down at her display again, then back up, and Drift could almost see her triangulating in her head. 'Yup, definitely that one.' She squinted at the screen. 'The *Gewitterwolke*?'

'The "w"s will be pronounced as "v"s,' Drift corrected her absently, scratching at the skin around his right eye. 'But yeah, that's the one.' A tapping noise caught his attention, and he turned to see Jenna working busily at her terminal. 'What are you doing?'

'Slicing,' she replied, chewing on a strand of red-blonde hair at the corner of her mouth. 'Their ident's an overlay, and a good one, but I can—'

'Don't,' Drift said firmly, taking two quick steps

to her terminal and planting a hand in the middle of her screen. She looked up at him, surprised.

'But I thought we didn't know—'

'Let's keep it that way,' Drift told her quietly. 'Two hundred grand says we don't want to know that ship's real name, or who it belongs to.'

She stared at him for a moment, then shrugged. 'Aye, Captain.'

'You're never normally *that* bothered 'bout the contract conditions,' Apirana rumbled. The big Maori was taking up most of the space in the cockpit doorway and watching the panorama of sky slowly move in front of them as Jia orientated them on the distant vessel.

'I don't normally stand to make this big a loss if someone decides we've broken the agreement,' Drift told him, moving away from Jenna's terminal.

'Don't really see how y'can lose something you ain't got yet,' Apirana shrugged, 'but I catch your drift.' He paused for a second, then grunted. 'No pun intended.'

Drift just nodded at him, and returned to hovering behind the pilot's chair. Jia cast an exasperated look back up at him, then returned her attention to the read-outs in front of her.

'I *can* pilot a ship without a babysitter, you know.'

'I'm not watching you,' Drift lied, although he was also scanning the darkness and trying to pick out every moving blink of light which might indicate another ship, looking for encirclement patterns. 'Anyone shadowing us?'

'No one on sensor,' Jia replied, 'so either we're alone, they're sitting on our *pìgu* so tight they'll be getting a roasting from the thrusters, or they've got a perfect blind field.'

'Good,' Drift muttered. He looked out of the viewshield again. The winking star of the *Gewitterwolke* was starting to resolve into the multiple running lights of a vessel under power as they got closer, and he thought he could make out the faint gleam of surfaces reflecting the system's star. 'C'mon A., let's get down to the cargo bay.'

'Gotcha,' the Maori replied, easing away from the door frame in a manner which reminded Drift vaguely of an iceberg he'd once seen calving from a glacier during a flight over the Polar Ocean of New Shinjuku. Watching the huge man's broad back as they walked focused Drift's mind on exactly what might happen if his gamble failed and his secret got out. How would a man with a temper as legendary as Apirana's react?

He felt his heartbeat quicken a little. 'Actually, you go on. I'll catch up in a second.'

''Kay,' the Maori replied over his shoulder, and kept walking. Drift stepped sideways, palmed his cabin door open and slipped inside. He made a beeline for the bottle of whisky by his bunk and sloshed a measure into a glass, then sank it in one practised motion.

The liquor burned its way down his throat and he felt his nerves loosen a little. He debated another shot, but decided against it. He was confident he knew his limits, but there was no point tempting fate. He just needed to get through this rendezvous, and then . . .

Then what? Sit on a secret all the way to Old Earth, lying to my crew? He cast a rueful glance at the bottle. *I don't know if there's enough whiskey on board.*

He took a deep breath. He was Captain Ichabod Drift now, and he didn't *need* whisky. He just liked it. This ship was the closest thing to a stable home most of his crew had ever had, and it was his duty to them to keep it that way. It was in everyone's best interests. That meant making sure Kelsier didn't go telling tales which might damage their trust in him, and it meant getting the job done without anyone finding anything out which could link him to the old politician.

Especially Micah. He's the only one who'd know the name.

He took another breath, held it, let it out again, and stepped back out of his cabin. Time to go and play nice.

The *Jonah*'s cargo bay was several times Drift's height and spacious enough to hold three large freight containers (so long as the crew breathed in when squeezing around them). Apirana was waiting, of course, and Rourke, Micah and Jenna emerged from the stairway which led down from the canteen just as Drift arrived. Rourke nodded once at him, which he couldn't help but interpret as *This had better go well, or I'll rearrange your face.*

'Jenna, you get the doors,' Drift instructed as Rourke climbed into the cab of their small, tracked loader. 'Micah, A.: Tamara will bring 'em aboard, you shift 'em into place.'

The two men nodded as Jenna headed over to the door control, while Drift tucked his thumbs into his belt. Long-standing cautiousness meant he always wanted his hands near his guns when a deal was going down, but it was best to find some sort of excuse for them to be there. If that meant looking like a hick farmhand posing for a picture, then so be it.

Seconds dragged by into minutes, until Jia's voice crackled over the comm speakers. +*They've opened the bay for us. Taking us in now.*+

Drift felt a sudden forwards momentum as the retros fired, braking the *Jonah*, then the hum as the electromagnets in the hull powered up to counteract the gravitational effect of the larger craft's own sub-deck Heim field. There followed some thirty seconds of what seemed like no motion at all, although Drift knew – or at least, hoped – that Jia was simply manoeuvring carefully to avoid hitting anything.

+*Setting down now.*+

There was a jolt, albeit a minor one, as Jia powered down the mags and the *Jonah* sank to meet the deck of the *Gewitterwolke*, then their craft's engine throttled back and died as Kuai acted on his sister's instructions. A few more seconds passed.

+*They're pressurising the bay.*+

There was silence for about half a minute.

+*It's quite a big bay . . .*+

Micah rolled his eyes. Apirana shifted on his feet and worked his shoulders. Drift looked over at Rourke, who met his gaze with the impassivity of a particularly unreadable statue. Jenna tried to look attentive. Then the lights over the bay door changed from red to green, and Jia's voice crackled over the intercom again.

+*Okay, sensors say you're good to go. You've got*

a welcoming party, too; looks like . . . a Muslim woman and some goons? Four of them. They've got some crates.+

Drift nodded, more to himself than anyone else, then directed a more definite tip of his head at Jenna. 'Let's go meet them.'

Jenna hit the door release and a section of the *Jonah*'s thick exterior shielding started to swing downwards to form a ramp. There was a faint hiss as the pressure outside and inside equalised, and then harsh white light began to filter in through the widening gap. Drift's right eye instantly adjusted to the rays hitting his face, although his natural left one took a couple of moments to catch up.

By the time the ramp was halfway down he could see the faces of their welcoming party. Kelsier's assistant was clad in a niqab again, and the datalens was still in place over one eye. Meanwhile, the two men who'd accompanied her to get him off the street and into the bar had been joined by another man and a woman, both with their own cybernetic augmentations. The appearance of the group wasn't uniform – in all honesty, it was more like they'd been attacked by the vengeful and possibly parasitic contents of a scrapyard – but nor was it that uncommon. Manual workers often had replacements or enhancements to limbs to give added strength or endurance for their tasks, or sometimes had them completely replaced by specialist tools, and a bunch of cargo haulers might well pick up the variety of additions he could see in front of him. Then again, it was easy to conceal a weapon in a mechanical limb, quite apart from the potential damage the limb itself could do. The group in front of him didn't appear to be armed, but Drift would have bet the *Jonah* that was a false impression.

Jenna gave a faint squeak and he saw her pull back, away from the edge of the ramp and into the corner of the cargo bay, out of sight of the welcoming party. He shot her a questioning look but she merely pressed one finger to her lips in a universal gesture for silence, eyes wide and scared in her pale face, then turned and ran for the stairs. There was no time or opportunity to seek an explanation: Drift filed it away under *things to ask about later* and stepped forwards to the head of the ramp, eyes on the men and women in front of him and thumbs tucked into his belt.

'*Hola*,' he greeted them, then focused on the niqab-clad woman. 'I'm afraid I didn't catch your name before.'

'You may call me Sibaal,' she replied, with no other motion of acknowledgement. She gestured to the four large, gunmetal-coloured oblong boxes behind her, each resting on a humming maglev bed which kept it slightly off the metal deck. 'The cargo is here.'

Drift nodded, although he was still surprised that a cargo this small could be worth two hundred grand just for delivery. Then again, each crate was easily large enough to contain a person, and pieces of microart no bigger than his thumb went for millions, so who was he to judge? 'Well, this shouldn't take long. If you want to set them down, we'll get them on board with the loader.'

'No need,' Sibaal shook her head, 'you may take the beds also.' She gestured, and her four companions split two to a crate and started pushing. The crates slid easily forwards through the air, but when the electromagnets on the beds registered the sloping ramp and started to tilt upwards, it became clear that they were heavy; even the augmented haulers were showing effort as they pushed.

The first crate cleared the top of the ramp and nudged into the cargo bay just as Drift realised that Rourke had slipped out of the loader and was at his elbow. He hadn't heard her move. Again.

'What's up with the girl?' she murmured.

'No idea,' he muttered back, 'but you might want to keep an eye on things while I go talk to Miss Personality down there.' Rourke nodded and took up station by the door release controls, while Drift sauntered down the ramp towards Sibaal, stepping aside to clear room for the second crate and its straining handlers.

'You have the money?' he asked, not feeling particularly inclined towards further pleasantries. She reached one hand into the opposite sleeve and pulled out a shiny, dark red oblong which she held out to him.

'I assume you take plastic?'

Drift retrieved his datapad from his pocket and slotted the credit chip into the reader. The information instantly sprang up: one hundred thousand USNA dollars credited to it, with no details of creditor or recipient. The piece of plastic itself was virtually worthless, but the electronic watermarks and security notes assured the viewer that it was a genuine, unsliceable (allegedly) Interstellar Credit Chip, which meant the currency programmed into it was as good as cold, hard cash in the hand.

Drift nodded, and tried to look as though being handed this much money was an unremarkable event for him. 'That'll do nicely.'

'Then we have a deal,' Sibaal said, extending a hand for him to shake. Drift automatically returned the gesture with the practised ease of someone who'd sealed innumerable deals in a variety of different ways, despite the fact that actual physical contact was a long way down the list of things he'd expected from her. Her hand was small in his, but her grip was firm.

He heard her sniff, and she withdrew her hand. 'You've been drinking.'

'And you've been party to blackmail,' he replied, smiling humourlessly. 'We all have our little character flaws.'

A faint shifting of fabric suggested an aggravated exhalation, but she made no further comment and simply proffered a small data chip. 'Your destination and timescale.'

Drift tucked the credit chip into his pocket and scanned the data as it uploaded to his pad. A building address – the Van Der Graaf Centre, Ookmeerweg, Amsterdam, The Netherlands, Old Earth – and confirmation of the date and time Kelsier had already told him.

'Remember,' Sibaal was saying, 'the cargo must be delivered *on* time – neither early nor late.'

'Yeah, Kel—' Drift stopped himself just in case anyone was listening, but the rest of his crew were still inside the *Jonah* arranging the last of the crates. He lowered his voice nonetheless. 'Kelsier drove that point home well enough. He'll get what he's paying for.'

Sibaal's eyes studied him coolly. 'See that he does. Under most circumstances an employer would promise further work for a job well done. However,' she tilted her head slightly to the side, 'I believe you said you would not welcome such an offer.'

'If it had been an *offer* rather than being grabbed off the street, held at gunpoint and threatened, then this might have all gone differently,' Drift countered, then decided to change the subject. 'Is there anything about the cargo we should know?' Sibaal's eyes narrowed slightly, and he sighed. 'Just . . . do the crates need storing at a certain temperature, or are they particularly fragile, or—'

'The contents are packed well and are not unduly sensitive to temperature or vibration,' Sibaal replied. 'So long as the crates remain unopened . . . and you don't crash into anything . . . then there should be no problems.'

'Well, that's encouraging,' Drift said, wondering about a farewell smile but deciding against it: regardless of the fact that his skiff was currently sealed inside her ship and a harmless pleasantry might not go amiss, Sibaal annoyed him. He looked back over his shoulder and saw the crate handlers returning down the ramp for the last time, with no indication that they'd gone storming through the ship trying to abduct Jenna or caused any other trouble while on board. 'Looks like it's time to go.'

'Indeed,' Sibaal agreed. 'Safe journey, Captain Drift.'

'Thanks,' he muttered, waiting for her goons to tramp past before ascending the ramp himself. He exchanged nods with Rourke on the way past and his partner slapped the button to bring the ramp up again with a whine of hydraulics, then tapped the comm in her ear.

'All aboard, Jia. Take us out.'

+Roger that,+ their pilot replied. +*Just waiting for them to clear the bay . . . Okay, bay is sealed and they've already started depressurisation.*+

There was a hum as the electromagnets kicked in and a faint wobble as the *Jonah* rose off the deck, then a deeper throb as Kuai started the main engines ready for his sister to feed power to the manoeuvring rockets when the bay doors opened.

The sound of an airlock opening made Drift look up, and Jenna's face and its accompanying tangle of red-blonde hair appeared over the gantry.

'Have they gone?' the girl asked, her voice thick with apprehension.

Drift gestured at the bay, empty except for the *Jonah*'s crew and their newly acquired cargo. 'Yeah. You want to tell me what that was about?'

'Not really,' Jenna replied, although she appeared to relax a little.

Drift sighed. 'Look, I just need to know—'

'You don't need to know anything!' she shouted, causing him to take a step back in surprise. Her mouth moved behind her lips for a moment before more words tumbled out, cutting off his half-formed sentence. 'That's your rule, right? You don't ask about someone's history unless they talk about it first? That's what you and Tamara told me when I first came on board.'

Actually I think we told you to let Tamara hold your hair back while you threw up, Drift thought, but decided not to voice that particular correction. 'Well . . . yeah.'

'This is my history,' Jenna said. Her voice was level again and her eyes met his. There was no aggression there, but there was the sort of determination which was practically palpable. 'You do *not* need to know it.'

Drift nodded slowly. 'Fair enough. But you understand that you're a member of this crew, and that means you have responsibilities. If your reactions mean you can't fulfil your responsibilities, then at best you won't be flying with us for long and at worst . . .' he shrugged, 'you get us all killed.'

'I understand,' Jenna replied firmly. Her eyes flicked past him, to Micah, Apirana and Rourke, all of whom were hanging back and looking as unobtrusive as possible . . . which wasn't very, especially when one of them was the big Maori. 'Now, if you'll excuse me?'

She turned away and disappeared from view, back towards the cabins. It shouldn't have been possible to slam a button-activated airlock behind her, but Drift got the distinct impression that she'd tried.

'Well, that was just the piece of weird we needed to top this day off,' Micah opined dryly, then shrugged dismissively. 'Eh, whatever.'

'Actually, I think we could stand to know a little more about exactly what's going on inside our slicer's head,' Drift countered. *Not least because it'll focus attention away from me.* He looked at Rourke. 'Do you want to have a word with Jenna, see if you can find out what that fuss was about?'

'Not particularly,' his partner replied, frowning in

confusion. 'What makes you think I'd be any good at that?'

Drift looked at her for a second, then nodded. 'Good point. Still, we need to have *some* idea what it was that set her off. I've blown it once, Micah's an asshole—'

'You only pay me to shoot things,' the Dutch mercenary grumbled, 'I don't see where being polite comes into it.'

'—Jia's going to be busy—'

'And is a raging egomaniac,' Rourke put in.

'—and Kuai is . . . well, Kuai,' Drift finished lamely. Their mechanic was good with machines and would win an inter-system passive-aggressive championship, but he wasn't the sort of person Drift would ever turn to for wheedling a secret out of an unpredictably prickly young slicer. Handling people was usually *his* strongpoint. 'Who's left?'

There was a moment of silent consideration. Then, as they all turned in unison, Apirana Wahawaha folded arms which were roughly as thick as Rourke's thighs and glowered at them.

'You guys *gotta* be kidding me.'

'There she is,' Apirana rumbled, startling Jenna out of her reverie. 'Home sweet home.'

She'd sat in her cabin for an hour or so, but it wasn't a large space and she'd started to feel claustrophobic – thankfully not a common occurrence, or space travel would not have been a good option – and had come back to the canteen. She'd expected to be confronted by Drift again, but apart from Kuai grabbing a coffee the rest of the crew had been absent until Apirana had appeared a few minutes previously and begun to do something with a pan. She could see a blaze of lights through the porthole, but one cluster in particular was growing as the *Jonah* swung in towards it.

'You actually think of it as home?' Jenna asked. Starship crews rarely had homes planetside of course, but she was still adjusting to this transient life. The notion that she might one day view the *Keiko* as the place she belonged was both distant and mildly alarming.

'Her,' Apirana corrected gently. 'Yup, pretty much. Been on the *Keiko* five years now, longest I've been anywhere since . . . well . . .' He tailed off and busied himself stirring his pan again, leaving Jenna to focus on the ship looming up to meet them.

The *Jonah* was a skiff, nothing more; a small, atmosphere-going vessel which could survive re-entry into a planet's atmosphere and with enough kick to achieve escape velocity again, but it couldn't make the jumps between star systems. To do that, you needed a much bigger craft. The *Keiko*, left parked at one of the Carmella System's huge waystations, was just such a beast.

The universal feature of any inter-system vessel was an Alcubierre drive and its ability to warp space-time around the ship, but that had to be generated by the large, encircling doughnut-shaped construct which meant such a vessel would never be able to survive atmospheric re-entry intact. As a result the *Keiko*, like the rest of its ilk, would never encounter anything except the void and so had no need for aerodynamics. This model had been built to be a sort of rounded cube, with only faint cosmetic curves and the position of the thrusters giving an indication as to which end was the nominal front.

'Hope the bloody door opens this time,' Apirana ventured from by the hob. 'Coupla years ago the system had gone offline or something. Me an' Kuai had to suit up and go out t'do a manual override.'

Jenna watched the *Keiko* grow larger, and saw a

crack appear in the dark grey surface as bay doors began to pull apart in response to a remote signal sent by Jia in the *Jonah*'s cockpit. The gape was cavernously dark for a few moments before internal lights flickered on in response to the motion. 'Well, you won't have to do that this time.'

'Thank the skies,' the Maori grunted, looking over his shoulder, 'I hate void suits. Only ever found one that even sort of fits me, and it's hot as hell.'

Jenna sighed. Apirana had never been unfriendly, but this smacked of conversation for conversation's sake, and she could only think of one reason why he had suddenly become chatty. 'The Captain asked you to talk to me, didn't he?'

'That obvious?' Apirana asked, looking up with a wry grin. Jenna nodded, and the big man shrugged. 'Well, I ain't gonna lie, he asked me to have a word, yeah. Which ain't to say I didn't have concerns of me own, but I might've waited a little before broaching them with you.'

'No one here is eager to talk about their past,' Jenna pointed out, trying not to let her irritation show too much, 'why do I have to be the exception?'

'Well, if that's what's bothering you,' Apirana shrugged. 'Can't say as I know much about the others, nor is it my place to say anything even if I did. Can tell you about why I'm here though, although it ain't exactly a pretty story.'

'That doesn't mean I have to tell you anything,' Jenna warned, but the big Maori just shrugged again.

'Gotta show trust to get trust, I know that well enough. Don't see a problem with you knowing, anyhow.' He turned the hob off, scraped the pan's contents – eggs, as it turned out – onto a plate and came over to sit opposite her.

'Don't know about yourself, but apart from the Changs I'm the only one on this boat who was born on Old Earth,' the Maori began. 'Little place called Rotorua in New Zealand's North Island. Far as I'm concerned, New Zealand is the most beautiful country in the galaxy.' He looked up at her, eyes bright in his dark, tattooed face. 'You ever been to Japan?'

Jenna shook her head. 'I've never been to the First System.'

'They ran out of room there before the Great Expansion,' Apirana said, applying his fork to his eggs, 'built on damn near every inch of land they had. New Zealand never got like that. There's still wilderness there: forests, valleys, mountains. An' a bloody great lake o' sulphur, which is where Rotorua is.' The Maori's mouth quirked in a grin, but there was a wistfulness there too. Jenna was a child of Franklin Minor, a world sculpted into a pale shadow of Old Earth with a breathable atmosphere but the barest fraction of its biodiversity imported, yet she'd still felt pangs of homesickness since leaving so abruptly. She could only imagine what the big Maori might feel, looking back through the years at his beautiful, ancestral homeland.

'I'd have loved to grow up there,' she said, honestly.

Apirana's face twisted.

'Even the best places can be hell, if you make 'em that way.' His fork scraped across the plate. 'My father was a demon, and a drunkard. He thought the world was out t'get him cos he was Maori. Could be there were some truth to it, too. But that didn't excuse how he treated me mother. An' me.'

'Did you run away?' Jenna asked softly, trying to picture the hulking man in front of her as a frightened child. It wasn't an easy feat.

'Sort of,' Apirana shrugged, 'but . . . maybe not soon enough. You gotta understand, my father weren't a big man. I get my size from the men on my mother's side, apparently, but they cut all ties to her when she married him. So yeah, he weren't *big*, but he had this . . . way about him, I guess. You didn't stand up t'my father. My mother got the *tā moko* here,' he gestured at his own face, 'which a lot o' people don't care for. But it hid the bruises better.'

Jenna winced.

'So one day when I'm fifteen, he has a bottle or two and cuts loose again,' the big Maori continued, 'but for some reason, this time I stood in front of me mother an' told him t'fuck off.' His lip curled. 'He didn't take it well.'

'What happened?' Jenna breathed.

'Well, my father thought he could put me in my place like he could when I was a kid. He belted me enough when I were small that since then, one look and a word would shut my face right up. So he swung for me again.' He swallowed, although there'd been no food in his mouth. 'But I was big by the time I was fifteen, bigger than him. An' when he hit me, an' I was still standing afterwards, suddenly I realised that. Another thing I realised, too late, was that I'd got his temper, an' I din't need the beer to bring it out.'

Around them, Jenna was dimly away of the black-

ness of space being replaced by the lights of the
Keiko's docking bay, but she found her eyes fixed on
the man in front of her.

'I'm not entirely sure exactly what happened next,'
Apirana admitted, looking down at his plate. 'After
a while, I realised my mother was screaming. At me.
To stop.' He sat back, fiddling with the fork which
suddenly looked tiny as Jenna registered just how big
his hands were. Those fists were nearly as big as her
head, and the knuckles were battered and scarred.

''Course, now when I look back at it, I see it from
her side,' the Maori said, a bone-deep weariness in
his voice. 'She'd lived in fear o' this man for years,
hoping every time he told her he loved her that this
time it would stop him from doing what he'd done
before. Watching for every little sign he might be
turning aggressive again. Blaming herself every time
he blew up. I don't think she cared about herself after
a while, just for me when he hit me, or when I saw
him hit her. She must've hoped that I could get clear
of him some day. And then that day . . .'

His voice had grown thick. Jenna found herself
looking at his cheek, at the way the whorls of his
tattoos moved as he spoke. She couldn't bring herself
to meet his eyes.

'That day, she saw me do worse to him than he
ever had to her, or to me, an' without even the alcohol
for an excuse. She must've despaired. But t'me, all
I heard was that I'd finally grown a pair big enough
to protect her, an' now she wanted to protect *him*.
I was an angry kid in a man's body, so I turned on
her, yelled at her. An' just like that, she was looking at me like she'd always looked at him.' His

mouth twisted. '*Then* I ran. Out our front door and into the streets, with just the clothes on me back.'

Jenna wanted to say something, but couldn't find the words.

'You'd think the streets are no place for a kid, an' you'd be right,' Apirana continued, 'but for a big, angry young Maori, there's people who'll take you in, shelter you from the cops, give you food an' a place to sleep. 'Course, they got their own reasons for doing it, and by the time you realise what they are you're in too deep to find an easy way out. For me, it were a gang called the Mongrel Mob. Started up middle of the twentieth century an' the authorities have been trying to stamp 'em out since, but it never worked. Once the Great Expansion started, well, that were that. The Yakuza are the power in the West Pacific Nation systems, sure enough, but the Mongrels run an operation too.'

Jenna found her voice. 'So you . . . became a criminal?'

'I was more'n a criminal,' Apirana rumbled, 'I was a gangster. Once they'd worked out I had a fuse, well, all they had to do was point me at someone and I'd go off. Thug, bodyguard . . . anything that involved violence, I could do. Bought into the myth that Maori were meant to be warriors. Picked up a way of speaking which stuck. Got my face done. Part o' me knew what I was doing were wrong, o'course, but they were the only *whānau* I had, an' the only thing shelterin' me from the law. It was do what they said, or do time.'

'So what changed?' Jenna asked. The *Jonah* was setting down, guided by Jia's expert ministrations.

Apirana laughed humourlessly. 'I did time. I was running drugs by that point, out in Farport. Cops caught up with me, an' so did about seven years of crimes. They pinned everything they could on me. Sentenced to thirty years, served fifteen. First two years, I raged against the system. Next five or so, I blamed my father. For a couple o' years after that I was blaming the Mongrels, but finally I ended up putting the blame where it belonged.' He tapped his massive chest with one finger. 'Here. Weren't easy. When you got a powerful anger like I do you can end up self-destructing if you turn that on yourself, but I reached a balance in the end. When I came out o' jail, I was gonna make a new life.'

'So you took up with this crew?' Jenna frowned. The *Keiko* might not have been organised crime, but it was hardly like they only ever took on legal employment.

'Didn't exactly mean to,' Apirana admitted, looking a bit shamefaced. 'Ended up in a bar on Farport. I weren't drinking, but trouble found me anyway. Three Mongrels had tracked me down. Even after all that time they wanted me back working for 'em, and they didn't fancy taking no for an answer.' He shrugged, idly massaging the knuckles of his right fist with his left hand. 'You can probably guess how that turned out.'

'Not well?' Jenna ventured.

'Could say that,' Apirana chuckled ruefully. 'About the time the third one went through a table I remember thinking to meself, "A., this has got to be the shortest resolution ever." But the Captain were in the bar that night, an' he hustled me out before any of 'em got back up again an' before the cops arrived. Offered me a berth on his ship if I were willing to lift when stuff needed lifting, look menacing when we needed to hold our own, and get stuck in if someone tried to take what was ours. Seemed like about as fair a deal as an ex-con like me could've hoped for, so I signed up.' He shrugged. 'An' here I am, five years later. This is my *whānau* now.'

Jenna thought back to what she could remember of the night she joined the crew. 'Do all starships recruit from bars?'

'More'n you might think,' Apirana grunted. He looked down at his plate, and at the now-cold eggs on it. 'Hell, I never was much of a cook. Think I'll ditch this and see if I left any chocolate stashed in me cabin on the big girl.' He stood up, made his way to the waste disposal in the galley and scraped the eggs off into it. 'You coming?'

'I thought you'd be asking me about . . . things,' Jenna said in surprise. The big Maori shrugged.

'Captain asked me to talk to you. I've talked to you. Well, talked *at* you, really.' He stepped back around the galley, briefly blocking out the light as he did so. 'You ain't the only one with a past, it's true. Maybe there's things you're ashamed of, I dunno. But as far as I can see, on this boat that just means you know you ain't alone in that. I got my temper under better control these days – much better – but that don't mean I've mastered it. Every now an' then, I'll still lose it. The others know that, they understand it, they can make allowances for it. But we can't plan for what we don't understand. You wanna be understood, you're gonna need to talk t'someone. Maybe that'll be me, maybe that'll be someone else. But I'm telling you that I will listen t'you. An' now you know that no matter what is in your past, I am in no position to judge you.'

He turned and walked away, his heavy tread receding down the corridor.

VOID STATION PUNDAMILIA

The lights above the crew hatch turned green and Drift spun the wheel which released it, then swung it inwards to reveal the short docking corridor beyond. He turned back to face the rest of the crew, leaning on the hatch with his usual lazy grin. 'Everyone know what they're shopping for?'

Jenna nudged Apirana. 'Why don't we get supplies at a registered supply station?'

'Because all of the registered supply stations are on government-controlled worlds,' Drift replied before Apirana could speak.

'An' since there's jackshit of use to anyone in this part o' the galaxy there's no government-controlled worlds here,' Apirana explained, looking down at the slicer, 'so we'd have to take the long way around t'get to Old Earth, an' that'd mean not making our delivery deadline.'

From his other side, Kuai sighed in a long-suffering

manner. Apirana couldn't exactly blame him; void stations, those metal monstrosities thrown together by enterprising 'businessmen' to fill the gaps where no government had colonised, were in International Space and therefore, at least theoretically, beyond any government's jurisdiction. What that meant in practice was that any laws they might have were set and enforced by the owner and whatever security he'd hired, so such trifling niceties as trade descriptions and quality control were often more myth than reality. That would obviously be of some concern when purchasing things like engine parts, fuel and, of course, air.

Then again, rogue traders on government-controlled worlds would usually have some sort of legal protection from an outraged mob of disgruntled customers, even if it was only the threat of theoretical arrest and sentencing after the event, while merchants with a pitch on a void station enjoyed no such luck. In addition, there was always the risk that the person you'd just cheated might turn out to be a *mafioso* or similar, in which case you might just as well walk out of an airlock without a suit and save yourself some hassle. As a result, the only sensible course of action for trade on a void station was to talk loudly, swagger noticeably, wear your weapons openly and check everything twice; or, failing that, see who the people who could manage those things bought from and do the same, on the basis that those merchants were likely to be fairly honest at least some of the time.

'Let's get to it, then,' Drift said, glancing at his wrist chrono. 'We don't exactly have a lot of time, and if we all want to still be breathing by the time we hit the First System then we need to source some oh-two from somewhere.' He fluttered a hand impatiently at the hatchway. 'Go!'

The crew moved forwards, minus Jia, who would be staying behind to mind the *Keiko*. Thieves were rather more common at void stations than the regulated and patrolled in-system waystations such as the one they'd been berthed in over Carmella II, so it paid to have someone on board rather than putting their faith in security access codes alone. Apirana was, of course, needed to loom menacingly, so he shuffled along into the docking tunnel behind Kuai and Jenna. It was a struggle not to lengthen his stride and walk naturally, but to do so would mean trampling his smaller crewmates so he hung back and moved at their speed, dawdling though it seemed to him.

'So,' he said quietly to Jenna as they stepped out of the tunnel and into the void station proper, and Drift, Rourke and Micah headed off in the other direction, 'you worked out where we're goin' yet?'

'The Van Der Graaf Centre is a conference facility in Amsterdam,' Jenna replied, 'but that's all the Spine had on it. I've no idea what it's going to be used for on that day.' She shook her head in mild frustration: despite its name, humanity's galactic databank was essentially a fractured series of individual, static records, updated on a system-by-system basis and only when a new courier arrived with the next download. Up-to-date information was only accessible about things within the same star system and something as trivial and fluid as a certain conference centre's itinerary was never going to be available from further afield, no matter how good a slicer you were.

'That's a damn weird place to smuggle something into,' Apirana muttered, absent-mindedly rubbing the knuckles of his right hand with the fingers of his left. 'Private addresses, warehouses, bars, the dark side of moons; we've delivered to all of 'em. Never done a dark run to something like this, though.' He grimaced. New experiences were all well and good, but he preferred to be slightly more in control of them. 'Feels kinda . . . exposed.'

'And during the day, too,' Jenna noted. 'That can't be regular for a smuggling job, right?'

'Not usually,' Apirana admitted, 'Although a lotta places, once you're through the borders you're better off looking like you've got nothing t'hide; cops get attracted to sneaking around.'

'I suppose that makes sense,' Jenna nodded slowly, 'but this whole thing still seems really odd to me, it's like . . .' She trailed off, blinking in surprise as she looked around them properly for the first time. 'What the *hell*?'

Kuai snorted, and Apirana felt a smile playing over his lips. 'You never been to a void station before, huh?'

The outside of a void station was covered in moving, flashing lights, mainly because they were always so far from a star and any corresponding external illumination that they wouldn't be seen otherwise. The inside wasn't much different as the assembled vendors tried to attract custom, and in that respect they superficially resembled the bustling, frenetic markets of any big city on any inhabited planet or moon. Once you started looking at the goods on offer, however, you realised quite how different it was.

Jenna was staring at a small stall which was quite openly displaying drugs, and illegal drugs at that . . . only of course, out here in International Space, outside the heliosphere of any inhabited system, they *weren't* illegal. A small notice in English, Russian, Mandarin, Spanish and Swahili declared that the stallholder was not responsible for any difficulties which might arise from taking the merchandise across interstellar borders, but the rather large sign which simply read five translations of 'WHOLESALE RATES AVAILABLE' clearly indicated that they were geared up to provide the raw materials should you be prepared to try your luck.

'And that's just . . .? Well, I guess it would be,' Jenna finished, answering her own question and tailing off a little lamely.

'Some of the governments don't like it, an' the USNA tried to stamp it out a while back,' Apirana told her, 'but everyone else got a bit itchy about them trying to put their laws on International Space.'

'And they liked the idea of the USNA *claiming* large chunks of International Space even less,' Kuai put in. 'The Red Star Confederate actually threatened war.'

'Luckily for everyone, the Free Systems breakaway started an' the USNA got caught up in it,' Apirana added, 'an' the whole thing was pretty much forgotten about.' He put his hand on Jenna's shoulder and gently steered her away from the stall with its neatly arranged powders, leaves and pills, along with the machine for measuring the purity of what you were about to buy and the two serious-looking men holding starguns in case anyone was thinking of a smash-and-grab of the merchandise. 'Come on, we got a job to do.'

'Right.' Jenna slipped out from under his hand and hurried a couple of steps ahead. She clearly intended it to look like she was eager to press on at their assigned task, but Apirana was used to smaller people being uncomfortable with casual physical contact with him. *Then again, I did tell her what I did to my father . . .*

They drifted through the grid-like layout of the markets, looking for useful items among the stalls and vendors. All around them were great drapes of cloth ranging from old-fashioned, plant-derived fabrics through to the most modern poly-u sheets which changed colour in line with the temperature, or the programmable weaves that could flash up brand logos, gang signs or anything else the buyer desired. Boxes of protein bars and nutrient shakes pushed up against small jars of genuine Chinese spices and racks of roasted meats, salty aromas intended to catch in the throats of travellers too long subjected to longlife ship food. Small booths offered immediate beams of the Next Big Thing in music who probably hailed from halfway across the galaxy, or a vid-scope from New Hollywood on Washington Major . . .

'The pirates are back!' one stall holder shouted. 'The pirates are back!'

Apirana glanced over and saw, to his lack of surprise, racks of weapons ranging from the basic and mundane to the exotic and downright bizarre.

The vendor was a large *Pākehā* man, dark stubble standing out against his fair skin, with a sizeable gut and enthusiasm to match.

'You, sir!' he called, gesturing enthusiastically to Apirana. 'You look like a fighter! Best deals on shooting hardware this side of Old Earth, right here! Kit out the whole crew for a couple of grand, and you could stop Captain Gabriel Drake hisself if he came for you!'

'Drake's dead!' someone catcalled. 'The Africans killed him and captured the *Thirty-Six Degrees* years ago!'

'Is that so?' the stallholder retorted, turning on the speaker in a manner more appropriate for a villain in one of the Chinese melodramas Apirana knew Jia secretly watched. 'If Drake is dead, who's been hitting all those freighters in the Uzuri System?'

'I heard it was Annie Eclectic!' someone piped up. 'Mohamud Kediye!'

Apirana sighed and turned away as the names of various pirates and ne'er-do-wells, some probably fictional, began to fill the air. Remote though it was, Void Station Pundamilia was the only stopover point in this part of the galaxy, and as such it was still busy with travellers. A glance ahead showed that Apirana's two companions had disappeared from view while he'd been distracted, so the Maori grunted in annoyance, set his face in the stoniest glower he could muster and simply barged forwards. After a few initial angry words, hastily bitten back when the utterers turned to see who had jostled them, the crowd started to part in front of him like sheep before a dog.

He found Jenna in an alcove piled high with electronic goods and parts, face alight and looking like she needed more hands to both rummage and hold things to her satisfaction. He came up behind her and she turned towards him, two flattish metal boxes of subtly different shapes under one arm, a straggle of cables thrown over one shoulder and something small, sleek and black nestling in the palm of her left hand, which she showed him as excitedly as a naturalist discovering a new species.

'Do you know what this is?!'

Apirana blinked. 'No.'

'This is a Tannheiser KK-2490! A "Truth Box"! This isn't even *legal* anywhere except African systems, and it's reckoned they'll outlaw it by the end of the year too!'

Apirana frowned at the object in Jenna's hand. He couldn't see what it would do which was that miraculous, but then it sounded like some sort of slicer toy so he probably wouldn't understand even if she told him. He'd picked up enough rudimentary mechanics and electronics to fix small, practical problems with various vehicles, and he could access the Spine without a second thought, but people like Jenna lived in a different world ruled by data flow and code strings as long as his arm.

'Well, good,' he said, then paused as he registered exactly how aglow her eyes were. 'Was there—'

'I *need* to get this,' Jenna exclaimed, knees bending slightly in time with the emphasis in her voice. 'This eats through Jupiter-level encryptions in *minutes*, if I had this we could—'

'A.!' Kuai shouted, appearing past Jenna's shoulder

and jerking a thumb back the way he'd come, 'I've tracked down a backup power capacitor for the Heim generator, there's some slight corrosion—'

'—I mean, forget about orbital datalogs, there's—'

'—basically sound, I had to cannibalise the last spare and—'

'—have *no idea* how much safer this would make—'

'—then we're all going to end up on the ceiling when the primary—'

'*Turituri!*' Apirana thundered, and both of them fell quiet abruptly. To be fair, so did the surrounding market for a few metres in all directions: some sentiments transcended barriers of language. The people around them turned back to what they were doing when it was obvious that a fight wasn't going to break out immediately, and Apirana fingered the credit chip in his pocket programmed with a small portion of the upfront fee they'd been given for the job, and wondered why Drift couldn't have found someone else to babysit the slicer and the grease monkey.

'Now,' he continued in a more reasonable tone of voice, 'one at a time, and using words I've got some hope of understanding, explain to me why the Captain ain't gonna be mad if I let you blow some of our money.' He nodded at Kuai. 'You go first.'

Kuai started talking about the importance of immediately accessible spare parts and how he'd had to break something on the *Jonah* down to make a running repair, which in turn meant that if something now failed on the Heim drive then they'd all find themselves unexpectedly floating when the artificial gravity failed. Apirana winced: the infamous Boreas

III 'landing' had been one of the most unpleasant experiences of his life, and was the reason why Drift had subsequently ordered Jia to wear crash webbing at all times during a re-entry. The little mechanic seemed to have a strong case, and Apirana was about to nod his assent when he saw Jenna stiffen.

'Y'alright?' he asked, frowning. Her eyes were widening as she stared at him.

No, not at him. *Past* him.

Two things happened virtually at once.

First, Kuai half-raised his hand, like he was back in class somewhere in Sichuan Province, and hesitantly said, 'Uh, A.?'

Second, someone cleared their throat ostentatiously behind him.

'Hey! Mongrel!'

A pirana didn't turn. He didn't need to. He'd recognised the accent and knew what he'd see. Instead he looked at Kuai.

'Get out of here and call the Captain.'

Kuai's face took on an expression of puzzlement. 'But—'

'That weren't a suggestion,' Apirana snapped. The little mechanic bolted away obediently and Apirana nodded at Jenna, whose eyes appeared to be trying to escape from her head while she fiddled nervously with the sleeve over her right forearm. 'You too. Get back to the ship.' *Now* he turned, breathing deeply to fill his lungs and swell his already impressive chest, just in case it would be enough to make a difference.

The moment he laid eyes on them he knew it wouldn't be.

There were three of them, all in designer bodysuits which looked initially like the same charcoal-grey outfit any businessman might wear if he was confident about his physique. However, Apirana could see the subtle alterations, such as the grain and thickness of the fabric which marked it as high-level impact armour. An area of the suit would stiffen momentarily when struck; it was hardly perfect protection against a blade or a bullet, but it could turn a fatal wound into a severe one, and a severe one into an inconvenience. There was something odd about the coolant lines on the suits of the flankers, too. Had he been a betting man, Apirana would have put money that alongside the devices to keep the occupant at a comfortable temperature were ones which could inject adrenaline or some other, more volatile stimulant into the wearer's system.

All three were male and all three had the golden skin tone of an East Asian ancestry, but there the similarity ended. The one on the right was bald with decorative metal studs in his skull and had a mechanical arm, judging by the shape of it beneath the bodysuit and the metal fingers extending from the sleeve. He also had speakers in his throat to presumably replace a voice box, although it was anyone's guess whether that was a dramatic affectation or simply a result of cigarettes like the one currently clamped between his teeth. The one on the left had dark, slicked-back hair and what appeared to be replacement legs. He also had augmented eyes, but instead of one mechanical eye like the Captain he had a narrow visor. Apirana had heard of short-range laser weapons concealed in things like that, although he'd tended to dismiss them as legend. More likely it would allow the wearer some sort of different spectrum to his vision, possibly infrared to spot body heat.

The one in the middle appeared to be unaugmented and had hair that was bleached a pure white and stood up in two ridges at either side of his head. No skin was visible on any of them except their faces and hands, but Apirana knew that their bodies would be covered with tattoos even more intricate than his own.

They were Yakuza.

He sketched a quick bow and switched to Japanese, which along with English was the official language of the West Pacific Nations. 'Ah, good day. I am afraid you are mistaken.'

'I think not,' the man in the middle replied, touching fingers to his own face. Apirana had immediately pegged him as the leader; the other two were almost certainly bodyguards or enforcers. 'I know a Mongrel when I see one.'

Apirana sighed. Turf war between gangs and organised crime syndicates ran as a sort of dark counterpart to the border disputes between governing bodies, and while they might not have racked up the same sort of body count they were just as vicious, if not more so. It could be that this Yakuza clan ran Pundamilia, or they wanted to muscle in on it, or they'd simply seized on the opportunity to victimise someone they perceived as a Mongrel mobster. Whatever the cause, this had the potential to end very badly.

He tried again. 'These are not gang marks, they are my heritage. Not every tattooed Maori is a Mongrel.' If he could at least keep them busy long, enough for Kuai to reach the Captain then the game would change dramatically . . .

'Unlucky for you, then,' White Hair said, with a smile that Apirana didn't like the look of in the slightest. Well, that was it: he wasn't going to try to fight off three Yakuza in the middle of a void station, so since stalling them hadn't worked the only option left was running for—

'A.?'

Jenna's voice brought his head around involuntarily. The slicer was still standing in the electronics stall despite his instruction to get clear, and he was about to yell at her to run as a precursor to doing the same thing himself when she nodded sideways.

Another Yakuza was standing some ten feet away, and he had Kuai in an apparently effortless half nelson. The mechanic's head was pushed forwards and down at what had to be an uncomfortable angle, and Kuai's comm-piece dangled casually from the gangster's free hand.

Apirana looked again at Jenna, who'd now pulled her sleeve back and was doing something with the bulky, manacle-like bracelet she wore on her right forearm when not on the ship. He'd always assumed it was some sort of health monitor, although he had no idea what good she thought it could do now. 'Jenna, get out of here.'

'You can't take them all,' she replied, just loud enough for him to hear. The Yakuza holding Kuai was smiling at them, and Apirana could see the two augmented thugs advancing slowly in his peripheral vision.

'Then go get help!' he hissed. She was right, of

course, but he wasn't going to bug out and leave Kuai alone.

Jenna shot him a glance, her fingers darting over her bracelet and fiddling with the controls. 'Just keep them busy for a few seconds.'

He blinked. *What the hell was that supposed to mean?* But whether or not she'd actually gone mad, he was out of options. He *hated* being out of options.

He lunged sideways without warning, took three quick steps and barrelled into Voice Box. The Yakuza raised his metal hand to try to ward him off, but while Apirana might have lost an arm-wrestling match to the augmented thug there was nothing to be done about weight and momentum, and Apirana had a lot of both. He slammed into his opponent and used both hands to shove the man backwards into White Hair, sending them both sprawling to the floor.

Visor adjusted quickly to the unexpected disappearance of his companion and fired off a kick with one of his metal legs which slammed into Apirana's ribcage. It hurt – a lot – but Apirana managed to hook his arm under the artificial limb before Visor could withdraw it again, then simply slammed his fist into the Yakuza's face. The man fell backwards, legs thrashing desperately, but Apirana lifted one boot and stamped down hard on his chest. He felt something crack beneath his foot and heard the man's breath explode out of him with an agonised moan of pain, then stamped on the Yakuza's face in an attempt to smash his visor. He connected, but his attention was wrenched around by a scream behind him.

Kuai was struggling against his captor, a small,

red-stained blade in his hand – the mechanic's multi-tool, which he must have pulled from his pocket during the commotion. The Yakuza who had a hold of him was bleeding from his left thigh but the wound didn't look deep enough to cause him a major problem.

'Look out!' Jenna yelled, and Apirana whirled back around just in time to see Voice Box advancing on him, blue-white light crackling on his fist.

Knuckletasers. Shit.

He tried to dodge the blow, but the same mass which had allowed him to send a grown man flying like a ten-year-old tackled by a rugby prop forward worked against him and the punch hit him squarely in the chest.

The metal arm was like a piledriver. The force of the blow to his chest would have knocked him back anyway, but the added kick of the voltage left him on his back, staring at strip lighting and feeling like his lungs had been replaced by sieves. He managed to roll onto his side, despite his muscles seemingly having turned to jelly, and caught a glimpse of Jenna. She'd removed the bracelet from her wrist now, and she pressed one last button with an air of finality and threw it onto the floor in front of her. It landed with a clatter not six feet from where Apirana was sprawled, with one light flashing an angry red.

And every single light went out.

Total power failure on a void station meant one thing: Death. With no life support to pump and recycle the air, no heating to keep the deathly chill of deep space at bay and no way through the docking hatches back to the ships which would provide a means of escape, everyone on board would essentially be doomed. Understandably, the sudden blackout was met with screams and shouts of alarm.

Apirana staggered up to his feet. Give it a second . . .

Emergency lights flickered into life, dimmer than the originals but still bright enough. He'd hoped that the Yakuza would be caught off-guard, but what he saw surprised him so much that he himself just stopped and stared.

Voice Box was clutching at his metal right arm with his flesh-and-blood left hand, but the prosthetic was hanging limp and apparently useless at his side. Apirana got the distinct impression that the man would have been swearing at it, but the speakers in his throat were apparently not working either. Meanwhile, Visor was pulling himself away across the floor, his legs trailing behind him.

Apirana took that all in, then took a quick two-step run-up and did his best to drive one of his boots clean through Voice Box's chest. The kick sent the panicked Yakuza flying again, this time into a stall apparently selling tools and spare parts which collapsed onto him with a sound like an avalanche in a scrapyard.

White Hair clearly didn't like the way the fight was going and turned to run for it as soon as Voice Box was buried by falling metal. Apirana let him go and turned around to find Kuai panting hard and holding his multi-tool, with his assailant having apparently come to the same conclusion as his boss. Visor, meanwhile, was calling out for his friends in a pained, piteous voice; it appeared that he'd lost the ability to see as well as the ability to walk, but

Apirana wasn't certain if that was thanks to Jenna or his boot.

He fixed Jenna with an incredulous stare. 'What was *that*?'

'High-intensity, short-range EMP,' the slicer replied absently, stooping to pick her bracelet up gingerly: Apirana got the impression that it had suddenly become rather warm. She saw his confused expression and elaborated. 'Electro-magnetic pulse. I figured if half their bodies weren't working properly you could probably take them out.'

'Lemme get this straight,' Apirana said, pinching the bridge of his nose. 'All this time you've been carrying about a . . . an EMP, on your fucking *arm*?'

'Only when I was off the ship,' Jenna explained hurriedly, 'and it takes a very specific keycode to activate it.' She looked over at the immobile Yakuza, still wailing in Japanese. 'Let's get out of here. Probably best not to draw any more attention than we already have.'

Apirana grunted and took a quick look around them. He was used to being the subject of stares, but there was more than just casual interest being directed towards the three of them and the damage his fight had caused. He also saw a bulge in one pocket of Jenna's flight suit, roughly the size of the Truth Box she'd mentioned earlier, and did his best to suppress a slight smile as he nodded.

'Right. Let's go find the Captain.'

The return of the lights had headed off the immediate hysterical reactions, but a lot of people were still moving in a determined manner towards wherever their ships were berthed. Apirana, Kuai and Jenna fell in with the general push of the crowd but he kept a close eye on their surroundings as he pulled out his comm and keyed in Drift's ident, alert for anyone who looked like they might have any sort of Yakuza link.

Drift picked up after the second beep. +*A., where the hell are you? What's going on? Kuai was babbling something about trouble but then the call cut off, and I called you but you didn't pick up.*+

'I was probably fighting one of 'em,' Apirana replied grimly, looking down at his shirt and noticing the four small burn marks on it for the first time. He lowered his voice a little, trying to speak no louder than his earpiece needed to pick up the words. 'Four Yakuza, Cap. They decided to make trouble for me, an' at least two of 'em were augmented.'

+*You took them all out?*+ The Captain wasn't even bothering to try to hide the incredulity in his tone, and Apirana couldn't blame him; he'd been about three seconds from having his face caved in by a metal fist.

'Not me; Jenna did something fancy with an EMP an' crippled the circuitheads, an' the others lost the taste for it after that.'

+*She did* what? *Is that what knocked the lights funny a few moments ago?*+

Apirana blinked, taken back by the venom in the Captain's voice. 'Yeah, but it's okay, the backup power came on—'

+*She couldn't know that! I don't care how fucking smart she is, she couldn't have known that! Tell me you've got whatever-it-was that made it.*+

'Uh, no,' Apirana admitted, casting a glance at the

bracelet which Jenna had now refastened onto her wrist.

+*Do it.*+

'I don't really think I need to—' Apirana began.

+*Me cago en la puta A., just do it! And meet us back at the ship as soon as you can. If we can get through the damn airlock after her little stunt.*+ The connection clicked and died. Apirana frowned in surprise. It wasn't like the Captain to be that . . . tetchy. Especially not where Jenna was concerned.

'Problem?' Jenna asked tensely.

'You might wanna gimme that bracelet,' Apirana muttered, holding out his hand. The diminutive slicer looked up at him, confused.

'It's one-use only.'

'Yeah, even so,' Apirana said. 'Captain din't sound pleased, so let's show him you ain't gonna be doing it again.'

'I . . . *what?*' Jenna spluttered, 'those bastards were—' She stopped, looked around quickly, then moderated the volume of her voice. 'They were trying to *hurt* you. What the hell was I supposed to do, let them?'

'Well, they din't manage it,' Apirana told her. 'Much,' he added, rubbing his chest ruefully. 'Look, I'm damn grateful, but just gimme the bracelet t'keep the Captain happy for now an' we can discuss it with him when we're outta here, right?'

'Fine.' Jenna uncoupled the bracelet and passed it over to him, but he could tell she was seething beneath her attempt at a calm exterior.

They reached the docking corridor without further incident, but the door didn't release when Apirana punched in the code. He grimaced and tried again, with no luck. 'Ah, hells. This anything to do with you?' Looking around, he could see that other doors seemed to be similarly inconvenienced, judging by the reactions of people clustered around them.

'Maybe,' Jenna said shortly, pulling a screwdriver from somewhere. 'Move.' He stepped aside to give her access, then stood as casually as he could between her and the rest of the station so his large frame hid as much of her as possible from view.

It was while he was stood there scanning the crowd for trouble that he saw Drift approaching, his face thunderous. Micah and Rourke followed behind him, with the Dutch mercenary wheeling a trolley bearing tanks of oxygen, but the Captain was striding out in front with an expression Apirana had rarely witnessed before.

'Any time now would be good,' he murmured, hoping Jenna could hear him while Kuai hovered nervously. The only reply was a metallic whisper and a sudden sensation of space at his back; he looked over his shoulder to see the door sliding aside and Jenna screwing the cover of the control panel back into place, her face still sullen.

He turned back towards the others, who were now only a few metres away. 'You get enough air?'

'The recycling system's working pretty much one hundred per cent efficient, that should be fine,' Kuai replied hastily, casting a worried glance at Drift's face.

'Take it through,' Drift said, not looking at them. He jerked his head; Apirana grimaced but moved to one side to reveal Jenna, whose defiant stare faltered a little when she saw the Captain's expression.

'What the hell do you think you're playing at?' Drift demanded flatly as the others filed past. 'We're on a void station in the middle of nowhere and you start playing around with an EMP? What if the backups hadn't kicked in? How would you have sliced your way out of something when there's no fucking *power* for your precious little systems to work? Then we get stuck here, which means we don't make the delivery deadline, which means—' He cut himself off, apparently in frustration, but this was an emotion Jenna clearly shared.

'I wasn't "playing around",' the slicer snapped, 'I was protecting our crew!'

Drift folded his arms. 'You're wouldn't have been protecting us if you'd knocked the station's entire power system out! And why have you been carrying an EMP around on my fucking *ship*? Why have you even *got* one?'

'It's impossible to set off by accident!' Jenna replied. 'I built it when I was on Franklin Minor because that's, like, circuithead central and they've all got more metal than sense.' She glanced around hurriedly, then leaned forwards with a conspiratorial air. 'Okay, fine: look, the reason circuitheads freak me out so much? There were a bunch of abductions of young women by a gang of augmenteds when I was doing my Masters. One of the victims was a fellow student and *she never showed up again!* I built this to knock out enhancements in case anyone tried it with me.' She folded her arms in return and stared back at Drift, who didn't seem impressed.

'You built it? Just like that?'

Jenna rolled her eyes. 'I *am* pretty smart. And I

was studying in a posh research facility at the time, you have *no idea* the kind of kit you can get your hands on if you know what you're doing.'

Drift's jaw moved as he chewed at the inside of his mouth, a habit which always made Apirana wince. Then his face set into a look of resolution.

'I'm leaving you here.'

'*What?*' Jenna's face drained of colour, and Apirana fought to contain his own immediate response. What was the Captain thinking? He was about to open his mouth and protest when he became aware that the three of them were no longer alone. Drift seemed to notice at the same time, and they turned together to find themselves looking at a pair of men in red body armour and open-face helmets, both cradling starguns across their chests.

Station security. The void stations all had their own enforcement gangs, who paid no attention to interpersonal altercations but would stamp down violently on anything that might threaten the station itself. Such as, Apirana realised, the power being knocked out.

He saw their eyes widen as they focused on his face, and their guns started to raise to cover him. *The tats. Someone gave them a description of me . . .*

There were two shockingly loud explosions next to him, and both men's features exploded in blood and bone. He whipped around to look at Drift, who was already holstering one of his smoking pistols.

'On board,' the Captain snapped, 'now!' He grabbed Jenna's arm and dragged her into the docking corridor. 'You too. Move!'

'But you said—'

'I wanted to see how you'd react,' Drift growled,

slamming the door control to shut it as Apirana hurried over the threshold. The moment the heavy door had slid shut, Drift put a bullet into the control panel on their side. 'We *were* going to have a conversation after that, but that option's off the table now.'

'But you killed them!' Jenna blurted, wrenching her arm free of Drift's grasp.

'Yes,' the Captain snapped, turning away from her and striding towards the other end where the *Keiko* was attached, 'welcome to the galaxy! What do you think they were going to do to you and A. once they'd worked out it was you who nearly knocked this place dead? You want to stick around and find out, be my guest: otherwise, hurry the fuck up or they'll scramble something which can shoot us down before we make the jump away from here!'

Apirana broke into a jog, wincing at the pains in his chest as he did so and trying to ignore how easily Jenna outpaced him as she ran towards her only ticket out. *That's two dead on this run already . . .*

They'd parked the *Keiko* at a waystation above Mars, and gone the rest of the way in the *Jonah*.

Jia had needed to calculate an emergency jump to get away from the void station before its small fleet of defence fighters could launch, and it had sent them off course: not by much, but their schedule was tight enough that by the time they'd reoriented themselves and got back on track they were running behind. Drift had chafed at the delay, but there wasn't really anything to be done about it. The First System was still the busiest in the galaxy, and the risk of collisions with other ships became too great for anyone to risk making an Alcubierre jump inside the Martian orbit. Besides that, of course, was the fact that they wanted to avoid attention. Luckily, despite teeming with ships and undoubtedly the last place they would want to be if they ended up being pursued, it was possibly the best place to be ignored in the first place.

The First System was the only inhabited system in which no individual government held sway over the interplanetary space. How long that would have lasted without the technology to colonise beyond the stars was anyone's guess, but the availability of a whole galaxy of raw materials had led to the controversial ice mining operations on Saturn's rings and Europa being closed, most of the First System being declared a Humanity Heritage Area and the whole vast expanse being treated with the same cautious diplomacy as Antarctica had been, centuries before.

In truth, though, it wasn't just the delay which had been rubbing Drift's nerves, for all that he could feel the weight of Kelsier's threat around his neck. The other reason his whisky supply had taken such a battering was the last few seconds on Void Station Pundamilia.

Oh, it was probably true enough what he'd told Jenna; if the station enforcers had found out that she'd let off an EMP then they probably *would* have killed her, and Apirana, and perhaps the rest of them for good measure. They were the only law on a void station, and by the same token Drift had committed no crime any government would recognise by gunning them down first, but Ichabod Drift had always had a fairly hazy approach to laws in any case. That wasn't what was eating at him.

He'd killed people before, of course: you couldn't run on the shady side long without getting into fights, and you certainly wouldn't last as long as he had unless you'd won most of them. And perhaps in the old days, when he'd been flying under a different name, he might have reacted to a problem by shooting first. These days, though . . . Well, the fact was that there was no real certainty anyone *would* have realised that Jenna had done anything. It wasn't like young women wandering around with an EMP device were a common occurrence, and under most circumstances he'd have fancied his chances of talking his crew's way out of 'misunderstandings' without needing to resort to violence. But that would have taken time, and time was a luxury that Ichabod Drift didn't have.

Besides, Kelsier's threats had changed things. He might be keeping the truth from everyone around him, but he was capable of being honest enough with himself to admit that. If keeping his past buried involved shooting a couple of void station thugs when perhaps he might not have technically needed to then that was a price he would pay, but not gladly, and not without a bitter twist in his soul directed at Kelsier and his manipulations.

'Why haven't we been challenged yet?' Jenna asked from her seat at their main terminal as the blue-green orb of Old Earth grew slowly in front of them. Things were still a little brittle between the two of them, but one good outcome from his shooting of the enforcers was that she did at least seem to appreciate how serious he was about this job: her EMP bracelet was under lock and key in his cabin, and she'd raised no further protests about it. He'd wondered about trying to get her to turn out the rest of her possessions just to make doubly sure she wasn't sitting on anything else potentially disastrous, but had finally decided against it. He still needed her expertise, and no good would be served by alienating her. Once they'd delivered Kelsier's package, however, he was intending to have a conversation to lay out some new ground rules for her presence on his ship.

In the meantime he'd spent a fair chunk of their journey from the void station cautiously repairing their relationship, when he hadn't been quietly cursing Nicolas Kelsier or evading questions from Apirana and Rourke about his apparent short temper. Rourke in particular had been concerned at how quickly he'd resorted to lethal force; not because she disagreed with him, but simply because it was out of character. He wasn't entirely certain he'd managed to convince her with his responses.

'With no single body controlling all the flight paths, no one pays you much attention until you get into their bit of sky,' Drift replied to her question. 'If you're quick, you can use that to your advantage. Who are we at the moment, anyway?'

'The *Erathirea*,' Jenna replied, double-checking the data screen in front of her. She frowned. 'What does that even mean?'

'No idea,' Drift answered honestly, 'it might be Greek. Or something.' He waved a hand dismissively. 'It doesn't matter. Just get ready to switch idents when I give the signal.'

'When *I* give the signal,' Jia corrected him. She'd adopted what Drift always thought of as her 'pilot hat', a battered thing of brown leather with a shiny peak and a faux fur-lined flap on each side to cover the ears, although at the moment they were tied up.

When he'd first asked her why she wore it in the climate-controlled cockpit she'd simply tutted at him and said 'pilot reasons'. Given she only put it on when she was about to do something tricky and had nearly had a meltdown at her brother when he'd hidden it once, Drift could only assume that she considered it lucky but was too embarrassed to say so outright.

'When Jia gives the signal,' Drift agreed, knowing better than to needlessly contradict Jia when she was zoning into her megalomaniacal piloting mindset. He then turned to Jenna, pointed at himself and silently mouthed *When I give the signal*. Jenna sighed and rolled her eyes, but nodded.

'Where are you thinking of entering?' Tamara Rourke asked, appearing in the cockpit doorway.

'Over the North Pole would make sense,' Drift said, tapping at the terminal in front of him. 'Come down somewhere no one watches that closely, skim over the North Sea between Norway and Britain, and straight into Amsterdam. The weather's good at the moment, too. Well,' he amended after a second, 'as good as we're likely to get.'

'You expect me to skim over a couple of thousand miles of ocean?' Jia snorted.

'Why, can't you do it?' Drift asked in surprise.

'Never said that!' Jia fired back over her shoulder. 'But that's a long way for us to go under radar, is all. Norway's got those really steep valleys with the sea in around the northern edge, right?'

Drift could feel himself looking blank. 'Uh . . .'

'Fjords?' Jenna piped up.

'Yeah, fjords!' Jia confirmed. 'They should hide us,

then once we're in the Europan system we can switch idents just in case and head overland, right?'

'I don't know if we've got the time,' Drift muttered, checking the chrono with a tight feeling in his gut. 'We can come in fast over the sea from the North Pole as there's not much traffic from that direction. The overland flight lanes will have speed restrictions and we'd be risking official attention if we break them.'

'Well, we hit a freak wave while I'm trying to skim for a couple thousand miles at well over the speed of sound then we're going to be . . .' Jia trailed off for a second as though searching for a suitable word, then settled for '. . .*fucked*.'

'Noted,' Drift replied, perhaps a little shortly. He checked the chrono again. 'How long until we can make atmo?'

'If you'd told me *beforehand* that you'd wanted to avoid the moon then we'd have had more time,' Jia snapped.

Drift scowled at the back of her head. 'I figured you'd have remembered that it's got sensor emplacements all over—'

'Of course I remembered!' Jia cut him off. 'But you never said you wanted to *avoid* it until we were already on course, so don't—'

'I don't *tell* you to avoid crashing into stars, either!' Drift retorted. 'But I figure you might have worked out that since we're doing a goddamn dark run we—'

'*How. Long?*' Rourke shouted over both of them.

There was a second or two of silence.

'About ninety minutes,' Jia said, her voice level but laden with enough sulkiness to float a battleship.

'Tight,' Rourke commented, coming up behind Drift and glancing over his shoulder at the chrono. 'How much of a window do we have?'

'Window?' Drift snorted. 'That's hopeful. We just have to aim to get there on time.'

'What if we don't?' Rourke asked quietly, bending down to speak into his ear. He could read the question beneath the question. *How badly is your old employer going to take it?*

'Run,' Drift murmured, then added, 'and hide.'

'You always did love the quiet life,' Rourke snorted. 'I'll tell A. and Micah to get loaded up in case the reception party is planning to cause problems.'

'Do that,' Drift agreed. One of the frequent balancing acts his crew trod was being ready for a potential double-cross without being so aggressive that they sparked a confrontation themselves. Thankfully Rourke, Micah and Apirana were all fairly level-headed and unlikely to shoot first unless the situation really warranted it.

'We got details on the venue yet?' he asked Jenna, looking over at where the young slicer was sitting.

'It seems to be hosting some sort of scientific convention today,' she replied, looking up from her screen with a frown. 'Do you normally "deliver" to that sort of thing?'

'First time for everything,' Drift replied easily, but he couldn't shake a nagging worry. Kelsier's rationale had made sense – someone involved in clandestine dealings for a government might indeed not have access to official governmental couriers – but it was still a very open, very public location to be carrying an unknown cargo into. 'Okay girls, look alive; we're coming into the outer customs territory, but there's just too much traffic for them to stop everyone up here. We can't afford a boarding, so if it looks like we've attracted attention I'm going to need the best evasive flying and data wrangling you've got, right off the bat.'

'Quit trying to tell me how to do my job,' Jia said, flexing her fingers, 'and just listen to that radio.'

The next hour was a lesson in relativity for Drift, as the *Jonah* seemed to crawl through space while the ship's chrono raced on, surely far quicker than mere seconds would allow. However, when his paranoia led to him double-checking it against the one on his wrist it was still depressingly accurate. New lights appeared all around them; other ships, few and distant at first but then increasingly more numerous and closer. Despite the sheer volume of space around Old Earth, its position as the hub of humanity meant that there was still enough traffic for the skies to get crowded.

'Verification check incoming,' Jenna suddenly piped up. Drift swallowed and looked over at her. The slicer had rewritten some of their ident overlay codes after joining the crew: they'd held up fine on the last smuggling job the *Jonah* had run, but that had been in a small, backwater system rather than the centre of galactic civilisation.

There was a few seconds' tense pause. Then Jenna puffed out her cheeks in relief, her exhalation briefly blowing a few strands of hair away from her face. 'Green-lighted.'

Drift echoed her sigh with one of his own. 'Right, so they believe we are who we say we are—'

'Idiots,' Jia put in absently.

'—so now we just have to look uninteresting,' he finished.

'You sure you still want to do your North Pole route?' Jia asked without turning her head. 'Do we have the time?'

Drift checked the chrono again and grimaced, a bitter taste in his mouth. 'No. But what option have we got? We can't just be seen to make atmo over Europa or we'd be a prime target for a mid-air customs check, we've got to sneak in from somewhere else so they think we're already in the system.'

'Where's the patrol boat which just scanned us?' Jia asked. Her fingers were suddenly skittering across the control relays, faster than Drift's eyes could follow. She was setting something up, but . . .?

'The boat!' Jia snapped. He jerked his gaze away and checked his screen, then passed the data to her display.

'Starboard one-eleven, elevation forty-two.'

'Beautiful,' Jia cooed. Drift winced. He'd heard that tone of voice before, usually right before she did something terrifying.

'Jia, what—'

'Find me a storm system over Europa,' the pilot snapped, not looking at him, 'the nastier the better.'

'I . . . what?'

'Just *do* it!'

'Fine,' Drift muttered. He'd learned from bitter experience that once Jia was in full flow she'd do whatever she wanted anyway. Your best option was to just give her the information she demanded so at least she had the greatest chance of not killing everyone. 'O-kay, looks like the coast of France is taking a battering.' He slid that to her read-out as well, watched her hat dip as she glanced at it and nodded.

'That'll do. Hold on.'

Drift instinctively took a firm grip on the sides of his panel, despite the fact that the artificial gravity from the Heim generator would save him from being thrown about. Still, his stomach did lurch slightly as Jia did something and the sky suddenly pinwheeled across the cockpit. 'What are you—'

'Ship!' Jenna screamed. 'Ship!'

'I *know*!' Jia shouted back, as a large cargo cruiser veered into view, shockingly near. 'What do you think I'm aiming for?'

'Why are we getting this close?' Drift yelled, alarmed despite himself. He could see the dents and scratches in the leviathan's hull, and the black blooms from where it had experienced countless re-entry heatings.

'Because,' Jia replied with an unmistakeable note of satisfaction in her voice, 'I've been watching its vectors and it's about to do . . . *this*!'

The cargo cruiser's rockets flared and its nose dipped towards the planet which was, from one perspective at least, below them. Jia dived the *Jonah* at the same moment, throwing them after their larger neighbour.

'You're entering *now*?' Drift demanded incredulously, strapping himself into his chair.

'This *pángrándàwù* is giving us cover from that patrol boat,' Jia said easily, as though shadowing a cargo cruiser during an impromptu atmospheric entry was something barely worthy of her attention. 'We stick close enough, we should avoid detection from the ground as well – only an idiot would try to slip-stream into atmo, right?' Drift caught a flash of white as she bared her teeth in a fierce grin. He groaned quietly, then keyed the comm.

'Buckle up, everyone. Jia's taking us down ahead of schedule, and incidentally has lost her fucking *mind.*'

'I heard that.'

'You were meant to.' He looked over at Jenna, who had gone even paler than usual, and made a slicing motion across his throat. 'As soon as we hit the comms blackout, kill the ident broadcasts; if anyone sees us pulling this fool stunt they'll know we've got something to hide anyway, so we might as well fly silent and pretend we just disappeared. But,' he added, figuring that a task might take the young slicer's mind off whatever further insanity Jia was planning, 'go find that shipping log system and see if you can patch us an easy ticket off this rock.'

'Aye-aye,' Jenna replied. Her voice was a little shaky, but she fixed her eyes to her station. A few seconds later she looked back up. 'We've lost comms.'

'Good,' Drift muttered. On this occasion, the bubble of ionised air around them which would temporarily affect all transmissions was their friend. He looked over at Jia. 'If you're going to just ignore my orders as Captain, at least tell me that you have a plan.'

'Don't I always?'

'No,' Drift replied, 'hence my worry.'

'If I tell you, you'll only worry more.' Jia turned her head to grin at him.

'Just watch the damn cruiser!' he yelled, gesticulating furiously beyond the *Jonah*'s nose. Jia tutted, but returned her attention to the hull shuddering in front of them. They danced like that for a couple of tense minutes, Jia nudging them this way and that to keep them close to the cruiser's concealing mass and stay out of its super-heated turbulence as far as possible, without risking collision with the ship itself.

'Comms are back,' Jenna reported, looking up and then hurriedly lowering her eyes again as she saw how close they were to their huge companion craft. Her voice drifted into the presumably unconscious sing-song she adopted when concentrating. 'Okay then, databank . . . where are you?'

'You'd best not tip anyone off to where we are,' Jia warned her, 'or all my fancy flying's for nothing.'

'Which would be why I'm currently setting up three proxies through different communications providers across this hemisphere,' Jenna retorted, sounding nettled. 'I don't tell you how to fly a few thousand tons of metal, you don't tell me how to slice: deal?'

Jia just grunted, but Drift was sure he caught the faintest ghost of a smile on Jenna's lips.

'Right, ready to roll.' Jenna frowned in concentration for a moment, then her expression cleared. 'There you are . . . really? Oh, that's just embarrassing . . .'

'If you're going to talk along, can you at least tell us what you're doing?' Drift asked irritably. He hated feeling helpless, and right now he was stuck between two consummate yet infuriatingly idiosyncratic professionals.

'Their security protocols are *shocking*,' Jenna said pityingly, glancing up at him for a second. 'This is barely fit for purpose, I could have sliced it in high school . . . but I might not even need to . . .' She tapped something, waited for a few seconds while idly drumming her fingers somewhere unimportant, then brightened as her terminal buzzed at her. 'Aha! Got an echo from the ping!'

'Meaning?' Drift asked, starting to feel that he needed to install an 'English or Spanish only' sign in the cockpit.

'Meaning someone's connection isn't secured and I can piggyback in on it, which will throw them for an even bigger loop if they try to trace me,' Jenna giggled happily. 'Although I wouldn't like to be this guy when they do, whoever he is . . .' She looked up at him again. 'Yeah, we're in. There's however many thousand idents in here, all logged and tagged. We can be any one of them on our way out, and so long as the real one isn't trying to leave at the same time we'll be good to go.'

'Sounds great,' Jia commented, although her tone of voice suggested otherwise.

Jenna snorted. 'Haven't you got us down yet?'

'Girl,' Jia said grimly as Drift put his head in his hands, 'you are going to regret saying that . . .'

RIDERS ON THE STORM

'How long are you going to shadow them for?' Drift asked, trying not to sound too agitated. It was testament to Jia's ridiculous piloting abilities that she hadn't either collided with the cruiser or been thrown aside into its wake, but he wasn't sure how much longer his nerves could take the strain of being this close to something so potentially dangerous.

'And what happens if they tell someone we're following them?' Jenna added.

'You see any windows at the back?' Jia snorted. 'We're too close for their instruments to pick us up, and they sure as hell can't *see* us. But in answer to your question,' she added, looking over at Drift for a second, 'not for much longer. These boys aren't going where we want to go.'

Drift checked their location on his terminal screen, then looked out of the viewport. The horizon was growing larger (or possibly smaller) and less obviously curved, and more and more detail was becoming apparent on the ground below. He sighed. 'We're coming down over Europa, aren't we?'

'In a manner of speaking,' Jia admitted. She shot a glance back at Jenna. 'We're still running radio silence, right?'

'No broadcasts,' Jenna acknowledged. Jia nodded decisively.

'Right then.' She keyed up the intercom with a grin at Drift. 'Attention all hands, this is your fantastically talented pilot speaking. We will shortly be experiencing turbulence, so you'd all better hope that my useless brother does exactly *what* I tell him *when* I tell him to, or we may all just crash and die.' She cut the link again, killed the cockpit lights, then muttered something under her breath in Mandarin and wrenched the helm to the right, just as Drift found that he was suddenly feeling unusually religious.

The turbulence from the cruiser caught them instantly, buffeting the *Jonah* through the air like a leaf on the wind. Jia's knuckles whitened but she wrenched their nose around, bringing the ship onto something like a smooth approach vector again, then checked her scopes. 'We're coming down into the troposphere.'

'And we're suddenly one dot in the middle of the sky,' Drift said grimly. 'Jia, what the *hell* were you thinking? We're going to get stopped for sure!'

'They can't stop us if we can't stop,' Jia replied cryptically, then keyed the comm again and spoke in a rattle of Mandarin too fast for Drift to completely follow. There was no mistaking the confusion in

Kuai's answer though, or the emphatic nature of Jia's snapped response. He tried to replay what he'd just heard in his head, and had just picked out the word for 'stop' or 'cease' when everything suddenly became very quiet.

'Was that—'

'—the engine?' Jenna finished his question for him, her voice rising in alarm, although it didn't really need to be asked. The steady rumble and roar of the *Jonah*'s relatively economical and almost always reliable jets had abruptly dropped out of hearing. Inside a cockpit shielded heavily enough to survive atmospheric entry there wasn't even wind noise, just the patchwork sight of Europan fields, forests, mountains and cities looming silently up at them.

And, ahead and below them, the ugly purple and grey bruise of the storm currently hammering in off the Atlantic Ocean. Although it wasn't looking like it was going to be either ahead of them or below them for very much longer.

'Jia,' he said urgently, 'if you don't tell me *right now* what the hell you think you're doing, I swear to any god you care to name that I will shoot you in the head and fly this thing down to the ground myself.' He wasn't entirely certain that he wasn't serious, either.

'We didn't have time to take a detour if we're going to make your appointment,' Jia said, adjusting controls. The *Jonah* did have flaps to control altitude and inclination, just like any terrestrial aircraft, but Drift couldn't see how she could hope to glide their stubby boat with any success. 'We can't get down without being noticed, so we break our cover as late as possible. Now we look like debris, or hell,' she shrugged, 'like a ship that's lost power. So we head for the biggest storm we can, the place which is going to mess with as many instruments which might be monitoring us as possible, and when we hit it,' she snapped her fingers, 'we disappear.'

'Yeah, because we *crash* and *die*!' Jenna yelled in alarm.

'Only if my brother doesn't turn the engines back on when I tell him,' Jia snapped. 'Right now we're not broadcasting anything and we have no drive emissions to track. No one would voluntarily power down and head for a storm system, am I right?'

'No one with any sense,' Drift growled.

'So when we get to the roughest, nastiest bit, we fire the retros to kill our forward momentum, drop like a stone then kick everything back in,' Jia said matter-of-factly, although Drift couldn't help but notice how hard she was having to fight the controls. 'We start broadcasting a new ident, head up coast towards Amsterdam and we look like a domestic craft which just took off. Presto, we're inside Europan airspace looking like we belong, while anyone who *was* watching us is still waiting for that piece of debris to kill a whole bunch of people.' She beamed, white teeth flashing in a tight grin. 'Damn, I'm good.'

'You're insane,' Drift told her flatly, double-checking the crash webbing he'd buckled around himself.

'Insanely *good*,' Jia retorted. 'Oh, here comes the wind. Hold on!'

Sure enough, they were running headlong into the first outriders of the storm and the *Jonah* was beginning to shake as this new form of turbulence started to jostle it around the skies. Jia began to whisper; at first Drift thought she was swearing under her breath, but as the measured litany continued he realised that she was actually counting down in Mandarin. Beneath and beside them, and now above them, grey fingers of cloud were drawing closer and obscuring their view of the world. A spattering of water on the viewports announced the arrival of rain, although they were flying through it rather than it falling on them, and the speed of their travel sent it streaking back upwards.

'Aren't we ready yet?' Drift asked nervously, checking his instruments again. It wasn't that he didn't trust the Changs not to bicker at a critical moment, but . . . well, actually he didn't, when it came down to it.

'*Sān, Èr, Yī* . . .' Jia whispered, then hit the comm button again. 'Hold tight!'

She pressed an innocuous-looking button on the control panel. Something lit up and blazed outside, casting strange new shadows on the viewports, and suddenly an invisible giant had hold of Drift and was trying to pull him clean out of his chair and through the *Jonah*'s nose cone. There was a clattering sound behind him as some unsecured item rolled across the cockpit and *clanged* off the edge of a console some-where. He grunted, and tried to keep the blood in his face by sheer effort of will.

'*Fuuuuuuuu—*'

'Kuai,' Jia called, one wavering finger on the comm switch again, '*cǐ shí!*'

There was a moment of gut-wrenching silence, and

then the welcome rumble of the *Jonah*'s main engine started to reverberate through the hull again. The great forward pressure started to relax; Drift scanned his instruments again and saw their speed was reducing rapidly. However, so was their altitude.

'Jia?'

'Nearly there,' their pilot replied, her face lit in strange blues and red from the control panel beneath in the rain-shrouded darkness of the cockpit. She flicked a switch and one batch of retros ceased firing; the *Jonah* began to swing around, even as its fall through the clouds became more and more prominent in Drift's mind.

'Jia!'

'And go!' Jia grinned, killing the other retro and feeding power to the main drive. Now Drift was pushed back in his seat again, although this was a mere nudge compared to the forces he'd been experiencing a few seconds ago. Their descent levelled out into what would have been a gentle downward glide, were they not still in a storm system and being battered from the side.

'Jenna!' Jia barked, flicking the lights back on. 'Give us an ident!'

'Ready and waiting,' the slicer replied. Drift looked over at her; she looked a little green, but hadn't passed out or thrown up, or anything else inconvenient. 'We are now the *Risky Gamble*.'

'I don't recognise that one,' he frowned. Jenna grinned at him.

'I just made it. It seemed appropriate.'

Above them and to starboard, flashing lights indicated search and rescue craft scrambling in the direction of their previous trajectory. Jia looked over her shoulder at him with an expression so smug it could have walked into a job in a stock exchange.

'Am I good or *what*?'

The *Jonah* cruised north-east, loosely hugging the shore of the English Channel on the Continental Coastway. The flightline's boundaries were marked by floating, flashing beacons – red for port and green for starboard – which constantly transmitted their locations to the craft travelling on it. The flip side was that the buoys in turn were continually monitoring the traffic, keeping track of who joined when and who left where, so Drift was glad all over again that they'd picked up a slicer who could manage a higher-quality ident-job than his own mediocre skills could muster.

'Why's it so slow?' Jenna asked, looking over Drift's shoulder out of the front viewports. They'd unstrapped themselves from their seats now their descent was over, and the *Jonah*'s stabilising systems along with Jia's hands at the controls were preventing the high winds from being much more than a nuisance, despite the Heim drive being deactivated so they were once more fully subject to a planet's gravity. On their right, the French coast was flashing by in a succession of ports, cranes, rain-lashed skyscrapers and even the occasional stretch of undeveloped beach or flat, green marshland.

'This is fast compared to most of the continent,' Drift snorted. 'The stupid thing is, air travel has got much *slower* on Old Earth because there's so many ships and flyers everyone gets in each other's way now. The flightlines are where you can open it up a bit, but compared to somewhere like the Carmellas where most people are poor, can't afford flyers and live under the surface anyway . . .' he shrugged. 'You're limited to going fast along the flightline routes, or cutting overland and sticking to the "safe" speeds.'

'Or ignoring them,' Jia put in.

'And getting pulled over by the Justices,' Drift told her sternly. 'You want all that fancy flying to be ruined by breaking a speed limit?'

'Pfft, like they'd catch us,' the pilot scoffed. She glanced over her shoulder and clearly saw Drift's expression. 'Relax, I'm joking.'

'I'm not sure I believe you,' Drift told her, honestly enough. He glanced at the chrono and grimaced. 'We're still going to be cutting it fine. I can't believe I'm saying this, but push it as hard as you can get away with.' He pretended not to see the grin spreading across the reflection of Jia's face in the front viewport as he got up out of his seat.

'Where are you going?' Jia asked him as he tossed his commset to her.

'I'd better check on the cargo and our fearless

warriors,' Drift replied, easing his neck from side to side. 'Keep an ear out for anything which sounds like trouble until I get back.' In all honesty he suspected there was nothing which would need doing that Rourke had not already done, but he was already getting the restless feeling which signalled a job on the shady side was approaching completion.

Sure enough, his business partner looked up briefly from her stripped-down rifle as he walked into the cargo bay, then back down at the magazine in her hand. 'What are you doing here?'

'And what the hell is Jia playing at?' Micah demanded angrily. 'A. nearly threw up on me!'

'Did not,' the big man protested, slapping his gut. 'Gonna take more than a little up and down to upset this Maori's *puku*.'

'I did tell you she'd lost her mind,' Drift replied mildly. He looked around. 'Cargo's okay, I hope?'

'Maglocks held fine,' Rourke confirmed. 'Are we going to be on time?'

'Might still be touch and go,' Drift acknowledged, 'but there's no help for that now except to hope Jia can step on it a bit without getting us flagged down.' He sighed, and scratched at the skin around his right eye. 'The way I read this, we should be safe until the moment we open those doors. That's when we'll get a double-cross, if one's coming.'

'These are pretty sturdy,' Micah commented, kicking one of the metal crates to demonstrate. 'Reckon they'll stop most bullets. Could be that they're thinking to open up, take us out and the cargo should survive?'

Rourke nodded slowly. 'Could be the way of it.

I'd still be surprised to see a gun squad waiting in a goddamn conference centre loading bay, though.'

'And why pay us the hundred kay up front?' Apirana put in. 'We could have spent it all, for all they know.'

'Then we'd probably have spent a lot of it on goods,' Drift pointed out, 'there's only so much whisky and women a crew can go through when travelling from Carmella to Old Earth on this kind of deadline. Plus if they take us out they'll get the *Jonah*, and they'd be figuring on finding the access codes which would get them into the *Keiko*, too. That's a whole new ship to sell on. No, they could get their goods transported for them and still make a profit, if they could pull it off.'

'But still,' Rourke repeated, 'a gun squad?' She shook her head. 'A lot of other places, certainly. Not in a conference centre in Amsterdam in the middle of the day.'

Drift shrugged. 'Stranger things have happened.'

'Name one.'

'You slept with that guy with the moustache, somebody Moutinho . . .?'

'Shut up,' Rourke advised, slapping the magazine into her rifle pointedly. She looked over at Apirana, who had an amused grin on his face. 'And you.'

'I din't say anything.'

'You didn't need to.' She glared at Drift. 'Go back to the cockpit and listen to the radio, dickface.'

'Ma'am,' Drift replied, bowing low to hide the smile he could feel creeping across his face. He turned away, but behind him he heard Micah's voice, tinged with curiosity.

'Who was—?'

'*Shut up.*'

Drift didn't go straight back to the cockpit; instead he headed aft and poked his head into the engine room, where Kuai was intently studying his holo-reader. At first Drift had thought Kuai was simply very dutiful at studying his manuals, but then he'd seen over the engineer's shoulder once and realised that he was actually engrossed in the adventures of anthropomorphic animated ponies.

'Everything okay?' he asked out of habit, although he knew that if it hadn't been then Kuai would be out of his seat and fixing it. Jia's brother was far too paranoid about her tendency to abuse the engines to leave anything in poor repair, and far too interested in being able to breathe properly to neglect the care of the life support.

'We're good,' Kuai replied, looking up. 'What's my idiot sister been doing this time?'

'Believe it or not, it was actually a pretty good call on her part,' Drift told him. Kuai snorted and lowered his eyes to his screen again, shaking his head.

'You know she's going to kill us all one day, don't you?'

'So why are you still here?' Drift asked, leaning against the bulkhead. 'You're a good engineer, Kuai. Even if your sister's the totally irresponsible thrust-erhead you think she is, *you* could go get a job on some respectable shipping firm somewhere, make your parents proud.' *And while it would be a shame to lose you, I think Jia might be a little less rash if she didn't have you around to wind up with it . . .* he added silently.

Kuai looked up at him again. 'You got any family?'

Drift shook his head. 'None left that I know about.'

Kuai nodded, but didn't press. 'It would kill my parents if anything happened to Jia,' he said instead, shrugging, 'so I try to keep her out of trouble as much as possible.'

'Good luck with that,' Drift snorted. The floor tilted slightly, as if on cue, and the rumble of the engines took on a slightly more urgent note. 'Yeah, I'd better go.'

'Have fun,' Kuai said dryly, already studying his reader again. Drift jogged back up to the cockpit, where instead of a cloud-darkened sky he found that they'd emerged into sunshine.

'Clear of the storm?' he asked, receiving his commset back from Jenna and settling it into his right ear.

'Still got high winds, but we've outrun the clouds now,' Jia reported. 'Should be clear running into Amsterdam from here, according to the weather scan. I'm getting us there as fast as I can, but it's still going to be close.'

Drift sat at his terminal and scanned the frequencies, searching for any sign that they'd attracted unwanted attention. The closer they got to their destination the more concerned he was becoming about the possible outcomes. There was obviously *something* in those crates Kelsier wanted delivered, and couldn't deliver himself at that: had he simply been looking to steal their ship then the landing bay doors of the *Gewitterwolke* wouldn't have let them out again. The same went for this being some sort of revenge plot for Drift dropping off the radar so thoroughly, as the Laughing Man could have saved an awful lot of time by pulling his trigger in the bar on Carmella II and no one in there would have blinked. And yet . . .

Many years ago, Drift might have told himself he was being paranoid. These days he was more inclined to listen to the paranoia until it had proved unjustified. Listen to it, but not be ruled by it; a lot of the people the crew of the *Keiko* did business with were only intermittently trustworthy, so you just had to be a good judge of timing.

But let's not forget that we're almost certainly smuggling in something *which will get us in trouble if we're caught,* he added to himself, *so there doesn't need to be a double-cross for this to go bad.* Still, the emergency frequencies had been empty of anything except the usual chatter, and even the rescue craft behind them were starting to call off their scrambled search in the teeth of the storm. To all intents and purposes, the *Risky Gamble* was just another flyer on the Continental Coastway.

That didn't prevent him from keeping the commset on and scanning channels until they reached Amsterdam, of course.

'We've just passed Rotterdam!' Jia called eventually. Drift looked at the chrono and winced.

'We've got one minute.'

'Then we're going to be late,' Jia told him flatly. 'We're coming up on the Amsterdam exit any second, but we're going to have to go across town.' She keyed the comm. 'Stand by for braking, folks.'

The retros flared as the *Jonah* swerved out of the Coastway's boundaries, and Drift had to grab on to his terminal to prevent himself from being thrown out of his chair at the sudden deceleration. He bit back an angry comment – she *had* warned everyone, albeit only a second beforehand – and turned to Jenna. The slicer had apparently either predicted the move or simply distrusted Jia's flying more than he did, as she'd refastened her crash webbing.

'Can you see anything on the feeds which suggests we're walking into something?' he asked her. The chatter in his ear was still the usual mix of inane and desperate, but none of it seemed at all relevant to them. A fire somewhere, vehicles responding . . . a groundcar crash somewhere else, one person dead . . . a dwelling burglary somewhere he wasn't even going to try to pronounce, and he was glad all over again that English had won out as the official language of the Europan Commonwealth: he'd spent a bored week in transit once trying to learn Dutch from Micah and had found it largely impenetrable, although that was possibly partly due to the qualities of the 'teacher'.

'Nothing,' Jenna replied, shaking her head as her hands skated over her terminal. 'The conference isn't really making the news, there doesn't seem to be any particularly heightened police presence . . .' She looked back up at him. 'It looks clear.'

Drift grimaced. 'Never say that.'

'I just said it *looks* clear, not that it *is* clear—'

'Even so,' he cut her off, waving a hand, 'this is not a ship where we *ever* say something "looks clear". Do I make myself . . . um, clear? It's bad luck.'

'And you laughed at my pilot hat . . .' Jia muttered. Drift ignored her and turned back to his own terminal.

The chrono in the corner ticked over to the next minute and stared at him accusingly as the ball of nervous tension which had been building in his chest sank abruptly through the pit of his stomach. He had a sudden impulse to yell at Jia to hit the afterburners and to hell with the flightlanes, but that would simply pull down a response from the authorities and Kelsier's factors, whoever they were, would doubtless melt away even if the *Jonah* could get to the rendez-vous before it was flagged down.

Something flickered on his terminal. He frowned at it and pulled it up: a new broadcast signal had started up from nowhere. The read-out showed that it wasn't an audio transmission. It read a little like the weak Spine signals they'd been passing through ever since coming off the flightline and into populated areas, but stronger, and given the timing he was in no mood to take chances. 'Jenna. You getting this?'

'Hmm?' She looked up at him and he slid the read-out across to her terminal. She frowned, red-blonde strands falling across her face and being absent-mindedly tucked back as she studied it. 'That's odd. Gimme a second.'

'You've only got seconds,' Jia called over her shoulder, 'we're a few blocks away now.' She jinked slightly and swore at someone unseen who'd presumably been, however briefly, where she'd wanted to fly.

'It's a data transmission,' Jenna said, without looking up. 'Encoded.'

'Source?' Drift asked, scanning out of the different viewports. Nothing looked any different to how it had a second ago, but his paranoia was screaming at him.

'Close,' Jenna answered immediately. 'Within a . . . few . . . blocks.'

Drift looked at her, mouth suddenly dry, and saw that she'd reached the same conclusion as him.

'*Shit.*'

'Whoah!' Jenna's eyes widened and she tapped at her terminal again. 'It's being answered, there's a two-way stream now.'

'Source?' Drift said again, mouth dry and scrambling across the cockpit to look over her shoulder, as though he'd be able to understand half of what she was looking at. *Come on girl, at least tell us which way to run . . .*

She turned her head to look at him, expression filled with uncertainty and what looked uncomfortably like dread.

'Our cargo bay.'

There was the taste of bile at the back of his throat. He stood still for half a second while his mind raced at different angles, then suddenly his gun was in his hand.

'Jia!' he barked. 'Stay course, but eyes on the sky! Get ready to burn! Jenna, with me.'

The slicer slapped at her webbing release, grabbed her pad from the console and followed him at a dead run towards the cargo bay. They pelted past the galley and clattered down the steps towards where the four metal crates sat innocently in the middle of the floor, while Rourke, Micah and Apirana looked up in confusion and growing alarm.

'What's the problem?' Rourke asked, swinging her rifle up into a ready position.

'Something out there started broadcasting, and

something in here started talking back,' Drift replied grimly, eyeing the crates.

'In here?' Micah queried. 'As in . . .'

'In *here*, yes,' Drift nodded impatiently, 'the cargo bay. So unless one of you have activated a transmitter for some reason . . . ?'

All three shook their heads.

'Well,' Rourke said softly, dark eyes sliding to their cargo, 'that changes the game.' She looked sideways at him. 'It *could* be something completely inconsequential which your contact just failed to mention would happen.'

'It could,' Drift agreed. 'Do you think that?'

'Do I look like I was born yesterday?' Rourke snorted.

Drift nodded. 'Yeah, me neither.' He looked up. 'A.? Tools.'

'You're gonna open 'em?' the Maori rumbled, taking three large steps to an equipment locker and pulling out a cutting torch which he casually tossed across the bay. Drift caught it in one hand, then the pair of goggles which followed it in the other, and pulled them over his head.

'Damn right. And you're going to start at the other end.'

He fired the torch up and narrowed the flame down to a thin blue cutting blade, which he applied to the lid corner of the crate nearest him. The metal started to glow a cherry red, succumbing to the torch's powerful heat, and he dragged it down one side.

'Jia?' he heard Rourke ask behind him. 'How long?'

+*Unless you want me to stop dead and tip off*

*anyone watching us then we're talking a minute, tops.
What the hell is going on back there?+*

'Tell you in a minute,' Rourke replied absently.
'Ichabod?'

Drift finished his circuit of the crate and applied
his boot to the lid, kicking it on one glowing edge
to knock it clean off onto the bay floor with a clatter.
He leaned over and looked in, heedless of the powerful
heat still rising from the newly cut rim. Dark, twisted
shapes came into view.

'Scrap metal.' He reached in, confused, and pulled
up a hunk of something which might once have been
an exhaust component for a vehicle of some kind,
then dropped it back in. 'What . . . ?'

'Camouflage,' Rourke said decisively, looking past
him. 'Keep going.'

'I've got scrap too!' Apirana shouted. Drift didn't
look up, but from the noise it sounded like the big
Maori had kicked his lid considerably further. 'What
the fuck is going on here?'

'Get that last one open!' Rourke ordered him, even
as Drift was attacking the third crate. Down one side,
down the second, the third, the last . . . He stepped
back, kicked the lid off . . .

. . . and was greeted by the sight of a sleek, metallic
cylinder with a few visible wires and a couple of
flashing lights, linking it to what appeared to be a
small terminal and digital broadcast unit. It filled
nearly the full length of the crate, and was possibly
as wide around as Apirana.

It was like nothing he'd ever seen.

'Erm . . .'

'*Fuck!*'

The scream – and it was a *scream* – had come from Tamara Rourke. Drift's eyes snapped to her and he felt his heart rocket into overdrive. He had seen Rourke angry, disappointed, dejected, delighted, determined and reflective, and sometimes he even thought he'd been able to tell the difference. He had *never* seen her scared.

She pointed one quivering, dark-skinned finger at the crate. 'It's a *nuke*!'

Drift blinked. 'What?'

Her eyes, wide and white with fear, flashed to his face. 'It's a *fucking nuke*!'

'But . . .' This was impossible. There had to be some mistake. 'How do you *know*?'

'There is a *nuclear bomb* in our cargo bay!' Rourke yelled at him. '*Why are we still having this conversation?!*'

'It's transmitting,' Jenna said, looking up at him from her pad, face pale, 'which means it was receiving.'

'Which means it's activating,' Drift finished grimly. His mind whirled. What was Kelsier's game? Was this a test? Some way of seeing whether he could, whether he *would* follow instructions, no matter what they were? *No, we were supposed to be handing this over right now. We shouldn't have known about it activating at all.* So why would a Europan agent be sending an active warhead into a Europan city . . . ?

Unless they really fired him. Holy shit, they really did fire him for corruption, and this is the bastard's revenge.

There was never meant to be a way out of this for us.

He looked around desperately. 'Micah! Bomb

doors!' If they could deactivate the maglocks on the crates and open the drop-down doors which ran beneath their feet, they could—

'No!' the Dutch mercenary shouted. Drift stared at him.

'What? Why?'

'This is *Amsterdam*!' Micah roared. 'You're not dropping a bomb on *my* country!'

For a split second, Drift considered shooting the mercenary dead and opening the doors himself, but common sense prevailed. He might miss, Micah would shoot back, the mercenary was wearing an armavest anyway . . . and besides, when it came down to it, the Dutchman was right.

This isn't the old days anymore.

'Jia!' he snapped, activating his comm. 'Full burn for the North Sea, *now*!'

+*What? But*—+

'Do it!' Drift yelled. 'We've got an activating nuke down here and we need to drop it into the ocean! I don't care if you have to—'

He was cut off as the *Jonah* lurched and tilted, sending them all sprawling across the floor, then sliding helplessly towards the aft bulkheads as their pilot threw power to what felt like the main boosters normally used for escaping a planet's gravity well.

+*You had me at 'activating nuke', boss.*+

'Gah!' One of the cutting torches, now mercifully deactivated, skittered across the floor and bounced up towards his face. He shielded himself with his hand at the last moment, but simply succeeded in punching himself in the cheek instead as the metal canister hit him. Meanwhile Jia had apparently left the comm channel open and they were treated to a tirade of abuse, presumably thrown at other flyer pilots.

+Cào nǐ! Cào nǐ mā! Cào nǐ māde bī! Cào nǐ zǔzōng shíbā dài. . .+

'Head for the North Pole, and don't brake until I tell you!' Drift yelled at her, fighting up to his feet against the acceleration. The last thing he wanted was for Jia to fire the retros as soon as she was over open water and them all to tumble the other way across the cargo bay, potentially accompanied by any crates they'd managed to unclamp. He straightened, took one step towards the crates and then stumbled sideways as Jia banked momentarily. 'Damn it!'

+*I need to go* around *things,* bai chi!+

Drift growled and fielded Jenna as she staggered into him, then pushed the young slicer away again and lunged for the crates. He clawed his way past the first one, the top of which had thankfully cooled from the red-hot state he'd left it in, and slapped at the release mechanism on the maglock at the corner of the bomb's container. It buzzed, and the green light blinked out. Rourke came down on the other side of it, hitting the floor and the release in one barely controlled motion.

+*We're over the ocean!*+ Jia's voice came over the comm. +*Ditch it!*+

Drift scrabbled to the other end of the metal container and slapped again. Another green light disappeared, and a second later he heard the *smack* of Rourke's hand disconnecting the fourth and final lock.

'Get clear!' Apirana roared. The big Maori had

fought his way forwards to the controls for the bomb doors, the nickname proving unfortunately apt on this occasion, and was standing poised by them. Drift took two stuttering steps and then a leap, landed hard on the cargo-bay deck . . .

. . . and behind him, the floor dropped away.

The wind noise was immediate and deafening, and the entire ship started to judder as its aerodynamics were compromised and great gusts of air and spray slammed up into the bay. The salty smell of the sea hit his nostrils; a wild scent and shockingly strong, and Drift's mind suddenly flashed backwards as he wondered how long it had been since he'd breathed air which hadn't been recycled and filtered hundreds of times before.

Of more immediate concern, however, was the fact that the opened crate with the ominously blinking bomb had slipped through the gap and vanished into the rushing blue-green blur flashing below them. He waved at Apirana to shut the doors again and the big man obliged, jabbing at the control which started to bring them back up with a whirr of motors and hydraulics barely audible over the wind noise. Drift activated his comm again.

'Jia, it's off! Get us clear!'

+*Trying! Incidentally,*+ the pilot added ominously, as the roar of the engines went up another notch, +*we've got company.*+

'Company?' Drift demanded, pushing himself upright once more and heading for the stairs. A moment after he hit them he heard a second set of boots behind him, and looked over his shoulder to see Jenna following him.

+*Yeah, looks like we ruffled some feathers. We got Europan fighters scrambling to intercept.*+

Drift grimaced. There was little chance of fighter aircraft having the sheer thruster muscle to catch a craft capable of breaking atmo, but it was unwanted attention nonetheless. 'Lose them.'

+*Working on that too.*+

It was only a few seconds later that Drift made the cockpit and launched himself into his seat. He pulled up the frequency logs, scanning through for anything which might be relevant to them . . .

. . . and behind them, the whole world went white.

MUTINY

The explosion of a nuclear bomb in the North Sea had predictably chaotic consequences, the most immediately obvious being a titanic blast of water and steam which had engulfed the fighter aircraft pursuing them and caused every single radio channel to start shouting at once. Another was that all aircraft in the vicinity of the explosion immediately began fleeing with no regard for rules or regulations, meaning that the *Jonah*'s screaming flight northwards had suddenly become entirely unremarkable. Jenna had switched aliases again on the basis that for at least a few seconds everyone was going to have something else to worry about, and so it was that the *Tamsin's Wake* changed direction abruptly and headed over Britain to touch down at a refuelling station in Birmingham.

Against the odds, they'd got away without being shot down or apprehended, which Drift considered to be a minor miracle in and of itself. However, it just made the fact that one of his own crew was holding a gun to his head all the more galling in comparison.

'Tamara . . .?' he said, trying to keep his voice steady. Jia had only just throttled back the engines and their whine was still dying away when he found himself staring down the deceptively small barrel of the one-shot palmgun Rourke seemed able to secrete just about anywhere. He'd even seen her pull it out of her underwear once.

'"Tamara" nothing. You have some explaining to do,' Rourke said. Her voice was quiet, but her eyes were like chips of dark ice.

'Is now really the time?' Drift protested. It wasn't just an evasive tactic on his part; they were still on Europan soil and, so far as he was concerned, at risk of being picked up by the authorities. He risked a glance sideways: Jenna's face was shocked while Jia's was rather less readable, but neither of them seemed about to jump up and attempt to disarm Rourke. He couldn't really blame them, given that neither pilot nor slicer were experienced in combat and Tamara Rourke could incapacitate someone twice her size with her bare hands.

'Jia,' Rourke said without turning her head, 'get on the comm and call the boys to the cockpit.'

'Gonna be kind of cramped,' Jia commented. 'Apirana ain't small. How about we move to the canteen? Also, if you shoot him and the bullet goes through him it won't damage something valuable if we're in there.'

'Thanks,' Drift said bitterly. Jia just shrugged.

Through the viewport behind her left shoulder Drift could see huge tankers crawling back and forth on the asphalt outside, massive hoses feeding fresh fuel into hungry tanks.

'She has a point,' Rourke conceded. 'Get up.'

'To go somewhere you are *more* likely to shoot me?' Drift snorted. 'It doesn't appeal.'

'Ichabod,' Rourke said softly, 'I've flown with you for, what? Eight years? I am really, truly hoping that you can explain to all of us why you took on a job which nearly destroyed a city, but I'm not going to wait for that explanation until you've had time to cook up one of your cover stories. Let's go to the canteen so you can give us whatever good reason you have for me to lower my gun and apologise. Keep stalling, and I *will* shoot you, and then burn off this rock before anyone tracks us down.'

'We can't,' Jenna put in timidly. 'Word on the Spine and the radio is that the sky is closed.'

Rourke frowned, but to Drift's disappointment neither her gun nor her gaze wavered. 'What?'

'Nothing leaves atmo without a scheduled launch window,' Jenna said heavily. 'Not just Europa; all governments have bought in. Looks like everyone's got a bit twitchy about a surprise nuclear explosion; there's talk of it being a Free Systems terrorist attack.'

'Shit,' Rourke muttered with feeling. Drift saw a moment of indecision flicker across her features before it was replaced with her usual calm determination. He knew that look, and it didn't bode well for someone at the other end of a gun. 'Come on, Ichabod. Slowly. I don't think you're fool enough to try anything with me, but I don't know how desperate you are right now. Let's get to the canteen where you can explain yourself.'

Pretty damn desperate. 'Okay,' he replied instead, and started to rise. He could pretty much feel the noose tightening around his neck. He'd kept it at bay for nearly two decades, long enough to hope that maybe he'd outrun it, but perhaps he'd only ever been living on borrowed time. He couldn't help but appreciate the irony of it being a mutiny which finally brought him down, though. He briefly considered trying to jump Rourke as Jia activated the comm and called Micah, Apirana and Kuai up to the canteen, but quickly thought better of it. It was the same choice as he'd faced with the Laughing Man: almost certain immediate death, or a chance to play things out and live a little longer, hoping that his luck would see him through somehow.

Granted, it hadn't exactly worked how he'd hoped so far.

He'd half expected the trudge to the canteen, held at gunpoint with the three women behind him, to be some sort of never-ending ordeal. Instead it seemed to be over quicker than blinking, and he still hadn't started to think through what he was going to say to his crew.

His friends.

Probably.

He usually leaned casually against the counter which separated the galley's floorspace from that of the canteen while addressing his crew, and he instinctively took that position again now. The main differences were that he felt far from casual, and instead of lurking by the door Tamara Rourke stood in the middle of the floor with her gun still levelled at his face. Micah, Kuai and Apirana appeared in the doorway behind her and stopped dead at what they saw.

'What the hell?' Apirana asked, clearly taken aback.

'This job's smelled bad since we took it,' Rourke said flatly, 'and I think we all knew it a bit. Secret cargo, secret employer, our Captain's been edgy and smelling of whisky and happy to shoot a couple of void station enforcers in the face instead of try to talk his way out of trouble like usual. But we all gave him the benefit of the doubt because whatever else has happened, he's usually seen us right before. And then everything goes to hell, and I can't be the only one wondering exactly what's been going on.'

To his own surprise, Drift felt a stirring of at least semi-righteous anger in his belly. 'You knew! Don't play the innocent! *You* knew that *I* knew who was hiring us, and you let it go!'

'Because I trusted you!' Rourke shot back at him.

'You *did* know?' Apirana rumbled. Drift experienced a sudden quiver of fear as he almost felt the Maori's gaze harden and definitely saw his jaw tighten. Apirana's loyalty had always been rock-hard, but if the big man felt his trust had been abused then Drift didn't like to think how he'd react. *Great, now I've got two of them mad at me.*

'Ichabod,' Rourke was saying firmly, 'someone's used us, and I'm not going to stand for it. In fact, someone's going to die for it. I'd rather that someone be the man who hired us, but if you won't give me his name then so help me, it will be you.'

Drift scanned the room. No help was forthcoming.

His crew had been forged together into a working unit by necessity and, yes, a certain camaraderie he'd deliberately nurtured, an 'us against the galaxy' mentality which had found fertile soil in the souls of this particular group of second-chancers. It was hard to believe, for a moment, that they'd turn on him like this.

At least, until he realised that right at this moment, he wasn't part of 'us' anymore.

'I'm suddenly wondering exactly who *you* are, Tamara,' he said darkly. 'You can identify a nuclear bomb just by looking at it; how many people can do that?'

'Don't you dare try to make this about me,' she warned, gun still steady, but she was hiding something. He could practically taste it.

'What other mysterious talents do you have that we never knew about?' he demanded, warming to his theme. 'How many times have we nearly died because you *didn't* tell us something you knew—'

'*GIVE ME HIS NAME!*' Rourke roared.

The voice which answered her belonged to Jenna. 'Nicolas Kelsier.'

Drift blinked in shock. Then, as one with the rest of the room, his gaze turned towards their young slicer.

J enna faced their stares awkwardly, abruptly
aware both of how tempting the open canteen
door looked and exactly how impossible it would
be to reach with the rest of the crew in the way.
Rourke was studying her as though she were some
sort of alien life form. Apirana's face radiated a
mixture of surprise and distrust, and Drift's . . .

Ichabod Drift looked absolutely stunned.

'Who the hell is that?' Kuai asked the room. Rourke
raised an eyebrow at Jenna.

'Well?'

'I don't know *who* it is,' Jenna clarified hastily. She
looked at Drift. 'You remember when you told me
to stop slicing the *Gewitterwolke*'s ident?'

He nodded.

'Well, you were sort of too slow,' Jenna admitted.
'I'd already seen that it was actually the *Langeschatten*,
and it was registered to someone called Nicolas Kelsier.'

Rourke looked back at Drift, who'd apparently been too stunned to move out of the line of fire of her palmgun when she was distracted. 'Well, Ichabod? We have the name now, and I can see from your face that it's the right one.'

Drift hesitated.

'There's a terminal linked to Old Earth's Spine in the cockpit,' Rourke said dangerously. 'I could put this bullet through your brain right now, then walk up there and find out for myself.'

Micah coughed slightly, and raised a hand. 'Nicolas Kelsier used to be ETRA Minister in the Europan Commonwealth.' Seeing their blank faces, he elaborated. 'The Extra-Terrestrial Resource Acquisition department. As in, the ones who sent me out to shoot people to stop them from taking anything they thought belonged to them.'

'Fine,' Drift said, his voice suddenly tired. Jenna frowned; the showy, charismatic ship's captain seemed to fade a little, and she was abruptly struck by the hollowness of his cheeks and the lines around his eyes, especially the natural left one. He looked older, and not a little hard, as he eyed Rourke belligerently. 'I'm getting a drink. You want to shoot me in the head, do it. Otherwise, put the gun away and wait, and I'll tell you what you want to know.'

'Be quick,' Rourke told him. They watched Drift throw some brown powder into a mug, add steaming water to it and then pour in a generous slug of whisky from his hip flask.

'I'm waiting.' Rourke had her hands on her hips and an expression of impatience on her face.

'Micah's told you that Nicolas Kelsier was the

ETRA Minister for the Europan Commonwealth,' Drift said heavily, taking a gulp of his coffee. 'About twenty years ago the EC was in a state of unofficial warfare with the Federation of African States over a couple of disputed systems. They didn't start deploying the Frontier Defence Unit until later,' he continued, with a nod at Micah, 'so at this point it was all diplomatic posturing and bullshit about "peaceful solutions" while behind the scenes, both sides made it as difficult for the other as they could in the hope that the other one would give up and get out.'

'God, I love politics,' Micah snorted.

'One of the main tactics the Europans started using was hiring privateers,' Drift continued, looking into his coffee. 'Private citizens offered commission to act as pirates against the merchant craft of a certain nation. Some of your take went to the Europans, but in exchange for that you had protection: denial of your activities, denial of your existence, refusal to extradite and so on, so long as you only hit the targets ETRA picked out. If you got indiscriminate then you were a liability; more than one privateer ended up full-blown pirate because they took an opportunity to hit the wrong ship from the wrong government.'

'The USNA did the same thing at one point,' Rourke nodded. 'So what are you saying, you were a privateer for the EC? Why the EC?'

'I'd taken on with a captain called Swift, out of Telamon,' Drift said, 'but after we got underway we found out he was a bastard of the first water. There was a girl who'd signed on at the same time as me, and Swift took a fancy to her. We were running at sublight again and four days out of New

Keswick when Swift got impatient and actually made a grab for her in the canteen. She'd ignored everything else, but as soon as he laid a hand on her she swung for him: damn good punch too, laid the bastard clean out.' He gave a humourless laugh. 'Of course, that didn't go down well with the first mate, who was Swift's crony and even nastier than his captain. He went for her in a flash with a carving knife.' Drift placed one finger almost tenderly against his ribs. 'Caught her right here with the point.'

'So, me and Tommy Hernandez and Ginger Ell and old Capshaw the navigator rushed him. Swift tried to save him, so we took him down too. We . . . weren't gentle.' He grimaced. 'Two minutes later and both of the officers were dead, but she was bleeding out as well. The ship's medical facilities were basic, and there wasn't a lot we could do about a knife through the heart. We flushed the two bastards out into the void but kept her with us, hoping to give her a proper burial.'

'Of course, we weren't thinking clearly. Not that it would have mattered if we had been; Swift was running a legal shipping business for all that he was an abusive shit, and we had no slicer on board. So we made port on a Europan planet in a ship registered to a dead man, with the captain and first mate absent and another dead body on board. We were immediately arrested as mutineers and suspected murderers, and were expecting to get slung into prison.

'And then we got a better offer.'

'From Kelsier?' Rourke asked. Drift nodded.

'This old guy came to see us while we sat there in

handcuffs. Two military troopers with him. Introduced himself, nice as you like; Nicolas Kelsier, ETRA Minister for the Europan Commonwealth. "Happened to be in the area", which since it was one stop over from a contested system I guess meant he was checking out the lay of the land. Said we could either serve a joint sentence for mutiny and triple murder – they were pinning all three deaths on us, you see – or we could work for him as privateers. We would attack ships from the FAS as designated by his department in exchange for yadda yadda yadda, you get the idea.' He shrugged. 'I'd just turned twenty. I could look forward to most of my life in prison, or I could stay flying and comparatively free. I took the second option. So did the others.

'The Europans were thorough: they took geneprints of us all, with promises that if we broke the deal we'd be hunted down and dragged back to serve our sentences, and our details would be forwarded to all other governments as escaped murder suspects. Whether they'd have followed through or not, I don't know, but we didn't chance it. I was nominated as captain, we took on some new hands who weren't averse to the idea of some violence, and . . . off we went.'

'Off you went?' Kuai said, looking a little sick. 'Off to kill people? Just like that?'

'No!' Drift snapped, eyes flashing, 'Our brief was to *steal resources*. You don't need to kill people for that. One good hit to the Alcubierre ring and a ship can't make a jump away from you. Usually we'd get them to launch a shuttle with the cargo on board which we'd pick up, then let them go on their way.

A couple made a fight of it, of course, but once crews realised they'd be left alive if they handed over their cargos . . .' He tailed off, looking uncomfortable.

'There's only a couple of pirates who had that rep,' Rourke said, picking up on what Drift had apparently unintentionally revealed. She was studying him intently, dark eyes fixed on his face. 'What name did *you* fly under?'

Drift looked back at her, and Jenna saw what looked like resignation settle over his features. 'The ship I took from Captain Swift was called the *Thirty-Six Degrees.*'

Jenna felt her eyes widening. But that meant . . .

'And your name?' Rourke demanded, although she must have already known.

Drift folded his arms and stared at her defiantly. 'I took the name Gabriel Drake.'

'*Bullshit!*' Jia erupted. She pointed a quivering finger at Drift. 'You are *not* Gabriel Drake! Drake's dead! The FAS killed him and his crew and captured the *Thirty-Six Degrees* in the Ngwena System ten years ago!'

'They *think* they did,' Drift replied coldly, 'but they never had a description or geneprint of me. I escaped.'

'Except that the FAS never killed them,' Rourke said quietly. 'The *Thirty-Six Degrees* was found in orbit in an ice belt around Ngwena Prime, all hands suffocated due to a catastrophic air leak. Everything else is just FAS propaganda.'

'And how would you know that?' Drift asked, his voice no louder than hers. The Captain and his business partner stared at each other across the room for a couple of seconds, eyes searching each other's faces.

Then Rourke shrugged, an almost mocking twitch of her shoulders.

'You're not the only one with contacts, Ichabod. Their story's a lie. Do you want to tell us what *actually* happened?'

Jenna saw Drift's jaw clench, and for a terrifying moment she thought he was going to launch himself at Rourke. 'How do you know it's a lie, Tamara?'

'The FAS don't guard their secrets as well as they should, and I had a reason to go looking,' Rourke replied sharply. Her palmgun was visible again, although she wasn't directly pointing it at Drift yet. 'What happened off Ngwena Prime, Ichabod?'

'Damn it Tamara, I've told you what you wanted to know!' Drift yelled, pushing away from the counter and taking a step towards her. Rourke brought the gun up instantly to point at his face: Drift stopped moving, but didn't stop shouting. 'Kelsier saved me from prison but kept it over my head as a threat to make me commit more crimes! Then I thought I'd got away from him, but he found me again on Carmella and threatened to go public if I didn't take this job! I'd have been arrested, everyone else probably would have too, and the *Keiko* would have been confiscated!'

'So you were trying to protect us?' The note of sarcasm in Rourke's voice was strong.

'You, me, all of us!' Drift protested. 'Is that so hard to believe?'

'I don't know,' Rourke said softly. 'Tell me how your last crew died, Ichabod.'

Drift glared at her, jaw working as he chewed the inside of his cheek.

'Now!' Rourke snapped, gesturing with her gun. 'I'm not giving you time to think up a cover story! I've read the file: the FAS used a merchantman as bait for Gabriel Drake then sprung a trap with two frigates which crippled the *Thirty-Six Degrees*' Alcubierre drive. It limped off and hid in the rings of Ngwena Prime, but by the time they tracked it down everyone on board had suffocated. Tell me what happened, or—'

'*I didn't want to die!*' Drift roared. 'That's what happened!' Jenna shrank back involuntarily from the fury in the Captain's face, but Rourke stood firm and her gun didn't waver.

'If the FAS found us, we were dead,' Drift continued, the words tumbling out fast and harsh, 'and if they didn't we were still dead, because we couldn't make port in that system without being caught, couldn't jump anywhere else, and we would run out of air, water and food.' His face had a hunted look, and for a moment Jenna pictured what it must be like to be stranded in the stars waiting for the end. 'So I grabbed an escape pod and spent three weeks in it on my own, nearly going mad while I waited to see if the frigates would notice me and shoot me down, and whether I'd calculated right and I'd intersect the orbit of a little shithole of a moon called Ngwena III.'

'What, and your crew just let you go?' Jia scoffed.

'My crew by that point were a bunch of violent bastards who'd signed on to get rich, not because some Nordic bastard had blackmailed them,' Drift spat. 'They blamed me for things going wrong, and I didn't have to be a genius to see what was happening. When I heard them talking about trying to buy their way free by handing me over to the FAS, that was it.' He grimaced. When he spoke again, every word seemed to carry the weight of a bullet.

'So that night, when it was my watch, I put on a sealed suit, overrode the safety mechanisms and opened the airlocks.'

'You did *what*?' Apirana rumbled dangerously. Jenna stole a glance at him and saw his huge fingers starting to curl into fists. Drift didn't seem to have noticed; his gaze was locked with that of Tamara Rourke.

'And did they all deserve that, Ichabod?' Rourke asked softly. 'Were they all looking to betray you? Every last one of them?'

Drift's lip curled, but his voice was ragged. 'You know I don't have an answer for that, Tamara. And don't think I haven't asked myself the same question, every night for years.'

Jenna just stared at him. Ichabod Drift, the Captain, the man with the ready smile and a lazy quip, the man who'd taken her on with no questions asked, was one of the most notorious pirates in the skies. A sudden memory hit her, almost dizzying in its intensity: she was still a child, sitting eating dinner with her parents and her brother, and the newsfeed was on. The announcer's voice was speaking in clipped, measured tones about an FAS transport ship attacked by Gabriel Drake, the crew killed. Her father looking up from his meal and declaring that 'someone should do something about that monster' and Jenna knew, even at that age, that the someone was never going to be *him*. Her father lived in a world where 'someone' was always 'someone else'.

Of course, Drift had said he didn't kill the crews. Maybe that had been another bit of FAS propaganda, which the USNA broadcasts had repeated unquestioned? *No,* her mind whispered to her, *he never said he didn't kill the crews. He said he didn't need to . . . and he's just admitted to killing all his old crew. Every single one of them.*

Rourke was just staring at Drift, her face unreadable. Drift held her gaze, defiance in his eyes. The rest of the crew simply stood hushed, unwilling to move or make a noise which might shatter the delicate tension in the air.

Except for one.

'*E kai nga tutae me e mate! Upoko kohua!*'

Apirana shouldered forwards, face contorted with rage and, before anyone could react, had reached one huge hand out to clamp it around Drift's neck.

SOMEONE SHOULD DO SOMETHING

Drift's hands flew up reflexively but uselessly as he was slammed back against the galley's worktop: the Maori's wrist was as thick around as his Captain's biceps, and beneath the fat layered over his frame Apirana had slabs of iron-hard muscle and tendons you could anchor a spaceship with. Jenna heard a wheeze as the Captain tried to speak, but Apirana's fingers were squeezing off his air.

'A.!' Rourke snapped, and suddenly the one-shot was aimed at him. 'Let him go! We might need him to—'

She never got to finish the sentence. Apirana's tattooed face snapped towards her and his other hand flew out with shocking speed, seizing her wrist and twisting it viciously. Rourke cried out in pain and the gun clattered to the floor, which caused the Chang siblings to dance aside, presumably out of worry about it going off and shooting one of them in the foot. The huge Maori then wrenched Rourke effortlessly towards him, releasing her wrist at the last moment and throwing his arm up to clamp around her neck. Crushed against his ribcage, Rourke tried to punch him in the back but he didn't so much as grunt.

'You *fucking* bastard!' Apirana roared at Drift, having switched back into English. Ignoring Rourke except to almost casually restrain her with one arm, he wrenched the Captain bodily across the room and onto the galley's table, pinning him there by the throat. 'All this fucking time I've been working for you!'

Jenna looked around desperately as the Maori continued to rant and Drift's face grew redder and redder, despite the best efforts of his clutching fingers on Apirana's wrist. The Changs had backed away as far as they could, while Micah had reached down to pick Rourke's one-shot up but then casually pocketed it and stood back again with an unconcerned air. None of them looked like they were going to jump in and stop what was rapidly progressing towards murder.

Someone should do something. The words echoed in her head, one of any number of times she'd heard her father say them, each time with the same emptiness of meaning. It had always been the verbal equivalent of a shrug: once voiced, the responsibility had been passed elsewhere.

She gritted her teeth and stepped forwards. '*Apirana Wahawaha!*'

The big man's face turned to her, twisted in anger and lips flecked with spittle from the force of his bellowing. His eyes practically bulged from their sockets, white and furious, framed by the dark lines of tattoos which no longer looked like body art but instead turned his features into something savage and primal. Jenna felt like she was staring down the throat of a volcano or at an onrushing tsunami; a force of nature untameable and unchallengeable, by which mere humans like her would be crushed and thrown aside.

She slapped him on the jaw, as hard as she could.

Apirana had told her once that the head was sacred to the Maori. The worst curse in the Maori language was telling someone else to 'go boil your head and eat it', not just for the disrespect of the original act but also the indignity of shitting it out again after-wards. To touch anyone's head without permission was a long way from polite, but to a Maori it went far beyond that.

Apirana's right hand left Drift's throat and drew back, fingers clenching into a fist roughly the size of Jenna's head. She took a deep breath, shut her eyes and waited.

Two seconds later, she cautiously opened them again. To her left, Drift was still on his back on the table and making a noise like a malfunctioning air-con unit as he desperately sucked in oxygen. In front of her, and far more prominent, the massive form of Apirana stood frozen in place. The big man's face was still wild, but there was recognition in his eyes. Recognition, and desperate indecision.

'I'm sorry,' Jenna said quickly, 'I'm sorry but you were going to *kill* him! And I don't think you want to do that. Not really.'

Apirana stared at her, teeth audibly grinding.

'Let her go,' Jenna said gently, nodding towards Rourke. 'Micah's got her gun. She won't shoot you.'

The big Maori just looked at her for a moment longer, then abruptly lowered his raised fist and shoved Rourke away. She fell to the floor and hit it groggily, breaking her fall with her hands but staying down.

'*Fuck!*' Apirana screamed. He seized the plastic seat of one of the chairs which were, like the table, welded to the canteen floor to prevent them from flying around during mid-air manoeuvres in a planet's gravity well; there was an ugly snapping noise and he wrenched it clean off its metal base, then hurled it at the galley where it impacted with a crash of pans.

'*Fuck!*'

Drift's coffee mug was seized up and shattered against the far wall a second later, leaving brown spatters where it hit. Jenna stood aside as the Maori stormed forwards, and felt the gust of air as his left arm passed within a couple of inches of her. That same arm rose up to slam a palm into the wall with a sound like a gunshot as he reached the doorway; then he was through and disappearing down the corridor, although a series of bangs and roared swearwords marked his departure towards his cabin.

Jenna took a deep breath, trying to calm her racing heart. Beside her, Drift struggled up to a sitting position, legs dangling over the edge of the table.

'Thank you,' he rasped, the wheezing tone not concealing the gratitude in his voice. 'I thought the big bastard had my number there.'

'I didn't do it for you,' Jenna told him, still staring at the doorway. 'I did it for him.'

'I don't care,' Drift said, getting to his feet, 'you still probably saved my life. How did you know he wouldn't hit you?'

'I didn't,' Jenna admitted, 'but A. seems to have issues about having his trust betrayed by people he sees as authority . . . or with being threatened,' she added, nodding at Rourke who was getting back to her feet. 'He's three times my size and I'm the youngest member of this crew. I have no authority, and I'm no threat to him.' *Plus we seem to get along well*, she added silently. She was in no hurry to repeat the experience, though.

Drift's eyes were studying her; the mechanical one was as unreadable as always but the living one looked to be weighing her up. Then he nodded slightly. 'Well, thank God you've got some brains, and guts enough to use 'em.' He glanced over at Tamara Rourke. 'You alright?'

'I've been better,' she muttered, rubbing at her neck.

'Yeah, well, join the club,' Drift told her. He looked up at the rest of the crew, eyes scanning over Micah and the Changs and coming to rest on Jenna. 'Well? Anyone else looking to kill me?'

His words were met with silence.

'Good.' He twisted his neck, as though still trying to iron out something damaged by Apirana's grip, then held out his hand towards Micah. 'The gun, please.'

'That's mine,' Rourke said dangerously. Micah looked from one to the other, but didn't move.

'Micah,' Drift said matter-of-factly, 'first of all, this

is my ship and I'm the Captain. Secondly, and I suspect rather more importantly so far as you're concerned, I hid the credit chip with the remaining money on before we entered atmo. So if you want to get paid, you'll be taking orders from me.'

Micah pursed his lips for a second, then shrugged and tossed the one-shot underarm to Drift, who caught it deftly. Rourke's eyes flashed, but Micah just spread his hands. 'What? He ain't the only one who used to take orders from Kelsier.'

'He killed his old crew!' Kuai protested.

'A decade ago!' Drift yelled, causing the mechanic to flinch away from him. 'What do you want me to say? That I'm sorry? That I wish I hadn't done it? Fine!' He threw up his arms. 'Consider it said! But if I hadn't bailed Jia out, would you have been able to raise the cash for her? And what sort of sentence would she have got if she'd been left there?'

'You're Gabriel Drake,' Kuai spat, 'if you think I'm going to fly with you now . . .' He shook his head, unable or unwilling to finish his sentence, and folded his arms defiantly.

Drift exhaled in apparent frustration, then look at Kuai's sister. 'Jia?'

The pilot looked uncertain, but stepped up beside her brother. Drift's face fell further. 'Micah?'

'I go where the money goes,' Micah shrugged, taking a couple of strides to stand by the Captain's side.

'You think he'll be earning much now?' Rourke demanded, now flanked by the Chang siblings. 'He's wanted twice over.'

'He's got a ship,' Micah pointed out. 'What've you got?'

'A pilot, a mechanic and Apirana,' Rourke shot back, 'plus a slicer. Right, Jenna?'

Every eye turned to her. Jenna had a sudden and thoroughly incongruous memory of being in an amateur dramatic performance at high school where she'd stepped out onto the stage, seen the audience and completely forgotten her lines. This was why she liked code so much, it never taxed her emotionally or asked her to make impossible decisions. Drift was Drake, and Drake was a . . . *had been* a feared pirate. Rourke was sensible and responsible, but Rourke had always seemed to view her as an asset: valuable, yes, but not a person to talk and laugh with. The Captain had made a real effort to make her feel at home on their ship, his recent snappiness notwithstanding.

And then there was the non-too-small matter of the ship itself. It was Drift's ship, and the ship was their best chance for freedom, but could he fly it without the Changs? *And is it going to stay his . . .?*

The bracelet on Jenna's left wrist chimed a warning note. She felt her cheeks burn but was grateful for the distraction; at least, until she read the text scrolling across its polished surface.

'What's that?' Drift asked, brows lowering. 'That's not another—'

'No,' Jenna said, cutting him off before any of the syllables of 'EMP' could cross his lips, 'it's a processor and display unit slaved to the main terminal in the cockpit. And yes, I built it.' She reread the words crawling over it and felt something ice-cold sink through her stomach. 'We need to go. The Europans are pulling up protocols to detain all *Carcharodon*-class shuttles at anchor.'

'How do you know?' Rourke demanded. Jenna gave her a look of the sort she'd used to reserve for her brother when he was being particularly dense. It had got a lot of usage.

'You hired me to slice. The Spine on any world has unregulated backchannels slicers use to distribute information, and I tapped into them as soon as we were in atmo, then set up alert tags.' She tapped her bracelet. 'Luckily for us, someone somewhere saw what the Europans are doing and passed the word out. I don't know how long it will take for them to get that protocol activated, but we can't be on the ground when they do.'

Rourke nodded once, her expression grim. 'We need to take off, then find somewhere to hole up since we can't leave the planet at the moment. Does anyone have any contacts on Old Earth? Jia? Kuai?'

'Only our parents,' Jia replied, shaking her head, 'and we can't exactly hide the *Jonah* in their apartment.'

'Micah?' Rourke asked, but the mercenary just shook his head.

'I don't think anyone Apirana knew here would be happy to see him,' Jenna volunteered, to a rueful nod from Rourke. 'I could try to chase up a safe house through the slicer channels, but I wouldn't really know where to start.'

'You don't need to,' Drift said firmly, eyeing Rourke. 'This is still *my* ship, damn it. Let's get in the air.' He strode forwards without waiting for a response, past Rourke and the Changs and heading out of the canteen.

'And go where?' Rourke demanded of his retreating back.

'Atlantic City!' Drift shouted over his shoulder, disappearing towards the cockpit. 'I've got an idea!'

They looked at each other for a couple of seconds. Then Rourke hissed in frustration. 'Kuai, abort the refuelling and get the engines running. Jia, get to the stick and make sure he doesn't try flying us out of here himself. Jenna, get on the channels and watch for *anything* which suggests we've been made. Micah, arm up and . . . shit, see if Apirana's still even on board, and if he is, whether he's going to go ballistic if we take off.'

'What, you trust him again?' Kuai demanded, pointing in the direction Drift had gone. Rourke scrubbed a hand across her forehead, which was about as emphatic a gesture of emotion as Jenna had ever seen the older woman make.

'Damn it, I don't know,' Rourke admitted, 'but trust him or not, it sounds like he has a plan. And stars help us, that's more than I have right now.'

Ichabod Drift felt . . . odd.

He'd been holding a secret in his chest for over a decade, so tightly that more than once he'd felt like the weight of it would smother him. The fear of being discovered hadn't faded over time: if anything it had grown, because as he forged more independence and put more and more distance between him and his old life there'd been that much more to lose. When he'd staggered out of his escape pod on Ngwena III and headed for the closest speck of civilisation, he'd been resigned to getting picked up by the authorities, tried and summarily executed as Gabriel Drake, and the bitter remorse he'd felt for opening the *Thirty-Six Degrees*' airlocks meant he wouldn't have argued the sentence. He had never been lower.

But then he'd heard the news: Gabriel Drake and his entire crew had already been killed in a heroic boarding action off Ngwena Prime. He was just another Hispanic face in the crowd, the Federation of African States' eagerness to claim credit for his treachery providing him with a security he'd never have enjoyed had they launched a manhunt for any possible fugitives with no background story. He'd taken passage out of the system on the first transport he could find, gathered up some of the credit chips he'd carefully stashed away in a variety of secure locations, and set about using the profits from Gabriel Drake's career as a privateer to start a new life for Ichabod Drift.

He couldn't get away, though, not completely. Not just because the funds to purchase the *Keiko* and the *Jonah* had come from his old life, but because his secret had been buried in his heart like a worm in an apple. How many times had he woken in fear in case he'd muttered something in his sleep which would have tipped off whoever had been lying beside him that night? How many reasons had he found never to hire someone from the FAS just in case he'd attacked a ship they'd been on, or their brother or mother or cousin had been on? How many times had he desperately wished he *could* tell someone, to explain what had happened? For someone to listen to the tale of his life and nod and say that yes, his hand had been forced and they would likely have made the same choices in the same situation? He'd never had the courage, though, nor what he felt would be the right audience.

Everything was out now, though. Not out as he'd have liked it, not shared to a close confidante, but dragged out of him at gunpoint to a room of people he'd hoped were his friends but had ended up looking for someone to blame. All the same, he felt oddly . . . free.

'What's in Atlantic City?' Tamara Rourke asked from behind him. He fought down the urge to retort sharply, to mock or to demand an apology. Jia pushed past him and dropped into the pilot's chair, fingers darting through the preflight checks, and the sudden vibration in the floor told him that Kuai had brought the main engines online. Three people who had been in stark opposition to Gabriel Drake a minute before had fallen back into old habits because Ichabod Drift offered them a way out, and he had no intention of pushing his luck with them.

Now he just needed it to work.

'A spaceport called Star's End,' he replied, turning to face her. Her face still showed distrust, but she hadn't choked him out from behind to get her gun back so he was prepared to call that a win for now. 'It's run by someone I used to know.'

Rourke's face clearly showed what she thought of people he used to know. 'And this friend of yours will just let us hole up in his place even though the entire planet's looking for us?'

'He's no friend,' Drift corrected her, feeling the floor shift slightly beneath him as Jia started to take off, 'but he owes me his life, and he's too proud to forget that no matter how much we used to dislike each other. I don't care how angry the Europans are, they can't lock Old Earth up forever. The other governments might hold to it for a couple of days, tops; after that there'll be riots if the launches don't restart and the trade stops coming in. We lie low for a few days, then we should be able to sneak off-world.'

'Star's End?' Jenna was already tapping at her terminal, calling up the information from the Spine. 'Proprietor . . . Alexander Cruz?' She looked up, doubt writ large on her face. 'It doesn't look very . . . nice.'

'It probably isn't,' Drift acknowledged, 'but it'll be a place we can duck out of sight until the skies clear a bit, and Alex won't tip anyone off about us.' He tried to sound casually confident, although he was anything but. The fact remained, however, that they needed *somewhere* to hide and there was no purpose to be served by having his crew rebel against the only viable option.

'Fine,' Rourke nodded after a second, 'but our conversation isn't over.'

'I can't wait,' Drift told her, unable to keep some of the sarcasm out of his voice, 'but let's focus on getting out of Europa for now, shall we?' He frowned. 'Wait . . . what about A.?'

Rourke grunted and activated her comm. 'Micah? How'd it go?'

+*The big man's still on board*,+ the Dutch mercenary's voice replied. +*Either that, or his cabin's learned how to swear at me in Maori on its own.*+

'Roger that,' Rourke replied, then keyed in another frequency. 'Kuai? How did we do on the refuel?'

+*Mostly topped up. What's the plan now?*+

'The sky's shut for the moment,' Rourke told him, eyeing Drift, 'but the Captain thinks he knows a place we can hide out until there's a window.'

+*Does it have any bombs? I've pretty much had my fill of bombs.*+

'If it does, I'm going to personally shove them down his throat.' Rourke clicked the comm off again, still looking at him. Drift decided not to rise to it.

'Stations then, people,' he said, picking up his earpiece and activating the frequency scanner once more. 'Let's head for Star's End and hope we can stay off the radar.'

They took off and flew south, over the Celtic Sea and into the stream of air traffic heading across the Atlantic Ocean from France and the Iberian Peninsula, chasing the sun westwards faster than it could travel across the sky. The channels in Drift's ear suggested that the Europans were concentrating their searches in the north, particularly around Iceland and the Finnish border with Russia, and he was very grateful the *Jonah* had changed direction when it did.

The flight was a tense one. Drift half expected a hail over the radio at any moment calling on them to change course or, worse, the sudden appearance of interceptor aircraft on an attack run. Added to that was the fact that even Jia's prodigious reserves of concentration were starting to get taxed by the long planetary approach, atmospheric entry and their various shenanigans into and out of Amsterdam, and there was still the bitter aftertaste of confrontation in the air. He found himself wired to jump into action at any moment in case someone's temper snapped or their pilot fell asleep at the controls and, as a result, when Jia spoke up to announce they were approaching the Eastern Seaboard he nearly jumped out of his seat, half-expecting some disaster to be announced.

'You okay?' Jenna asked curiously.

'Better now we're on the final stretch,' Drift replied

honestly, trying to look like he'd been snapping to alert. He jabbed a finger at his earpiece. 'Can you throw me over a channel for Star's End?'

'Here.' The calltag appeared on his terminal screen. He tapped at it, activating the connection and trying to surreptitiously moisten his mouth. This was where it could all fall apart, and if his promised bolt-hole proved to be unwelcoming then he didn't fancy his chances either with his crew or escaping the Europans. Still, there was no way he was going to take them inside without getting some assurances. The line crackled into life and a bored female voice spoke into his ear with the familiar twang of North America flavouring her words.

+*Star's End Spaceport?*+

He carefully schooled his vowel sounds to match hers; people always reacted better to a familiar accent. 'This is the *Tamsin's Wake* requesting berthing and an open line to Alexander Cruz.' He said it casually, as though it were the most natural thing in the world, and it certainly seemed to wrong-foot the person on the other end.

+*Excuse me, sir?*+

'My ship requires a berth,' Drift explained, 'and I need to speak to Alex urgently.' He was careful to keep his voice brisk and businesslike, and free from any patronising or belligerent tone. Someone less skilled at talking their way through obstacles might have tried to bully or shame the operator into doing what they wanted, but Drift was of the firmly held opinion that you rarely opened doors by offending people. 'He is still running Star's End, isn't he?'

+*Uh, yes sir,*+ the operator replied, uncertainty still

audible, +*but Mr Cruz is not available to take incoming calls.*+

'I quite understand,' he said reassuringly, 'and believe me, I wouldn't ask unless it was very important.' He hesitated, but he didn't have many options. 'I'll tell you what: could you please contact him and tell him that Gabriel needs to talk to him about Tantalus? If he won't take my call, I won't trouble you any further.'

+*I . . . Very well, one moment, sir.*+

'Tantalus?' Jenna asked, looking up.

'It's a planet,' Drift shrugged casually, muting his headset's microphone, 'someone named it that because parts of it look green from orbit and scientists originally went loopy about finding extraterrestrial life, but then it turned out to just be some chemical element in the mud, or something. I pulled Alex's bacon out of the fire there once, although he won't thank me for reminding him about it.'

'Won't she just come back and say that he still doesn't want to talk to you?' Jia put in, without looking around. 'You gave her an easy out there.'

'I gave her a way to pass the responsibility on without either putting me straight through or ditching a call her boss might actually want to take,' Drift said, eyeing the approaching New Jersey coastline of steel and concrete. '*That* is the easy out.'

'You want me to start taking her down anyway?' Jia asked, starting to swing their nose towards the towering blocks with dancing, metres-high advertisements blazing out across the ocean at them.

'Hold until I get a reply,' Drift told her. Now the pilot *did* look over her shoulder at him.

'Don't tell me you've had me fly us here and—'

'After what's just happened, let's make sure this is a safe place,' Drift cut her off. 'Alex is a bastard, but if he says he'll shelter us, then he'll shelter us. If I don't get that assurance, we may be better off taking our chances elsewhere.' His comm buzzed and he activated the connection again before Jia could retort. 'Hello?'

+*This is Alexander Cruz. Who's speaking?*+

'Alex, you know very well who it is,' Drift said, losing the New Jersey accent and putting an edge into his voice. Cruz wasn't a bored bay coordinator who needed buttering up; the man had always been steel and ice wrapped in a curious moral code who wouldn't budge unless he was pushed, and Drift doubted that would have changed now he owned some real estate and a superficially legal business. Besides which . . .

There was a pause.

+*You're dead.*+

The words weren't a threat. The tone was that of a man who was struggling to believe the evidence of his own ears.

'Then you've just become a fucking medium, congratulations,' Drift snapped, the sound of Cruz's voice triggering old memories and bringing Gabriel Drake's old vocal mannerisms back to the surface. He didn't try to suppress them; he needed the other man to believe him, and quickly. 'I've got a ship I need landing, and I could do with some coffee too.' He saw Jenna's eyebrows quirk, but ignored her for now.

+*Listen, whoever you are—*+

'Alex, shut the fuck up,' Drift spoke over the other man's attempted indignation. 'You owe me a favour and I'm calling it in. I don't expect you to like it, and I give you my word I will be out of your hair as soon as I can and everything between us will be square, but until that time don't try to fob me off by pretending I'm not who I say I am.'

+*Sweet shitting Jesus. It really is you, isn't it?*+

Drift felt a grin spread across his face, although he was careful to keep it from creeping into his voice. 'Now you're getting the idea.'

There was another pause for a few seconds.

+*I suppose you'd best come down then. I'll find you a mug.*+

tar's End Spaceport occupied a large, flat area which might have been a bay or lagoon of some sort long ago, before the water was pumped or diverted away and the whole thing surfaced over. The port itself was a multilayered affair, with curved walls which made it look a little like an enormous sports stadium from the exterior and served to contain the blast from any catastrophic accidents. As the *Jonah* crawled into position over it, Drift saw the other purpose of those walls: berth bays were built into them, like the comb of an enormous beehive or, perhaps, a vast wine rack. There was a steady chatter over his earpiece as ships of varying sizes were given clearance to take off or land in certain sectors, all activity monitored to minimise the possibility of two vessels attempting to fly through the same piece of air at once.

'This is *huge*,' Jenna commented, peering out of

a viewport. 'Even Franklin Major doesn't have anything like this.'

'There's ports like this all over the continent,' Jia snorted. 'Every continent, really. Well, not so many in Africa, but then they've got the space elevator.' She checked her read-outs, then tapped the internal commswitch. 'Okay people, we're heading down. Hope you're not claustrophobic.' A couple of seconds later the *Jonah* started to sink, swivelling in the air as Jia prepared to fly backwards into their assigned berth – carefully, or so Drift hoped.

'What was the "coffee" thing about?' Jenna asked him as the walls rose up above them.

'Mmm? Oh, it's a code. Or was a code, anyway,' Drift corrected himself. 'People like Alex and me used to use it, along with the ports we tended to dock in. If the authorities were after you and you needed somewhere to lie low then you'd head for someone you knew – and you'd only ever be offered sanctuary by someone you knew – and ask for help. But there's no point announcing it over an open channel, of course, so when you hailed them you'd ask for a drink when you got down. It didn't matter what it was, so long as it wasn't alcoholic.'

'And if they said you could have some, then you were okay?' Jenna asked. Drift smiled and shook his head.

'No. If they said they'd get you a cup, a mug, a glass or whatever, *then* you were okay. If they ignored you or responded with anything else, even if they said you could have some but didn't mention anything to put it in, then you either wouldn't be safe there or wouldn't be welcome. Probably both.'

'Sounds like a decent system,' Jia commented. 'Ever get any mix-ups?'

'Not really,' Drift replied. 'Like I said, no one would give sanctuary to someone they didn't know, and if you knew them then they'd know the code. It worked well.'

'Do people still use it?' Jenna asked. Drift shrugged.

'Not sure. I honestly don't know where most of those people are now, except Alex.'

'Everyone quiet,' Jia ordered, halting their descent, 'this is the tricky part.'

Star's End had various sizes of docking berth, and the one they'd been assigned looked uncomfortably narrow to Drift's eyes. Jia backed them in slowly, muttering under her breath in Mandarin and with her eyes flickering from one sensor read-out to another. There was a brief outbreak of hissed swearing at one point when something beeped urgently at her, but to Drift's delight – and mild surprise – she managed to get them in and set them down without hitting the walls.

No sooner had the main drive powered down than a thick steel security door began to lower across the entrance to the bay.

'Well, that's not at all worrying,' Jenna said uncertainly.

'It's standard,' Drift assured her. 'The doors protect the bays from any accidents outside or someone trying to fly into the wrong one, plus in this case it means no one can see in and work out who we are.' As if in response to his words – although more likely the growing darkness as the door continued its crawl downwards – lights flickered on inside the bay.

'Seriously, nothing to worry about.' He felt a small shiver of relief run through him. Finally, his feet were more or less on solid ground again and he wasn't reliant on other crew members to pilot or slice him out of trouble. Oh, there were problems hanging over his head, but right now he was back in the realm of dealing with people, and people was where he excelled.

The comm buzzed. +*Attention* Tamsin's Wake, *this is Star's End security. Power down all engines and prepare for docking inspection in two minutes.*+

'Roger that, Star's End,' Drift replied easily, 'our drives are already inactive and we'll have the doors open for you.' He got up out of his seat and stretched. 'Okay people, let's go and meet our hosts.'

'You mean I don't get to sleep yet?' Jia grumbled.

'Not quite,' Drift told her. 'Go round up your brother and bring him down to the cargo hold. I want everyone front and centre for this.'

'So they can shoot us all at the same time,' Jia muttered, but she stripped off her piloting gloves and headed out of the cockpit. Drift cocked an eyebrow at Jenna.

'On your feet, Tech Officer.'

'Tech Officer?' Jenna snorted, obeying.

'Hell, I figure you need a title beyond "slicer",' Drift shrugged as she followed him out of the cockpit back down to the cargo bay where they were greeted by the sight of what scrap metal hadn't fallen into the ocean when the bomb doors had opened, and Rourke and Micah rooting through it.

'I thought we'd better check to see if there was any sort of tracking device hidden in here,' Rourke said in answer to their unspoken query.

'Anything?' Drift asked, although he was sure he'd have already heard if there had been.

'Nothing,' Micah snorted, 'the other three crates were all just scrap.' He exhaled noisily through his nose and looked over at Drift. 'So what's our play now?'

'Right now, we're about to be visited by a security inspection which I suspect will be led by Alexander Cruz,' Drift told them. Rourke immediately reached for her Crusader, and Drift winced. 'I really don't think that's necessary.'

Rourke's eyes were cool as she pulled her hat down over them. 'I don't fancy any more surprises, Ichabod. I'd like to hear what this friend of yours has to say.'

'I told you he wasn't a friend,' Drift warned. Rourke shrugged.

'All the more reason to have a gun to hand.'

'No,' Drift said, surprising even himself with the sternness in his voice. Out of the corner of his eye he saw Micah stiffen slightly. 'This man owes me a favour. They've sealed the bay off, which is standard practice but also means we're locked behind a steel door in the middle of his spaceport. We are here on his sufferance and his sense of honour, which is probably not outweighing his sense of trouble by all that much, at the moment.' He nodded at Rourke's trusty rifle. 'Let's not give him a reason to decide we're not worth the hassle.'

Rourke studied him for a couple of seconds, face blank, then blinked and laid the weapon carefully back against the wall. 'Fine.'

Drift concealed his sigh of relief and turned to face

the Chang siblings as they walked in. 'Security inspection, Kuai.'

'Good job we've already offloaded the illegal military hardware, hey?' Kuai grunted. Drift spared him a moment's glare, then saw the shadow growing in the corridor behind him. A second later Apirana's huge frame loomed into view, towering over the Changs. Drift tried not to look at the big man's massive hands as he felt the ghost of them clasped around his neck and met Apirana's eyes instead, or attempted to: the Maori looked away after a second, shoulders hunched.

'Where are we?' Apirana muttered, shoving his hands into the pockets of his flight suit.

'Atlantic City,' Drift answered him, breathing a little more easily. He could deal with Apirana later. Currently there was a more pressing concern, and he turned to face the front of the bay as a buzzing noise indicated that someone outside was requesting entry. 'Everyone try not to look too suspicious.'

'Now he tells us,' Jia drawled. Drift ignored her and walked over to key in the release code, then stepped back and held his breath.

The seals detached and the loading ramp groaned downwards, meeting the floor with a clank. The bay outside was lined in metal so the mags of a ship could gain a purchase and a pilot wouldn't have to control the beast by thrusters alone, and was otherwise bare: understandable, given that the level of heat thrown out by a ship's thrusters would damage pretty much anything it touched.

Bare, that was, apart from the group of men and women arrayed at the bottom of the ramp. There were half a dozen of them in sober, dark blue uniforms, each one with a tazer gun cradled loosely in their hands and stun batons at their belts; clearly the security force. Drift's quick scan over their faces suggested they were relaxed and possibly a little bored, and there was no sign of the sudden rush he'd half been fearing which would have doubtless ended with the *Jonah*'s crew eventually being handed over to the Europan authorities.

The man slightly in front of them looked far from relaxed, however. Alexander Cruz was a far cry from the dashing rake of a man Drift had known a decade ago, and if it was strange to see him in the calf-high black boots, black breeches and crisp white shirt he'd apparently decided was to be his uniform as the spaceport's owner and manager, then it was even stranger to see him with a gut and the hint of a double chin. His eyes met Drift's and his face tightened a little, but he stepped away from his escort and advanced up the ramp on his own. He jerked his head at Drift, indicating he should move towards the rest of his crew. Drift obliged, happy to be out of sight and hopefully earshot of the security detail.

Cruz clearly still wasn't one for pleasantries. He stopped about ten feet away from the loose line of the *Jonah*'s crew, his cold dark eyes flickering from one to another of the ragged group that could have hardly contrasted more starkly with his uniformed team. His eyes barely rested on Drift even as he addressed him without preamble.

'What am I even supposed to call you these days?'

'Ichabod Drift will do fine,' Drift replied levelly.

'What sort of a name is that?' Cruz snorted.

'Less well known than the alternative,' Drift pointed out. 'You're looking well,' he added, in an attempt to steer the conversation elsewhere. It was true: Alexander Cruz still carried himself smoothly and easily despite the weight gain, and his skin held the tan of a man who got out into the comparatively benign light of Old Earth's sun on a regular basis.

'You look like shit,' Cruz replied baldly, 'but then if I'd just dropped a nuke in the Europans' backyard I'd probably be crapping rocket fuel too.'

Drift suppressed a sudden urge to shiver. 'That's an interesting allegation.'

'Don't try to play me for a fool when you're taking advantage of an old favour, *Drift*,' Cruz snorted. 'You've been off-radar for a decade or more. I thought you were dead; everyone thought you were dead. You've kept a low profile for a reason. You'd only show your face after all this time to someone who'd know it if you were out of options and desperate. You've got a ship to take you away from trouble, so I figure you just can't risk making orbit in case you get snatched . . . which means you're the one the Europans are looking for.'

Drift shrugged as lazily as he could manage. The man had always been smart even if not always sensible in his youth, and there was no point irritating him with further denials. 'And is this common knowledge?'

'No,' Cruz said, rolling his eyes, 'that's why my team are staying outside and are not party to this conversation, because they owe you nothing and I can't trust someone not to try getting a reward out of this. There's a description out on your craft, of course, but given there must be a few thousand *Carcharodon*-class shuttles in the sky over North America at any one time, that won't help the authorities much.' His eyebrows lowered into a scowl. 'I don't know what you do for a living these days, and I don't care. I have a business, and it's *legal*. God help me, I owe you for Tantalus, but you are gone from here within an hour of the USNA relaxing the launch restrictions for this continent. Am I clear?'

'Perfectly,' Drift nodded. 'Thank you.'

The portmaster pursed his lips. 'Okay then. Don't draw attention to yourselves: I won't rat on you, but if the Justices come asking questions I'll just be handing over the arrival log and I won't be taking any chances to tip you off that they're on their way.'

'Understood,' Drift assured him. Cruz stood there for another second or so, then nodded decisively.

'Well, I have a spaceport to run.' Those cold eyes met his once more. 'Goodbye, Mr Drift. I hope not to see you again.' He turned on his heel and strode away without another word, leaving Drift and his crew standing.

'You saved his life?' Jenna asked quietly as Cruz disappeared from view.

'I did,' Drift acknowledged.

'Why?'

'It seemed like a good idea at the time,' Drift snorted. 'And to be fair, I suppose it paid off in the end. This is the only spaceport we could expect to hide out in without difficult questions being asked.' He exhaled noisily, pulling his thoughts into order. 'Right. We're down and we're hidden, but we don't know how long we've got before Alex gives us our marching orders. So, when the time comes for us to move, we need to have worked out exactly how we're going to nail Nicolas Kelsier.'

There was a stunned silence for a second or so, and then the shouting started. Drift let it rise around him for a few moments before raising both hands and allowing some of Gabriel Drake's tone to creep back into his voice.

'*Quiet!*'

The added sharp edge worked; even Tamara Rourke closed her mouth again, although the look she shot him suggested that it was more from surprise than anything else. He let the sudden stillness hang in the air for a moment, just to ensure everyone's attention was properly focused on him. Other people might have found that expectation daunting, but not Ichabod Drift. Wherever he'd been, whatever name he'd adopted, he'd always used the same tool to get by.

Words.

'I'm taking it from people's reactions that they

don't think going after Kelsier is a particularly sensible thing to do,' he began. 'Let me put this to you another way: going after Kelsier is the *only* thing to do. We're a ship full of loose ends who know that he just tried to nuke Amsterdam. We were meant to die in the explosion and tie everything up neatly, but when he finds out what happened he'll know we're still alive, and then he will come hunting us.'

'Hunting *you*,' Kuai snorted, 'he only knows you! As soon as I walk out that door . . .'

Drift shook his head, a humourless smile on his lips. 'You're not getting it. He hired us to do a job: sure, he picked me to do it because he thought I might trust him, or he had blackmail material on me, but for some fucked-up reason he *needed* that nuke to blow up in Amsterdam. He needed a crew who could do a difficult smuggling job, to schedule. He's a careful man, which means he did his research, and *that* means he knows my crew. Odds are he knows all of us by name. And he already found us once.'

'Yeah, when we weren't trying to hide!' Jia argued. 'Why can't we just let this blow over?'

'Because it won't,' Drift answered bluntly. 'You don't know the man who hired us. I do. When he worked for the Europans and he was giving orders to people like Micah and me, he was very careful, very clever and *very* ruthless. That was when he was in a government with laws and rules and God knows what around him, even if he might have ignored some of them from time to time. You follow me? Now, imagine a man like that who only answers to *himself*, and ask yourself whether he's going to have got any more forgiving.' He looked over at Micah. 'Would you agree?'

'He's a psychopath,' Micah said simply, 'and the main reason I left the FDU.'

'Oh no, was he sending you somewhere you might have got shot at?' Kuai asked nastily. Micah glowered at the mechanic.

'Don't talk like you've ever picked up a gun in anger, little man,' the mercenary sneered. 'You expect the *staatslieden* to think of the big picture, yes, because they won't be doing the fighting themselves, but some of the orders coming out of ETRA . . .' He tailed off, shaking his head.

'Anyway, Jia, why are you suggesting hiding?' Drift demanded, turning back to their pilot. 'Someone cuts you up in the sky, you threaten to hit them so hard their children will be born bruised. Someone tries to *blow* you up and you're just going to run away and say "Please sir, don't do it again"?'

'It's not the same,' Jia growled, but Drift could see that he'd stung her pride. He scanned the faces in front of him and settled on Rourke's.

'Tamara. You were calling for blood earlier. I'm with you.' He spread his hands. 'Are you still in?'

'That was before I knew your history,' Rourke said flatly. 'How do I know I can trust you?'

'You might note that we've worked together for eight years *without* me killing you, or killing anyone else who's ever been on the crew, or even leaving someone to die,' Drift shot back. 'I mean, I didn't have to come back and get you on Severus Prime, did I?'

'No,' Rourke admitted.

'Or how about Benjamin, that time on Janus III? We didn't leave him behind, did we?'

'He died anyway.'

'Yeah, but that's because we couldn't get him to the med facility fast enough,' Drift countered. 'We *tried* to help him.' He waved his hands. 'Look, I'm not saying this will be easy, but Kelsier will be expecting us to go to ground. He won't be ready for us to come after him.'

'That might be because it's a stupid idea,' Kuai retorted. 'If he's got resources to find us if we hide, he's got resources to protect himself from one little ship. And how would we find *him*, anyway?'

'Alex might know where to start,' Drift shrugged. There was a moment's silence.

'Why,' Rourke said carefully, 'might Alex know?'

'Alexander Cruz was the captain of the *Dead Man's Hand*,' Drift replied. 'He was my main rival, I guess.'

'That pompous little toerag was the Butcher of Dawnside?' Apirana blurted out.

'You've brought us to a starport run by *another* of Kelsier's ex-privateers?' Rourke demanded incredulously, cutting over the Maori. 'How do you know he won't sell us out?'

'Firstly, because I had no choice,' Drift replied honestly, 'it was here or nowhere. Secondly, because he's a stubborn bastard with an overinflated opinion of his own honour and he owes me a favour. Thirdly, because if he'd been planning to double-cross us he wouldn't have been so hostile: he's not trying to get us to stick around to trap us, he wants us gone before we make his life difficult. I'm inclined to oblige him.'

'So am I,' Kuai snorted. 'Jia? Let's go.'

The pilot looked sideways at her brother, but didn't move.

'Do you have a plan, Kuai?' Drift pressed. 'Do you know what you're going to do next? Or are you just going to walk out into Atlantic City and hope you can find someone who needs a mechanic?'

'That beats hoping to find a terrorist,' Kuai retorted. 'Jia?'

His sister's eyes were fixed on Drift. He could see the uncertainty in her face, but there had always been a fire in the *Jonah*'s pilot which wasn't present in her sibling. Drift wasn't entirely sure if the Chinese had a word that exactly equated to 'forgiveness', but even if they did Jia didn't know the meaning of it.

'You think you can find him?' she asked him, ignoring her brother.

Drift nodded. 'Yes.' He deliberately didn't say how long it would take, but Jia's arched eyebrow suggested she'd caught on.

'You find out where he is by the time traffic's cleared to break atmo,' she said flatly, '*and* you have a plan for taking him down, or I'm finding something else to fly off this rock.' Only now did she meet Kuai's eyes: the mechanic said something sharp in Mandarin which Drift vaguely recognised to be a querying of her sanity, before Jia responded with an aggressive flurry he had no hope of understanding. He ignored the squabbling Changs and turned his attention to Micah.

'Well?' he asked. The Dutch mercenary grimaced. 'I don't like it.'

'Fair play,' Drift nodded, trying to ignore the sinking feeling he was starting to experience. He'd hoped Micah would be fully with him, but the disadvantage of having someone who could confirm Kelsier's ruthlessness was that the other person would also be understandably unwilling to tackle the old bastard's operation. 'Would you feel safer looking for Kelsier through your gunsight or over your shoulder?'

Micah blinked. 'Well . . .'

'Risk deserves fair reward,' Drift added, seeking the leverage he needed. 'He's got resources, and I'm intending to clean him out. Anything we take from him gets split seven ways, equally. After expenses.'

'*Equal* shares?' Micah's eyebrows quirked before he drew them into a frown again. 'You can't just blind me with money, you know.'

'You know him, at least by reputation,' Drift pressed. 'You know he'll be coming after us anyway; you might as well get *paid* for fighting his goons, surely?'

Micah grimaced again, then sighed and shook his head. He nodded sideways at Jia, raising his voice to be heard over the argument. 'Okay then, but I'm with her. You have a location and a plan by the time we need to move, and I'm with you. Otherwise I'll take my chances alone.'

Drift nodded gratefully, then eyed the arguing Changs with some irritation. Still, he was well aware that his authority as Captain was wafer-thin at the moment and the last thing he wanted to do was annoy Jia by telling her to be quiet and causing her to side with her brother out of sheer contrariness, so he turned his attention to the three remaining members of what was still at least nominally his crew.

'Jenna?' He grimaced, not needing to feign reluctance at the thought of her leaving. 'I know you haven't been with us long, but—'

'I've got nowhere else to go,' she answered, cutting him off. 'You picked up a drunk girl and gave her a ride and a job instead of robbing her or . . . worse.' She attempted a smile, although it was shaky and half-formed. 'Just try not to get me killed.'

Drift smiled, the same reassuring grin which had assured many a wary trader of his honesty. 'Wouldn't dream of it.' To his right, the squabbling in Mandarin had subsided, with Kuai wearing the sulky expression of someone who'd lost an argument. Which was, in fairness, exactly what Drift had been counting on: if the mechanic felt the need to 'look after' his little sister then he'd hardly abandon her if she was heading off into danger. And thinking of danger . . .

He turned to look at Apirana, trying not to let his unease show on his face. 'You're pretty distinctive, big man. Might find it hard to hide.'

Apirana just nodded, lips tight and face blank. Drift waited for a further reaction, but none came.

Except from Jenna.

'Oh, for goodness' sake,' the young slicer sighed. 'Captain, Apirana is sorry he let his temper get out of control and he wants to remain part of the crew, otherwise he'd be off the ship already.' She turned and addressed the big Maori, whose expression had rapidly slipped into 'stunned'. 'Apirana, the Captain wants you to stay or he'd have ordered you off the ship already, but neither of you are prepared to say anything unless you can work out what the other one intends, and goddamnit both of you suck at this!'

The shocked silence after Jenna's outburst was broken only by a snigger from, of all people, Tamara Rourke. Drift glared at her, then briefly at Jenna, then set himself and faced Apirana again.

'You want to stay?'

The Maori's mouth worked as though more words were trapped behind his lips, but the only one which emerged was a vaguely embarrassed, 'Yeah.'

Drift felt his guts get a little less fluttery. He'd honestly had no idea what the big man's intentions were; Apirana's emotions were usually so clear that the close-faced, silent Maori had quite thrown him. But if he was willing to stay, that meant he wouldn't be wandering around Atlantic City and sticking out like a sore thumb . . .

'Good,' he nodded firmly, trying to take it in his stride, 'you're a solid hand and I'm happy to have you. However, if you so much as threaten me again then you *will* be leaving this ship, immediately, no matter where we are at the time. Are we clear?'

This time Apirana's voice was firmer. 'Yeah.'

Drift held his gaze for another second, then turned to Tamara Rourke. 'Well?'

Rourke met his eyes, her stare weighing and considering. 'You've got a tall order, Ichabod.'

'I can do it. I *will* do it!' He heard some of his anger at Kelsier bleeding into his voice, and left it there. 'I've worked too hard to have to give everything up to run and hide. I've built a *reputation*, damn it! We all have, that's why we get work! If we're too

scared to tell people who we are then we lose all
that! Plus,' he added after a second, 'he has *really*
fucked me off.'

Rourke nodded slowly, casting glances to either
side of her. 'It seems you've talked your way out of
another tight spot, at least for now.' She met his eyes
again. 'Very well. If we have a location and a plan
by the time your "friend" Alex gives us our marching
orders, I'm with you.'

Drift tried to conceal the huge sigh of relief that
suddenly built in his chest. He might have only put
off the trouble, but he'd take the spectre of trouble
in a couple of days to the reality of trouble now. 'I'm
glad that's settled. Now, any questions?'

'Yeah, why the hell would anyone want to blow
up Amsterdam?' Apirana asked. 'What's this guy
Kelsier's play?'

'He told me he'd been fired by the Europans for
corruption,' Drift admitted. 'The way he said it made
me think that was just a cover for him being moved
into whatever secrets he was peddling now, but I
guess that was his intention.'

'Double bluff,' Rourke nodded. 'So are you thinking
this was a revenge hit? But why Amsterdam?'

'I know there was a group of Dutch politicians
who brought a lot of the charges against him,' Micah
put in, 'it might have something to do with that? I
mean, he must've been fired about three years ago,
but I reckon he's the type to hold a grudge.'

'I wouldn't be surprised if the old bastard's got
a record of everyone who's wronged him tucked
away somewhere,' Drift agreed bitterly, 'and God
knows he's careful enough to wait a year or two

until everything's planned out before he acts. Besides, I doubt even he could get his hands on an atom bomb just like that.'

'Get fired, blow up a city?' Jia asked incredulously. 'That's kind of an overreaction, ain't it?'

Micah grimaced. 'I never met him, but if the sorts of orders we got in the FDU were any guide then I can say Nicolas Kelsier doesn't exactly do "proportional response".'

Drift nodded. 'It was always effectiveness first, efficiency second. He didn't give much of a damn about collateral damage if what he wanted to get done got done; Cruz wouldn't have lasted, otherwise. I can buy Kelsier nuking an entire city to take out a few people. Besides, if he did something more specific people might start asking who had an agenda against those victims, and then it might get traced back to him.'

'And you're saying you got a plan to deal with this guy?' Kuai asked, his voice dripping with doubt.

'I've . . . got the beginnings of one,' Drift replied, and to his astonishment he realised that it was actually true. He pointed at the Changs, Micah and Apirana. 'First things first: you four go and get some sleep. We've all been wired too tight for too long.'

'Aye, Captain!' Jia shouted gratefully, turning on her heel immediately. 'I'll be in my bunk. Any of you wakes me up unless we need to fly somewhere, you'd best be prepared to duck.' She disappeared without hesitation, heading in the direction of her cabin. The other three turned to follow her, with grins from Apirana and Micah, and Kuai still looking ready to kick something.

Drift looked at Jenna. 'I know you'll be tired too, but I need you to get onto the Spine and see if you can do anything to fog searches for us. There'll be a hundred and one theories about what went down already, ranging from terrorists to aliens, so see if you can give credence to the ones which don't involve a *Carcharodon*-class shuttle. Then get your head down, too; I reckon we'll be needing you again.'

Jenna nodded wearily and headed for the cockpit, which left Rourke and Drift alone.

Rourke folded her arms. 'Well? I have to say, I'm intrigued as to what your plan can possibly be.'

Drift chewed over his words for a second. 'What do you know about the Laughing Man?'

Rourke's face went completely blank, even more so than usual. 'The Laughing Man? As in, Marcus Hall?'

'Unless there's more than one,' Drift shrugged uneasily. 'Kelsier had him running as his private attack dog when he cornered me on Carmella.'

'You're sure?'

'Flashed his electat at me,' Drift said, waving a hand at his face. 'Either someone out there's decided to get one as close to the descriptions as they can, or—'

'No one would dare,' Rourke said absently, her eyes starting to wander. Drift recognised the pattern; what he thought of as her 'planning' mode, where her senses automatically checked for threats or bugs while her brain started to work on a problem. She licked her lips absently. 'Well, that explains why you were so scared, at any rate.'

'I was *not* . . .' Drift saw her expression, and tailed off.

'Okay, I was a bit. Look, it's not that I didn't want to tell the others about this, but I wanted to talk to you about him first.'

'What do you want me to say?' Rourke asked, scratching her nose. 'I've no doubt you've heard the same stories I have. Not all of them are physically possible, of course, but either way it means we'll have to be doubly careful, and we know Kelsier's got some serious resources at his disposal.' She nodded slowly. 'That might actually make it easier, in a way. The larger his footprint, the easier he'll be to track down. If he can source a nuke and hire Hall . . .'

Drift made a vague noise of agreement, but noted to himself that Rourke hadn't answered his question. Something to be considered another time, perhaps. At present, however, he had to deal with another problem courtesy of the enigma that was Tamara Rourke. He still found her as hard to read as he ever had, but he had at least seen a crack in the shell. Granted, it had taken a nuclear bomb to achieve, but it was a sign that there was *something* under there. People and their natures had always fascinated Ichabod Drift, which was why he'd ended up so good at playing them when he needed to, and his interest in the one in front of him had been renewed. Possibly even enough to overlook what she'd just done, although that rather depended on how co-operative she planned to be.

'There's one other thing,' he said, bracing himself. 'I think you've left us with a few difficulties.'

'*I've* left us with difficulties?' Rourke snorted incredulously. 'I wasn't the one who—'

'I'm not talking about the job,' Drift cut her off,

raising a hand, 'I'm talking about the *crew*. I can excuse Apirana, once; everyone knows he's got a short fuse and sometimes he blows up, it's how he is. You, on the other hand: in the eight years since you've been on this boat you've demonstrated an emotional range roughly equivalent to that of a particularly stoic asteroid. Yet you still pulled a gun on me in front of everyone else, and held me to account. That's mutiny.'

Rourke blinked. '*You* are calling *me* out for mutiny?'

'Hello? Captain over here,' Drift pointed out, jerking a thumb at his own chest. 'I'm not in danger of starting another mutiny because I've got no one to mutiny *against*. This is my damn ship, and everyone on it needs to know that they do what *I* tell them, not what I tell them unless you currently have a gun held to my head! Sure, I'm not going to tell Jia how to fly or Jenna how to slice, or Kuai how to keep the engines running or Micah how to shoot someone, but . . .' He threw his hands up. 'That's why I hired experts, so I can tell them what I want doing and they work out how best to actually *do* it.'

'And Jia respects your authority so much,' Rourke snorted.

Drift shrugged. 'She always actually ends up doing what I've told her to do, she just gives me a heart attack in the process.' He waved a hand. 'Beside the point. If I tell a crew member to do something then they need to do it there and then without looking to someone else for approval, because sometimes that moment of hesitation could kill us. So if you want a part of coming to take Kelsier down, you need to respect that.'

Rourke's eyes searched his face, which he deliberately kept as blank as possible. Finally, she nodded. 'Very well. I want a crack at this man. But I won't be accepting vague answers in the future, Ichabod: trust is earned.'

'I agree completely,' he beamed. 'How did you know it was a nuclear bomb?'

Rourke's eyebrows lowered sharply. 'Excuse me?'

'You knew it was a bomb,' Drift continued. 'You didn't have to study it, take any readings from it . . . you just looked at it and went "Shit, nuke".' He shrugged. 'I'd always pegged your history as some sort of bodyguard, something like that. But that's not just the sort of knowledge you pick up. You know my dirty history now, so it's your turn. Where were you, *who* were you, before you became Tamara Rourke and stepped onto the deck of the *Jonah* for the first time?'

She hesitated.

'This is not an optional answer,' Drift added, in the most matter-of-fact tone he could muster. 'You and I make a damn good team, but I still own this boat. So either you tell me some feasible reason why you know what you know and then I give you your gun back, or you walk off right now.' He crossed his arms. 'What's it gonna be?'

The silence stretched between them. Rourke didn't move, or speak, but simply looked at him. He wanted to take the words back, because he'd got so used to having her at his side for backup, for advice, for the angle he hadn't considered, that he didn't want to take the chance she'd turn on her heel and leave without a word . . . but he could only be pushed so far. Even now, a small part of him he thought he'd left behind for good in the Ngwena System was whispering, *She's pulled a gun on you, what if she pulls the trigger next time? Drive her away and then shoot her in the back as she leaves. It's the only way to be sure she won't sell you out . . .*

He fought it down. Trust is earned.

Finally, Rourke sighed. Something in her face seemed to soften momentarily, and Drift braced himself. Anything which had taken that much thought was unlikely to result in an answer as simple as 'I took a summer-school course in nuclear physics'.

She started to hold up a hand, then hesitated. 'Tamara Rourke's the name my mother gave me, but as for *what* I was . . . just remember that you did say "before".'

Drift nodded.

She raised her left hand, palm outwards to face him. It didn't look remarkable: paler than the rest of her skin, marked by the calluses of someone familiar with manual labour.

Then, suddenly, something flashed into view, seeming to erupt from the lines of her palm. His first thought was *An electat.*

His second thought, as he recognised the image, was *Oh, shit.*

'**W**hy would you, of all people, want to know how to find Nicolas Kelsier?' Alexander Cruz had asked him. Well, after various curses and repeated assertions that he'd never wanted to see Drift again, anyway. 'The old man was fired for corruption years ago.'

'Help me out here and I'll owe you a favour,' Drift had told him. A snort had demonstrated what the portmaster thought of that. 'I know you, Alex. Your business here isn't going to be as legal as you pretend. Are you seriously telling me you'll never have any use for a favour you can call in from a crew like mine?'

Cruz had looked at him for nearly a full minute. Then he'd scribbled a name and address on a piece of paper and handed it over. 'If I hear a whisper that you told anyone I gave you this, your shuttle won't be leaving this spaceport.'

Drift had looked at it with a frown. 'Is this some sort of joke?'

'Best source of off-Spine information on the continent,' Cruz had told him with every sign of seriousness. 'You're lucky she's on this coast. I can't say what her price will be, though; rumour is her charges can be a bit . . . esoteric. By the way, do you remember Maiha?'

Images had flashed through Drift's head, a sensory hit straight from the hindbrain: long, straight black hair tangled in his hands, beads of salty sweat on golden skin, deft fingers plucking at his belt buckle, a gentle weight pressing his wrists into soft pillows belonging to the man in front of him. He'd forced himself to keep a straight face. 'Yeah, I think so.'

'As far as I know, she's some sort of chief aide there now,' Cruz had continued, with no sign that he had any idea what his old first mate had been up to on the rare occasions when the *Thirty-Six Degrees* and the *Dead Man's Hand* had been in port together. 'That might help you. Or hinder you, I don't know. Don't much care, either.'

And so it was that Drift, Micah and Apirana had travelled overland up the coast from Atlantic City on the train. It was a snub-nosed bullet affair riding a magnetic monorail which sailed high above the old streets of New Jersey and curved in long, graceful arcs between the towering skyscrapers. The buildings' sides were awash with light and colour which Drift knew from experience would be advertising holos trying to sell everything from the latest protein bars to sleek urban flyers, but they were for the locals only: at the speed the train was going the holos were little more than blurs that left a fleeting, contextless impression on the retina. Not that he would have been paying much attention anyway; the rest of his crew had got a few hours of sleep but he'd barely managed any after hammering out an alarmingly loose plan with Rourke, and his eyes felt like they were made of dust.

The line swung west, hugging the shore of Lower Bay, then turned back on itself to skirt the lower edge of the mess of starports and industrial wasteland which was Staten Island. Their carriage passed through clouds of refinery smoke and shimmering fuel haze, then burst out into the clearer air over the Narrows. Drift activated the magnifying window to look north and see Liberty Island, where the monument nicknamed the Plastic of Liberty stood tall on its pedestal. The original had been melted down centuries ago when the demand for copper in circuits and wires had become almost untenable and before large reserves had been secured elsewhere in the galaxy.

The train slowed to a final halt on the south shore of Brooklyn. Drift secured his rebreather mask in place as a precaution against the polluted air which sometimes washed over the city, nicknamed 'Staten smog' after its usual origin, and forced a somewhat reluctant sliding door aside to step out onto the platform with Micah and Apirana in tow. They found themselves on a steel grid platform some fifty feet above the ground, wire mesh surrounding them on all sides with an enclosed staircase down to street level at one end and a somewhat ramshackle-looking elevator at the other. The train pulled away and waist-height barriers automatically swung down across the holes in the mesh which lined up with the train's doors, the general notion being that if you were stupid enough to fall out of an obstructed hole fifty feet above the ground then you deserved what you got.

They took a second to inspect the elevator and then headed for the stairs by unspoken agreement. It was early March and there were mounds of dirty slurry at the side of the streets, the remnants of the most recent snowfall. The air was bitterly cold despite the amount of heat generated by Old New York's sheer presence, and Drift was glad he'd raided the *Jonah*'s clothing lockers for a thermojacket which he wore zipped up over his armavest. Micah had dug out his old combat fatigues, a temperature-regulating outfit effective against extremes of climate up to fifty degrees Celsius either side of freezing. With the regimental patches ripped off and his hair in thin dreadlocks instead of a military crew cut, the former FDU soldier looked like anyone else who'd picked up a bargain at an army surplus store, although the heavy automatic pistol holstered at his hip hinted at his violent past. Apirana, meanwhile, had disdained any form of thermal clothing and was simply wearing a hooded top over his utilitarian jumpsuit. With his hood up and rebreather mask on, his tattoos were mainly hidden and he was only conspicuous for his size, and for once Drift didn't feel like he was walking around next to a flashing beacon.

There was a thrumming buzz overhead and they

looked up to see a police flyer, decked out in white and blue with reflective chevrons, its twin rotor blades blurring in the centre of each stubby wing. One or two of the locals shrank back into the shadows cast by the towering hab blocks, five or six storeys of concrete and plastic, but most kept on as normal. This wasn't Manhattan, where the rich and well-to-do lived and worked behind a twenty-foot wall that encircled the island to keep out swimmers, and where the police were prominent and vigilant. As New York had expanded westwards and southwards, Brooklyn and Queens had been abandoned like a waste product with the residents largely left to their own devices, be that for good or ill. It would take something more akin to a riot for the NYPD to set foot on the ground here, which Drift found both comforting and worrying in almost equal measure.

The flyer banked away west, heading towards Jamaica Bay, and Drift took a moment to assess the state of the street once its shadow had gone. The locals who'd ducked away reappeared, but no one seemed to be taking too much of an interest in the trio of newcomers. He looked up at a street sign barely visible past a bird's nest of wires, where the residents had decided to take an enterprising approach to getting power by simply tapping the existing supply directly, and pointed ahead of them. 'The nearest metro's this way.'

Old New York's subway system was dilapidated and suffered from the sort of issues you'd expect in an often-subterranean transport system that had been in near-constant use for centuries, but it still more or less ran. It was certainly the best way to get into the heart of Old New York from the southern edge of Brooklyn, but when they disembarked from their rattling carriage at Tremont Avenue they didn't take the stairs up to the street. Instead they took a left at the Presbyterian Mission which occupied one corner, exchanged too-casual glances with two men lurking just past it whom Drift was convinced were going to try to sell them something narcotic until they caught a glare from a now de-masked Apirana, and headed for an elevator which only went downwards.

The moons of Carmella were far from the only places in the galaxy where humanity had started to dig in search of living space, although in the cities on Old Earth – even the badly polluted inner areas – it wasn't for fear of an unbreathable atmosphere so much as crippling ground rent costs. The newer tunnels, plazas and living spaces under the sprawling metropolis of ONYC were known as The Warrens, and demonstrated the usual disparity of good supply networks and plentiful transport links in the Uppers to the isolation and deprivation of the Lowers.

The elevator doors opened onto Level 17 of the Lower North Warrens and revealed a tunnel which reeked of damp, stale air, boasting intermittent lighting and, given how far they were beneath the water table, a slightly worrying leak in the ceiling.

'Looks homely,' Apirana rumbled quietly. Drift had found that he was still a little apprehensive about any sudden movements and was aware of Apirana's size in a way he hadn't been in years, despite the almost painful care the big Maori was taking not to appear threatening. Still, he'd given his terms for

Apirana's continued presence on the *Keiko*'s crew and Apirana had accepted them, so he felt that he owed it to the big man to treat him accordingly unless and until Apirana broke those terms.

'You're *sure* this is the right place?' Micah asked. The Dutch mercenary hadn't been keen on this jaunt but Drift had talked him into it, partially so he didn't have to be alone with Apirana but mainly because right at this moment Drift didn't fully trust him not to sneak out of Star's End and find some way of selling them all out for a profit.

'So Alex told me,' Drift replied, aware once more of exactly how much trust he was placing in a man who he knew had never liked him and who currently saw him as a potentially dangerous liability. 'Let's see what we can find.'

As it turned out, their destination was hardly elusive. Most of the doors were boarded over, and the ones which weren't were gaping black holes leading into cramped habs with not even a stick of furniture remaining. The central plaza, however, was another matter.

'The hell is this?' Apirana muttered as they caught sight of an entrance. The hollow silence of the tunnels was replaced with an indistinct mutter of noise through the steel-framed glass doors, the bass thud of music intermingling with the sound of many, many voices, and lights which cast long shadows from within.

'The way I heard it, the lady we need to speak to basically moved in and set up shop here,' Drift explained. 'Took over the businesses, took over the black market, took over everything. Everywhere below Level 10 in the North Warrens is hers, but she bought most of it legally and doesn't cause any major problems so the Justices leave her be.'

'And someone all the way down *here* is the best off-Spine source in North America, and can tell us where Nicolas Kelsier is?' Micah said. 'That takes some believing.'

'She's clearly got connections,' Drift shrugged, 'and rumour is that she often takes payment for information in information. What goes around comes around, I guess.' He worked his shoulders, adjusted the scarf he'd tied around his neck to hide the bruises left by Apirana's fingers, and marched up to the doors.

They opened easily with a push, affording him a view into what had once been the communal space of North-east Level 17. In truth, it still was, but the promenades and shopping booths had been remodelled into a more organic, chaotic space. There were still businesses, but hammocks swung from above their heads, the air conditioning whined as it sucked in smoke from firepits built into the floor, and cheers and jeers sounded from around what looked like a fighting cage.

And above it all, sitting in a heavily upholstered chair on a platform held aloft by the massive hydraulic arm of what had at one point been a maintenance vehicle, was Nana Bastard.

Drift closed his natural left eye and dialled up the zoom on his mechanical. Nana Bastard looked to be in her seventies, age-repellent drugs notwithstanding, and had two fat braids of silvery hair twisting down from either side of her head. She was approaching plump, her features were wrinkled and leathery, and something about the shape of them combined with the beadwork and fringes on her clothes suggested she might have some First Nations blood in her somewhere. What struck Drift instantly, though, were her eyes: dark and sharp, with no visible white from this distance, they reminded him of a predatory bird's as they darted here and there across the crowd of people packed into the plaza. A second after he'd focused on her, those eyes flashed up to him, he saw her press something on the arm of her chair and her lips moved inaudibly.

'Cap?' Apirana muttered, nudging him. He returned his right eye's vision to normal and opened his left, and instantly saw figures in the dark blue of what had once been plaza security uniforms pushing through the throng towards them.

'Nothing to worry about,' he replied, 'we're here to get an audience, after all.' He focused on the closest man, who appeared to consist mainly of an ambulatory chest, and pitched his smile between 'polite' and 'friendly'. 'Morning.'

'Morning,' the man replied automatically, his eyes flicking over them. He and his two companions, one male and one female, had clearly customised their uniforms: badges and patches sewn onto them presumably hinted at some sort of family, tribe or gang alliance, the sleeves had been removed to show well-muscled arms adorned with tattoos, and the epaulettes on the shoulders of the speaker had been replaced with a row of steel spikes an inch high. Each one had a shockstick tucked into their belt and a comm in their ear, but they didn't have the swaggering arrogance of any number of gangland enforcers Drift had dealt with in the past. Despite their appearance, they almost seemed . . . professional. 'Do you have business here?'

'I'd like to speak with Nana,' Drift said, hoping the title was the correct one to give. 'Ms Bastard' certainly didn't seem like the one to go with, no matter what name this extraordinary old woman had taken for herself.

'Nana's not taking new audiences until next week,' the woman spoke up. She had a tattoo under one eye, a swirling pattern which might have been tribal or could have been simply something she'd liked the look of. 'You can come back then, or you're welcome to make yourselves at home in the meantime.'

Drift masked his surprise with a cough. *Definitely not your standard gangland enforcer*, who usually revelled in making your life difficult. Phrases like 'you're welcome' were rarer than hen's teeth out of their mouths, unless flavoured with heavy sarcasm. Was this another surprising twist of Nana Bastard's regime? *No, I think I know exactly who's behind this.*

He played his hunch. 'Then I would like to speak to your commander. Maiha Takahara, unless I'm mistaken?'

The first speaker didn't even blink. 'Captain Takahara doesn't give audiences to members of the public.'

And here we are again, Drift thought wryly, *trying to get through bureaucracy to speak to the person I want. God, but this was simpler when we were all outlaws.* 'How many ask for one?' he countered.

'Besides, my business with Nana is business, but Miss Takahara is an old friend and this would be a social call. I'd be grateful if you could pass on a message that Gabriel would like to see her. Of course, I'll understand if work has to take priority for the moment.'

He deliberated for second. *Come on*, Drift urged silently, *you've been professional so far . . .*

'Hawkins to Control,' the man said, raising a finger to his comm. 'Is Captain Takahara available?' There was a pause for a few more seconds. 'Captain, this is Hawkins. We have three newcomers at the South Gate. One of them requested an audience with Nana, but has now asked to speak to you. He says he's an old friend of yours, and that his name is Gabriel.'

Drift waited as Hawkins nodded in response to whatever was being said into his ear. He hadn't wanted to mention his old name, but it wasn't like Hawkins would twig; there were many Gabriels in the galaxy who'd never had the second name Drake. Besides, it couldn't be helped, as Maiha Takahara was unlikely to have the first clue who Ichabod Drift was. Of course, this would mean letting another person know that he was still alive, but Rourke and Jenna would be in Europa waiting for the green light by now and he didn't have a week to waste on an old lady's schedule.

Hawkins looked up at him and his hand dropped from his comm. *Something's wrong*, Drift thought, seeing the man's eyes, an instant before Hawkins drew his shockstick. His two companions followed suit a second later, thumbing the activation studs to send blue light crackling up and down the batons' lengths.

'Gentlemen,' Hawkins said firmly, holding up a pair of cuffs, 'I need you to come with me, please.'

REUNION

D rift sat on a cold, bare steel chair, hands pulled back behind him and cuffed to the rod which curved up from under the seat to support the back. His shoulders were already starting to ache, and the cuffs had so far proved resistant to everything Rourke had ever taught him about slipping out of such restraints.

There'd been no question of fighting, of course: one hit from a shockstick could drop a man, and two would do even for Apirana. If he'd pulled a gun then he'd have likely had to shoot all three guards dead, and he'd had enough of shooting security personnel for doing their job. Besides, any stray shots into the crowd could have sparked a riot which would have sealed their death warrant, quite apart from any injuries or fatalities they might inflict.

Most importantly, though, he had to speak to Nana Bastard, and he had a greater chance of doing that as an obliging prisoner than he did either dead or having killed three of her guards.

The 'Capt. Takahara' nameplate on the desk in front of him stared at him mockingly. So he'd been captured by Alex Cruz's old first mate and handcuffed to a chair in her office, with its tidy bookshelf and modern-looking terminal and other things which generally seemed quite incongruous this far below ground in Old New York City . . . but where was she, if she'd ordered this? People were always more pliable than steel cuffs, and he rated his chances higher with dialogue than with escapology.

The door behind him clicked open and someone walked in, their steps swift and light over the floor. Another click signified it shutting again, and was followed by a faint buzz which the deepening shadows helped his brain translate into windows darkening to opaque. Now the only illumination came from the desk lamp. A snap of fingers from behind him caused the head to turn towards him automatically, flooding his eyes with a stark whiteness. He heard the faint whine of lenses as his mechanical right eye tried to compensate, but failed to completely manage it.

Steps again, now moving around behind the light. He squinted, but couldn't make anything out other than a vague shape. 'Is this strictly necessary?' he asked, trying not to sound too plaintive.

'That depends,' a voice replied, seemingly from out of the light. 'It's not every day a ghost turns up on my doorstep.' The voice had changed, of course, but he knew it at once.

'Maiha,' he said, relief warring with irritation in

his tone. 'I know you didn't exactly expect to see me, but—'

'*Shut up.*'

Drift shut up. When handcuffed to a chair with a light shining in your face so you couldn't see what the other person was doing, compliance was usually a good idea.

'Gabriel Drake was killed by FAS forces in the Ngwena System,' the voice of Maiha Takahara continued, a little less harshly but still with an audible edge to it. 'Everyone knows that. It was well publicised. Yet the man sitting in the chair in front of me looks remarkably like how I think Gabriel Drake would look, if you took away an eye and added a dozen or so years and a fucking stupid haircut.'

Drift winced; he'd forgotten Maiha Takahara's irrational hatred of people who dyed their hair. Back in his privateer days he'd worn his short, tidy and in his natural black, unlike the violet lengths which straggled down either side of his face now. Besides which, his roots were probably *awful*.

'So either the FAS are a bunch of incompetent, lying assholes,' Maiha's voice said, almost conversationally, 'or I've got a fairly determined and well-informed plant in front of me, pretending to be a dead man who thinks he knew me.'

'Of those two options, which do you really think is most likely?' Drift asked earnestly. 'C'mon Maiha, the FAS were hopeless at dealing with privateers like us; all they could do for years was posture and bullshit. If we hadn't had it so easy Kelsier wouldn't have kept his job for half as long. They got their act together in the end, of course, or I bet you'd still be flying around in the *Dead Man's Hand* terrifying merchants.'

'Let's say I believe you're who you say you are,' Maiha said after a second. 'How did you find me?'

'I promised a favour to Alex Cruz, after calling in the one he owed me from when I saved all your backsides over Tantalus,' Drift replied promptly. For all he knew Maiha could have contacted her old captain for verification right before this conversation, so it would pay to be truthful.

There was a pause, then an amused snort. 'Oh Gabriel,' Maiha Takahara said, her voice no longer containing any hint of hostility, 'you can't even try to make this any fun, can you?'

'*Fun?*' Drift tried not to grit his teeth. 'Your goons handcuffed me to a damn chair! How is that fun?'

'Looks fun from where I'm standing,' Maiha said. She clicked her fingers again and the desk lamp returned to its original orientation, casting a subdued light more evenly over the office and bringing her properly into view for the first time.

Alexander Cruz had tried to turn himself into the very image of a professional businessman, but his former first mate had clearly not had the same priorities. Her sleeveless jacket and her trousers were the same navy blue as the guards who'd arrested Drift and his colleagues, but red and golden dragons snaked all over them, matching the inked beasts which crawled up her bare arms to disappear under the short sleeves of her shiny black collared shirt. Her hair was shaved on one side and swept over into a fall of vivid red, with three metal studs set in a line along the length of her skull on the bare side. More metal glinted in her nose, her lips, her ears, at the corners of her eyes and even in the sides of her neck.

'And you had the cheek to talk about *my* hairstyle!' Drift said, startled. This was a far cry from the deceptively demure-looking young woman off New Shinjuku whom he'd known over a decade ago. That person was still there in the lines of her face, though; older though she might be, Maiha Takahara's beauty had matured rather than altered or disappeared.

'People change,' Maiha shrugged, 'some more literally than others. I hadn't expected you to get a whole new eye, though.'

'I . . . for crying out loud, why do people always think this is a fashion statement?' Drift protested. 'I *lost* it.'

'Careless,' Maiha tutted. She made her way around the desk and leaned down in front of him. 'This doesn't suit you, by the way.' She reached out and untied the scarf around his neck, then pulled it away. Drift winced slightly, the soft rasp of the fabric enough to make the bruises left by Apirana's fingers flare up, and Maiha whistled in surprise. 'Well now, someone's been a bit rough with you, haven't they?' She started refastening the scarf around her own neck, apparently absent-mindedly.

'Maiha,' Drift said, struggling to keep his voice level, 'could you uncuff me, please?'

'Why?' Maiha asked. She sat down on the edge of her desk, shrugged out of her sleeveless uniform jacket and threw it casually onto the back of her office chair, which Drift couldn't help but notice was rather better-padded than the one he was restricted to. 'Were you planning on going somewhere? I thought you told Hawkins you wanted to make a social call on me.'

'Well, yes,' Drift agreed, 'but—'

'You hardly need your hands free to talk,' Maiha pointed out, playing with the end of the scarf. 'Of course, Hawkins also said that you'd asked to see Nana . . . and that you asked that before you asked to see me. So maybe you only wanted to see me in case I could get you in to see Nana before next week?' She looked up at him. 'Is that it?'

'I'd certainly be grateful if you could organise anything like that,' Drift admitted. There was no point lying in this situation. 'I do need to see Nana as soon as possible, because some associates of mine need some information I think she can provide. Once that's out of the way, though . . .' He shrugged. 'Believe it or not, I actually would be interested in having a catch-up with you.'

'I don't believe you, as it happens,' Maiha said firmly. 'I mean, let's be honest, you and I were never exactly *close*, were we? We exchanged more bodily fluids than pleasantries.'

'Well, we didn't have much of a chance,' Drift pointed out. 'You'd have been in trouble if Cruz ever found out what we were doing, so we couldn't exactly be friendly where everyone could see. And when anyone couldn't see, well,' he shrugged, 'we had better things to be doing.'

'True.' Maiha gave a throaty chuckle. 'Remember the time we did it in his cabin?'

Drift laughed despite himself. 'I nearly wet myself trying not to laugh in front of him when he asked if

I remembered you. Egotistic little bastard had no idea what was going on, did he?'

'Not a clue,' Maiha agreed. 'I thought he'd rumbled us that time in the engine room when we were berthed on Amina IV, when I came out and walked right into him. But he believed me when I said I was sweating so hard because I'd been . . . hell, I can't remember what I said, I made up some sort of mechanical jargon and hoped. He never knew what half the parts of a ship were anyway, let alone which ones were big or heavy.'

'That was not, I have to say, one of your better choices of venue,' Drift informed her dryly. 'Too much cold metal.'

'You don't like cold metal?' Maiha said in mock-astonishment. 'That's a shame, given where you're sitting now.' She rose to her feet again and shrugged her shoulders, and her shirt slipped down her arms to the floor. *What the hell? When did she undo that?* Then Drift's brain caught up with his eyes, which were focusing on the dragon tattoos winding down Maiha's ribs and across her belly, and the glint of metal in her naval and through each nipple. *Oh.* Maiha's body had altered in other ways besides the addition of piercings and ink, but her belly's softening had brought with it a heavier swell in her breasts and a pleasing curve to her behind which had been absent from the stick-limbed, athletic frame of her youth.

'Captain Takahara,' he said, determined not to be struck dumb by what really shouldn't have been that unexpected a turn of events, given their history, 'are you trying to seduce me?'

'*Trying?*' Maiha snorted with laughter, then reached down and grabbed his crotch. 'Don't flatter yourself, Gabriel; your cock's the only part of you which has never lied . . . and yes, I seem to have its attention.' She straightened up again and placed her thumbs in the waistband of her trousers, then started to draw them downwards. The desk lamp behind her cast deep shadows beneath her hip bones as they surfaced. Drift found his throat dry.

'I'll get you in to see Nana,' Maiha said, almost absently, 'because I *did* always like you, but you have to tell me what you're going to ask her first.'

'Deal,' Drift said instantly, trying and failing to tear his gaze from the fabric descending over her smooth curves. Her thumbs slid past a thin line of black cloth on either side of her body, leaving them in place as her trousers continued their path downwards. *Underwear?! Goddamnit, she never* used *to wear underwear . . .*

'But you won't get to see her for an hour or so anyway, no matter what I do, so you've got a bit of time to kill,' Maiha continued. The delicate black scrap of her underwear remained anchored between her legs, which now came into sight as she bent over in front of him, hair falling to cover her face and affording him a view of her back for the first time: more dragons, running red and gold across the faint bumps of her spine. She straightened again, kicking her trousers away: he dimly noticed that she was barefoot, but couldn't have said at what point she'd removed her shoes, or even be certain that she'd been wearing any in the first place. His concentration was not what it sometimes was.

'So,' Maiha said, straddling his legs and sitting down, warm on his thighs but out of his reach, 'what do you want to do?'

Drift managed to work some moisture into his mouth. 'Is this some sort of . . . test?'

'Test?' Maiha sniggered, the motion causing interesting movements in her chest. 'Hell no. This is me being horny and you still being pretty, even with a few lines on your face and that metal eye. I'm just having fun seeing how long it takes before you're incapable of forming words.'

'Let me out of these,' Drift challenged her, rattling his restraints and forcing himself to look her in the eyes. 'I reckon I can still make you forget how to speak.'

'Promises, promises,' Maiha laughed. 'But I'm not a foolish young girl anymore, Mr Drake. I know better than to uncuff the most notorious pirate in the galaxy. No, you'll have to do without your hands this time around.' She quirked an eyebrow. 'Maybe after you've got your answer from Nana we can see how you do on a fair footing.'

'Fine, then,' Drift managed. 'But there's one thing.'

'Mmm?' Maiha picked up the end of the scarf which was still around her neck and drew it slowly across his face.

'My crew,' Drift said as firmly as he could. 'You've got two of them locked up, I imagine. Now you're satisfied I'm not an imposter I'd like you to let them out, please.'

Maiha's eyes took on the sort of intensity Drift had always imagined was only possessed by industrial welding lasers in orbital shipyards. '*Excuse* me?'

Drift raised his eyebrows in response. 'Did I stutter?'

'You've got a naked woman sitting on your lap—'

'Actually, you're not *technically* naked ye—'

'—and you're thinking about your *crew*?' Maiha frowned. 'The only crew you used to care about were the ones you were planning on sleeping with, and even then "care" is a strong term for it. I'm starting to wonder if you might not be an imposter after all. Unless you've decided you prefer men these days.' Her eyes widened suddenly. 'Is that it, you've taken up with the beefcake I saw out there? I like the big guy's tattoos, actually; he's Maori, right? And the other one's *very* pretty.'

Her tone was jokingly severe, but Drift could tell it was a double bluff of sorts; she was genuinely offended that he'd been able to turn his thoughts to his crew with her on his lap. In truth, he was somewhat astonished himself.

'Mai,' he said carefully, 'this is just business before pleasure, that's all.'

'You *have* changed.'

'Yeah, I grew some loyalty and a conscience.' He frowned. 'Hang on a second. You think Micah's *pretty*?'

'Is that his name?' Maiha asked casually. 'Ooh, *yes*. I have to wonder what I'm doing here with you actually, I imagine he might be more welcoming . . .'

Drift gritted his teeth and tried to persuade himself that he was doing the right thing. Certain parts of him remained unconvinced. 'Mai, they're both members of my crew, and I owe them.' *And I* really *need to keep on their good sides.* 'You and I can have as much fun as you want, or . . .' He gritted his teeth. 'Or you can go and find Micah, if that's what appeals to you. But it wouldn't be right for me to leave them locked up.'

Maiha's face had taken on an odd expression, and one that Drift was unfamiliar with. She studied him for a few seconds, then pursed her lips. 'Stars above, you're actually serious, aren't you?'

He nodded.

She sighed. 'Fine.' Her eyes rolled upwards for a second, as though trying to perform complicated mathematics in her head, then she focused on him again. 'It's done.'

Drift frowned. 'Just like that?'

'Skull chip,' Maiha grinned at him, tapping one of her cranial studs. 'This pretty little head of mine is full of surprises. It's not like I can do anything really complex, but flashing up an "all clear" alert on a containment cell, locking or unlocking doors, sounding or silencing alarms . . .'

'Dimming windows and turning lamps?' Drift asked.

'Exactly.' She smiled smugly. 'Envious, Gabriel?'

'More than a little,' he admitted. 'And thank you.' Then something dawned on him. 'Oh, uh, by the way. My name's not really Gabriel Drake.'

'I never really figured it was,' Maiha replied lazily, 'mine sure as hell isn't Maiha Takahara. But what's a name to people with a history like ours?' She sighed irritably. 'Fine, since I'm going to have to introduce you to Nana, how are you known these days?'

'The name's Ichabod Drift,' Drift replied.

'Ichabod Drift?' Maiha frowned and shook her

head. 'I hate to tell you, that's not the sort of name I can hear myself screaming.'

Drift tried not to show how offended he was by her casual remark. 'I promise you, you'd be in good and plentiful compa—'

He was cut off by her leaning forwards and planting her lips on his, one of her hands reaching around to knot her fingers in the hair at the back of his head. He kissed back enthusiastically, instinctively. They remained locked together for long, searing seconds until she pulled away, leaving him trailing after and brought up uncomfortably short by the handcuffs which still secured him to the chair.

'I haven't been in good company since I was seventeen,' Maiha told him, as conversational as though the kiss had never happened, 'why should I want to break that habit now?' She leaned forwards again but this time crossed her arms over his breastbone, so their faces were held a few inches too far away to make contact. 'Now, Drift? I've heard worse names, I'll grant you, but Ichabod?'

'What's wrong with Ichabod?' Drift protested, refusing to be fazed by her behaviour. His sporadic sexual encounters with Maiha had always been an odd mix of illicitly snatched and strangely competitive, and it seemed she was feeling nostalgic.

'Well, it doesn't exactly roll off the tongue, does it?' She stood up suddenly, and her fingers went to work on a tiny bow tied at one side of her underwear.

'Speaking of tongues . . .'

'You managed to persuade her, then?' Apirana muttered, rubbing his wrists. The huge Maori seemed even bigger in the enclosed space of the elevator, which was currently taking them up to the top storey where Nana Bastard gave her audiences.

'Apparently so,' Drift agreed cautiously, 'but I'm not expecting any other favours. We're still not exactly among friends here.' Even back in the day, if Cruz had ordered the crew of the *Dead Man's Hand* to fire on the *Thirty-Six Degrees* then Maiha would have undoubtedly done so without hesitation. A familiar face and some sex would count for nothing against any orders from her current employer.

'The list of people who know you're still alive is growing, you know,' Micah pointed out, as though that could have escaped Drift's attention. 'Can you trust her?'

'No more than I can trust Alex Cruz,' Drift replied, although he hoped that wasn't true. After all, he and Mai had kept a secret for the other for several years. 'They're both in the same boat as me, though; stones and glass houses, et cetera. We're all better off just keeping our heads down and hoping no one ever figures out who we used to be.'

'So there's no chance the Guard Captain won't pass the details of your former identity on to the biggest source of off-Spine information in North America,' Micah said. 'I mean, it's not like there'd be any loyalty there, or anything.'

'You're starting to sound like Kuai,' Drift told him absently, earning himself a glare from the mercenary. The elevator *dinged* and the doors slid aside, allowing them to exit onto what had once been a high-level promenade of shop fronts. Huge air-con pipes ran overhead, branching off over the open spaces and plunging into walls. Ahead of them, two guards with shocksticks stood flanking Maiha Takahara at a place where the safety railings had been removed. Beyond them, looking to be floating in mid-air from this angle, was the chair in which rested Nana Bastard. She beckoned them forwards.

'Why're *we* here, anyway?' Apirana asked quietly as they stepped out of the elevator. 'I thought you'd see her on your own.'

'Nana's request,' Drift shrugged. 'Maiha said she insisted.'

'Oh, that don't sound good,' the Maori rumbled. 'My face don't lie as well as yours.'

Crap. 'You know, you might be on the money there,' Drift muttered. He hadn't even considered that possibility, but it made sense. You often got the most telling information from the reactions of the person in a group whom you *weren't* talking to. 'Just try to look angry to start with. Micah, look bored.'

'Waaay ahead of you,' the Dutchman drawled.

Nana did something with the arm of her chair and the platform glided forwards until it rested against the edge of the walkway with a faint *chunk* sound. Maiha waited until Drift and his two companions were about six feet away, then held up a hand. Drift stopped instantly, and Maiha stepped aside to give them their first proper, close-up view of the old lady who ran everything below Level 10 in the North Warrens.

Closer to eighty than seventy, Drift thought instantly, taking in the ravines at the corners of her eyes, the sagging dewlap of skin beneath her jaw, the swollen knuckle joints on her fingers. *But just as dangerous as Old Man Kelsier, if not more so.* Especially since his wits were still feeling fuzzy; he'd snatched an hour or two's sleep after his liaison with Maiha had concluded and before she'd arranged this audience, but it hadn't been enough to recharge his batteries properly. He carefully sketched a bow. 'Nana.'

'Captain.' Nana's voice was strong, almost fruity, and dripped with an Old New York accent so strong you could use it to flavour coffee. 'I wasn't going to see anyone else this week, but Captain Takahara here put in a good word for you and that got me curious.' She chuckled. 'Truth to tell, most things make me curious, you know? So, what do you need?'

Drift looked sideways at the guards, and at Maiha's expressionless face. Mai had denied all knowledge of Kelsier's whereabouts and had expressed roughly the same incredulity as Alex Cruz upon learning of his query, but he hadn't expected to be conducting this conversation in front of her, let alone two drones in uniform.

'Ignore them,' Nana advised, waving a hand after following his gaze, 'confidentiality is *very* important to me, and all my employees know it.'

Drift didn't ask what happened to those employees who broke it; he reckoned he could work it out. He'd also thought very hard about exactly how to phrase his question, in order to avoid any useless answers which were nevertheless technically true, and had come to the conclusion that the safest course was to avoid an actual question at all. He cleared his throat. 'I need to know how or where to find the Europan Commonwealth's former Minister for Extra-Terrestrial Resource Acquisition, Nicolas Kelsier, with the smallest possible chance of him knowing that I'm looking for him.'

Nana didn't answer immediately. One of her hands came up to rub thoughtfully at her chin, while those beady old eyes studied him intently. When she did speak, her voice had lost its previous chatty tone and taken on a far more businesslike manner.

'That's an interesting request. As I understand it, the EC's been trying to track him down for a time now.'

'I wouldn't be surprised,' Drift said, trying to keep his expression as neutral as possible. Nana's eyes had rested on his, and he returned her – no, wait. Both of her eyes were focused specifically on his *right* one. He thought for a moment, then kicked up the zoom as far as it would go. It treated him to a disorienting, lurching view of the old woman's eyebrow in the right side of his vision while the left side saw her face as normal, but the adjustment of the lenses clearly drew her attention to what she was doing. She started slightly – although he probably wouldn't have noticed it had he not been looking for it – and the ghost of a smile touched her lips, perhaps with a hint of apology.

'Well, Captain Drift,' Nana said, as though the little exchange had never occurred, 'are you acting for yourself here?'

Drift frowned. 'Excuse me?'

Nana pursed her lips, as though his lack of comprehension vexed her. 'The whereabouts of this man is something actively sought by at least one government. I'm simply trying to ascertain whether you're here because someone told you to be, or because you've got a hankering to see Mr Kelsier your own self.'

Drift studied her face. Why was she asking this? Would the price be higher if she thought he had a government backing him? Or would the threat of that sort of clout loosen her tongue? *She makes a living off information, maybe she's planning to sell everything on to Kelsier as soon as she can . . .*

He smiled at her. 'I couldn't possibly comment.'

'Hmm.' Nana's face was as blank as his for a few seconds, before it moved into an expression of resignation which matched the sigh that escaped her lips. 'Well, nothing for it then, I guess. We'll play it your way.' She straightened in her chair, fidgeting with a cushion behind her back. 'As it happens, I *do* know where you can find Nicolas Kelsier . . . or at least, where he holed up after his little "misunderstanding" with the Europans, and where he was until at least relatively recently.'

'And the cost for this information?' Drift enquired. There was still a fair chunk of Kelsier's original hundred grand left, and what he'd managed to gather about Nana Bastard was that her information was usually worth the price: as it would have to be, for her to have any hope of making a living off it.

'You see that cage down there?' Nana said, nodding to her right. Drift frowned, took a couple of steps and looked over the safety rails. Beneath him was the fighting cage he'd seen earlier: a grim-looking thing of wire mesh and sweat-soaked mats, spattered here and there with blood. It was a far cry from the sterile, advertisement-plastered rings of the Intergalatic Fighting League, whose roster competed in environments ranging from Zero-G grappling bouts to full-contact, full-grav, knock-down-drag-out affairs.

'Yes?' he replied, uncertain and unhappy about where this might be going.

'One round,' Nana said simply. He looked sharply back at her, saw her eyes studying him intently.

'What?'

'One round,' she repeated, 'that's my price to you, Captain Drift. We'll find you an opponent and you try to last one round against him. No submitting, no quitting early. You don't have to win, you just have to survive, and then I'll tell you what I know.' She leaned forwards, and suddenly the resemblance to a predatory bird was back in her face.

'Let's see how badly you want this information.'

'This,' Drift said, looking at the cage in front of him and fiddling with the padded gloves which left his fingers free, 'is insane.'

A crowd was gathering and regarding him with some considerable interest, but he was more interested in where he was going to be spending the next five minutes. It didn't look big and scary. It might have been better had it looked big and scary. In fact, to his eyes it looked rather uncomfortably small, with very little room to manoeuvre.

'What the hell is this going to prove, anyway?' he demanded, not necessarily expecting an answer.

'You step in that cage and take a beating, Nana's gonna get a pretty good idea how bad you want this,' Apirana shrugged. 'Most men don't get paid enough to take a shit-kicking for five minutes, no matter how much their boss wants a piece of information. You go in there and you stick it out, she knows that your beef with Kelsier is personal.'

'And what does she get out of that?' Drift said helplessly. 'Beyond some sick sense of satisfaction, I mean.'

'Information,' Micah said. The Dutch mercenary wasn't looking at the cage at all, but around them. Drift glanced at him and saw his eyes moving from point to point, taking in the guards, the crowds, the raised promenades: everything, in fact. 'And information gives her protection.'

'What the hell is that supposed to mean?'

'She's scared of something,' Micah said, matter-of-factly. 'We've got an entire community living down here in a goddamn *shopping mall*. There's a whole team of guards, all professional, with your old friend in charge who's set them at the right places to block access to Nana . . . but it's not these people she's scared of. She's surrounded herself with a crowd which knows its neighbours and knows each other, and somebody's always going to be awake. They're like a giant early warning system, because no stranger's going to sneak in here without someone seeing them.' He saw Drift's expression and shrugged, as though his explanation was the most natural thing in the world. 'Only reason I can think of to know so much is because you really, *really* want to make sure you know about something before it happens to you.'

Drift stared at him, then shook his head. He didn't have time to think about that now, and wasn't sure how it would benefit him even if it was true. Instead he focused on the ripple of movement passing through the crowd which seemed to indicate an opponent was on his way.

He'd been expecting some sort of giant, a man the size of Apirana who'd corner him and pummel him with rib-breaking force. Instead, the fighter who stepped into view was perhaps an inch or so shorter than him, although more heavily built, with a flattened nose and ears which looked to have taken more than their fair share of punishment. His hair was short and blond, his fair skin was marked with a smattering of tattoos including one on his chest of a tiger's face, and he bounced lightly on his feet as he met Drift's gaze.

'Whaddya know,' Apirana grunted, eyebrows raised, 'you might not die after all.'

Drift snorted. 'Thanks.' He nodded at the man, and got an acknowledgement. Still, just because the man wasn't huge didn't necessarily mean he wasn't a bloodthirsty maniac; or just very, very good.

'*Attention, everyone,*' Nana's voice rang down from above. Drift jumped, and looked up to see that she'd gained a headset from somewhere. Her voice was projected from what seemed to be speakers underslung from her raised platform. '*The man in front of you came to me with a question. I have set the price for his answer at lasting one round with Jonathan Limberg. May you all be my witnesses on this.*'

'Old lady plays it straight, at any rate,' Drift muttered. He unzipped his armavest and slipped it off his shoulders, then passed it to Apirana. 'Fine. Let's get this over with.'

He wondered what the Maori was frowning at for

a second before he remembered the scratch marks down his chest.

'Oh, so it was *that* sort of "persuasion",' Micah snorted. 'I might have known.'

'Worked, didn't it?' Drift muttered, not feeling in the mood to discuss it any further. Micah opened his mouth to reply but then shut it again; Drift only realised why when Maiha appeared at his shoulder.

'No nutshots, no biting, no headbutts, no eyepokes and no strikes to the throat,' she informed him matter-of-factly, with no hint of her earlier provocative manner. 'Disqualification is instant.'

Drift blinked. 'There are *rules*?'

'Of course there are rules,' she snapped. 'What do you think we are, barbarians? Two of our fighters have gone on to join the IFL! Shoes off.'

Drift knew better than to question or argue, so he bent down to untie his boots. When he'd pulled them off and stood straight again Maiha inspected him thoughtfully, then motioned to Apirana and Micah.

'Step away, please.'

'Do it,' Drift told them, and the Dutchman and Maori obediently stood back. Maiha stepped forwards and started to frisk him, her palms passing over him with a businesslike briskness completely at odds with their previous, private encounter.

Drift sighed. 'Do you *really*—'

'Shut up and listen,' Mai hissed as she reached around him, fingers feeling down his back for some sort of subdermal weapon, presumably. 'Limberg is good, but you'll have reach on him, you lanky fucker. Keep moving and keep your jab active in his face. He'll wait for you to drop your hands and then kick you in the head, but if he gets frustrated he'll try to get you on your back, and when he does that he tends to leave his neck open. Grab it and squeeze it, and you *might* get out of this one. Oh, and he's left-handed, but his stance won't tell you that.' She stood back, her face showing nothing but professional satisfaction. 'He's clear,' she announced loudly.

'*Gentlemen*,' Nana's voice declared, '*into the cage, if you please. That's if you still want to go through with this, Captain?*' Drift looked up and met her gaze; there was no mockery or gloating there, simply interest.

'Why the hell not?' he retorted, loud enough for her to hear him. Limberg was stepping through the door which had been swung open for him, and Drift jogged up to the cage to follow him in. He tried not to hear the *clank* of it shutting behind him as the sound of a prison cell. *Although in fairness, in prison there's always the chance that your cellmate won't be trying to knock you out.*

'You know the drill!' Maiha shouted at Limberg from outside the fence, who nodded. Then she turned to Drift. 'Keep going until you hear the horn!'

'Sure,' Drift muttered, taking up a stance he dimly remembered; left hand and leg forwards, right leg back, right hand cocked by his ear to swing or ward off punches, chin tucked into his chest. Sure, he'd done this sort of fighting before, but that was the best part of twenty years ago when he was fresh out of high school on Soleadovalle, and he and all his friends were in the gym thinking they were going to be the next 'Lightning' Nik Alvarez. In the intervening years his main involvement in physical altercations had consisted of hitting anything *with* anything until the other person was unconscious or, in more recent times, until Apirana finished off whoever he'd been dealing with and came to help.

Sadly, that scenario was not an option. It wasn't as though he hadn't asked, either, but Nana had been very clear that it had to be him going into the cage rather than the huge Maori.

'Fight!' Maiha yelled. Someone pressed a button on an airhorn and Drift strode forwards towards the centre of the ring, mainly because he remembered that the one place he really didn't want to be was backed up against the cage wall with nowhere to go.

Drift had forgotten the peculiar tunnel vision which took over at times like these. He'd been in his share of fights, of course, but that had always been something more organic; a firefight when an FAS freighter crew had decided to make a stand once the *Thirty-Six Degrees* had overridden their airlocks and forced a boarding, or a brawl breaking out over a payment dispute at a smuggling drop-off. In those situations everyone was involved and threats could come from anywhere, so you relied on your crew to watch your back while you watched theirs. This situation, where you were surrounded by bodies making noise but the only one you had to concentrate on was standing in front of you . . . this was unfamiliar.

The lines on Limberg's chest moved suddenly, the tiger roaring silently. Drift stared, caught off-guard for half a second by the unexpected electat, and in that half-second Limberg darted forwards with a leaping left hook.

Shit! Drift back-pedalled hastily, feeling the breeze as the punch cleared his nose by a fraction, but Limberg wasn't done. He kept moving forwards, that lead left hand pawing at the air, and Drift remembered just in time what Maiha had said: with his power hand advanced Limberg would have a potentially knockout jab, while his weaker right would get a full wind-up behind it. He backed off again, then suddenly became aware of the cage behind him.

'Circle!' a voice shouted, probably Micah. 'Left!' it added a moment later. Drift obliged, since moving towards Limberg's left hand didn't seem like a good plan in any case.

'Fuckin' hit 'im, bro!'

That would be Apirana, then.

Limberg had eased off his pursuit since his initial straight-line rush hadn't worked, but was still uncomfortably close and looking for an opening, matching Drift's sideways movements with his own to pressure him backwards. Drift tried to concentrate and get back into a long-forgotten groove as his opponent's left fist flicked out in an attempt to judge the distance between them. It fell short and Drift jabbed back with his left hand, surprising himself as the hasty punch glanced off Limberg's jaw. It had no substantial effect on Limberg except to make his eyes narrow in annoyance, but it did wonders to settle Drift's nerves a bit. He jabbed again; Limberg swayed back out of reach, but Drift could see that Maiha had been right about the reach discrepancy. He pressed forwards and fired off two more jabs, then swung a sloppy haymaker with his right hand which Coach Hernandez would have bawled him out for.

Limberg had barely watched it whistle by when his kick caught Drift in the ribcage like a gunshot.

Although actually, some gunshots he'd taken had hurt less than that.

Nonetheless, he staggered sideways and nearly dropped his guard, only just raising his hands to catch the swift one-two of punches which followed. He flung out his left hand again, *jab jab*, and Limberg stood back to let him punch thin air, then kicked him again. This time Drift dropped his right arm to block it, and got the feeling of someone sledgehammering his bicep for his trouble.

He tried to hide the pain by going on the offensive: he kicked at Limberg's leg but the other man pulled it back just in time, so he tried to rush him. One, two, three punches fired at Limberg's head, which were either harmlessly blocked or simply avoided, and a swinging elbow aimed at the temple which Limberg ducked under. On his way past, the fighter hammered Drift's ribs again – a punch, this time – and Drift stumbled face first into the mesh which surrounded them. He turned back with his guard up, but a right hand slid through and glanced off his cheekbone with stinging force. As he retreated along the cage wall he felt a warm wetness trickling down his face, and knew he'd been cut.

'One minute gone!' Micah shouted. Drift cursed inwardly. His ribs felt like they'd been set on fire, his lungs didn't seem to be doing their job properly and his opponent was barely even sweating. There was no way he could survive another four minutes of this. He was a starship captain, not an athlete; he might not put on weight, but the only regular exercise he got was in the beds of beautiful women. And even that wasn't as regular as he'd have liked.

Limberg was holding back for the moment, but he'd start unloading in earnest as soon as he realised that Drift really didn't pose a threat to him. At that point, no matter how badly Drift wanted the information that Nana supposedly had, all bets were probably off. He didn't like pain in general, he didn't like getting punched in the face in particular, and he didn't think he possessed some sort of magical constitution which would prevent him from getting knocked unconscious.

He tried to manoeuvre around Limberg, but the other man matched his sideways movements and kept him pinned against the cage, then fired off a one-two at Drift's face only to put all his weight into another kick which caught him in the ribs again. Drift staggered again, unable to keep his legs in order, but couldn't get away from another hammerblow of a kick which he took on his arm leaving it momentarily numb.

Then the feeling came back into it, and it was a feeling he could have easily done without.

Limberg was studying him, as if sizing him up for the next attack, and Maiha's words came back to him. *He'll wait for you to drop your hands and then kick you in the head*, she'd said.

But Limberg didn't know that he knew that.

Drift let his right arm hang at his side, as though it were broken or otherwise incapacitated – which in fairness, wasn't *that* far from the truth. He raised his left hand so the back of it was facing his blood-smeared right cheek, the desperate defensive position of a battered man fearing a vicious left hook and seeking to ward off the inevitable for a few more moments.

Limberg stepped forwards and swung another kick, this time with his right leg, aimed at Drift's ribs on the other side of his body. Drift pulled his left hand back and down in an obviously futile attempt to block it, but it had only ever been a feint; a leaping step which ended in Limberg's left leg whipping upwards towards Drift's now completely unprotected jaw.

Drift ducked then, as the surprised fighter was carried around by his own momentum, tackled Limberg from behind and bore him to the mat.

The fights Ichabod Drift had been in generally had not consisted of standing in front of a trained fighter and exchanging punches and kicks. Certainly not without the ability to kick them in the testicles or poke them in the eyes. Choking someone out quickly and silently so they couldn't raise an alarm but you didn't have to actually kill them . . . ah, that was far more in the *Keiko*'s playbook.

He swarmed on the startled Limberg like a spider, wrapping his legs around the other man's waist and snaking his left arm over Limberg's shoulder and around his throat. Then he anchored his left hand on his throbbing right bicep, gritted his teeth and squeezed.

Limberg knew what he had to do, he was simply a little too late to do it; he hadn't expected to be suckered into the headkick, and he hadn't expected the apparently incompetent man he'd been beating up to know how to apply such an expert blood choke. His fingers clamped around Drift's forearm, but he was already a step off the pace and panic made him sloppy. Drift watched his head turn a deeper and deeper red, felt his struggles losing power and urgency . . .

The horn sounded.

Drift let go and rolled off Limberg, who didn't move. Somewhere in the distance he heard a roar which could only have been Apirana, but his own head was pounding loudly enough that everything sounded like he was underwater. He registered feet running into the cage and someone bending down to check on Limberg, then someone else helped him sit up. He found himself staring into the steady, dark eyes of Maiha Takahara and opened his mouth to express some sort of thanks, but was stopped by a furious widening of her eyes and tightening of her mouth, and an almost imperceptible shake of her head. Her gaze flickered upwards for just a second.

Right. Can't let the boss know you spoiled her game. Guess I'd better play my role, then.

He gave her the finger.

t was approaching midnight in Prague, and it was raining. In fact, 'raining' was possibly an inadequate term; great sheets of water were dropping from the sky until it seemed that the air was comprised more of liquid than of gas, or that the Vltava had risen from its bed and come looking for a night out in the Old Town. Tamara Rourke was more grateful than ever for her waterproof body glove, especially since her coat was definitely getting rather sodden. She flicked the brim of her hat and sent droplets scattering out of the relative shelter of the archway and into the downpour, where they were immediately swallowed.

Weather. No wonder most of our species left this planet behind.

Lightning arced across the sky above the city, bright enough to cancel out the advertising holos dancing in the air above the street and accompanied immediately by the tearing boom of a thunderclap. Behind Rourke, Jenna jumped noticeably. Franklin Major and Minor were two of the relatively few planets in the galaxy where terraforming had been completed, but their breathable atmospheres boasted comparatively calm climates. The sort of storm currently breaking over Prague was rare indeed in their skies.

'You alright there?' Rourke asked over her shoulder. Jenna nodded, but the rain-slicked strands of red-blonde hair sticking to her face suggested otherwise. The girl's lips moved, but Rourke didn't hear the words over another peal of thunder. 'What?'

'Why did we have to come outside?' Jenna repeated, in what would have probably been a whine were it not for a conscious effort on her part.

'Because it's loud,' Rourke replied.

'But why's that important?'

'Because when Ichabod calls me, I don't want any fancy bugging techniques being able to pick up what he's saying,' Rourke told her. Jenna frowned.

'Why would anyone be bugging *us*?'

'Not necessarily us,' Rourke said, gesturing up the street to where lit windows threw rectangles of illumination across the ancient, drenched cobbles of the street surface. 'Bars can be bugged, particularly if someone in government is feeling paranoid. Then there's Listeners, who are basically walking microphones, loads of subdermal implants. They go and hang around anyone they think looks suspicious and the handlers process the audiofeed, see if they can match it to any surveillance data. A lot of surveillance cameras have directional audio pickups too, and you'd be surprised how accurate they can be.'

'Okay,' Jenna said slowly. Rourke could see her trying to keep her face neutral, but knew that somewhere under there was an expression indicating that the girl thought Rourke was paranoid. To be fair, Rourke wouldn't have believed half the surveillance tricks possible had she not used most of them herself in the past. 'But why would the Captain *call* you?' Jenna added. 'Can't he just send the data using the cryptkey I gave him?'

'Sure he can,' Rourke sighed, 'but if he's sending us anything it means he's got a chance to boast about how he got the information, and that means he'll be calling.' She grimaced as the thunder crashed again. 'Good grief.'

'Are you sure it was a good idea to leave just Jia and Kuai on the *Jonah*?' Jenna asked suddenly.

Rourke frowned. 'Why?'

'Well, Kuai wanted to just leave,' Jenna pointed out. 'What if he convinces Jia that they should take the ship and go?'

'It had crossed my mind,' Rourke admitted, 'but Jia would never agree to it. She wouldn't try to pilot it without at least someone on comms with her, and given the searches going on for *Carcharodon*-class shuttles at the moment she'd be mad to take off without a slicer on board. Plus, that girl's out for blood; I could see it in her eyes.'

'Okay,' Jenna said, seeming slightly reassured. She appeared about to say something else, but Rourke held up a finger to forestall her as the comm in her ear beeped. She activated the link as Jenna tapped her wrist console, linking her own comm into the conversation.

'Go ahead,' Rourke answered.

+He's in the Olorun System.+

Drift's voice sounded weary, even allowing for the slightly distorting effect of the comm signal being encrypted at source, bounced off a satellite or two and then decrypted again, not to mention atmospheric interference. Rourke bit back the reflex to ask what had gone wrong; even with a supposedly secure signal, they didn't want to give anyone who might be listening any more information than they had to about who they were or what they were talking about.

'I don't know it,' she admitted.

+It's not inhabited yet. It's nominally FAS but it's next to the Perun System, which is Europan. Apparently he hides out in an asteroid.+

'What, like that smuggler base in the Albus System?' Rourke asked. 'Do we have any verification on this?'

+Not for the asteroid. As for the system, the Perun was where I did my last few drops for him; it had always been a different rendezvous before that. If he was already crooked and skimming resources off by that point then the Olorun would have been a suitably short trip to stockpile them out of sight. I think it's solid enough to move on.+

Rourke nodded reluctantly. 'I'd like more, but I have to agree with you. Are you sure you want us to go ahead with our part?'

+Are you?+

The question took her off-guard, which was a surprise in its own way. Until that moment she hadn't realised exactly how uncertain she was about the whole business. She thought it might be an echo of what Drift himself had gone through, although inverted; he'd abandoned an infamous name and taken up an unknown one, whereas she had swapped deliberate, enforced secrecy for the comfortable obscurity which came with being mostly unremarkable.

She felt Jenna's eyes on her and composed herself. Old training died hard, and she doubted the girl would have even noticed the momentary hesitation which was all the reaction she'd betrayed. 'It's probably our best shot at this, but you realise that it's still not very likely to work, don't you?'

+*That's why Jenna's there.*+

Rourke nodded again, noting the slight tightening of her companion's features. 'True. Wish us luck, then.'

+*Good luck. And stay safe.*+

Drift cut the link, leaving Rourke and Jenna with no sound but the hammering of the rain on pavement and a distant rumble as some other part of the sky was split by a million volts. She looked at the young slicer. 'Are you ready?'

'I'll just be dealing with terminals,' Jenna answered, trying to pull her coat more tightly around her, 'they're predictable. You're the one with a person to handle.'

Rourke just shrugged, and tried to make her voice sound more confident than she felt. 'They're predictable enough.'

The walk south from the archway was short, but undeniably wet. Rourke tried to keep to narrow alleys where possible to give the sky as narrow an angle of fire as she could, but there was only so much to be done against the elements. Prague's streets were virtually deserted by pedestrians with only a couple of other souls braving the fury of the Czech skies, although there were still some electric cars purring through the wet. In one respect that comforted Rourke, but with less potential witnesses came less chance of blending into a crowd. She felt particularly exposed as they crossed Národní, the wide road with its maglev tram tracks which marked the border between the Old Town and the New Town. This was a sketchy plan thrown together on the fly, even by the standards of the *Keiko*'s crew, and for a moment she missed the sense of reassurance from when she'd had a supervising officer, a support team and the nominal protection of a government. That had been an illusion, at least in part, but she still would have been a hell of a lot better prepared for this sort of insanity.

You made that decision a long time ago, girl. Focus on the here and now.

An automated booth lit up at their approach, offering tourist-guide downloads at a price well above reasonable and just below the ridiculous, but they ignored it and zigzagged through the avenues and junctions of the New Town. Rourke had memorised several different possibles routes to and from their destination in order to avoid looking indecisive or suspicious, something her training had drummed into her long ago, but she took the quickest one now. It was only a couple of minutes until they reached their goal, a stout door of red-painted wood which was raised above street level by three well-worn marble steps.

The building towered over them by five storeys, bracketing the entire length of the narrow street with its equally imposing opposite number. Only the slightly differing external décor occurring every four or so windows along its length hinted where the wall of stone was divided internally. It seemed strangely huge, despite the fact that she'd seen larger buildings on half a hundred worlds including this one; over a certain scale, humanity's edifices seemed to be processed by her brain as oddly regular geography instead of artificial constructs. However, this narrow canyon of a street was still small enough to be human in scope, and she felt dwarfed.

Jenna stepped smartly up to the lock while Rourke crowded into the space behind her, facing out into the street while doing her best to surreptitiously shield what the girl was up to with the sweep of her coat. She was about to quietly enquire how long it was likely to take when the door buzzed and a huff of effort from Jenna indicated the slicer pushing it open.

'That was quick,' Rourke commented, slipping through behind her crewmate into a hallway of warm light and neutral decoration. The floor was tiled in a brown and cream pattern and a couple of inoffensive, mass-produced holos in frames broke up the expanse of the walls. There were locked boxes of dark steel attached to the wall for when the building's tenants received any form of physical mail, and ahead of them a staircase with bannisters of rich, dark wood began its climb to the upper floors.

'I could have got through that blind drunk,' Jenna snorted softly, pulling her jumpsuit's sleeve back over her wrist console.

'I remember,' Rourke replied, feeling a slight smile

tug at her lips. Jenna's cheeks coloured slightly, and
she coughed to cover her embarrassment.

'Where now?'

'Top floor.' Rourke nodded at the stairway, removing
her hat and shaking the water from the brim. 'Flat
Nine. You're certain she won't be here yet?'

'The House is still in session,' Jenna said, brushing
a strand of sodden hair back behind her ear as she
consulted her wrist again, 'and given recent events
she's going to have to be there.'

'Good,' Rourke nodded. 'Let's get on with it, then.'

The climb to the top floor wasn't as easy as it
would have been thirty years ago, or even twenty: it
wasn't that Rourke was getting out of shape as such,
but she was starting to notice things like knees, which
she had previously taken for granted. Still, she was
reportedly older than she looked and definitely older
than she felt, so she wasn't going to be complaining.
Indeed, she seemed slightly less out of breath than
the young slicer at her side by the time they reached
the top corridor with its two doors facing each other,
both darkened by decades of age and varnish but
nonetheless solid for that.

'This one.' Rourke nodded to the door on the left.
Jenna stepped up smartly and did . . . something.
Rourke still wasn't too sure exactly how the girl's
wrist-mounted console worked or connected, but it
did the job and that was the main thing.

There was another buzz and click. Jenna stepped
back slightly and Rourke shrugged her coat off into
the girl's hands, then went through the door fast and
silent, her palms aching at the absence of a gun. Not
that she'd have wanted to use one even if she came

across someone unexpected – her custom-modified, silenced Smith & Wesson might have just about escaped notice by neighbours in this storm, but she wouldn't have liked to chance it – but the simple threat of a firearm could stop someone from making a noise before they started. However, the Europans had taken a dim view of people bringing in guns even before they'd had a suspected terrorist attack in their backyard, and with the *Jonah* locked up in Star's End and no active smuggling contacts on Old Earth, she and Jenna had had to come in through customs like respectable people.

She ghosted through the flat, checking corners and possible hiding places on instinct, most of her attention listening for telltale sounds: a startled breath, a challenge half-formed in a throat, a click or scrape as something was hurriedly set down or seized up.

Nothing. Beside herself, and Jenna standing outside the door, there was no-one here.

The apartment was quite large, but also largely empty. This wasn't a home full of heirlooms, half-forgotten presents and books bought to read on a day which had never come. This was a functional stopover point, a place where a busy professional could stay when work kept them away from the family pad. In the case of Anna-Marie Císař, the Europan Commonwealth's current Minister for Defence, that was certainly likely to be true for the immediate future.

Rourke took note of the layout: bedroom, living room, a kitchen diner, bathroom and, as they'd predicted, a second bedroom turned into an office which housed the apartment's terminal hub. She moved back to the front door and pulled it open again by a crack. 'Clear.'

'Good.' Jenna hustled inside, shutting the door behind her and absently thumbing the 'lock' button. 'Honestly, you'd have thought she'd have better protection in place.'

Rourke frowned at the lock's control pad. 'I thought SecuriTop was a good make?'

'They are,' Jenna acknowledged, 'this is, like, four times harder to crack than the lock downstairs.' She shrugged, looking around. 'But for someone who knows what they're doing, that's like the difference between . . . between you shooting a target at five feet and twenty feet.'

'Right,' Rourke nodded.

'You want a secure house, you put a damn great metal lock on it,' Jenna added, passing Rourke her coat. 'The only people who trust computers alone to keep them safe are the ones who don't know much about them.'

'You know what to do?' Rourke asked, cutting her off before the girl could expound her opinions on the limits of technology any further.

'Yeah.' Jenna's grin lit up her face with a mix of eagerness and mischief. 'This is going to be *fun*.'

Rourke stopped her with a hand in the centre of her chest. 'Just do the job. Don't get carried away, and for all our sakes, don't leave any traces.'

She was slightly surprised when Jenna brushed her hand away with an annoyed look. 'You want to come and babysit me, be my guest,' the girl snapped, 'but you won't know what the hell you're looking at. So you let me do what I do, and you do what you do and lurk in the shadows.' She brushed past and headed for the minister's office.

Rourke sighed. She'd never liked dealing with external specialists anyway; they had a tendency to be unfocused, or lose focus easily, and have an unduly high opinion of their own value. Still, they'd always been a necessary evil, and over the last eight years on the *Keiko* she'd become inured to all but the most extravagant extremes of personality.

Tamara Rourke made a quick and more specific search through the apartment, found what she was looking for, and settled down to wait.

I t was, in fact, close on three more hours before the lock on the flat door buzzed and gave Rourke the split second of warning she needed to prepare herself. She rose silently to her feet from the chair she'd been occupying in the living room and took a breath, counting on the noise of the door being opened and closed to obscure the faint sound – far too many people underestimated how noticeable breathing was when it wasn't expected – and waited, out of sight of the main door. There was a rustle of clothing as a coat was hung up, a slight clatter of something hard being placed carelessly onto the hallway table – probably the key card to gain access to the block in general and this flat in particular – and then a pause.

This was when so many people would blow it, that agonising moment where the mark was *so near* and yet not quite in the right place for the game to proceed, an unexpected delay which preyed on the nerves. This was when some would betray themselves, either unconsciously through an unintended movement or noise or by deliberately making their move before the correct time, an act borne of frustration. Rourke didn't move and didn't breathe; there was no way she should be detected, and there was no reason to panic. What was the woman doing? It didn't matter, not to her. All that mattered was that Císař was not yet in the right place, and so Tamara Rourke would wait.

A grunt of effort from the hallway, a faint slithering sound, a muffled thump of something being dropped on carpet. Rourke frowned ever so slightly, but then the noise was repeated. *Boots. Taking off her boots. Now, where will she go?*

This was the first unpredictable element, no matter how confident she'd hoped to sound to Jenna. The front door opened onto a hallway at right angles with the main bedroom and the bathroom at one end and the second bedroom – now an office – at the other. In order to access the kitchen and diner Císař would have to come through the doorway almost directly in front of her, into the living room; that was the gamble Rourke had taken. Despite the doubtlessly harrowing day she'd just had, Anna-Marie Císař was unlikely to turn in straight away, and would surely not head straight for her office; she'd just come from work, after all. She might stop into the bathroom, true, but that would only be a brief delay. No, most likely was that this hard-worked and currently highly stressed politician would head straight for the kitchen to make herself a coffee, perhaps with a dash of something alcoholic, and possibly prepare a meal . . .

The faint noise of stockinged feet on carpet, a shadow suddenly growing in the patch of light thrown into the living room's dark interior. Rourke forced herself not to tense, waited as still as darkness behind the door, saw the back of the woman's head appear, *five feet seven inches barefoot, one hundred and twenty to twenty-five pounds, blonde dye over a natural auburn and last coloured one week to ten days ago,* watched her take another step, *unlikely to be trained in martial arts judging by musculature on arms and legs, slight limp in left leg possibly caused by blister,* and thumbed the safety button on the handgun she'd found in the top drawer of Císař's bedside cabinet with an audible buzz.

'Please do not raise your voice,' she said firmly. Arming the gun was a showy move straight out of the holos, but it was a recognisable noise which would register with anyone who had a familiarity with fire-arms. Císař froze in place, hands slightly raised from her sides and fingers extended.

'Are you from the Free Systems?' Her voice was hoarse and the accent of her native land was strong, at least in this moment of stress.

'Not at all,' Rourke replied. 'I wish you no harm, and I apologise for the manner of this intrusion, but my presence here must remain a secret and that wouldn't be likely to happen had you attacked me or screamed. Please, Ms Císař, by all means turn around.'

Císař turned in place, carefully, bringing her face into Rourke's view. The thin lines of her eyebrows showed the rich auburn of her natural colour, her eyes were green and largely unlined, *but dark-rimmed from lack of sleep, which the expensive make-up hasn't fully concealed,* her cheekbones high and her cheeks smooth, *probably taken Boost a time or two, as the cut of her clothes and the seniority of her office don't quite match the youthfulness of her face; a little vain, then.*

Císař's eyes flickered to her own handgun, which was held loosely in Rourke's gloved hand and pointing at the floor. 'So you would not have shot me?'

'I simply needed to get your attention, Minister,' Rourke admitted. She did not, however, put the gun down.

'What do you want?' Císař's eyes narrowed suspiciously, but Rourke could see the thoughts running through her mind, that Rourke could have already robbed the apartment or harmed her had she wished to . . . at least, that's what Rourke *thought* the other woman was thinking. This was why she normally left such negotiations and manipulations to Drift; the man could read people's moods as easily as she could spot a feinted punch or a concealed weapon. He relied on her to get them out of trouble when it started, and she relied on him to make sure it never started in the first place. After all their years of working together so smoothly she still couldn't quite believe he was . . .

Focus, Tamara.

'I want to help you,' she said to the minister's frown. 'My employers have come into possession of the name and current location of the man who was behind the explosion in the North Sea.'

Císař's eyes widened. 'What?! Who? Where?' Then her eyes narrowed once more. 'Who are you, and who are your employers?'

Rourke raised her ungloved left hand. It had been so long since she'd activated the electat that she'd almost thought her palm would remain blank when she'd tried to show it to Drift, but his horror-tinged expression of shock had quickly reassured her that it had worked. She gave her left hand the same mental prod now, and watched as surprise crept over the other woman's face.

'The GIA.' Císař's nostrils flared in anger. 'The USNA think they can simply send an agent into *my* apartment?'

'With respect, Minister, there are very few places we *don't* get sent over the course of our careers,' Rourke replied levelly. 'The reason I am here waiting for you is because we cannot be seen to be directly involved in this affair.'

'When is the Galactic Intelligence Agency ever seen to be directly involved in *anything*?' Císař snorted.

'Exactly.' Rourke allowed herself a small, tight smile. *Now give her the freebie, before she gets too angry.* 'We know that the man who sent that bomb was a former employee of your government.'

'Impossible!' Císař snapped.

'Nicolas Kelsier?' Rourke asked.

Confusion clouded Císař's expression. 'Kelsier? I don't . . . he was . . .'

'—fired,' Rourke finished for her, 'for corruption. After skimming off quite a large amount of money, or so it seems, which he's used to finance this spiteful attempt at revenge.'

'How do you know this?' Císař demanded. Rourke smirked as smugly as she could. It didn't come easily.

'We . . . "picked up" the ship which botched the bombing. It seems the captain was unaware of what he'd been called on to deliver, but he was very clear on who had hired him: his old employer, Nicolas Kelsier. This captain was one of your old privateers.'

'Privateers?' Císař's face went blank. 'I don't know what you—'

'Let's not be coy, Minister,' Rourke snapped, 'do you really think the GIA wasn't aware of Kelsier's private pirate fleet? We might accept protestations of ignorance from a junior undersecretary perhaps, or the Minister for Education, but the Minister for Defence? You might not be a part of ETRA, but your departments work hand-in-hand.'

Císař's gaze shifted, not meeting Rourke's eyes. 'That was before I was in office.'

'We don't care,' Rourke said, waving a hand dismissively. 'The point is that you know what I'm talking about. Do you see the delicacy of the situation now? We have a pirate, a man who may well have committed offences against *our* shipping as well as the Federation of African States, who has the nav records and data trails to suggest he really was hired by Nicolas Kelsier to deliver a nuclear device into Amsterdam.'

'Then with the greatest respect to your agency,' Císař said, the tone of her voice indicating a certain sarcasm, 'why do you care?'

Rourke took a deep breath. 'Because we believe Nicolas Kelsier may be partially funded by or even fully involved with Free System separatists, and that is a far greater priority for us than one pirate.'

Go on. Swallow the lie.

She and Drift had debated this fiercely. Her GIA electat was the only even vaguely credible form of authority they had, but even that wouldn't persuade anyone of importance in the USNA to do what they needed. The Europans were the nation least likely to automatically arrest Drift if the truth of his former identity got out, and the fact was that they might need to throw as much truth as they had at this in order to get the lies to stick, but no one would believe that the GIA were throwing a bone to another government with no angle for themselves. In the end, the Free Systems were the only viable patsy.

All the colonised systems in the galaxy had been claimed by one of the governmental conglomerates from Old Earth, and it was those conglomerates which set the laws and, crucially, levied taxes. Predictably, however, this empire-building hadn't gone unchallenged, and when certain systems had enough of sending percentages of their GDP back to Old Earth, they'd staged local variations of the Boston Tea Party. Rourke herself had played a small part in the series of events which had culminated with the Yangtze System throwing off the yoke of Red Star rule, but the GIA had stopped laughing when USNA systems started rebelling as well.

At that point it had become a giant exercise in galactic hypocrisy, as every conglomerate tried its best to quietly prevent cessation from its own ranks while vocally supporting the rights of everyone else's subject systems to break away in the interests of democracy.

Some of the Free Systems were war zones, others were fully independent, many were somewhere in between with the citizens fighting among themselves and bombing each other when they couldn't agree on whether to stay or break away. However, some freedom fighters inevitably decided that the best way to 'send a message' was to hit a prominent government target elsewhere . . . and the USNA had taken several of these hits in the last few years.

'Separatists?' Císař either couldn't or didn't bother to hide the grimace which twisted her lips. Her first thought upon hearing a gun armed behind her had been of the Free Systems, which boded well.

'So we believe,' Rourke lied. 'If Kelsier is working as a mercenary, using the resources he stockpiled when stealing from your government to complete jobs for others, he is as big a potential threat to us as he is to you. However, even our authority has limits; we could never mobilise even a small amount of USNA troops after this man on the testimony of a former Europan pirate who was involved in a bombing attempt on another government's territory. You would have a rather stronger case.'

'That's what you're suggesting?' Císař looked incredulous. 'That I should authorise *military action* against a former employee of my government based on second- or third-hand intelligence?'

'A small, discreet action only,' Rourke assured her, 'the USNA has—'

'The USNA has a history of shooting first and finding out the truth second,' Císař spat, then raised her eyebrows mockingly. 'Well? I imagine you may be recording this conversation, but my remarks are as deniable as your government infiltrating my *home*. Give me the surveillance data, give me the interrogation transcripts – with the screams edited out, if you please, I know how you work – and give me this 'captain' himself, with his ship and his logs. Then, and only then, will I decide whether or not I have a case with which I can pursue further action.'

Rourke felt the growing void in her chest and tried to ignore it. They'd been banking on Císař's desperation to produce something, gambling that she would jump at a chance to show a result in the aftermath of the largest terrorism scare to hit the Europan Commonwealth in living memory. 'With respect, Minister, my agency cannot simply—'

'Your agency works with lies and misdirection, and shows no respect to *anyone*,' Císař declared forcefully. She pointed a slightly quivering finger – from anger rather than fear, if Rourke was any judge – at the flat's front door. 'Put my gun down and get out of my home. You needn't fear that I will shoot you in the back with it; I value my career as minister too much for that, which is precisely why I will be ignoring this poorly concealed attempt to get us to do your dirty work for you. *If* you have hard evidence of a connection between any individual and this bombing attempt, then your superiors may submit them to us through the usual channels. Now get out.'

Rourke debated arguing further but decided against it. Even Drift couldn't have salvaged this mess, although the odds were good that he wouldn't have let it get this bad in the first place. Then again, perhaps the web of bullshit she'd been trying to spin had simply been too tenuous in the first place. She placed the gun on the table beside her without a word and moved to the front door, pressing the release button with her gloved thumb and pulling it open. Only once she was halfway through did she take the gun's magazine from her coat pocket and drop it on the doormat with a mocking tip of her hat to the Minister for Defence.

She reached the ground floor in less than twenty seconds (her old instructor had used to say that only two sorts of people were intelligent enough to realise that sliding down bannisters was quicker than using stairs: children and agents), wrenched open the front door and ran out into the rain, which had settled down from its thunderous beginnings into the kind of solid drenching which could keep up its steady precipitation through the night and well into the next day. She headed south-east for the nearest rail station as fast as she could, hoping that Císař would decide the paperwork involved with arranging the detention of a GIA agent simply wasn't worth it. As she ran, she activated her comm.

+Go.+ Drift sounded like he'd recovered a little from whatever had been causing him problems earlier, but he clearly wasn't in the mood for chatting. Which was good; perhaps for once he'd adhere to proper communications protocol.

'No deal,' Rourke said, trying not to puff as she turned a corner. 'It's up to the girl now.'

Hroza Major was Perun IV's largest moon and it glittered when viewed from space, as though someone had washed large parts of its surface with diamonds. In reality the effect was caused by the extensive transparent roofs of the miles of bio-domes which sheltered the human populace, containing the oxygen they needed and trapping the weak rays of the Perun star to bring the temperature up into an acceptable range, much like greenhouses on Old Earth. Drift thought it was unusually beautiful for something so practical.

'I'm still amazed you and Jenna didn't get grabbed boarding the flight out of Europa,' he said to Rourke, who was standing in the cockpit doorway.

'It's not how these things tend to work,' the former agent replied with a shrug. 'The USNA and the Europans are on pretty good terms, and I was polite. It's the sort of incident that will get the softly-softly treatment, because the Europans won't want to admit publicly that a GIA agent just swanned into a Minister's flat. So they'll drop hints in diplomatic language that they're not pleased, and then the GIA will take time to interpret those, and then they'll do an internal investigation to find out if any agent matching my description had been authorised to be there, and *then* they'll have to convince the Europans of that . . .' She snorted. 'It probably took a week or two for both parties to stop dancing and work out that I wasn't there under orders from anyone.'

'That seems remarkably inefficient,' Drift noted.

'Welcome to the thrill-a-minute world of inter-galactic espionage,' Rourke said dryly. 'It was an awful lot of doing nothing for a very long time while everyone worked out what was happening, and then doing everything very quickly and in something of a panic.'

That sounded familiar to Drift. Thankfully it had only taken two days for the USNA to break ranks and open the skies above their shores to traffic again, at which point a whole slew of delayed craft had gone spacewards as fast as possible, including the *Carcharodon*-class shuttle currently known as the *Tamsin's Wake*. Alex Cruz had studiously avoided any contact with Drift, but the fact that their bay door had opened mere minutes after the lockdown had finished was hint enough that the portmaster wanted them gone post-haste. They'd broken atmo with every apparent intention of heading to the aster-oid belt to take on some minerals for shipping, before turning aside to rejoin the *Keiko* at its way-station above Mars instead. Jia had plotted them the fastest possible course to the Perun System as soon as they'd got back aboard the freighter and they'd taken off as though all the hounds of hell had been behind them.

And then they'd done nothing for three-and-a-half weeks while the Alcubierre drive had bent space-time around them.

It hadn't been easy. The usual bored atmosphere of a starship in transit had been replaced with the quiet tension of seven people who were used to moving in the shadows but were now being forced to step out of them. Jenna had busied herself in fiddling with her wrist console, Rourke and Micah sparred on mats in the cargo bay, and Kuai effectively quarantined himself in the engine room after a third explosive quarrel with his sister. By the time they got to their destination, Drift was so eager for action he wasn't really sure if he'd have cared if the entire Europan starfleet was waiting to arrest them.

They weren't, of course, which meant it was time for the next piece of outrageously ballsy chicanery.

'You're sure these codes are still legitimate?' Drift asked Rourke, his finger poised over the transmission button.

'They *were* legitimate, and that's the important thing,' Rourke told him firmly. 'It's a GIA ident code. I wouldn't like to try using it in a USNA system, but for a foreign government?' She shrugged. 'It should be fine. Especially since it's not the only piece to the puzzle.'

'Well, here goes nothing,' Drift said, and started the transmission. It wasn't like they had much of an option, anyway.

It couldn't have been thirty seconds before the comm crackled into life. +*This is Glass City Starport Control to shuttle* Jonah, *please come in, over.*+

'Glass City Control, this is the *Jonah*,' Drift answered crisply, 'go ahead, over.'

+*Shuttle* Jonah, *you are broadcasting a USNA government ident code. Please confirm your identity and purpose, over.*+

'Control, we cannot discuss this over an open channel,' Drift replied, 'but we believe your security forces should be expecting us. Please advise on how to proceed, over.'

There was a pause.

+*Shuttle* Jonah, *you are cleared to begin atmospheric entry to make landfall at Glass City. Hold at thirty thousand feet for an escort, over.*+

'Roger that, Control,' Drift acknowledged, giving Rourke a thumbs-up, '*Jonah* out.' He looked over at Jia. 'You heard the lady, take us down.'

'No stunts, either,' Rourke added firmly. 'It's going to be hard enough convincing anyone that you're all GIA specialist contractors without you going all thrusterhead over the capital.'

'Yeah, yeah,' Jia muttered, angling the *Jonah* nominally downwards, 'whatever.'

Drift blew his cheeks out and turned in his seat to look at Rourke. 'Taking orders from you is going to be *weird*. And you're sure they're not going to think it's odd that there's only one actual GIA agent in the whole lot of us?'

'I'm not *sure*, no,' Rourke replied, with strained patience. Admittedly, Drift had been asking variations of that question since they started putting the plan together. 'But it's general practice. There's an awful lot of galaxy to cover and only limited resources available, so an agent with a long-term brief will often need to put their own team together out of whoever they can find.'

'So it's just a case of whether the Europans know that?' Jenna asked.

'Pretty much,' Rourke admitted. She grimaced. 'Let's hope they're open-minded about my slightly eccentric hiring policy.'

'Just blame me,' Drift grinned, 'I'm a far more believable eccentric than you.'

Hroza Major's atmosphere was naturally occurring, unbreathable and thin, that last meaning there was little resistance to their descent surfacewards. Jia brought them down with a minimum of turbulence until Glass City was stretched out beneath them, then hit the retros to keep them hovering.

'Glass City Control, this is the *Jonah*,' Drift broadcast, 'we are holding position and awaiting escort, over.'

+*Roger, shuttle* Jonah, *escort is approaching now.*+

'Boss, we got two fighters on intercept,' Jia reported, unable to keep a hint of nervousness from her voice. Drift couldn't blame her; it ran against all his instincts to sit still and wait for official attention, but the die was now well and truly cast. The only thing left to do was see how their gamble paid out.

+*Shuttle* Jonah, *this is Escort 1,*+ a new voice announced. +*We are sending coordinates for your landing point now, please keep yourself between us at all times, over.*+

'Roger that, Escort 1,' Drift replied, trying to keep

his voice calm. The coordinates flashed up and he slid them over to Jia's read-out. 'We'll follow you down, over.'

The two sleek, slate-blue Europan patrol ships led them over Glass City and past the commercial spaceports to the red stone hills at the conurbation's northern edge. Here they peeled away to each side and left Jia to take the *Jonah* down onto a landing pad decorated with the circle-of-stars emblem of the Europan Commonwealth.

'And now,' Rourke said, unhooking her rebreather mask from her belt, 'let's see if we've flown into a trap.'

They assembled in the cargo bay, masks on and comms activated. If they'd been planning to spend any significant time outside in Hroza's sub-zero temperatures or if the atmosphere had been toxic, corrosive or completely absent, then the crew would have donned heated full-body suits. As it was they could handle being a bit chilly, although Drift made sure to zip up the thermojacket he'd worn in Old New York.

'Remember,' Rourke said, standing by the ramp control, 'let me do the talking where possible and don't make things up or improvise unless you absolutely have to. We're using real names and real identification because we can't afford to be caught in any falsehoods, so stick as close as you can to your real history if you're asked about when you joined the crew, where you joined the crew, anything like that. If they get suspicious, that's it for us.'

'No pressure, then,' Micah grunted as Rourke flipped the switch to lower the ramp.

They started down the ramp as soon as it had reached horizontal, by which time the welcoming committee was already in place. Drift counted half a dozen void-suited soldiers with alarmingly efficient-looking rifles, and while the barrels were not pointed at the *Jonah*'s crew they weren't shouldered cere-monially, either. Standing in the middle of that loose semicircle was a woman with the three pips of a captain in the Europan Armed Forces on her shoulder.

Rourke didn't let the other woman speak first. Instead, she peeled off her glove and held up her hand while they were still walking, presumably willing her electat into existence. 'I'm Agent Rourke of the United States of North America's Galactic Intelligence Agency, and this is my team.' Her tone was business-like and almost bored, the voice of someone getting a necessary formality over with.

'Captain Rybak of the Perun System Defence Force,' came the response. 'We received a message from the Minister for Defence advising us to expect you.'

Drift held his breath. This was where they found out if Jenna's backup plan had worked.

Captain Rybak inclined her helmeted head in a slight nod. 'We've been instructed to act in accordance with you in an attempt to apprehend the terrorist Nicolas Kelsier. Please, come inside.'

'	I'm starting to hate this place,' Micah muttered
	from behind Drift's left shoulder. The Dutch
	mercenary was fiddling with the straps on his
armavest and scowling as the *Jonah* descended
towards the surface of Hroza Major again.

'What's wrong with it?' Drift asked mildly.

'I hate it because we shouldn't *be* here,' Micah
growled. 'We should be in the Olorun System trying
to find Kelsier, not messing around in Glass City like
a bunch of *toeristen*. You said we'd be looking for
the old bastard, not waiting for him to come find us.'

'You want to go hunting through the Olorun
System for a "big asteroid"?' Drift demanded. 'We
wouldn't even know where to start. We know he's
there—'

'According to some old woman underneath Old
New York,' Micah muttered.

'—so someone somewhere nearby will have had

some sort of contact with him or his operation,' Drift finished. 'He needs to get supplies, and common sense would say from nearby. If we ask enough questions, we'll find a lead sooner or later.'

'You remember that we might not have much "later" to play with, right?' Micah said. 'Rybak might have bought our schtick but you know she'll send a message to Old Earth at some point, a progress report or something, and when they get a reply this whole house of cards is going to collapse around our ears.'

Drift sighed. 'Just go and get ready to move the cargo.' He watched Micah leave the cockpit, the mercenary muttering under his breath in Dutch, then cast a glance at the back of Jia's head. 'You're uncommonly quiet.'

'He's right, you know,' Jia replied without looking round from her controls. 'We're on borrowed time. We need to get something soon, or running and hiding is all we've got left.'

'I've been living on borrowed time for the last couple of decades,' Drift told her grimly, 'and no one's managed to collect the interest yet. Bring us down into the Low Docks; we'll offload this lot and see if we've had any bites since we've been away.'

The Low Docks were a large area of metal grill-work, open to the skies and capable of taking several dozen atmo-capable shuttles at once. Jia piloted the *Jonah* down into an empty bay, engaging the mags and gradually killing the thrusters as they descended the last distance vertically. Drift pulled his rebreather mask on and activated the comm, wedging a plug into his other ear to avoid discomfort from the low atmospheric pressure.

+*I can't believe you took us off on a five-day ore run.*+ Micah's voice was just as sullen over the commnet.

+*I can't believe I'm hearing you complain about earning money,*+ Apirana put in.

Drift sighed as he came through the doorway into the cargo bay and took the steps down to the floor of the hold, which was filled with large shipping containers of copper and nickel ore mined from the considerably warmer inner planet of Perun II. He still had hope that they could track Kelsier down, but he needed his crew to keep the rather fragile faith he'd apparently managed to reignite. The significance of Micah's grumbling – well, grumbling more than usual – was not lost on him.

+*You can't spend money when you're dead,*+ Micah was arguing, +*and I'm not planning to retire into a grave. We should have been—*+

'Earning money for bribes?' Drift cut in sharply, feeling the warm puff of his own breath reflected onto his face by the rebreather. 'Allowing time for word to get around? Letting Tamara and Jenna see what goes on while we're out of the picture? Because that's what we've done, Micah. Besides which, if this *does* go south and we *do* need to get out in a hurry then we're going to need all the cash we can scrape together.' He looked up to see Jia appearing from the cockpit and sealing the door behind her, rebreather already in place. Kuai's masked visage appeared from the direction of the engine room a few moments later so Drift hit the button which would pull the breathable air from the cargo bay.

When most of their air had been removed Drift

lowered the gang ramp to reveal mechanical loaders already waiting to retrieve the goods, piloted by operators who were unmasked and presumably snug in their sealed, heated cabins. The forewoman approached, a stern-faced lady with a blunt fringe and hair darker than the night sky, and handed Drift a credit chip without preamble. He slotted it into his pad and nodded as the numbers flashed up: seven thousand Europan was hardly a fortune but was still a decent wage for short-range cargo haulage.

It took barely two minutes for the ore containers to be unloaded, although Drift's ears and fingers were already complaining about the cold by the time the work was done. He sealed the *Jonah* behind him and threaded his way through the docks towards where the rest of the crew were already waiting for him on the other side of a pedestrian airlock. The gust of warm air which hit him when the inner doors opened practically brought him out in a sweat.

Glass City was in some ways very similar to the underground warrens of Carmella II, yet totally unlike. Both consisted of townships constructed inside arcing roofs, but the Hrozan settlement lacked the claustrophobic, dank atmosphere. Instead, the views of open sky above lent it a feeling of space despite the constraining glass structure. There were no atmo-scrapers here either, as the architects behind Glass City had envisaged a relatively low-level, low-density settlement. In short, the entire place felt like a middle-class suburb and Drift kept finding himself fighting the urge to track down something valuable to steal.

'All okay?' Apirana asked as Drift removed his

mask and they headed for the nearest tram terminal, which would take them through the city to where Rourke was waiting for them.

'Fine,' he replied, patting a pocket: not the one where he'd actually concealed the credit chip, as he had no illusions that the crowd around them wouldn't conceal pickpockets despite the city's genteel appearance. 'Say what you will about honest work, at least you rarely have to shake anyone down for your wage. Given recent events, it's almost enough to make me consider registering as a haulage ship and becoming . . . respectable.'

'You'd get bored,' Jia sniffed.

'I'd get bored,' Drift admitted.

'An' too easy to find,' Apirana added.

'Also that.'

The Low Docks tram stop was busy, despite the spaceport being only one of three in Glass City: Hroza Major's three cities were tourist attractions for those with the money to travel and an interest in eclectic architecture which blended function with aesthetics. The crew of the *Jonah* joined the throng to wait for the maglev, a silver, bullet-nosed affair with enclosing walls and roof, not to protect passengers from the non-existent elements but for the rather more mundane purpose of preventing people jumping on and off between stops.

They'd rented a small suite of rooms in the grandly named Lakeview Royale, which succeeded in having a view of one of Glass City's artificial bodies of water but utterly failed in providing anything other than decidedly standard accommodation for what was still a substantial price: Hroza Major was not a place for those of limited means. Drift and his crew would normally have stayed in their bunks aboard the *Jonah*, for the security of the ship as much as to save money, but the hunt they were on required them to be somewhere more immediately approachable than behind a couple of feet of metal and surrounded by an unbreathable atmosphere.

'How do we know Nana Bastard was even telling the truth?' Micah asked as the tram wound its way up through the Low Markets. 'We've come halfway across the galaxy on her say-so but Kelsier might not be anywhere near here. She might not even know who he is!'

'Everything I found out about her before we went there suggested she's honest,' Drift assured him with the conviction of a man who'd stepped into a fighting cage off the back of that information. 'She's been known to admit ignorance when people have asked her stuff she doesn't know. It won't help her rep if we poke around out here a while, find nothing and then go back and denounce her as a cheat. If she made a habit of doing that then I'm pretty sure her custom would have dried up a long time ago.'

'Yeah, yeah,' Micah muttered, although there was some genuine acquiescence in his manner, 'I *know* that, it's just . . .'

'It would be nice to be sure,' Drift finished for him. 'Well, that's an inconvenience we're going to have to live with until we get a solid lead, so—'

'Boss,' Apirana broke in, his deep voice lowered until it was nothing more than a gravelly whisper. Drift glanced up at him, saw the Maori's eyes flicker sideways for a second. 'Looks like someone's scoping us out.'

Drift turned to follow the direction the big man had looked in and found his gaze meeting that of a young woman, perhaps in her early twenties. She was pale-skinned with straight, nut-brown hair cut in an asymmetrically choppy style which didn't reach her shoulders, and was dressed in dark blue overalls with a logo over her left breast. She could have worked for any one of the numerous warehouses or goods merchants scattered throughout the market districts, and as such would have had perfectly good reason to be aboard the same tram as them, holding onto an overhead rail at the other end of the carriage. However, she didn't look away from him and in fact started to make her way down the tram towards them, bracing herself against the turns to avoid being dumped into the laps of fellow passengers.

'You Captain Torres?' she asked in a low voice, when she was about three feet away from him.

'That's me,' Drift nodded easily, his mind already sorting through the names he'd used. 'Torres' had been asking about Nicolas Kelsier and a niqab-wearing woman possibly called Sibaal in the Flats Markets. The markets themselves were no flatter than the rest of Glass City's gently undulating ground, but had gained the name due to mainly selling the fruits, vegetables and other edible plantstuffs grown in the artificially enriched soils of the Equatorial Flats to the south, where Perun's light and heat was at its greatest and most easily collected by the moon's glass structures.

'My boss said you were in last week,' the girl

continued, 'he told me to come find you and say he might be able to help you now.'

'Is that so?' Drift couldn't keep a slight smile from his face. He glanced at the badge on her overall – trying not to let his eyes linger too long on the curves beneath, which the sturdy fabric did not entirely hide – and nodded thoughtfully. 'Lavric's, eh?' He searched his memory. 'Tall guy, looks about sixty or so? Grey hair, dark eyebrows?'

'Yeah, that's him,' the girl nodded. 'So, you wanna come talk to him? He said he's going to be very busy after today and he might not be able to see you.'

'That so?' Drift scratched at the skin around his right eye. He cast a glance sideways at Micah, who nodded fractionally. 'Okay then. We need to go and pick up the last member of our crew, because if your boss can help us we might need to leave fast.' He looked out of the window as he felt the tram slow and smiled when he saw a stop approaching. 'We'll come find him this afternoon, I think I can remember where your business is. It's on, ah . . .'

'Mr Lavric said to bring you myself,' the girl replied, shrugging. 'I don't know why.'

'Okay then,' Drift gestured towards the approaching stop. 'Why don't you get out and wait for us here? We'll pick you up on the way back and then you lead us like you're meant to. What's your name, anyway?'

'Natalija,' the girl replied, flicking her hair out of one eye.

'A pleasure to meet you, Natalija.' Drift gave her a smile which sat somewhere between friendly and flirtatious; she was probably technically too young for him, but that had never really mattered a damn. She smiled back, perhaps out of polite reflex and perhaps not, and he casually nudged the door release with his elbow as the tram slowed to a stop in the area known as South Lake Shore, picturesque even by Glass City standards. 'We'll try not to keep you waiting too long.'

'Don't hurry for me,' the girl grinned, 'I'm getting paid anyway, and this beats hauling shit around the warehouse. See ya.' Drift stood aside and she slipped through the door, then headed towards a bench just vacated by would-be passengers now waiting to board. Drift didn't even try to disguise watching her backside as she threaded her way through the crowd.

'You're impossible,' Jia told him severely.

'Merely improbable,' Drift replied cheerfully, folding his arms. 'So . . . trap?'

'Trap,' Apirana grunted, while the others nodded soberly. Drift sighed, and activated his comm. The call was answered almost immediately.

+*About damn time.*+

'Nice to hear your voice again, too,' Drift replied happily to Rourke's grumpy tones. 'It looks like Lavric's in the Flats Markets may have something for us.'

+*I see. What's the arrangement?*+

'We have a guide,' Drift informed her. 'She's been told to take us to see her boss. We've left her at the South Lake Shore tram stop and we should be with you in about ten minutes.'

+*I'll start putting our affairs here in order then.*+ There was a pause. +*This 'guide'. What's she like?*+

'Oh you know; young, pretty . . .' Drift grinned. 'Nice ass.'

+*It's almost like the person who sent her knows you, Captain Torres.*+

A WATCHING BRIEF

The van parked at the edge of the Flats Markets was cramped, over-warm and not exactly fragrant, what with the various bodies which had been packed into it for some time now. It was also not a van, apparently; it was, in fact, an Unmarked Mobile Technical Support Unit, but so far as Jenna could see it was a goddamned van, and that was how she was going to persist in thinking of it.

Her five companions in the van's interior were a mixed bag. Captain Rybak had two troopers with her, kitted out with armavests and open-face helmets, which reminded Jenna slightly of the void-station enforcers Drift had gunned down at point-blank range. However, these two had uniforms of slate-blue instead of red, and rather than starguns they carried a dual-purpose weapon combining a high-powered semi-automatic rifle with a tazer, depending on what manner of response was needed.

The main reason they were so cramped was the large, powerful terminal, which took up a fair part of what would normally have been a roomy cargo area. Sitting in front of it and surveying a plethora of display holos were Martin Karhan and Sara Vankova, two local officers who were a study in contrasts. Karhan was older, greying and had the rounded physique of someone who'd been sitting doing hi-tech surveillance work for most of his working life, often in extended bouts with little exercise and poor access to appropriate nutrition; Vankova was close to Jenna's age, had her dark brown hair done up in a complicated plait at the back of her head and appeared to so far be staving off an expanding waistline to match her supervisor's through the combined forces of a youthful metabolism and boundless enthusiasm. Jenna had already fielded several excited questions from her on what it was like to be part of a GIA field team with variations of 'I'm not supposed to talk about that'.

Of more immediate concern was the fact that everyone they were working with in Glass City, from Vankova and Karhan to Rybak and her unit with all their associated guns, were only helping them because of one particular communiqué indisputably sent with the authorisation of Anna-Marie Císař. That message, which had preceded the *Keiko*'s arrival by about a week, instructed them to aid the GIA team led by Tamara Rourke in bringing Nicolas Kelsier to justice for his role in the near-bombing of Amsterdam . . . but it had been sent by Jenna using the access protocols she'd gleaned from Císař's home terminal, and was as fake as one of the *Jonah*'s ident overlays.

They'd been hoping to get the Europan Defence Minister to buy their scheme, but Jenna had always been the fail-safe. The question was how long they had before their deception was realised. Even if Rybak had responded with an affirmative immediately, that would probably not have reached Old Earth yet, and it would take more time for any message or arresting force to return . . . assuming, of course, that no one ever found traces of the slicing she'd done in Císař's apartment.

Jenna had been gone from Císař's flat well before the minister had returned for her ill-fated conversation with Rourke. She also knew she was good; better than that, she was *really* good. But good enough to have left absolutely no virtual fingerprints on a terminal's datalogs? Nothing to be detected if the best tech security experts in the Europan conglomerate were called in to double-check that a rogue GIA agent hadn't gone snooping around where she shouldn't?

Probably not.

So she sat in the van, within five feet of two men with guns who were more than qualified to use them, and waited for the call she wouldn't hear over the comm system she didn't have access to which would bring everything to an abrupt and almost certainly bloody close, simply because she'd somehow slipped up in Prague. All in all, it was good that she could blame the temperature of the van for the sweat beading her brow and forming damp circles beneath her arms.

'This has got to be the most backwards way to

conduct an operation I've ever heard of,' Martin Karhan muttered, adjusting the focus on one of the surveillance feeds from a camera embedded in the frame of the glass roof high above them. The market was a press of bodies funnelled through streets narrowed by the presence of stalls, and from this top-down viewpoint it put Jenna somewhat in mind of diagrams of blood cells flowing through veins, albeit more geometric in layout.

'It's a sting,' Vankova argued, 'it's just a pretty daring one. They got any tails yet?'

'Nothing yet,' Karhan replied, shaking his grizzled head. 'And yes, it's a sting, but whoever heard of throwing a whole team in as bait? No disrespect to Agent Rourke,' he added, glancing briefly over his shoulder at Jenna, 'but how do you know this Kelsier's guys won't just shoot them all straight off?'

'Because I'm not with them,' Jenna replied, feeling her stomach tighten and hoping to hell that their gamble would pay off. 'Kelsier knows I'm part of the team hunting him, and wants to get us all; if they kill the others they won't find me. Besides, we've done this before.' *Except it was only the Captain in the net that time, and I don't think Gideon Xanth was as smart as Kelsier.*

'That seems like a big risk, if you don't mind me saying,' Karhan shrugged, 'but it's not my team or my life, so . . .' He broke off, frowning. 'Okay, we've got movement; looks like two tails have joined from Trader's Way.' His finger traced the progress of two heads, now following the cluster of *Keiko* crew through the crowd at a slight distance.

Rybak leaned forwards. 'Are you sure?'

'Hold on.' Vankova brought up a replica of the feed on another screen, then wound it back. Jenna watched the heads of Rourke, Drift and the rest shuffle backwards through the market, bodies moving in an odd waddle. 'Yup,' the younger surveillance officer nodded, 'look, these two are just standing around until Agent Rourke's team go past, and on opposite sides of the junction. That would have to be a hell of a coincidence.'

Rybak grunted and leaned back, then spoke softly into her comm. Jenna fought down the urge to wipe her palms on the legs of her jumpsuit, and tried to get her breathing under control. She was supposed to be part of a GIA team – perhaps not a fully fledged agent, but at least a trusted external contractor. Then again, surely it wouldn't be that surprising if the slicer was at least a little nervous at the thought of danger?

'Right boys, let's take a look at you,' Vankova muttered. Her braid was flicked forwards over her right shoulder and she started to chew on the end in what was presumably an absent-minded manner as her fingers danced across the terminal's controls. Jenna watched as the perspective of the monitor changed to a feed from street level, one of the many cameras situated on buildings dotted throughout Glass City. Hroza Major might have a prosperous, largely peaceful population and a low crime rate, but that didn't mean the Hrozan government wasn't of the opinion that prevention was better than cure.

A flash of violet hair caught her eye: Drift, apparently in easy conversation with a girl wearing overalls who was leading them through the market. The Captain's olive-skinned face looked relaxed, but then he'd always been good at dissembling. Rourke, a pace behind, was wearing a grim expression, but that wasn't out of character either. Then came Kuai and Jia, the former nervously fiddling with his dragon pendant and the latter skulking along with her 'pilot hat' pulled down firmly over her ears. Behind them was the massive shape of Apirana, his hood largely hiding his face from the cameras but still easy to pick out due to looming well above most of the crowd. Finally, Micah brought up the rear, seemingly in deep conversation with Apirana. Jenna could see that he was looking around a lot, to all intents and purposes at the market's wares, but she'd have put money on the mercenary's true motivations being to watch for ambushes. He didn't seem to have picked up on the men following them, however, and it was these two that Vankova was focused on.

The young surveillance tech did something which highlighted the two tails on the overhead view and tagged a floating star above their heads on the street-level feed she was watching, then rewound the footage. One of them came into plain sight a few seconds later: a thickset, jowl-faced man with studs on his forehead.

'Got you,' Vankova muttered, and dragged her thumb and forefinger over the man's face on the display in a pinching motion. The shot flashed up onto yet another tertiary screen which had until now been mostly blank, while images flickered up alongside it as the unit attempted to match his features against security camera feeds from the docks. While it was working she skipped back over a few more seconds of street-level feed until the other man came into view; taller and thinner, with a shaved head, his face was also selected and appeared alongside his companion's.

'We've got a route deviation,' Karhan spoke up suddenly. He pointed to where the party had headed straight on at a junction instead of turning left towards where the icon for Lavric's warehouse sat.

'A mistake?' Rybak asked.

'The girl's supposed to work for Lavric,' Jenna pointed out, 'she shouldn't get lost showing people to where she works.'

'Damn,' Karhan muttered, tightening the focus on some of his cameras, 'we figured the ambush would be at the warehouse and the girl was just so they knew the timing. It's going to be somewhere else.'

'And soon,' Jenna added, 'they must know the Captain would notice if he was being led too far off course.'

'The Captain?' Rybak was looking at her with a puzzled expression, and she silently cursed herself.

'Drift,' she clarified, 'he acts as the captain as . . . part of Agent Rourke's cover. We've sort of got used to calling him that. What I mean is, Kelsier's people would think he's in charge, and he's known to be smart, so—'

'There,' Rybak cut her off, finger jabbing at a plaza filled with stalls and kiosks on the overhead camera shot. 'They'll take them in St Methodius' Square. Open ground, time to shoot a runner before they can make one of the alleyways and get away.' She swore in a language Jenna didn't know and looked over at her. 'I hope you're right about them wanting to talk first.'

'So am I,' Jenna replied, her eyes glued to the screen. *It wasn't supposed to be in the square, it was supposed to be at the warehouse . . .*

'You thought about what you're going to do with your share of the money?' Micah asked as they traipsed through the streets of the Flats Markets, attracting some stares in the process. The Dutch mercenary's armavest looked a little out of place but at least he wasn't carrying his immolation cannon. Hroza Major's status as a frontier planet meant the Europan gun controls were looser, partially in case the Federation of African States decided to try to grab itself some more territory, but that sort of military-grade hardwear was still out of the question in such a supposedly respectable place as Glass City.

'The money?' Apirana replied, a little absently. Over his life, he'd largely got used to attracting attention, but he couldn't help but feel vulnerable and exposed despite the sizeable automatic pistol tucked into the small of his back under his top, the hood of which he was once more wearing up. Drift and Rourke had enough faith in the plan to be walking into what they strongly suspected was a trap, but Apirana was more than a mite uneasy about the whole thing.

'Yeah, the money we're going to get from Kelsier once we take him down.' Micah's eyes were enthusiastic, but at least he had the sense to keep his voice low as they pushed through the throng of Hrozans. Not that it would have probably mattered if he'd been bellowing in Apirana's ear; the surrounding traders and stallholders were doing a good enough job of hollering their wares that the sound of a small military engagement might have passed unnoticed.

Hopefully we don't have to test that theory, but I wouldn't place a bet . . .

'Honestly hadn't thought much about this past staying alive,' he admitted, turning side-on to squeeze through a gap between a stall of what looked to be red melons on one side and a table of unfamiliar tubers on the other. 'Why, you got your mind set on something?'

'I figure a man like that, he has to have a fair bit of cash tucked away,' Micah replied, 'and on an even seven-way split, that might be enough to retire on.'

Apirana blinked. 'Retire?'

'Yes,' the mercenary nodded, 'you think I want to be knocking around the galaxy for the rest of my life dodging bullets or waiting for Jia to fly us into something really solid?' He casually fended off a woman with a tray of what might have been aubergines. 'Think about it, A.: how long has the Captain been chasing a big score?'

'For longer'n I've been on the crew,' Apirana admitted.

'And has he ever managed it?' Micah asked. 'I mean, I've only been with you a couple of years, maybe you all got rich and then blew it.' The tone of his voice conveyed his opinion of how likely he felt that was.

'No,' Apirana sighed, 'something always seems t'get in the way . . .'

'Exactly.' Micah raised his eyebrows in what Apirana assumed was meant to be a meaningful way. The Maori felt his own creasing into a frown.

'I don't follow.'

'There's too many *complications* in this crew,' Micah said quietly, 'especially the Captain.' He cast a furtive glance ahead of them, where Drift's long-limbed, violet-haired shape could be seen walking alongside the girl sent to guide them. 'You've done your time for your crimes, am I right?'

'Yeah,' Apirana nodded, suppressing a slight grimace.

'*He never has*,' Micah pointed out. 'He's dodged or tricked or talked his way out of everything. And fair play, when we're in trouble he can be handy to have around because of that, but how many problems has his history caused us? I'm not just talking about this, now, I'm talking about all the jobs we haven't taken and all the places we've had to avoid without even *knowing* about it.'

Apirana grunted. This wasn't something he wanted to think about too hard; he still felt the cold bite of shame for how he'd behaved in the *Jonah*'s canteen. Once he'd calmed he'd started to realise that he'd always known the Captain must have had a shady history, and if he'd always been content to let it lie and had never been willing to ask the questions then what right did he have to get angry when the answers were unexpectedly revealed? But he'd felt foolish and his anger had risen automatically. His instinctive reaction to feeling stupid or incompetent was to place the blame elsewhere and get angry about it, no matter how much he came to regret it in the long run.

And he had nearly come to regret it immensely. He had a brief flashback of seeing Jenna's face turned up to him, eyes closed and features screwed up, her skin even whiter than usual as she waited for his fist to land. She possibly didn't even know how close he'd come to lashing out at her, how he'd teetered on the razor's edge for a long second, trying to fight down the impulse to obliterate this new provocation.

He became aware that Micah appeared to be expecting a response, and grunted noncommittally. 'So what're you saying?'

'I'm saying that if we stay on this crew then you and I are going to be getting shot at and busting our knuckles on people's faces for the Captain's schemes until we're too old to do it anymore,' Micah said quietly. 'I'm sure as hell not managing to save anything up. If we get a decent score off Kelsier's corpse, I'm thinking of cutting loose. You know, *invest*. Maybe buy a bar somewhere; borders change and politics shift, but people will always want liquor.' He grinned suddenly, a quick flash of white teeth in the darkness of his face. 'Present company excepted, of course.'

'An' you're telling me this because . . .?' Apirana asked, trying to keep an eye on what was going on around them. There were just so many *people* in this market . . .

'Wondered if you might be interested in throwing in,' Micah shrugged nonchalantly. 'You're a sound guy, not just a dumb *worger*, I reckon you've got a head for business. Besides, double the starting money means more choice of venue.'

'You're not considering the possibility that we might die first, then?' Apirana snorted as they emerged from the alley into a wider square awash with the weak, white light of Perun. The mercenary just shrugged.

'There's no point planning for a future in which you're dead. I just—'

'Then shut up a second,' Apirana cut him off, partially raising one hand while trying to reach casually under the back of his top with the other. Micah frowned, his own hand straying to the holstered gun at his belt.

'Problem?'

'Yeah, this place,' Apirana replied, looking around. 'Me an' the Captain didn't come through here on the way t'Lavric's last time. We're being taken by a different route.'

'*Verrek*,' Micah muttered. Apirana saw the mercenary's eyes flicker upwards, scanning the windows around them. 'We're sitting ducks here, I don't care what the plan is.' He raised his voice so the others could hear him over the bustle of the market. 'We need to get into—'

There was a hiss, and he cut off with a choking

sound. Apirana watched him in confusion for half a second as Micah's left hand rose towards his throat, but then a terrible comprehension dawned in the mercenary's eyes moments before the hissing sound came again and two of the Dutchman's fingers were sheared off by the passage of a second stargun disc into his neck. Micah dropped to his knees in front of Apirana's horrified gaze, his right hand still fumbling with his holster.

'*Ambush!*' Apirana roared, hauling his gun out and desperately searching for the threat. He saw it a moment later, through the crowd which had suddenly realised that guns were being drawn and fired in their midst and were starting to scream and run: a man with his stargun still raised and his face obscure by a virulently coloured mask . . . but it wasn't a mask, Apirana realised with a shock. It was an electat.

The Laughing Man.

How long had the Laughing Man been a figure of legend in the galaxy's underworld? Twelve years? Fifteen? Apirana had first started hearing tales of him in prison on Farport, when new inmates came in bearing dark rumours of callous executions and impossible assassinations. By the time he'd got out again, the man known as Marcus Hall was the unquestioned king of contract killers, a dark myth with an undeniably real core. Only one thing was really understood about him: if he'd taken a contract on you, you might as well arrange a comfortable way to die and save yourself some trauma.

Apirana had seen bad things in his life. Hell, he'd done more than a few. Even so, it was one thing to know that a man such as Hall existed, and quite another to see him walking towards you. His body reacted a fraction slower than it would have normally, sheer panic freezing his muscles for a split second. Long enough, as it turned out, for his hood to be snatched down from behind and something cold and round to be placed at the base of his neck.

'Drop it, big man,' someone snarled. Apirana risked a glance sideways and saw other members of the rapidly thinning crowd around him had also broken cover and were now holding guns on his crewmates. His anger flared for a moment, a brief crimson flash of desire to turn and wreak bloody vengeance on the man behind him, but he fought it down. He opened his hand to let the gun fall and stared straight ahead, hands raised to the sides of his head, guiltily grateful that the screams and shouts around him were largely obscuring the bubbling wheezes which were Micah van Schaken's last actions in life.

The Laughing Man's eyes flickered across the group, presumably checking that they were all covered by the motley selection of gun hands he had with him. Several of these were cybernetically enhanced, Apirana noticed; it meant they'd blended in well with the market's workers, some of whom would be hauling large crates or pallets of goods around, but it also seemed that Kelsier had a definite preference for metal in his employees. The girl Natalija was nowhere to be seen. Apirana wondered if she'd been a plant all along, or simply an innocent decoy told to take them by a certain route.

'Captain Drift.' Hall's voice was deep and oddly accented. Apirana had never had much of an ear for accents anyway, but it certainly didn't sound familiar.

'Mr Hall.' The Captain wasn't bothering to hide his anger, or his tension. His face looked thunderous, but Apirana could read the nervousness there too. Drift knew this stood on a knife edge now. 'You have a uniquely unpleasant way of announcing yourself.'

'Van Schaken was Europan Special Forces,' the Laughing Man replied matter-of-factly, 'I eliminated him because his presence might have severely disrupted this conversation. He was possibly an even greater threat than Miss Rourke here, although I hope you'll note that I've arranged to have three guns covering her.' The flat eyes in his multicoloured face slid sideways for a second to where Rourke stood, arms slightly splayed and nostrils flared in fury. 'Consider it a compliment.'

'Go fuck yourself, Hall,' Rourke spat.

Hall's expression didn't change, as least so far as it was possible to tell beneath the garish, distorted skull design covering his face. He simply turned back to Drift. 'Your crew's one short. Where's the girl?'

Drift's eyebrows quirked. 'Come again?'

'The slicer, McIlroy.' Hall's voice was hard, and Apirana suppressed a shiver of rage at the thought of him hunting Jenna down. 'She's not with you. Where is she?'

'She bailed on us back on Old Earth,' Drift replied, folding his arms. 'Didn't like the odds.'

'I hope for your sake that she didn't,' Hall said, his voice quiet. 'My instructions are to execute every member of your crew. I can either do that quickly and relatively painlessly, or I can hand the job over to these men, who will take their time. I suspect they'll leave you until last and make you watch, so I suggest *someone* tells me where to find McIlroy.'

Drift just glared at him, lips pressed so thin they'd almost disappeared.

'There is one other option,' Hall acknowledged. 'My employer values ingenuity and daring. He could find a place in his operation for you . . . or for Miss Rourke.' He turned back to face Rourke again. 'But only one of you. The first to speak up gets it.'

'You're scum, Hall,' Rourke snarled.

'I'm a *professional*, Tamara,' Hall replied without apparent rancour, 'and you have three guns pointing at you. As it stands, I look to have made the better life choices. But you can change your situation, if you want.'

'How come only they get the option to join?!' Kuai blurted out suddenly. The Laughing Man's gaze didn't waver from Rourke's face, but Apirana saw his lips purse slightly.

'If the engineer says anything which isn't telling us where McIlroy is, shoot him.' He sighed, then added, 'It doesn't have to be fatal.'

'You seem very unconcerned about the law,' Drift spoke up. 'Here we are, standing in the open with you holding us at gunpoint and one of my crew dead on the ground. Aren't you worried the authorities might be taking an interest?'

'My employer has a certain pull in these parts,' Hall replied, 'but you're correct, we should hurry. Yourself or Miss Rourke have ten seconds to accept my employer's offer, or someone tells me where to find McIlroy, at which point everyone dies efficiently and very quickly. Otherwise we take you somewhere unpleasant and these men set to work on you all until we find the slicer, which could take some considerable time. Ten.'

'Hold on,' Drift said, his face taking on a slightly desperate expression which Apirana could well identify with, 'we—'

'Nine.'

'—look, why—'

'Eight.'

'Just *hold on* a—'

'Seven.'

'We can pay—'

'Six.'

'Damn you, Hall—'

'Five.'

Apirana forced himself to breathe out and tried to relax some of his muscles. He was only going to get one shot at this. The slim upside was that if it went wrong he'd probably never know about it.

'Four.'

'You'll never—'

'Three.'

'*I accept.*'

Apirana stiffened again as the count stopped. The voice had belonged to Tamara Rourke.

'Tamara!' Drift cried, shock plastered over his features.

'You *fucking* bitch!' Kuai shouted furiously, a second before a gunshot went off and blood spattered from his calf. He went down in a screaming heap; Jia cried out in alarm and tried to move towards her brother, but was hauled back by her collar and had the barrel of a gun pressed to her cheek by her captor, a dark-skinned woman with her hair woven into narrow braids.

'*Don't* stop covering her,' Hall ordered the thugs, who obediently kept their guns trained on Rourke. The Laughing Man seemed to study her for a few seconds, then nodded very slightly. 'A good decision. I don't for a second imagine it's a genuine offer on your part, but that's not my call to make. My employer seems to think that you can be persuaded, given time, so that's what will happen. Where is McIlroy?'

'She's on the *Jonah*,' Rourke answered instantly, 'we needed her there monitoring the feeds, and to make sure no one could get into it even if they had the access codes. She'll have to open it from the inside.'

Hall exhaled. 'Which I imagine she would be unlikely to do for us. This explanation requires us to keep at least some of you alive and undamaged. How very convenient.'

Rourke's expression didn't waver. 'I can't change the truth just because you don't like it, Hall.'

The Laughing Man snorted. 'You're a former GIA agent, Tamara. You should be able to change *anything*, should you need to. Very well, we'll play it your way.' He nodded to the gun hands.

'We'll blow the ship up. Kill th—'

A shot rang out before the Laughing Man had finished speaking. Apirana winced automatically, but it hadn't heralded the brief swirl of red and black pain which was how he imagined taking a bullet to the brain might feel. Instead, one of the three thugs covering Rourke jerked and collapsed, his head exploding like one of the red melons they'd seen earlier being hit with a sledgehammer. Everyone froze in shock for half a second, but this time Apirana's body reacted fastest.

He spun to his left, his raised arm knocking the gun barrel away before the man holding it could pull the trigger, although he heard the report of other gunshots around him. He had a vague impression of a jowly, pale-skinned face with decorative studs across the forehead, and then his right fist slammed into the thug's jaw with an audible *crack*. The man went down and stayed down: Apirana threw himself as flat as he could, scrabbling for the gun he'd relinquished earlier with fingers which had suddenly become unhelpfully numb and tried to take stock of what was happening.

Several of Kelsier's gun hands were prone and not moving, red pools spreading out from their bodies across the flat stones which made up the floor of the market. Apirana saw a couple of backs disappearing into a side alley and raised his gun, but by the time he'd got it up they'd rounded a corner and the shot was gone. In a handful of seconds, the crew had gone from surrounded and held at gunpoint to being alone save for the dead and the dying. Jia dropped down beside her brother and for a moment Apirana felt his stomach clench in worry, but then the pilot pulled her jacket off and held it to the bleeding wound in Kuai's leg, which caused the little mechanic to cry out in pain again and Jia to scold him in Mandarin.

+*Come in, Agent Rourke.*+ A voice flavoured with Slavic vowels crackled in the comm in his ear, and he saw Rourke raise one hand to touch her own. Her other hand held the one-shot palmgun, which had been tucked up her sleeve the whole time. +*What's your situation?*+

'Took you long enough,' Rourke snapped. She glanced over at Kuai, who was still groaning on the ground, then at Apirana. 'A., you okay?'

'Fine,' he replied, levering himself up, 'jus' didn't fancy standing in a firefight.' He looked over at Micah, then looked away again with a flash of mixed guilt, anger and grief. He didn't need a closer inspection to see that the Dutch mercenary was beyond medical help. 'Micah's gone, though.'

'Poor bastard,' Rourke sighed, then addressed the unseen speaker on the comm again. 'We've got one in need of medical attention. What happened to Hall? I got a shot off at him, but then had to get down.'

+*We lost sight of him heading towards the north side.*+ There was a brief pause. +*We seem to have lost contact with our team there.*+

'Shit,' Rourke swore, exchanging a look with Drift. 'How many got away?'

+*We counted twelve in total, not including Hall.*+ Apirana looked around, counting the bodies. Two, four, five, six . . .

'Seven down,' Rourke reported, 'so five got away. Your other teams know what to do?'

+*They'll stand off unless there's a risk to the public.*+

'Good. Give Jenna the signal; this is the only chance we're going to have to get the intel we need.'

'Not quite,' Apirana said, looking down at the man he'd struck. A little overweight, dressed in unremarkable overalls, dark hair thinning on top and spiralling tattoos up both arms. He felt his anger fire up again; anger at Micah's death, anger at Kuai taking a bullet in the leg, anger at them being forced into this ridiculous situation in the first place. 'I only knocked this guy out. An' I think he's starting t'come round . . .'

Jenna bit her knuckle, willing her crew to notice that the trap they were expecting appeared to be closing around them sooner than they'd thought. The terminal *pinged* to her right, but she barely registered it.

'I've got a face match,' Vankova said. Moments later the sound came again. 'Make that two matches. Both of them from the day before yesterday, both came in from the Market Docks.'

'Got a ship ident?' Karhan asked, while he adjusted controls to track the progress of the *Keiko*'s crew through the market.

'Working on it . . .' Vankova replied, her voice a little testy. 'Right, both look to have come from the *Raggety Edge*, assuming that's her real name, currently in bay Alpha Two Nine—'

'They're in the square,' Rybak cut her off, leaning

forwards with one hand on the back of Karhan's chair. 'Where's the response team?'

'Too fucking far away!' Karhan snarled, gesturing at the highlighted location of Lavric's warehouse. 'Tell them to get moving or we might have the deaths of a GIA team on our heads!'

'A.'s noticed,' Jenna said, her voice sounding tiny and quavery in her ears as Rybak snapped something quiet but urgent over the comm. She watched helplessly as the big man's hood turned from side to side and saw one hand reach towards the small of his back where he'd stowed his gun. Beside him, Micah's fingers also began reaching for the pistol holstered at his hip, but then the Dutch mercenary seemed to jerk oddly. A second later and he jerked again, then collapsed.

'No!' Jenna shouted uselessly at the screen. 'For fuck's sake, get out of there! *Run!*'

'Man down,' she heard Rybak say tightly. 'Where's the shooter?'

On the overhead view, Jenna saw a small blotch of red starting to form where Micah had fallen, and she bit down on her knuckles to prevent herself from crying out again. She saw Apirana pull his gun out, sweeping the crowd with it as he looked for their attackers, saw the ripples of panic spread through the market-goers around them . . .

'Shit!' Karhan gasped, and the tone of shock in his voice was so pronounced that she looked away from the bird's-eye view to where the veteran surveillance officer was pointing. Another holo display showed a view across the square, and moving towards Apirana and the others was a man with a raised weapon and a riot of colours for a face.

'*Jezus Kristus*,' Rybak breathed in horror. 'The Laughing Man.'

Jenna stared at the image with a sick feeling building in her stomach. She'd never heard of the Laughing Man until a few weeks ago, and even then not in detail. None of the crew would tell her more than the barest details about him, not even Apirana. Somehow, she suspected that the leering, neon skull obscuring his face was all the detail she needed.

'They're surrounded,' Rybak said grimly. Jenna looked back at the overhead view and saw to her horror that she was correct: while the rest of the crowd were fleeing, some of its members had pulled hidden guns on the *Keiko*'s crew and got the drop on them. One of the two tails they'd identified now had a gun to the back of Apirana's head, and she waited in horror for him to pull the trigger. Then the moment passed and the Laughing Man moved towards where Drift stood, unnaturally still.

'He's going to talk,' Karhan breathed, 'thank God.'

'Too late for Micah,' Jenna snapped.

'Small mercies,' Karhan grimaced. He looked up at another screen, showing a group of blue-armoured shapes making their way through the streets towards St Methodius' Square. 'I hope that "Captain" of yours can keep him busy for a couple of minutes.'

'Talking's what the Captain does best,' Jenna said absently, nails digging into her palm.

'They've got some damn cheek, pulling something like this in the open,' Rybak muttered angrily. 'The police here must be corrupt as hell.'

'Not all of them,' Karhan retorted sharply. He started selecting members of the Laughing Man's gang, highlighting them on the system and seeking camera angles which would show their faces. 'Sara, we need idents on all of them, and ships of origin.'

'Including that bastard,' Rybak growled, indicating the assassin talking to Drift. Karhan focused one of the street-level cameras on the Laughing Man again, who'd apparently said something to infuriate Rourke.

'It won't pick him up!' Vankova exclaimed in frustration.

'What do you mean?' Karhan demanded, looking over at her display. Jenna followed his gaze: sure enough, face after face was appearing and being run through the records, the roar of the terminal's cooling fans rising as it accessed more and more processing power, but the Laughing Man's wasn't among them.

'It just won't pick him up!' Vankova said again, helplessly. 'It must be the electat; all those fucking colours are throwing off the contour recognition software.'

'Okay, fine,' Karhan muttered, 'so we track him back to a time when he hasn't activated the electat, he can't have just been walking around like that all day—'

'They've shot Kuai!' Jenna exclaimed in horror as the little mechanic suddenly dropped to the ground. She breathed slightly more easily a moment later when he writhed around clutching his leg instead of lapsing into a horrible stillness as Micah had, but nonetheless the sick, impotent feeling was threatening to overwhelm her. 'How long until your team get there?!'

'Maybe thirty seconds until they're in position,' Rybak replied.

'To hell with "position",' Jenna snarled, 'just—'

'If they start shooting too early then *they* will die and *your team* will die,' Rybak cut her off harshly. 'They need to hit these bastards all at once so they're either dead before they can think to pull a trigger on your friends or they're running away. Besides, they need the right angles of fire; bullets will go straight through a human body.'

Jenna bit down on a retort. What the Europan captain said made sense, but she still couldn't bear the thought of her crew being in danger for a second longer. She had to fight the impulse to try to snatch one of the trooper's weapons and run through the streets herself, even knowing that she'd never get it, find her way there in time or probably be able to hit anything even if she did. She watched Rourke and the Laughing Man exchange silent words, trying to read meaning from a pair of faces seemingly carved from granite for all the information they gave away. Then the assassin looked away from Rourke, nodded to someone—

There was a spatter of red and Jenna saw one of Kelsier's thugs drop; she barely had time to draw breath before more followed. In a moment, the picture changed from the *Keiko*'s crew surrounded at gunpoint to them turning on their ambushers while unseen marksmen picked off anyone still upright. Anyone, that was, except for four figures racing for the south side of the square.

'Team One, fall back and *do not engage*,' Rybak snapped over the comm. 'Let them out; they're our leads, over.'

'Where's the Laughing Man?' Vankova asked nervously. 'Did they get him?'

'Headed north,' Karhan replied. His fingers danced over the controls as the views on different screens zoomed in, zoomed out, panned around . . . 'Damn it! Where the hell is he?'

'Team Three?' Rybak spoke and waited. 'Team Three, come in, over.'

There was a pause.

'Team Three, please respond, over.'

'Shit!' Karhan slammed his fist into arm of his chair, clearly not needing to wait for his captain's confirmation. 'How the hell did he—'

'Never mind him for now,' Jenna said grimly, getting to her feet and picking up her slicer's bag. The Europans stared at her in astonishment, except for Vankova who was still scanning the displays.

'Never mind him?!' Rybak asked incredulously. 'He must have just taken out one of my teams!'

'And he just killed one of my friends!' Jenna shot back angrily. 'But I've got a job to do, or this will have been for nothing! Hunt him down if you want, but for now tell me what ships the other four came in on!'

'We've got . . . one from the *Raggety Edge*, one from the *Child of Winter*, and it looks like two from the *Early Dawn*,' Sara Vankova replied crisply. She looked around at Jenna, her expression a mix of nervousness and sympathy. 'The *Early Dawn* and *Raggety Edge* are closer to them; *Child of Winter* is in the Low Docks.'

'Two of them came in on the closest ship, that's probably the one they'll make for,' Karhan said, biting his lip. He narrowed his eyes as he looked at Jenna. 'You up to this?'

'I'm going to have to be,' Jenna replied, although her stomach seemed to be suggesting that throwing up would be a good move right about now.

'Right then,' Vankova said, getting to her feet and picking up a bag of her own. She gave Jenna a smile which might have been made of spun sugar judging by how fragile it appeared. 'Let's do this.'

RUN RABBIT, RUN

The *Early Dawn* was an imposing, *Sei*-class multi-use vessel; larger and bulkier than the *Carcharodon*-class which the *Jonah* belonged to, it could take nearly twice the cargo but had a reputation for engine trouble. Jenna adjusted the thermal hood of her dock-tech jacket and checked the read-out on her Hrozan-issue pad, then looked up at the craft's snub nose again. 'You're *certain* this is the right one?'

+*Trust me*,+ Sara Vankova's voice came over the comm in her ear, +*this is the bay. Besides, this is an illegal vessel; there's hatches for concealed weapons in that bow, or I'm a Member of Parliament.*+

Jenna blinked, her eyes seeing nothing but what looked to be standard heat shielding. 'Really?'

+*Look, just read the ident then.*+

Jenna tapped some keys and the lines of text flashed up on her pad. Sure enough, the ship was purporting to be the *Early Dawn*, although Jenna would have bet circuits to static that it was officially registered as something different. She took a deep breath, tasting the rubber and plastic of her breath mask as she did so, and pulled back her sleeve. This exposed the flesh of her arm to the chill not-air around her, but she needed to access her wrist terminal. A few quick taps synced it – and more importantly, the Truth Box she'd quietly pocketed during the ruckus on Void Station Pundamilia and which formed the basis of her wrist-mounted and thoroughly illegal slicing rig – with her Hrozan pad. Suddenly she had the ability to slide through the shuttle's security systems without looking like she was using a device with anywhere near enough processing power for such a task.

+*How long is this going to take?*+ Vankova asked nervously. A surveillance officer's presence was necessary because Jenna didn't know how to operate the devices in Vankova's bag, and wouldn't have been entrusted with them anyway; Vankova was here instead of Karhan simply because she was smaller and quicker, so could run away and hide more easily if it came to it. That said, Jenna got the impression that the veteran might have been a more reassuring companion, especially given that she herself was trying to pretend this was the sort of thing she did all the time as a supposed GIA operative.

'Not long,' she answered, a flash of smugness momentarily overriding her nervous nausea as the pressure seals released and the entrance ramp started to lower. To anyone else it would look like two Hrozan dock-techs were being allowed on board by someone in the cockpit: it certainly shouldn't have been possible to slice their way inside in such a short period of time using a basic pad. 'Let's go.'

+*That was impressive,*+ Vankova said admiringly as they waited for the ramp to reach the deck. +*How'd you do that?*+

'Product of a misspent youth,' Jenna replied honestly, taking a quick look from side to side. The docks were bustling with their usual business and there were no signs of desperately fleeing thugs, but given the sheer amount of people, crawlers and ships around, Kelsier's goons might have been a hundred yards away and she wouldn't have known. 'Come on.'

They hurried up the ramp as fast as they dared. If anyone working for Kelsier was watching this ship then the game was as good as up anyway, but the last thing they needed was some well-meaning bystander to decide something suspicious was going on and poke his nose in. Jenna called it up behind them, leaving them standing in the *Early Dawn*'s cavernous bay. There were a couple of cargo containers, one with its doors open and looking to be empty, some equipment lockers on the far wall much like the ones in the bay of the *Jonah*, a small haulage buggy with two wheels at the front and tracks at the rear, and an overhead crane system which looked to have considerably more durability to it than the slightly ramshackle one Jenna was used to.

+*This way,*+ Sara said, heading for the airlock which would lead them towards the bridge. Jenna followed her, the rushing of air growing louder as the atmosphere thickened around them, the *Early Dawn*'s pumps working to make the cargo bay breathable again. By the time they'd climbed up the four flights of steel steps the light over the airlock was glowing green and the doors slid open with a faint whine to grant them access to the ship beyond.

The first thing which greeted Jenna's eyes as the corridor lights flickered on was a gun rack, lined with half a dozen assault rifles and a couple of starguns; an unpleasant reminder of Micah's recent fate, not to mention what would happen to her and Sara if they were caught. She swallowed and pushed onwards, peeling her thermo-hood back and the rebreather off her face. The galley was on their left and some of the cabins on their right, with more sitting directly over the main cargo bay – the cramped crew conditions, despite the large size of the ship, was another reason why the *Sei*-class wasn't a hugely popular model except with captains eager for a high capacity-to-size ratio – but the bridge lay directly ahead. A second set of doors slid aside as they approached, these ones with a slight grinding noise suggesting that something somewhere was thinking about giving out, and then they'd reached their target.

'Right,' Jenna muttered, shrugging out of her thermojacket, which was rapidly becoming too warm, 'navigation terminal.' She looked blankly at the unfamiliar layout of seats and terminals. 'Any ideas?'

'I thought you were a slicing expert?' Sara said worriedly. The Hrozan's fringe was stuck to her forehead, sweaty from her hood, nerves, or both, and she was digging about in her bag.

'That doesn't mean I know what they look like from the *outside*,' Jenna pointed out, perhaps a little

more sharply than she'd intended. She tried to
picture the *Jonah*'s bridge and keep herself from
peering out over the snub nose of the shuttle to see
if she could spot any sign of its owners approaching.
Come on, Jenna, think. There were two chairs at
the very front of the cockpit, but one was considerably more worn than the other and the controls in
front of it had marks scratched onto them, presumably noting where the optimum thrust points were,
or flap angles or . . . whatever, she was making
things up now. 'Right, that must be the main pilot's
chair, which means it would make most sense for
the navigation console to be . . . this one.' She hit
the start-up button on a terminal and watched it
flicker into life, biting her lip until it became painful
to try to stop herself from fidgeting.

'*Goddamnit*, where's the transmitter array?' Sara
hissed behind her.

'Pull a schematic off the main system,' Jenna
advised her absently, focusing on the screen in front
of her. *Aha . . .*

'I'm not a slicer!'

Jenna hissed in frustration – *How was it possible
to be a surveillance officer and not even know how
to find a schematic on a system? It didn't even involve
any slicing* – but tapped her pad a few times and slid
something over to Sara's. 'There.'

She focused on the navigation terminal, for so it
had proved to be, and opened the log. Of course,
the *Early Dawn* didn't have the processing power to
calculate Alcubierre jumps – that would be done by
whatever carrier ship was waiting for it in orbit –
but nevertheless, its navigation systems would still

faithfully keep track of where it was at any given time, and more importantly where it *had* been.

'It's near the engine room,' Sara said, sounding frustrated. 'Why the hell would it be back there?'

Jenna rolled her eyes. 'I don't know, but you'd better get a move on if you're going . . .' She heard boots leaving and turned around to see an absence of Sara Vankova, the surveillance officer apparently having taken her advice before she'd finished giving it. She shrugged and turned back to her work, slapping the comms terminal into life and acutely aware of how sweaty her fingers felt on the keys, and saved the last two months of log data from the navigation console into a separate file. She slid that file over to the comms terminal and started narrowing the broadcast band. Drift had encoded a very specific frequency into her wrist console before they'd split up a week prior and she'd gone undercover with the Europan authorities. In a few moments she'd have dropped this file over to the *Jonah* and...

. . . and those four people were pretty much running towards the *Early Dawn*.

She ducked instinctively, despite the fact that the refraction of the thick spaceshield would render her invisible from outside at such a low angle, and looked again. Yes, four of them, three men and a woman so far as she could tell under the bulky clothes and rebreathers, coming straight for her.

Oh shit.

'Focus,' she muttered to herself, wrenching her gaze away. Check frequency again; send the nav log; *comeoncomeoncomeon*; while that's transmitting, remove record of file compiling from nav console; shut down nav console; *you bastard, why do you take longer to shut down than you did to start up?!* File sent! Remove transmission record from comms terminal log; check outside again . . .

Shit! We're not going to make it!

She stared blankly at the hurrying shapes for one second, two seconds, trying to comprehend what her brain had already realised.

We're not going to make it.

Jenna took a deep breath, let it out again.

Okay. So we hide.

Heart hammering, she turned back to the comms terminal. Check transmission record is deleted; turn terminal off; *don't make me pull the plug on you*; access main system through the pad and depressurise cargo bay again, or they'll know someone's been on the ship . . .

Somewhere behind her there was a faint whine as the fans started up again, emptying the cargo bay of the oxygen they'd dumped into it scant minutes before. The nav console's display winked out: Jenna turned and scanned the cockpit, snatching up her thermojacket from where she'd let it drop and desperately searching for anything else incriminating which either she or Sara might have left. She saw nothing and scrambled out of the door, sealing it behind her, then headed for the stairway which would take her up and over the cargo bay into the crew dorms. She paused at the airlock to peer through the narrow window; sure enough, the ramp was starting to drop away to let the ship's rightful owners on.

She didn't dare use her comm to try to contact Sara, just in case Kelsier's crew were monitoring channels or simply using the same one by coincidence. She also wished that she'd used the ship's comm to send a message along with the nav log, even one which just said 'will try to hide', but there was no use for that now. Instead she stuffed her thermojacket into her bag as well as she could and ran up the steps to the dorm corridor, fumbling with her pad to call the ship schematics up again.

The door at the top of the steps seemed unwilling to open at first, although that was probably her imagination. She ran past half a dozen cabin doors, three on each side, almost before the lights had time to register her presence and flicker on, then was brought up short by the door at the other end. She hammered the release button and for a heart-stopping moment thought she'd broken it, but then it grumbled reluctantly aside and she nearly fell down the steps towards the infirmary.

She paused for a moment to grab a look through the airlock on this side of the cargo bay. Three of the crew were running up the steps on the opposite side towards the bridge, but only three.

Which meant the other one was likely heading for the engine room.

'Sara!' she yelled, trusting that the airtight seal on the cargo-bay door and the hopefully still-thin atmosphere within it wouldn't let the sound give her away. 'Find somewhere to hide! *Now!*' She raced past the infirmary, turned a corner in the corridor and nearly collided with the Europan surveillance officer, who was fiddling with a panel in the wall. Sara's head whipped around to look at her, her thick braid colliding with the metal panelling with a soft *thunk*.

'What?' the other girl asked, eyes wide in panic.

'They're on,' Jenna hissed, grabbing her by the shoulders. 'Find somewhere to hide, come on!'

'But I haven't... wait, they're *on board*?!' Sara's eyes widened further, if that were possible.

'Yes, and one's coming this way!' Jenna gave up on words and began propelling the Hrozan towards the engine room. She slapped the door release, prayed to whatever deities might be listening that the faint noise of it either opening or shutting wouldn't give them away, and bundled Sara through it.

The lights in the engine room flickered on and Jenna was faced with two roughly chest-height banks of metal running away from them down the length of the room, presumably enclosing pistons or . . . something, this really wasn't her area of expertise. There were various panels of switches and levers scattered around, as well as bits of pipework and what looked like large, shiny hoses, but there was only one immediately obvious hiding place. Well, two.

'Down the end!' she snapped at Sara as the door started to grind shut again. 'Get behind one of these metal things, crouch down and keep quiet!'

It was perhaps thirty feet away, but it felt like the longest dash Jenna had ever made. At any moment she expected to hear a shout from behind them, or a gunshot. They'd be boxed in, and what chance would they have had even if they weren't? A slicer and a surveillance officer against four armed thugs?

There was no shout, and no gunshots. Sara dived to the right and Jenna scrambled to the left, pulling her bag and jacket in after her and tucking her feet in to minimise any chance of being seen from the other end of the room. Sara mimicked her, and for a moment the only sound was that of the other girl's ragged breathing.

Then the door hissed open again.

Jenna desperately pressed her finger to her lips in an attempt to get Sara to breathe more quietly, even while her mind repeated a panicked mantra: *Please don't notice the lights; please don't notice the lights; please don't notice the lights* . . .

Whoever had followed them in clearly had too much on their mind to worry about lights already being on, however. There were some frantic scrabblings and what sounded like dials being twisted or adjusted, then a voice which sounded shockingly loud as it echoed around the metal confines of the room:

'Come *on*, you piece of shit!'

A deep mechanical cough answered this plea, which was delivered in a desperate male baritone, and Jenna felt the floor shudder beneath her; then a rumble started up, growing in volume and power as the engine of the *Early Dawn* roared into life around them. The voice returned, shouting now to be heard over the noise.

'Okay, we've got power!'

There was a crackling noise, barely audible above the engine: a comm broadcast, some of the words inaudible.

+*What about . . . can we . . . if . . .?*+

'How the hell should I know?' the voice demanded angrily. 'Jensen was the mechanic! You want to wait for her? No? Then get us in the fucking air and let's get out of here before the authorities wake up!' Jenna heard steps, boots on metal, and then the faintest of noises just audible above the engines signifying the door opening again. She waited until she heard it shut, waited a few more seconds to be sure, and then peered very cautiously around the edge of her hiding place.

They were alone.

The breath rushed out of her and she almost collapsed against the cold metal of the engine bank; not pressed tight up against it in fear, but the loose-limbed, jelly-muscled slump of abject relief. Seconds later though, the tightening in her belly returned. Yes, they were alone, but they were still trapped in a non-too-large shuttle about to head for space, with four people who would probably kill them on sight. And that might be if they got lucky.

'What do we do now?' Sara asked, her voice barely more than a squeak. 'How do we get—' There was a jolt beneath them. 'Oh *God*, are we taking off?!'

Jenna sighed. She was used to thinking of herself as the newbie, the one out of her depth in any situation except when slicing was directly involved, but she was quickly coming to realise that there was a world of difference between what she'd been through in the last year and Sara Vankova's experience of watching screens showing events as they happened to other people.

'We sit tight, we stay out of sight, we wait,' she said, as calmly as she could manage. 'I got the log broadcast off; your team and my crew will be following this ship.'

'I didn't attach the transmitter yet though!' Sara hissed. Jenna shrugged uncomfortably.

'Well . . . we're not going anywhere. I'm guessing you'll get another chance.'

Sara sat back, her head knocking against the metal behind her. 'Oh, Jesus.'

There was silence for a few seconds, or as close to it as the engine room would get now until they were swallowed up by whatever interstellar transport was waiting for them. Then Sara spoke again.

'So . . . what do we do if they find us?'

Jenna reached into her bag and pulled out the gun Drift had insisted she take with her. She wasn't too familiar on the make or model, but he'd told her that it had a fully loaded magazine of twenty shots and had made sure she remembered where the safety was. It was meant as a last-resort measure only, although had she known she was going to be unintentionally kidnapped by their targets she'd have asked for a couple of spare magazines just to be on the safe side.

She glanced over at Sara, who was looking at the gun as though it were an intemperate viper. 'Can you shoot straight?'

'Not really,' the surveillance officer replied in a small voice. 'I just do cameras and bugging. Stuff like that.'

'Oh. Good.' Jenna looked away from the Hrozan girl and closed her eyes. 'Neither can I.'

THE LAUGHING MAN

Despite himself, he was impressed.

It was utterly infuriating of course, and he was disappointed with himself that he hadn't seen it coming, but he still couldn't help but feel a sneaking sense of admiration that the crew of the *Keiko* had bluffed the Europan authorities into their pockets. It was the work of people who knew their backs were against the wall and had gambled everything. He'd never been a gambling man. He'd never seen the point of trusting to luck.

That was, for example, why he'd run for it the moment it became clear that things were not as his employer had planned. It was also why he'd been prepared for a lack of omniscience on his employer's part, and had brought his usual selection of equipment with him. The five-man Europan fireteam he'd encountered during his flight had presumably been expecting terrified, disorganised thugs instead of the galaxy's top assassin with a primed, military-issue stun grenade. Their moments of disorientation in its immediate aftermath had cost them their lives: regrettable deaths, of course, but if they'd been truly concerned about their own mortality they presumably would not have joined the armed forces in the first place.

Unless, of course, they'd signed up to fight their government's enemies with lethal weaponry but had thought that they were somehow special, and would live charmed lives. He shook his head briefly at such a ridiculous notion. He'd been an indifferent student of physics at best, but so far as he was aware death was one of the constants of the universe, like gravity. If you placed yourself in a position where you were at a higher risk of death, you could hardly claim surprise if it found you earlier. It was like jumping off a cliff on a planet with a strong gravity well and being surprised that you hit the ground. Of course, a career as an assassin might also seem likely to end his life prematurely, but the point of being an assassin was that you didn't wear a uniform and you didn't stand in front of your enemies.

Well, except in special circumstances.

He'd found a way into the sewers shortly after disposing of the fireteam and had followed the schematics on his pad to come up through an access panel in a residential block. The Europan authorities might work out where he'd gone eventually, even though he'd used flash-strips to weld the first manhole in place behind him. All he needed was a little time and some cover. Once the trail was broken they would be reduced to scanning their surveillance feeds to see where he emerged.

The odds of anyone coming into the boiler room in the short period of time he'd be in there were minimal, but he left his stargun close at hand anyway while he pulled out his travel mirror. It was a sheet of silvery cloth, six feet long and three wide, with adhesive clamps at each corner, which he attached to the wall. A press of the activation switch tautened the cloth instantly and the small current transformed it into a near-perfect mirrored surface. It was meant as a space-saving travel accessory for those who didn't feel they could do without seeing their outfit in full, but he had another use for it. He quickly stripped off all his clothes and stood in front of the mirror, then concentrated.

The electat on his face, the leering skull trademark of the Laughing Man, had been allowed to subside the moment he'd got into the sewers. That was how the outside world identified him, and in many places once he'd discarded that uniform he was nondescript. Here though, on this rich Europan world with its face-scanning technology, he would need to be more subtle. He knew that his facial electat would have thrown off their scans while it was activated but they would be able to trace him back, sooner or later, to when he'd arrived plain-faced.

Time to change the game.

His skin started to change as he brought his *other* electat to the fore, the electat which covered his entire body, from the top of his head to the soles of his feet and all the nooks and crevices between, from eyelids to crotch. The process had been painful, and far longer than he'd have liked even with the use of tattooing machines. After all, there were certain sensitive areas which had needed to be done by hand. It had been expensive as well; even though he'd killed the artist shortly afterwards, he'd paid him first. The man had done the job well, after all, and he might have had a family to take care of. However, he simply couldn't afford any word to leak out. The galaxy knew of Marcus Hall the Laughing Man primarily by the leering skull, but it also knew that he was dark-skinned.

Once the electat was completely activated, the man who stared back at him from the mirror had skin the colour of milky coffee. He turned in place, inspecting himself to make sure that the work hadn't faded in any way, but it appeared to be unbroken. That would help a lot, but there was always the possibility that the face-scanning would see past skin colour.

First, he drew a laser depilator over his scalp to remove all his hair. Second, he broke his own nose. The pain made his eyes water, but with his electat activated he wasn't concerned about bruising giving it away as a recent injury. Then he inserted a lens into his left eye, changing its colour from his natural dark green to a grey-blue. Finally, he retrieved a custom-made prosthetic mechanical eye fitting which he placed over his right eye. It wasn't a true augmentation of course – both his natural eyes were in perfect condition – but it looked like one. The most expensive mechanical eyes fitted neatly in the natural socket and looked almost real unless they were studied closely, but the cheaper ones – such as the one sported by Ichabod Drift – were bulkier and had external structures on the face itself. That should be enough to throw off even the most ardent surveillance technology.

Of course, his fake eye couldn't be bonded to his skull while he was sedated, as was usual procedure for the real thing. Instead, multiple tiny barbed hooks pierced his skin to secure it in place. The pain made him bite his lip, but it was necessary. If he suffered a blow to the face then it would be torn loose and he could be badly wounded, but otherwise the barbs could be retracted with minimum damage when needed. The other option would have been adhesive, but that would take longer to dissolve and remove. Although painful, the flesh anchors meant the 'eye' could be taken off in a matter of seconds if necessary.

The clothes he'd been wearing during the ambush would have to be abandoned. He'd prefer to burn them, but starting a fire in here might set off the building's smoke alert systems. He tucked the top and trousers into a dark bend of pipework where no one would go looking unless they had good cause to, and redressed himself from his supplies. It was surprising how easily you could carry a change of clothes, if they were a thin fabric and vacuum-packed.

The stargun gave him more pause. It was an excellent weapon but an uncommon one, and possibly too distinctive after his killing of van Schaken. A random check might lead to dangerous suspicion being cast on him, even disguised. Besides, if he got into a situation from which he needed to fight his way free then the game was as good as up. He had no tertiary identity to turn to here.

He reached a decision: he would abandon his weapons. Many people went armed on Hroza Major – especially now, most likely – but by no means all. He needed to get off-planet as soon as possible and would just have to take the chance that his disguise would get him by any Europan checks before the authorities found his tools.

He went back to the manhole he'd climbed out of and dropped his remaining munitions in. It would signpost where he'd exited, but only if they'd already worked out that he'd taken to the sewers. That done, he stepped out into the fading light of the Hrozan day and headed for the nearest starport with the air of a man who had nothing to hide.

He wasn't going to report back to his employer. He'd decided that as soon as the first Europan shots had been fired. He'd been tiring of this long-running engagement of his services anyway, let alone using him as a common menial with a gang of thugs. He got paid, eliminated his target and moved on; that was how he'd always worked. So let Drift, Rourke and their crew play their dangerous game with the Europans. Had he been a gambling man, which of course he was not, he might have put money on them succeeding in running their quarry to ground. He wished them luck, for it would save him having to take any action himself. If his employer – now ex-employer – survived the *Keiko*'s crew's quest for vengeance and learned that the Laughing Man was still alive and had broken his contract, that might damage his reputation.

The streets were crawling with Europan police; not the counter-terrorism armed forces he'd recently killed five members of, but the regular law enforcers. He nodded amiably at two of them and received an absent-minded acknowledgement in return as they bustled past him.

So far, so good.

CONFLICTING FORCES

'What do you *mean*, you can't find him?'
      Tamara Rourke was seething. The inability
of the Europans to track Hall down had
stoked her cold rage until it felt like there was a small
star burning in her chest. She was a patient woman
– it was a lesson she'd learned painfully – but even
she wanted to go out and start tearing down Glass
City to find someone she could hurt for all the shit
she and her crew had been through in the last month
or so.
  Captain Sonja Rybak met her glare, although not
completely happily. She was clearly uncomfortable
about her forces' failures so far, but was pugnacious
enough to take the unspoken attitude that since she
was the one in command of the armed troops she
wouldn't be apologising for anything. Rourke forced
herself to remember that not only did they need this
woman to help find and eliminate Kelsier, they also

needed not to antagonise her sufficiently for her to start asking difficult questions.

'Glass City is large,' Rybak replied to Rourke's question, 'and I hope we can at least agree that the Laughing Man has been able to evade everyone sent after him so far in his "career"?'

'We can,' Rourke replied bitterly. A single well-placed bullet from her palmgun could have ended Hall's legacy, of course, but he'd reacted faster to the Europan counter-ambush and fled before she could get a shot away. She took a deep breath and, with an effort, pushed back her desire to get revenge on Micah's killer. *Another body to lay at Hall's door. There'll be a reckoning eventually.* Her living crew still needed her, one more than the others. 'I suppose you've learned nothing about Kelsier's location from the man Apirana was able to capture?'

'He's resisted our attempts to get information from him so far, although we've had barely any time,' Rybak replied. Her mouth twisted slightly, as though she'd suddenly encountered a bitter taste. 'Would your team . . .?'

It took Rourke a moment to realise what the Europan captain was implying, but then she shook her head firmly. 'No. I'm aware of the reputation the GIA has in some areas, but we're not all torturers and interrogation experts.'

Rybak managed to look both pleased and disappointed at once. Rourke could understand why; they desperately needed information, but handing over that sort of critical detail to a foreign team would rankle, quite apart from unease at the rumoured methods the GIA used. Still, there was nothing for it.

She'd hoped that Hall might prove more tractable if he was captured – he at least would owe Kelsier nothing, whereas it was anyone's guess how deep the captured thug's loyalty ran – but that option was closing to them as well.

'I think we need to proceed according to the original plan,' she told Rybak. 'It's been ninety minutes since the *Early Dawn* took off. We should start the pursuit.'

Rybak frowned. 'If we can just lay our hands on Hall—'

'We can't wait for that possibility,' Rourke cut her off. 'You said yourself, he's evaded every attempt at capture so far. We need to work with what we have, the nav data Jenna managed to transmit to us before . . .'

'Before she was kidnapped?' Rybak finished grimly. 'Agent, I don't know what sort of qualities your slicer may have, but Vankova isn't one of mine. She's local law enforcement, and won't have had training on resisting even the most rudimentary forms of torture. There's every chance the men and women on that ship know what our plans are and will simply set a different course to avoid Kelsier's base completely. Without the homing beacon Vankova was meant to set up, that nav data will only get us into roughly the right area. If it's an asteroid *field* then we could spend the next hundred years looking for our target!'

'You're thinking like a military commander now,' Rourke said, shaking her head. 'These aren't soldiers, Captain, they're criminals and terrorists. They might just abandon Kelsier if all seems lost, yes, but the man you've got in custody isn't spilling his guts yet and that makes me think the others will stay true, at least for now. They might disable the homing beacon, but they'll head back to the closest thing they have to safety. Your ships will be faster than whatever transport brought them here, even to a system next door. We'll be there on their tails, ready to see what they do and where they go.'

'*Our* ships might,' Rybak conceded, 'so would you be riding with us? Forgive me for saying, but that freighter of yours doesn't seem too spry.'

'You might be surprised,' Rourke smirked. It was true, too: the *Keiko*'s Alcubierre drive had been souped up to allow for faster transit between systems, although that had been done for more mundane commercial purposes than the sort of unseen GIA enhancements Rybak might assume it carried.

Rybak drummed her fingers on the desk, staring down at the plan of Glass City as though willing it to give up the location of the Laughing Man. Rourke had already done plenty of that though, and could see no obvious place for him to be hiding. Then again, an obvious hiding place wouldn't be a good hiding place . . . unless, of course, Hall was going for a double bluff.

She exhaled in frustration. Trying to second-guess the galaxy's most infamous assassin was a good way to drive oneself mad. 'Captain, I think we must leave the apprehension of Hall to others.' *Besides, the longer we stay here the more likely it is a message will come from Old Earth and blow our cover completely.* 'Homing beacon or not, element of surprise or not, our best chance now is to follow the leads we have before they go cold.'

Rybak nodded slowly in reluctant agreement. 'And your man van Schaken?'

'I believe he favoured cremation,' Rourke replied, a little uncomfortably. This was something an agent should know about her team, but Micah had never really been one for deep conversation. 'He never gave us specific instructions. Each of my crew know that there's no guarantee of returning their body to their home planet if they die in my service.'

'I'll make arrangements,' Rybak said. She looked up at Rourke questioningly. 'I assume you're happy for that to wait until we return?'

Rourke adopted the careful mask she'd used so many times over the years. There was no question of the *Keiko*'s crew returning to the Perun System after they'd left it, so Micah was likely to go to his rest alone and unmourned. However, somewhere out in the void, Jenna McIlroy was trapped on a hostile ship with nothing for support but an inexperienced surveillance technician and a handgun she'd shown no evidence of being able to fire effectively.

'Captain,' she said firmly, 'my duty now is to the living. Let's go find our terrorists, and get our people back.'

The time spent cramped behind a piece of uniden-
tifiable equipment in the engine room of the *Early
Dawn*, limbs tucked in awkwardly, barely daring
to speak in case someone came in at exactly the
wrong time, terrified of discovery, in near-total darkness only slightly alleviated by the light cast from
various control panels, constantly subjected to the
vibrations transmitted through the metal floor and
the casing she was pressed up against and really, really
needing to piss was, without a doubt, the most miserable period of Jenna McIlroy's existence so far. It
even beat out zero-gravity hockey in seventh grade,
which she'd been fairly certain was the most painful
and emotionally ravaging experience it was possible
to suffer without stepping inside a well-equipped
torture chamber.

Her mind had been her own worst enemy during
the hours the *Early Dawn* took to reach its parent

ship in orbit, wherever and whatever that was. Her body was suffering, it was true, but it was her brain which insisted on continually presenting her with ever-more violent and horrific scenarios of discovery, interrogation, abuse and execution. She hadn't dared try to use her comm to contact Drift or the others in case the signal got picked up – the only thing saving them was the fact that no one else on board knew they were there – so there was no one to talk to, to get advice from, to reassure her that it would be okay or to talk through a plan with her. Sara certainly wasn't much use for it: the Hrozan girl had spent a reasonable portion of the flight crying, although at least she'd done so quietly. It was left to Jenna to try to organise her own thoughts.

She noticed immediately when the whine of the engines changed. They'd been pushing hard, insofar as she could tell, which made sense; now, however, the throaty rumble died back a little. Moments later she felt herself being pressed harder against the metal behind her by the unseen hand of deceleration.

'What's happening?' Sara asked, a movement in the shadows behind her hiding place suggesting that she'd looked up. The last time Jenna had seen her, just before the motion-activated lights had winked out a few hours ago, her minimal make-up had been smudged from tears and she'd looked terrified. Jenna was quite glad she didn't need to control her own expression right now.

'Someone's just hit the retros.' The pressure grew stronger. '*Hard.*' Jenna took a firm grip on her bag to make sure it didn't slide and skitter away over the engine-room floor. 'We must be about to dock in their ship, and that means someone'll be coming in to shut the engines down soon.'

'What do we do then?' Sara asked nervously. Jenna paused, running through things in her head, checking to make sure she hadn't missed anything obvious. She opened her mouth to speak again, but before the first words had formed they heard the hiss of the door opening and the lights came up once more, bathing them in illumination which seemed blinding after their time in the dark.

Both of them froze, apart from Jenna very carefully easing the safety off on her gun. The rate of deceleration was starting to slow, and they were surely approaching a dead stop by now. *Just hurry up and dock . . .*

'We on yet?'

The voice seemed so loud she jumped, and nearly hit her head on the metal behind her. It was the same male voice as before, loud and rough and impatient, and was answered by the hiss of a comm.

+. . . *a moment, so get ready for . . . chronising the Heim fields.*+

Jenna blinked. Almost every ship or waystation in the galaxy had a Heim generator to produce artificial gravity, but that naturally led to complications when one craft docked inside another. If the activation of one field was synchronised perfectly with the deactivation of the other then there were no problems, but it certainly wasn't the best time to be building a card pyramid, or eating soup.

Or hunkering down in a low, narrow hiding place . . .

She looked over at Sara again, braced herself as

best she could between the hard surfaces surrounding
her and mouthed 'Hold on'. The other girl looked
back at her in confusion, then her eyes widened in
shock as the familiarity of gravity disappeared and
she started to drift upwards. Jenna winced as the
Hrozan's expression slipped into one of terror, waited
for her to float out into view of their unseen
companion . . .

'What the—'

Gravity reasserted itself just as the man started
speaking. Sara dropped back to the deck, a fall of
only a couple of inches, and hunkered down into a
ball immediately as a thump came from the far end
of the room. Jenna felt her pulse rise so fast that it
seemed like nothing less than a hammering in her
ears, the individual beats barely distinguishable as she
clutched her gun with hands suddenly slick with sweat.

'What the hell sort of "synchronising" do you call
that?!'

+. . .*the fuck up, Marone, I warned you, didn't I?
We're on, so kill . . . ngine and let's get out of here.*+

'Prick,' the man apparently called Marone muttered.
The engine's rumble coughed and died and the door
hissed open and shut again, the second action cutting
off the thuds of Marone's retreating boots. Jenna let
out the breath she'd been holding with a sound like
the pressure cooker in the *Keiko*'s galley when Kuai
had been steaming vegetables.

'We've got to get off!' Sara hissed at her. Jenna
shook her head.

'There's no getting off; we're in orbit now, and
they'll be making an Alcubierre jump as soon as they
can.'

'We can't keep hiding here forever!' Sara protested, clearly horrified.

'We shouldn't need to,' Jenna countered. 'They'll leave the shuttle now, and we *should* have it to ourselves until they get to wherever they're going.' She checked her wrist chrono. 'Give them five more minutes to get off this boat, and then I think we can risk heading out.'

It was possibly the longest five minutes of Jenna's life.

Finally, when the display showed that her self-set timescale had expired, she forced herself up to her feet. Muscles screamed and protested after being bunched up for so long, and the less said about her spine the better. She groaned and staggered sideways, catching herself on the metal bank Sara had been hiding behind.

'Oh God, I am too young to be making noises like this,' Jenna muttered. She reached down and offered Sara a hand. 'Coming?'

'You should . . . *ow* . . . try yoga,' Sara offered, clearly not experiencing an entirely pain-free transition to vertical herself.

'Yoga? Seriously?' Jenna blinked at her. 'I'm not fifty.'

'Trust me, it might be different for you GIA types when you're running around all over the place,' Sara said, 'but when you're sitting in front of a terminal all day every day you need something to help you stay mobile.' She arched her back, and Jenna heard something click. 'Ohh, that wasn't good, that wasn't good . . .'

Jenna thought about pointing out the sudden banal

bent their conversation had taken, but decided against it. If talking about an exercise regime kept Sara's mind off their situation and prevented her from freaking out and running through the *Early Dawn* screaming to be let off, it was a price well worth paying.

'You know, my life isn't exactly like you think,' she said as they made their way cautiously towards the door. There was no sign of movement in the corridor from what she could see through the small window, and right at this moment she wasn't necessarily certain that she'd care if there was. Sara had been right, they could hardly stay huddled up in the engine room forever. 'I do a lot of sitting in front of terminals as well.'

'You say that,' Sara replied, her voice dropping as Jenna reached out to hit the door release, 'but I only met you this morning, and look where I am now!'

'Point taken,' Jenna acknowledged. The door slid open without any immediate shouts of alarm from the other side, so she stepped through and tried to match her movements to how she vaguely remembered Rourke behaving whenever she'd followed the older woman into potential trouble. Gun in both hands for stability, pointing low ('People start on the ground; you pull the trigger too early when you're bringing a gun up and you might hit a leg, which is better than shooting above someone's head when you're bringing a gun down'), sidling up to a corner and peering around it before moving into the open . . . she was certain that her interpretation would have caused Rourke to despair, but it was better than nothing, and it would hopefully give

Sara some confidence if she looked like she had a vague idea of what she was doing.

Each section of corridor was dark as they approached, before being bathed in light as the lamps flickered on. On the one hand this at least meant that no one had been this way for a few minutes, probably since Marone had left the engine room; on the other, it was going to be very obvious to anyone left on board that someone was approaching. Still, they got past the infirmary without meeting anyone, and Jenna was able to sidle up to the airlock which overlooked the cargo bay to peer through the window.

'Clear,' she breathed with relief. Sure enough, there was no sign of activity beneath them. 'Come on, let's get to one of the cabins.'

The corridor atop the cargo bay was deserted as well. To Jenna's immense relief the door for the first cabin they tried was not coded, and opened the moment they tried the release. She leaped in, gun waving in arcs to try to cover all angles, but she needn't have bothered. There was a single fold-down bed built into one wall, a desk with a simple terminal and detachable pad, some drawers bolted to another wall, and a door to the bathroom cubicle which, upon investigation, proved to contain not only a toilet and wash basin but also a shower pod just about big enough for a medium-sized adult to turn around in.

'I need to get this secured,' Jenna said, kneeling down and firing up her wrist-mounted hacking rig to connect it to the cabin door's simple computer brain. 'Can you black out the windows, or something?' Anyone could lock the door from the inside – that was the point of doors, after all – but there was always an override code to open it from the outside which the captain of the ship would normally have set; it was the work of thirty seconds to remove that from the memory and install a new access code. Later on she'd just rewrite the programming so someone familiar with the system wouldn't be able to pull the same trick, but for now they were still reasonably secure from anyone without heavy-duty cutting gear.

A few minutes later they'd activated the self-tinting glass in the cabin's porthole to prevent anyone outside noticing the light and were both sitting on the bed with a mug of water to combat the thirst which had built up during their self-imposed imprisonment in the engine room. Jenna found herself feeling relaxed and safe, and nearly laughed; they were nowhere near safe, but everything was relative.

'So . . . what now?' Sara asked. Jenna was getting a little sick of hearing that question, but snapping at her only ally wasn't going to do any good, so she took another sip of water and started to lay out their situation.

'Well, odds are they're running away to wherever they normally hide out, which will be somewhere in the nav log data I transmitted. If our guess was right then the jump shouldn't be more than a couple of days, but for that long we've probably got this place to ourselves.'

'What happens when they come back on board?' Sara asked. Her hands had found her braid of hair again, which was looking decidedly sorry around the end.

'With any luck it'll be a short run to wherever

they're docking,' Jenna said. 'Actually, if our info's right and their boss hides out in an asteroid then they might just fly the parent ship right up to it and anchor to it with a cable, then shuttle inside in this. If it's a short trip they won't even need to come into a cabin, and if the door for this one seems stuck they'll hopefully just assume it's a malfunction and leave it.'

'And when we're in the asteroid?' Sara said, her face betraying her nervousness. 'Doesn't that mean we're basically sitting inside a base full of people who'll kill us if they find us?'

'Essentially, yes,' Jenna shrugged, trying to sound more confident than she felt, 'but we've got two advantages over them.'

'They don't know we're here?' Sara asked.

'That's one,' Jenna nodded. 'The other one is that everything – this shuttle, the main ship, the asteroid – are all going to be controlled by computers.' She held up the arm with her hacking rig on and tapped it meaningfully. 'And what's controlled by computers can be controlled by *me*.'

GHOST IN THE SYSTEM

Something was digging into her ribs.

Repeatedly.

Jenna tried to ignore it but the sensation was an insistent one, and distantly familiar at that. She rolled over under the covers and flailed an arm to shoo Missy away. 'Damn it, cat . . .'

'Uh, Jenna?'

Wait . . .

Jenna reluctantly opened her eyes and found a bright blue pair staring worriedly back at her, above a mouth chewing on the end of a thick brown braid. The room she was in wasn't one she knew, either.

Shit. How drunk was I last night?

She experienced a half-second of terrified confusion until she realised that the person facing her was at right angles and therefore kneeling on the floor, rather than in the bed with her, and her memory threw up a name to go with the face as well as, thank God, some context.

'Sara? What . . . what's going on?' She yawned and sat up, and everything else fell back into place: the attempted trap, their unintended kidnapping by the remnants of Kelsier's thugs, taking shelter in the cabin . . . then the memory of Micah's death hit her like a bowling ball in the gut again, and her eyes misted momentarily.

'You said to wake you when we came out of the jump,' Sara said, pointing at the terminal in the corner of the room. 'It just pinged at me, so I think we're . . . oh.' The Hrozan trailed off as Jenna rolled out of bed, then belatedly remembered that she'd stripped off her jumpsuit before she'd gotten in. She covered her embarrassment as best she could by reaching for it casually – she had underwear on, damn it! – and pretending she wasn't embarrassed at all.

She checked her wrist chrono. 'Nineteen-hour jump. Sounds about right.' A quick zip-up and she was once more decent – albeit conscious that her underclothes hadn't been washed – and ready to face the world.

Whichever world that happened to be.

'There's no inhabited systems within nineteen hours of Perun,' Sara offered from her seat on the floor. 'I might not have left the system before but I know that much; it's at least four days' travel.'

'Then with any luck, we're in the Olorun system,' Jenna muttered, crossing to the terminal and tapping it. Before she'd fallen into an exhausted slumber she'd been keeping watch to allow Sara to sleep first, and she'd used that time to thoroughly poke around the systems of the *Early Dawn* – and by extension, those of the *Half Light*, the carrier ship they were currently riding inside. Their cabin's terminal was linked to the mainframe in the bridge, and while it might not have had admin access eighteen hours ago it most certainly did now. What was more, the same linking protocols which, among other things, enabled the Heim drives of the two crafts to be (clumsily) synchronised had given her a pathway to access the larger craft's systems. There weren't even any software defences in place, but then who would anticipate needing to defend a slicing attack from their own shuttle?

When I get back to the Keiko, *that's the first thing I'm setting up.*

The nav data flashed up at her request. Jenna was no pilot, but while a veteran stardog might have committed up to a dozen regularly used jump co-ordinates to memory or be able to work out roughly what part of the galaxy they were in from the pattern of the numbers thrown out by the nav system, most people would be blind without the computer's assistance. She ignored the meaningless stream of figures and focused on the annotated diagram.

'On target!' she muttered, unconsciously giving it the same emphasis as Chiquita Martinez, ever-beaming hostess of the popular Serenitan game show of the same title. She looked over at Sara and inclined her head toward the display. 'Approaching the fourth planet of the Olorun system. Did you fit the tracker?'

'Yeah, it's ready whenever we want it,' Sara replied, patting her bag. The device would now be snugly attached to the internal coils of *Early Dawn*'s main transmitter array. Originally it had been intended not only to pinpoint the shuttle's location when activated but also piggyback Jenna in to take control of whatever systems she could, but she now had a far better vantage point.

Of course, it came at the cost of being within the reach of a bunch of very unsavoury people, but she was trying not to think about that.

'Wonderful.' She sat down in the chair in front of the terminal, thinking. 'I guess we wait, then.'

'For what?' Sara asked.

Jenna looked at her and shrugged. 'Whatever seems like a good idea. I'm making this up as I go, you know.'

'You're doing an amazing job,' Sara said earnestly. 'Do they teach all GIA operatives to be so self-reliant?'

'Probably,' Jenna muttered. She felt bad continually lying to Sara, but what other option did she have? Admit that she and the rest of the *Keiko*'s crew were a group of chancers who were duping the Europans into clearing up their own mess for them? No, there was nothing to do but play the role she'd been assigned to the best of her ability, and hope to hell that Drift, Rourke and the rest would be following. Preferably with some sort of backup.

Time dragged on. They'd come out of the Alcubierre jump virtually on top of the gas-giant fourth planet, far closer than Jenna would have expected – presumably the *Half Light*'s crew were running scared of pursuit and didn't want to get caught in the open if they could help it – and it quickly became clear that their destination was not going to be the isolated, mid-system asteroid they'd thought.

'We're heading for the ring system,' she said after a while, checking the nav display.

'We are?' Sara came to look over her shoulder, although there was little to see.

'This course won't intersect any of the moons,' Jenna replied, tracing their approach with one finger to show the Hrozan, 'and we can't land on the planet, it's gas. Wherever we're going must be in the rings.'

'That tracker had better work,' Sara muttered. 'I don't fancy anyone's chances of finding us in there otherwise.'

The rings grew larger. Even shut in the *Half Light*'s cargo hold and only able to watch what was going on through the nav display, it still took Jenna's breath away to see a structure many times wider than her home planet stretching away across the sky. She chewed on a ration bar, one of the stock she and Sara had swiped from the galley: they'd taken a chance that no one would notice, on the basis that the piecemeal 'crew' would have other things on their mind and probably wouldn't be spending long in the shuttle anyway. Besides, they hadn't brought any food with them, not having expected to be on the *Early Dawn* for more than a couple of minutes.

'There,' Sara said after a while of them silently watching the almost hypnotic data returns, most of it a shimmering mess as the *Half Light*'s sensors reported a plane of particles so small as to be indistinguishable from each other. The Hrozan reached across and pointed towards a speck which was starting to stand out against the background noise.

'I think you're right,' Jenna nodded. The speck grew into a dot, then gradually swelled into something much larger. Before long their objective was filling the screen – an irregularly shaped lump which resembled nothing so much as a cratered potato spinning gently through its ice-and-rubble-strewn surroundings, except that potatoes didn't usually have hundred-metre-high, atmosphere-tight docking doors installed in one of their sides. Jenna pulled the nav data back and scanned through the rest of the *Half Light*'s read-outs, trying to make sense of what was happening simply through the activity taking place on its main computer. However, things became very clear when abrupt deceleration nearly pulled her off her chair.

'Jesus!' she muttered. 'I guess the normal pilot's not on board . . . Ah, they're going to deploy the mag-anchor.' She pointed, suddenly realising what one series of rapidly declining numbers meant. 'There must be a docking plate on the surface.'

'So they'll be coming on board?' Sara asked, a note of worry creeping back into her voice.

'I reckon.' Jenna left the terminal and went to check the lock on the cabin door to make sure her programming was still functioning. She needn't have worried; the ability to open from the outside had been deactivated when she and Sara had settled down for the 'night', and no one would be getting in now without explosives or a cutting torch. Nonetheless, she felt her heart rate start to rise. This was about to get very real indeed.

The main terminal *pinged*. Sara looked up at her. 'Main hatch has been activated.'

'Okay.' Jenna breathed out and tried to retain her air of calm. 'So we sit quiet.'

She tried to picture the crew moving through the

Early Dawn, working out how long it would take them to get to the cockpit and down to the engine room. She felt the vibration of the engines start up a little before she'd expected, and then a jolt as the mags disconnected and they rose up off the deck of the *Half Light*'s cargo hold. The shuttle jerked forwards almost before they'd got any clearance, and both of them tumbled sideways.

'What the hell . . .?' Jenna scrambled upright, fighting against the acceleration, and slapped the switch which controlled the tinting on the porthole. The viewport shifted from opaque to transparent just in time for her to see the doors of the *Half Light* flash by, followed by another momentary lack of gravity as the Heim fields were caught out by the speed the shuttle was travelling at. Then they were out and into the veritable blizzard of ice and dust particles which made up the majority of the ring structure, the gravity reasserting itself and dumping her down on her backside. 'Who taught these clowns how to fly?!' she hissed, remembering at the last moment to keep her voice down.

'Something's spooked them!' Sara offered. The Hrozan picked herself up off the floor, an expression of hope creeping over her face. 'Check the scopes!'

Jenna pulled herself up on the edge of the desk and swept through the read-outs, scanning their surroundings. The *Early Dawn*'s sensors weren't powerful: the *Half Light*'s were much higher spec and she still had access to them thanks to her piggy-backed jack-in, but the main ship's systems were starting to power down now the shuttle was clear of its bay. However, just before they went dark she caught sight of a small anomaly, nearly lost in the readings of the giant planet, which might just have been another ship. Or possibly two.

'Oh, thank God. Thank God, thank God,' Sara breathed. She grabbed Jenna by the shoulder, so hard that Jenna nearly reached up to peel the other girl's fingers away. 'They came after us!'

'Yeah, but these bastards have spotted them,' Jenna pointed out grimly, 'and our lot weren't expecting to have to hunt through a planetary ring.' She looked out of the viewport again and saw the dark brown, nearly black surface of the asteroid blurring beneath them. 'We need to attract their attention somehow so they know where to look.'

'Can we do that?' Sara asked.

Jenna shrugged. 'That's what the tracker's for. Besides, once we're inside I should be able to slice into the central systems and we could broadcast what we like.' She grimaced. 'Of course, I won't have a continent's worth of proxy options so it'll be fairly clear where it's coming from, and then it's just down to whether we can keep Kelsier's thugs out. Also, we need to be able to convince our crews that we're not being forced to lure them into a trap, and it'll have to be a short message so we can get it off before anyone can cut the signal.'

Something flashed on the terminal as the *Early Dawn*'s systems linked with that of the asteroid now they were approaching the docking bay. The huge metal doors came into sight through the viewport, the surface of the asteroid rolling across the sky as the shuttle aligned itself with the internal gravity so everyone wouldn't suddenly find themselves upside down when the Heim drives synced. Jenna followed the signal and logged it on the terminal, tracking the link codes to find a way into the asteroid's systems. The big rock had a tighter security system than the *Half Light* . . . but it still wasn't expecting an attack from within.

'What languages do you speak?' Sara asked suddenly. The question was so unexpected that Jenna sat blinking at the display, her train of thought abruptly derailed.

'Huh?'

The shuttle was now pointing at the asteroid, but the access doors were so large the edges of them were still just visible from the viewport and they were starting to slide open. The *Early Dawn* started to edge forwards before it probably should have done, and a proximity alert flashed up on the display.

'Languages,' Sara repeated. 'We need to get a message out, right? What about if we put it in a different language?'

'I just speak English,' Jenna admitted. 'Well, and a little bit of Spanish, but so does a third of the galaxy. And my grandmother taught me how to swear in Gaelic – my family's from Ireland way back – but a bunch of Gaelic swearwords won't help us. Besides, none of my crew can speak it.' She looked up. 'You?'

'Pretty much the same,' Sara replied, looking a little shame-faced. 'You know, schools offer optional courses on Our Historic Languages, Czech and Slovak and that, but hardly anyone ever *does* them.'

The *Early Dawn* was passing through the doors. Jenna caught a glimpse of a huge hanger bay cut into the naked rock, enormous fans perhaps half the size of the *Jonah* in the roof to pump atmosphere in and out as required, then she activated the tinting again just in case there was anyone with a vantage point to see in and wonder who the two nervous-looking girls they'd just caught a fleeting glimpse of were.

'We could try pig Latin, I guess,' Sara suggested. The gravity fluctuation beneath them was less obvious this time, merely a fleeting impression of added weight as the Heim fields overlapped for a microsecond. '*Omecay inway?*'

Jenna glared at her. 'That's not helping.'

'Well, sorry,' Sara humphed. 'I'm just a surveillance tech from Hroza Major, you're the one who's been around the galaxy and has a crew that speaks every language under the suns.' She shrugged. 'Although I guess we don't know what languages the people on here speak anyway.'

Jenna's eyes widened. Of course, the main languages of the galaxy – English, Spanish, Arabic, Mandarin and so on – were common enough that most people who'd travelled around would be likely to have at least a basic grounding in them, and a lot of the others had virtually died out.

But not all.

She got up and grabbed the startled Sara in a hug. 'You're a genius!'

'Excuse me?' Sara extricated herself and pulled back, confusion writ large on her face. 'What?'

'I know how to do it!' Jenna beamed, then sobered slightly. 'Well, probably. I think it's our best shot at getting a message out which the people looking for us *should* understand and the people in here with us almost certainly won't, anyway.'

'I'm not following, I'm afraid,' Sara admitted, looking a little uncertain. Jenna was about to explain, but then there was another jolt as the *Early Dawn* set down on the deck, and seconds later the residual thrum of the engines died away. They sat quietly and watched the display, waiting for the signal which would show the main hatch being opened.

'There we go,' Jenna muttered as it finally flashed up. Her stomach was starting to churn and her palms felt damp with sweat as she contemplated what she was about to try. Of course, she could just sit back, not attract any attention and hope Drift, Rourke and co. would come to the rescue, but there couldn't be a rescue if no one knew where they were.

Besides, she was part of a crew, and every member of a crew needed to pull their weight.

'Okay,' she said, flexing her fingers and looking at the screen. 'I'm going to be slicing into systems I've never seen before via a non-hardlined link, and trying to establish and maintain control against a hostile resistance while also making sure that no one can override the programming blocks I've put in place to get back into this shuttle and come shoot us. Does that make any sense?'

'Not really,' Sara admitted.

'Did it sound impressive?'

'Yeah, pretty much.'

'Good enough.' Jenna breathed out and eyeballed the display, then carefully lowered her fingers onto the control panel.

'I need a pilot hat . . .'

In the cold depths of the Olorun system, over the nominally north pole of a ringed, creamy-yellow gas giant which was unnamed so far as anyone within a few light years was aware, two interstellar-capable ships hung in space bound together by a docking link. One was a freighter, a StarCorp *Kenya* model running under the name of the *Keiko*, the shell of which must have been three decades old although the thrusters and Alcubierre ring had likely been either repaired or replaced since then. The other was Europan Commonwealth military vessel *Draco*: significantly newer, slightly smaller and with noticeably more guns. Guns which were, in fact, the current main topic of discussion.

'The plan has changed,' Captain Rybak stated firmly. She'd turned out to be young, especially by the standards of what Drift would have expected for the commanding officer of a Europan counter-terrorism force, and commanded her bridge with the sort of forceful personality one might expect from a precocious talent in a high-stakes environment. Rourke had dealt with her one-to-one while in Glass City, and words like 'stubborn' and 'mule-headed' had featured prominently in her descriptions of the Europan captain.

'That is not an acceptable solution,' Rourke repeated, a faint tilting of her head and narrowing of her eyes the only signs of her dwindling patience: signs just noticeable to Drift, but far too subtle for someone unfamiliar with her to pick up on. Drift was increasingly glad they'd left Apirana on the *Keiko*. They'd barely been able to restrain the towering Maori from taking revenge for Micah's death by beating the life out of the man he'd knocked out in the marketplace, and when Apirana had heard that the *Early Dawn* had lifted off with Jenna still on board his rage had turned positively incandescent.

'Look, Agent,' Rybak said, addressing Rourke, 'we haven't been able to locate the ship since we came out of the jump. We don't even know if we're in the right place, but even if we are, our cover must be blown by now. If we'd come out hot on their tail and still had a chance of taking this base by surprise, I'd be prepared to commit troops to an assault. As it is, I'd be very surprised if our target doesn't know we're coming and has had time to prepare, and I'm not going to send my men and women into a death trap. Even if we can find this rumoured asteroid, and that's a big "if" with the tracker beacon not deployed on the *Early Dawn*, we won't be able to open the door. We just blow the damn thing up.'

'You have one ship, and we have no idea how big the asteroid could be,' Rourke pointed out. 'This won't be like shooting up an enemy ship, Captain. I've seen smuggler bases like this before; it could be a hundred times your size. Anything solid enough to be habitable inside is going to be pretty resilient to firepower, so you might be able to blow in some windows if they have any, but they'll just sit tight behind airlocks in the middle. You'd need heavy-duty mining lasers to even make a real dent in that rock, and in the meantime they're almost certainly going to have defensive gun emplacements to shoot back at you.'

Rybak glowered at her. 'You're not convincing me that an assault on foot makes any more sense, Agent. If they can shoot us when we're shooting them, they can shoot down any assault shuttle we send in, especially since we *can't open the door.*'

'Not if they don't realise it's coming,' Rourke argued. 'We can set the *Jonah* to silent running and ghost in—'

'Silent running?' Rybak snorted. 'There's no way you could set that up from far enough out to avoid detection!'

'I have faith in Jenna,' Rourke replied firmly. 'She'll get the tracker working. Then we just line the approach up.'

'"Just line the approach up."' Rybak shook her head disbelievingly. 'Even powered down and on radio silence, they'll pick you up the moment you fire manoeuvring thrusters. So unless you have a pilot who can plot the approach trajectory from *outside sensor range* without needing to make any course adjustments—'

'Yeah.' Jia Chang didn't even look up.

Rybak blinked. 'What, you think that's easy?'

'Easy? No.' Now Jia did look up, meeting Rybak's eyes with a challenging stare. 'If it was easy, anyone could do it.'

Rybak looked questioningly at Rourke, the *Is she for real?* query plain in her dark brown eyes. Rourke just shrugged.

'I have a specialist crew. They come with certain . . . idiosyncracies.'

Rybak sighed. 'Fine. Assuming your *expert* pilot is capable of what she says, I still don't see how you're planning to get inside without the piggy-backed access to the central control systems your slicer was supposed to provide.'

'We ram the fucker in,' Jia spoke up again.

Rybak's eyebrows rose. '*Excuse* me?'

'We're gonna have to come in fast anyway,' Jia said, angling her hand through the air to mimic their approach. 'Less chance of being seen, less chance of getting hit. Odds are they'll have an internal hangar, cos most smuggler dens do; we don't know how big the doors'll be but they'll need to be at least big enough for a *Sei*, and that's twice our size. Bigger doors mean less . . . *Kàng lā qiángdù* . . .' She looked over at her brother, who was sitting sullenly in the corner. '*Wǒ rúhé shuō?*'

'Tensile strength,' Kuai provided. Jia nodded and turned back to Rybak.

'Yeah, that. Hit 'em dead centre at the sort of speed we'll be going and *pow*!' She smacked one hand into the other. 'Bust straight through.'

'And . . . you don't think that might damage the

craft we'd be going in on?' Rybak asked, her tone of voice the sort Drift might have used to speak to a child, had he ever needed to do such a thing.

'Nah, the *Jonah*'s got a reinforced nose,' Jia replied, tapping her own for emphasis. 'We toughed it up after we . . . had to do something similar before,' she finished a little lamely as Rourke's warning glare caught her eye. Drift breathed a silent and hopefully unobtrusive sigh of relief: the last time they'd needed to ram-raid their way into somewhere it had been a Europan government supply facility in orbit over one of the moons of Karibu, and he saw no reason why Captain Rybak should become aware of that particular piece of larceny.

Rybak herself was shaking her head slightly in what appeared to be disbelief. 'I have to say, Agent Rourke, one hears a lot of things about the GIA but this . . .' She gestured with one hand, a vague wave seemingly intended to take in their presence on her bridge, Rourke's stubbornness and Jia's flippancy all in one go. 'This, I did not expect.'

'Our chief weapon is surprise,' Drift commented gleefully, 'surprise and fear.' He waited, but there was no sign of comprehension dawning on anyone's face. 'Really? Have *none* of you studied the Classics?' Rourke shot him a look which was closely related to the one that had just shut Jia down, and he subsided as a GIA field operative would presumably be expected to when glared at by a full agent. 'Sorry, boss.'

Rourke turned back to Rybak and shrugged again. 'Specialist crew.'

Rybak's expression showed what she thought of

Rourke's explanation, but she turned to the two officers standing with her, whom Drift understood to be a first and second lieutenant. 'Gentlemen? What's your assessment of this . . . plan?'

'It's highly unorthodox,' the taller one said, scratching at the neat blond moustache which sat on his upper lip. Drift still hadn't caught his name properly. Hamann? Harmon? Something like that.

'Counter-terrorism doesn't lend itself well to orthodox,' the other, older man reminded him. This was First Lieutenant Yao, and from what he'd seen of the man so far Drift considered him trustworthy and reliable; so much so that he almost felt guilty about the rain of shit which would undoubtedly land on this force when their compliance with an unauthorised military operation was discovered.

Almost. Some moral obligations outweighed others.

'It'll be a risk, ma'am,' Yao continued, addressing Rybak, 'but if we're going to prosecute this mission successfully then we've got limited options now our original plan is no longer viable. Our troops are, at least, well-trained in the sort of close-quarter fighting we would encounter inside any such asteroid. The issue will be getting them in there intact, but while the agent's plan is risky it does provide us with the same element of surprise as if we could open their doors externally.'

'Very well,' Rybak said, nodding slowly and rubbing her chin with her index finger. 'If we go ahead with this . . . plan . . . to ram in the main hangar doors then the interior won't be pressurised, and the force of the crash could be devastating. We'll need all our people in suits, and braced; we won't have any crash couches, but magnetic crash webbing should keep them secure enough.' She straightened slightly, threw a last, brief sideways look at Rourke, and straightened slightly to address her two juniors.

'Lieutenant Yao, give the instructions for all troops to suit up in preparation for low-pressure combat. Every piece of magnetic webbing is to be throughly checked before it's deployed; one failure could mean several casualties.'

'Yes ma'am.' Yao saluted and turned away, and Rybak focused on the second lieutenant.

'Lieutenant Hamann, instruct navigation to extrapolate the likely coordinates of Kelsier's location based on the navlog information from the *Early Dawn*'s previous visits to this system, then set the sensor team to work identifying any bodies in that area. Soft and quiet; the last thing we need is for them to get wind that we're here if by some chance they're not expecting us.'

'Ma'am.' Hamann saluted in turn, then made his way down the steel steps to where various uniformed Europans sat at terminals. The *Draco's* bridge was far larger than that of the *Keiko*, consisting as it did of the command deck where they were standing and what Drift thought of as the 'business area' below where people actually *did* things. He supposed the frigate had more sophisticated sensor and communication equipment than a freighter like the *Keiko*, not to mention weapon systems, but even so he wasn't sure what there was to be gained by having everyone so far away from each other.

'Well, Agent,' Rybak said in a low voice, turning back to face Rourke, 'the wheels are in motion.

I hope to hell your shuttle can do what your pilot thinks it can.'

'When it comes to knowing the capabilities of the ship she's flying, I've never known anyone better,' Rourke replied steadily. 'Besides, as she says, this isn't the first time we've done this.'

'You'll have to tell me about that,' Rybak said, her expression serious.

'I'm afraid that's classified,' Rourke told her, with the closest approximation of a polite smile Drift had ever seen her muster: it still didn't reach her eyes. 'Just be assured that Jia doesn't have a death wish. If she's flying a boat into somewhere, she wants it to come out again.'

'Every man or woman I've led or followed into combat has wanted to come out again,' Rybak said quietly. 'I don't think I need to tell you that it doesn't always work out that way.'

'We know that well enough.' Rourke's smile had dropped away, and Drift didn't need to wonder why. It wasn't like they hadn't known the risk they were taking playing bait, and it wasn't like Micah had been particularly close to any member of the crew – the mercenary had been largely callous, bordering on thoroughly unpleasant at times – but no one deserved to die like that, choking on their own blood on the whim of a true monster like the Laughing Man. Drift hoped that the Hrozan forces had succeeded in apprehending the assassin, but wasn't going to hold his breath. Marcus Hall had slipped his way in and out of too many tight spots for there to be any likelihood of him being run to ground in such a relative backwater.

'Well then, Agent,' Rybak was saying, 'I need to oversee arrangements to ensure as many of my people come through this as possible. In the meantime, perhaps you'd like to ensure the shuttle they'll be going in on is thoroughly prepared?'

Drift knew a dismissal when he heard one, and had levered himself away from the bulkhead where he'd been leaning even before Rourke nodded her assent to the Europan captain. Jia offered an arm to Kuai, who took it; the bullet he'd taken in the leg had missed any bone but had torn up his calf muscle pretty badly, and despite prompt medical attention he was going to be hobbling for some time. The Changs had virtually stopped bickering since Glass City, although Drift couldn't say for sure if it was Kuai's injury or Micah's death which was the cause. He'd half expected the little mechanic to have been berating his sister for agreeing to this plan in the first place, but there'd been little sign of that, and he leaned on her without complaint or protest as the four of them – *only four now: Micah dead, Big A. in his cabin, and Jenna . . . God knows* – began to head for the door which would take them to where the docking link joined the two ships.

'Ma'am!'

The shout came up from beneath them. Rybak frowned and took two brisk steps to look down over the railing. Rourke paused and half-turned back, ostensibly to check the Changs were following but in all reality Drift knew his partner was as curious as he as to what had prompted the interruption.

Lieutenant Hamann came hurrying back up the steps, his words audible across the bridge.

'We're receiving a signal, ma'am: the tracker beacon. Comms are pinpointing the location now but it doesn't seem to be where we expected Kelsier's base to be. It's reading as close by, in the ring system.'

Rybak's brows furrowed immediately. 'I don't like it.'

'What do you mean, you don't like it?' Rourke interrupted, making her way back towards the Europans uninvited. Drift followed her as inconspicuously as he could, being roughly a foot taller and with violet hair to boot; the dirty look Rybak gave him showed that he had failed miserably. 'This is what we were waiting for!'

'But why *now*, Agent Rourke?' Rybak demanded. 'If the signal had been running when we arrived, that would be one thing. We've been here,' she checked her wrist chrono, 'seven minutes. To my mind, that means our target saw us arrive, has finished preparations and is now trying to lure us in.'

'Or Jenna and that Vankova girl have only just managed to activate the beacon,' Rourke replied, her voice audibly tight. 'It could be their last gasp, Captain.'

'It's too convenient,' Rybak snapped. 'We'll follow the signal, but if they've seen us already then your silent running idea is just going to get us killed. We shoot it to bits; if we can't do that then the *Draco* stays to take out anyone trying to flee and you take Lieutenant Hamann back to the Perun System to gather more ships with more guns.'

'By which time two of our own will certainly be dead,' Rourke bit out.

'It'll be more than two of mine dead if we get shot

down before we even make it inside,' Rybak replied icily. 'I appreciate your feelings, Agent, but I expected a more realistic attitude from the GIA.'

'You won't get any confirmation that you've found Kelsier,' Drift cut in, trying another angle of approach. 'The bodies won't be identifiable, any computer systems won't be accessible . . . you'll never know if you've actually completed your mission!'

'And I certainly won't complete it if my troops are blown up in a vacuum,' Rybak said, eyes flicking to him for a moment before returning to her staring match with Rourke. 'As ranking officer here, I—'

'Ma'am!'

Another shout came up from below. Lieutenant Hamann, seemingly grateful for the opportunity to remove himself slightly from his superior's argument, darted down the ladder and exchanged a few words with a commsman before returning apace clutching a piece of paper.

'A data transmission we've just picked up on the emergency frequencies,' he said when he reached them again. He passed the paper over to Rybak. 'It's text only: two words.'

Rybak glanced at it and shook her head. 'It means nothing to me.' She looked up, somewhat grudgingly, and handed it to Rourke. 'Agent? Some GIA cypher, perhaps?'

Rourke looked down and Drift peered over her shoulder. Sure enough, two blocks of letters were centred on the slip of white:

HAERE MAI

Rourke looked around at him, the whites of her eyes bright in the shadow cast on her dark face by her hat. Her expression was neutral, but he was good enough at reading her to know that she was as stumped as the Europans.

'Haere mai,' Drift muttered, trying out the sound of the unfamiliar words, if actual words they were. 'Haere mai.' Something plucked at the back of his brain, an infuriating, nagging sensation that he'd heard these words before. The vowel sounds seemed slightly wrong, somehow. He tried again with a different inflection. '*Haere mai.*'

Ahh. *That* sounded more familiar. Where from? He closed his eyes – the left physically, the right with a mental command – and tried to think. Somewhere on the *Keiko* or the *Jonah*, certainly, but he spent most of his life on one of the two so that didn't really narrow it down. A holo show? Maybe, but that wasn't what he'd been thinking of . . .

'Ichabod?'

'Sshh.' GIA operatives probably didn't shush their superiors, but it was too late for that. 'I'm thinking.'

For some reason he had a memory of hearing it when his right hand was hurting a bit. Why would that be? What was the context? It wasn't like he was Apirana and went around punching walls—

Wait.

He felt the beginnings of a grin creep over his face, and looked up at Rourke and the Europans. 'We know of nothing in this system that should be broadcasting anything?'

'It's claimed by the FAS, but they don't even have an outpost here so far as we know,' Hamann replied, shaking his head. 'If we were looking for an actual *asteroid* then it would be further afield, but the ring system of this planet has plenty of large chunks of rock and ice. If I were a betting man . . .'

'Well, I *am* a betting man,' Drift exclaimed, a fierce joy he'd thought he might have lost starting to stir in his chest again, 'and I'd place big money on us having a way into wherever sent this, but we need to get there now if not sooner.'

'But what does it *mean*?' Rybak demanded.

'It means "come in",' Drift told her with a grin, 'and it's come from Jenna, I guarantee it. It's in a language that only one person within about three systems of here will speak, and Jenna will have heard it every time she's knocked on his cabin door.'

He turned around and looked at the Changs, whose faces indicated that comprehension was starting to dawn.

'Jia? Go get Apirana.'

'**M**issile lock!' Drift shouted. 'Missile lock!'

'I heard you the first time!' Jia snapped.

'Yeah, well there were two!' Drift protested, watching the display with a sinking feeling in his gut. *Of all the ways I could choose to die, being blown into hard vacuum by an explosive device was a long way from the top of the list.* There was a sickening lurch as the *Jonah* corkscrewed to one side and at least nominally upwards, the change in momentum doing unkind things to Drift's gut despite the artificial gravity.

'Are there still two now?' Jia demanded.

'No,' Drift confessed. 'There're three now.'

'*Cào nǐ zǔzōng shíbā dài!*'

'I thought you said your slicer would be able to get control of their systems!' Rybak shouted. The Europan captain was dressed in a full atmo-suit except for the helmet and was 'supervising' their run from the doorway, although the notion of anyone having much of an input into proceedings once Jia had actually started flying was a convenient fiction Drift had been happy to go along with.

'Why do you think we suggested this?' Drift demanded, desperately scanning the screens. '*Dios!* Jia, one incoming!'

'If we reach that rock and Jenna's still alive, I'm gonna *qiā sǐ* that little bitch!' Jia spat, a term Drift didn't know the translation of but which didn't sound friendly. 'Hold on!' The *Jonah* changed course again, a roll-turn which sent them diving down towards the main layer of the ring structure. 'As soon as we hit dust, jam it!'

'Won't the—'

'Just fucking *do* it, *bái chī!*'

Drift hovered his hand obediently over the jamming switch: not a feature commonly seen on *Carcharodon*-class shuttles, but a certain level of paranoia was rarely a bad thing in a starship captain, especially when they might sometimes have to leave places in a hurry after doing something not technically legal. 'Ready.'

'Wait for it . . .' Jia muttered as the shifting, refracting plane of the ring loomed up towards them. With no sense of scale, Drift found his eyes swimming as he tried to focus and work out the distance to the mass of rock and ice shards. He glanced back at the display and saw to his dismay that the missile was closing in on them even faster than he'd feared, its radar tracking signal growing stronger and more urgent.

There was a sound like the most violent hailstorm

ever hitting the viewshield and he slammed his hand onto the jamming switch even before Jia's shout of 'Now!' His headphones were momentarily clogged with the blast of white noise from the *Jonah*'s own transmitters as Jia hauled them around yet again; the shuttle described a tight arc out through the bottom of the ring, which was merely a few tens of metres deep, and back up into it again.

'Status?' Jia barked.

'Yes!' Drift punched the air as the missile's signal faded, presumably passing them astern as its targeting system was confused by the combination of jamming and the radar-baffling particles of the ring structure. 'Lost it!'

'Great,' the pilot replied, her voice still tense. 'The others?'

'Uh . . .' Drift frowned at his screen, trying to make sense of what he was seeing. 'They've gone.'

Jia actually looked over her shoulder at him, the ear flaps of her pilot hat wobbling as she did so. 'Define "gone".'

'Nothing has a lock on us,' Drift told her, checking again to make sure he wasn't imagining it. Sure enough, the display remained suspiciously clear. 'They must have cleared when we went through the ring.'

'Or your system's glitched and we're about to get blown out of the stars,' Rybak put in darkly.

'*Or*,' Jia continued as they pulled up above the main ring layer once more and the dark bulk of the asteroid loomed up ahead, 'Jenna's got off her ass and is running the show now, which is why the doors are opening.'

'They're what?' Drift looked up from his station

and, sure enough, the gleam of metal now had a slowly widening dark line in its centre. Moments later there was a crackle of static over the speakers, followed by a familiar and all-too-welcome voice.

+*Shuttle* Jonah, *this is Jenna McIlroy. You are cleared for landing so long as you do it fucking quickly, because I am slicing like a goddamn bastard to keep control of this rock's systems from whatever techno-wizard they have on board. I'd appreciate you coming in and establishing a perimeter, or whatever it is you do, before I get someone else trying to burn their way into my shuttle.*+

'Jenna!' Drift's spirits, which had been dipping almost as fast as the *Jonah* trying to evade a missile, soared once more. 'Damn, it's good to hear your voice!' He frowned. 'Wait, did you say "someone *else*" trying to burn their way in?'

+*Uh, yeah.*+ There was a nervous and slightly manic laugh. +*But we're in the main hangar bay and, well, I needed to open the door for you guys which involved a security override* anyway so . . . *I guess it got kinda cold and hard for them to breathe, real quick.*+

Drift exchanged a sober look with Jia. That sounded to him like a Jenna who was stretched about to breaking point. 'We're coming in.'

'Damn right we are,' Jia muttered, throwing more power to the drive and activating the internal comm to address the crowd of Europan troopers in their cargo bay. 'Hold onto ya butts!'

'Better strap in,' Drift advised Rybak. 'When she brakes, she brakes *hard*.'

'I don't doubt it,' Rybak replied, following his suggestion and dropping into the seat where Jenna herself would normally be. 'I'll say this for your pilot; she can certainly fly.'

'Never say that until we're inside!' Jia shouted. 'Are we still clear?'

'Still clear!' Drift confirmed, seeing a welcome lack of targeting icons on his scope. At this distance they'd barely have any warning to evade, especially given how fast they were closing on the asteroid. Which was a point, actually. He swallowed nervously. 'Jia, aren't we going in a bit—'

Even given his warning to Rybak, Jia's application of the retros still caught him by surprise. '*Jesús Cristo!*'

'Told ya to hold on,' Jia snapped, 'not my fault if you din't listen.' The hangar mouth swallowed them with Jia still firing retros, and only a few hastily flicked switches activated the mags and cancelled the *Jonah*'s artificial gravity before the Heim field of the asteroid took hold of them. The bay itself was larger than any he'd seen except on the biggest ships, and held two other cargo shuttles besides the hulking shape of the *Early Dawn*.

'Jenna, we're in,' Drift wheezed into the comm. 'You can shut the doors and repressurise, if you can.'

+*On it. Hey, you okay?*+

'Yeah, you know what Jia's flying's like.' Drift ignored the snort from the pilot's chair, slapped at the release on his crash harness and turned to Rybak, who was breathing a little hard herself. 'Coming, Captain?'

'Certainly, Captain,' the Europan officer responded, disentangling her own arms from the restraints. She seemed to have got her head around the notion that the *Keiko* and the *Jonah* belonged to Drift, warranting him the title of 'Captain' despite Rourke still being addressed as 'Agent' and viewed as being in charge.

They came out above the cargo bay and its corresponding payload of nearly one hundred Europan troops in atmo-suits and maglock harnesses, some clamped upright to the walls and the rest lying on the floor, secured against whatever misfortunes might arise from rapid changes of velocity. Rybak adjusted her comm but still raised her voice slightly, probably unconsciously.

'We have breached the asteroid and are currently setting down in the main hangar bay! Standard sweep-and-clear, all contacts are to be treated as hostile and engaged unless and until they put down arms and surrender! We believe that the GIA currently have control of this rock's computer systems,' here she threw a look at Drift, who gave a hopefully encouraging thumbs-up, 'but that status is subject to change so I want everyone's suits to remain sealed until you have at least *two* airlocks between you and this hangar! Suit protocol from that point will be decided by your squad commander on an individual basis!' She paused for a second, then dropped her voice to little more than a fierce whisper.

'Go show these bastards what it means to start a war with Europa.'

'YES MA'AM!' the cargo bay roared back, mag harnesses being unfastened and weapons readied. Within seconds the entirety of Rybak's company were poised at the main ramp and Drift only just managed to stifle a truly incongruous giggle.

It had actually worked. The time since Kelsier's cargo had so spectacularly vaporised part of the North

Sea was a jumbled blur: week after week of shitting construction blocks, living by the skin of their teeth and fraying their nerves, trying to spin a web of bullshit fast enough and far enough to get clear of the clutching fingers which seemed to be closing in on all sides. And, against all odds, they'd nearly done it. Here they were, poised to unleash the military might of the old bastard's former government against him based on the strength of Drift's tongue, Rourke's old electat and a Defence Ministry communique forged by a girl just out of her teens with a knack for slicing and the view that, when it came to computers, laws were things which happened to other people. Now there was just one thing left to take care of: Nicolas Kelsier himself.

And this, of course, was far too important a detail to leave to the Europans. They might get it wrong.

The *Jonah* touched down and Jia immediately hit the ramp release, as per instructions. The fully suited Europan troops charged down it as soon as it tipped beyond horizontal, fanning out and sweeping the hangar bay with their weapons. A few shots reached Drift's ears, indicating that there were at least some of the asteroid's crew that hadn't realised exactly what magnitude of threat had come aboard in the slightly battered *Carcharodon*-class shuttle.

'Agent?' Rybak had finished fastening her own helmet in place and was walking down the steps to where Rourke was standing, her atmo-suit dark green and looking rather shabby in comparison with the Europans' slate-blue combat rigs.

'Captain.' Rourke looked even odder in an atmo-suit than most people did, and it took Drift a moment to realise that she seemed wrongly proportioned without her coat and hat. Rybak wasn't a particularly tall woman, but next to her Rourke looked almost like a child. Granted, few children would be handling a Crusader 920 with such familiarity. Hopefully.

'Let's go and see what we can flush out,' Rybak said, drawing a sidearm. A quartet of soldiers drew up around them on a bodyguard detail and, thus flanked, the two women made their way down into the hangar. Drift waited until they were out of sight, then activated his comm.

'Jia? Can you patch me through to Jenna?'

+*Done.*+

'Jenna,' Drift said, making his way across the gantry to the opposite airlock, 'how're you holding up in there?'

+*Your friends have certainly made my job easier,*+ the young slicer replied. +*Whoever was trying to take the systems back from me seems to have other things on their mind now.*+

'Glad to hear it,' Drift said agreeably. He reached the door and palmed it open. 'How about *your* friend? Is she still with you?'

+*Sara? Yeah, she's just gone to the galley to make some coffee now we don't have to worry about anyone breaking in.*+

'She's not in the room? Good.' Drift stepped through and let the door hiss shut behind him. Ahead of him, Apirana poked his head out of the *Jonah*'s own canteen with an enquiring expression. Drift gave the Maori the thumbs-up and his voice took on a more businesslike tone. 'Have you got access to schematics?'

+*Sure. What do you need?*+

'I need to know where Kelsier is,' Drift told her flatly, 'and A. and I need to get there before the Europans do.'

+*Gotcha. What does he look like? They've got cameras most places . . . well, they did, but I've decided they don't need to see the feeds. However, I've still got cameras most places . . .*+

'White, old, straggly pale hair to about his collar, mechanical right hand . . .' Drift paused. 'Wait. Where *haven't* they got cameras? Because I'd bet money the old snake doesn't want anyone spying on his private nest.'

+*We've got . . . ooh, that's interesting. It looks like . . . yeah, there's a few corridors and rooms on the schematics which I can't seem to find on camera,*+ Jenna confirmed. +*There's a little network in the middle of it all. It's pulling down a lot of power as well.*+

'Sounds like a good place to start,' Drift confirmed. Apirana appeared again, now with Micah's immolation cannon slung over his shoulders by its strap, and Drift barely restrained a wince; the indiscriminate firepower of the big gun would be devastating in the sort of narrow corridors the asteroid was likely to offer. Still, at least it was going to be on his side. 'How do we get there?'

+*You might be in luck. It looks like our Europan friends have already gone past one of the entrances without turning in, and they've been poking their noses in everywhere else. I'm guessing they're concealed.*+

'This is sounding more and more promising,' Drift

said, feeling a tight grin spreading across his face. 'Send your friend over to the *Jonah* so she doesn't see what's going on.' He looked up at Apirana. 'Okay big man, time to move.'

'Let's end this,' the Maori growled in reply.

Drift had wondered about taking a larger gun, but the asteroid was likely to resemble a starship's interior and he reckoned he'd had more experience of starship boarding than most. Firepower was useful, but speed of reaction was vastly more important than accuracy at range, so he trusted that his pistols would do the job. All the same, he couldn't help feeling slightly under-equipped as he watched Apirana carrying an assault rifle in one massive hand and steadying the immolation cannon with the other while they jogged across the hangar bay deck towards the *Early Dawn*.

+*Captain, I'm sending Sara out to you with the drive you'll need,*+ Jenna's voice crackled into his ear suddenly, +*so please don't shoot her.*+

'Gotcha.' The crew ramp began to lower from the *Sei*-class shuttle before Drift had finished speaking. He vaguely recognised the girl who appeared out of the *Early Dawn*'s cargo bay from the introductions back on Hroza Major and raised a hand in greeting. She returned it uncertainly, and seemed to be eyeing Apirana's weapons uneasily.

'Uh, hi. Jenna said to give you this.' She held up a small black device, which Drift took from her and tucked into a belt pouch. 'Where are you off to?'

'Just got to go and take care of something,' Drift said, as reassuringly as he could. He jerked a thumb over his shoulder. 'Our ride's there; go grab a snack and we'll be back with the rest of them.' He tapped Apirana's arm and the two of them turned away, heading for the nearest airlock entrance into the asteroid's interior.

'Do the soldiers know you're going in?' the girl called after them, sounding worried. Drift ignored her; he had more important things to concentrate on than lying to a surveillance officer.

As he'd expected, the asteroid's corridors bore a strong resemblance to those of a starship. They were lined with metal instead of being left open as bare rock, presumably to allow the use of mag-levs for the movement of heavy cargo, and the most obvious difference was the rows of pipes and wires, all of which were inside the main corridor since there was no space around it to run them out of sight as was normal practice in a ship. Apirana kept having to duck or sway to one side whenever they encountered a ventilation outlet hanging down from the ceiling like some sort of infeasibly regular stalactite.

They only had to turn one corner before they found their first bodies.

'The Europans ain't messing, are they?' Apirana said, casting an eye over the trio of dead pirates strewn across the corridor beneath a hail of bullet damage to the metal panelling on the wall. Drift saw his eyes narrow, and the Maori's face screwed up into a grimace. 'Two of these ain't even armed.'

'Do you see any reporters around?' Drift asked him, advancing to the next junction and trying to ignore the feeling in his gut which told him that these deaths were a direct result of his trickery. 'No one's watching this little war. That means no one needs to play by the rules.' He activated his comm again. 'Jenna, which way?'

+*You've got two entrances nearby which the Europans seem to have walked right past, even though they've cleaned out the rooms around you. Turn right to get to the closest one, it's just around the next corner.*+

'Sounds like a plan,' Drift agreed. He eyed the corridor ahead of them; perhaps fifty yards of no cover save the very slight insets of doorways into side chambers. 'You're certain the Europans cleared these rooms out, right?'

+*Trust me Captain, they seem to be killing everything they come across,*+ Jenna replied, sounding a little sick. Drift nodded grimly.

'Alright then. A.?'

'Right behind ya,' the Maori replied. Drift double-checked that his pistols' magazines were engaged and the safeties were off.

'Let's go then.'

They made it halfway down the corridor before Jenna's voice rang in his ear again, tight with urgency.

+*Captain, the entrance is opening!*+

'**S**hit!' Drift brought both his guns up to cover the corridor ahead as he and Apirana halted from their jogging pace. 'What's happening?'

+*There's three . . . no, five . . . wait, seven . . . guys, just get out of there, they're coming your way!*+

Jenna's warning wasn't necessary; Drift could now hear a clatter of boots ahead of them. There wasn't time to get back to the previous junction to take cover so he dropped to one knee and took aim at the corner, both guns outstretched. Behind him and to his right he heard Apirana grunt as the Maori hoisted the immolation cannon up to shoulder height.

The first man came around the corner, saw them and began to whip his rifle up into a firing position, but Drift's right-hand pistol barked twice and dropped him before he could bring it to bear properly. There were shouts of consternation and a gun barrel appeared around the corner, but the *whump* of the immolation cannon was followed immediately by its shell impacting on the wall edge. Some of the volatile gel spattered across the metal face Drift could see and started burning as it came into contact with the air, but the majority of the weapon's payload clearly found targets judging by the sudden screaming.

Drift grimaced: Kelsier's goons obviously hadn't expected them and had been driven back momentarily, but he and Apirana were essentially sitting ducks in the corridor should they regroup. They needed to end this, and quickly, and his mind flashed back to something particularly stupid he'd done when boarding a merchantman about fifteen years ago. He'd been younger and thought he was immortal, and he'd been trying to impress a gorgeous young new addition to his crew; she'd had hair like fire, slightly crooked teeth, and a pair of breasts which would have made the ancient sculptors throw their chisels away and start sobbing at their inability to capture such perfection in stone. A shame he couldn't remember her name.

'Cover me,' he told Apirana.

'Say what?'

Drift was moving before he'd even properly registered that the Maori didn't seem to have understood his instruction. He burst up from his crouch, took four or five quick steps and then slid on his back, feet first, past the line of the wall with both his guns raised.

The small crowd of the asteroid's crew – just over half a dozen, perhaps – were in some disarray.

He fired into the pack, trying to concentrate on the ones not distracted by clawing at their own flesh or clothing as the immolation gel burned away at them, but realistically he was hardly in a position for sharp-shooting. His sudden appearance prompted a spatter of wild shots but they fizzed over him, which was, in fairness, what he'd been counting on. He skidded by the man he'd shot down a second ago, praying to any deity who might be listening that he was either dead or well on the way instead of just winged, and ended up against the corridor's far wall with his legs bunched beneath him, both pistols dry and the gun barrels of the two men and one woman who were still upright tracking towards his now-stationary form.

At least, until Apirana stepped around the corner and pulled the trigger of the immolation cannon twice. One man took the first shell full in the face and was taken clean off his feet by the force of the impact; the second shot crashed into the woman's chest and enough spattered onto the man beside her to incap-acitate them both in the way that only flaming chemical incendiaries could truly achieve. God, but Drift sometimes wished he'd never let Micah bring that thing on board his ship. Still, it was undeniably effective. He ejected his magazines and fumbled for clips to reload, not least to put their former antagon-ists out of their misery and stop the damnable screaming.

Apirana beat him to it by taking two steps and stamping on the pair's throats with two audible and rather sickening cracking sounds, then turned to look down at him. The big man's mouth had developed a tic at its left corner and his eyes seemed just a little wider than usual. Drift recognised the danger signs; once Apirana's blood was up he started to behave like the Berserkers of Norse legend, at which point it was safest to just stay behind him.

'You okay?' Apirana asked him, breathing a little more heavily than was perhaps warranted by his exertion thus far.

'Yeah.' Drift pushed himself up to his feet. 'You?'

The Maori didn't reply. Instead, his face twisted into a snarl of rage and he brought the cavernous muzzle of the immolation cannon up with a shout.

Drift didn't waste time with questions: he threw himself forwards and sideways, trying to get out of the monstrous weapon's firing arc before Apirana could incinerate him, but shots rang out before he'd hit the steel decking. The shots were not the *whump* of the cannon however, but the sharp-edged hammer-blows of supersonic ammunition.

There was a shuffle of boots. Drift looked up to see Apirana stumbling sideways and then the Maori fell, a dark-skinned avalanche in ship fatigues. Behind Drift a rifle was wavering weakly in one hand of the first man he'd shot down, its owner still on his back and his face twisted in pain. Drift hadn't reloaded his pistols and the barrel was swinging towards him, albeit slowly and somewhat shakily, so he did what he always did in these situations and improvised.

He shifted his grip on the pistol in his right hand to grasp it by the barrel, and threw it as hard as he could.

Luck, fate or excellent hand-eye coordination was on his side and the metal missile struck the crewman square in the face. Drift himself followed it a moment later, launching himself at the wounded man with a yell and grabbing the rifle before it could be turned on him. His opponent fought desperately, teeth bared in a grimace, but his strength was clearly fading. Drift compounded this by punching him where he could see a bullet wound on the man's right pectoral, and that pretty much ended all resistance. Drift ripped the rifle out of his hands, stepped away from him and emptied the magazine up and down the pirate's body while screaming obscenities. Then, feeling slightly sick at himself, he threw the weapon away and dashed to where Apirana had fallen.

'A.!' He checked the Maori over quickly. There was a bullet wound in the meat of Apirana's right arm which was bleeding badly and a round had been stopped by the big man's armavest just under his collarbone, but he was most concerned about the one which had penetrated and left a dark, wet wound over what he judged was roughly the bottom of the left ribcage. Could that have hit a kidney, if it had penetrated far enough? His grasp of anatomy had never been a strong point. 'How bad does it feel?'

'Gah!' Apirana's breath was coming fast and shallow, and clearly paining him. 'Pretty *fuckin'* bad, bro!'

'Okay, hold on.' Drift grabbed the small, syringe-like dressing gun from the medkit on the belt of Apirana's armavest and sprayed sterile, fast-setting foam into both wounds. It was hardly more than a sticking plaster, but it would slow the big man's blood loss somewhat. That done, he activated his comm again. 'Jenna, you still there?'

+*I'm here.*+ The young slicer's voice sounded ragged. Of course, she would have seen the whole thing on the cameras. +*Is he . . .*+

'A.'s still alive, but he's wounded.' Drift tried to keep his voice crisp, although it was as much for his benefit as either of the other two's. 'Anyone else heading our way?'

+*It doesn't look like it. Kelsier's mob seem to have blockaded themselves in properly now and the Europans are having trouble getting to them.*+

'No one else coming through any secret doors?' Drift coughed; the acrid, chemical stench of the immolation gel was mixing with the stomach-turning scent of charred human flesh and hair, and the resulting cocktail was making it difficult to breathe.

+*Nothing I can see, Captain.*+ Jenna sounded a little more focused now, which was something.

'Right. Keep a lookout and shout at me if you see anything, okay?'

+*Roger that.*+

'Right.' Drift looked down at Apirana again, then up the corridor. 'Where's the entrance this lot came out of?'

+*About twenty metres away, on your left.*+

Drift grimaced and met the Maori's eyes. 'Think you can make it that far?'

'Not fucking dead yet,' Apirana growled, and held up his left arm. 'Gimme a hand.'

'Not a chance,' Drift told him flatly, 'you'd pull me over.' He holstered his second pistol and got behind Apirana, helped the big man into a sitting position (not without a groan of pain on the Maori's part), then threaded his arms underneath Apirana's armpits. 'Ready?'

Apirana nodded, and Drift hauled upwards. Or tried to.

It took two attempts, some truly sulphurous swearing from Apirana and black spots appearing in Drift's vision but he finally managed to get the Maori onto his feet, although even that was clearly a massive strain for the big man. He was leaning heavily even then, an experience for Drift which felt somewhat akin to trying to support a small landslide, and together they staggered towards what looked like an innocuous section of wall marked by nothing other than a small keypad which could have controlled anything from ventilation to lighting. However, Drift could see the slightly wider gap between wall panels which hinted at an opening.

'Jenna, any ideas?'

+*Access code should be 32519, if I'm reading this right.*+

Drift punched the numbers in and, sure enough, the wall panel swung almost silently inwards to reveal a tunnel: not regularly shaped and metal-lined like the corridors outside but simply the bare, dark rock of the asteroid, studded with intermittent lights and lined with cables. They stumbled inside and let the door swing shut again, but after a couple of steps Apirana hissed in pain and sank down against the wall.

'Shit . . .' Sweat was beading all over the Maori's head, visible even in the dimmer light that now illuminated them, and his breath was huffing out around gritted teeth. 'That's me done, bro. You go get the little fucker, yeah?' He reached up with a wince and unslung the assault rifle which until now had been dangling from its strap. 'Gimme your gun, take this one. I'll watch your back. No one's coming through here unless they're on our side.'

Drift felt his gut twist. Micah's death was still raw, and Apirana had been a part of Drift's life for far longer than the Dutch mercenary had. Despite his occasional terrifying rages, and even the recent near-strangulation Drift had suffered at the big man's hands, Apirana Wahawaha was a friend. Besides, quite apart from the pain and guilt involved, there was something terrifying about seeing someone as big and strong as Apirana reduced to a crippled wreck. His sheer size and vitality seemed like it should make him immune to all but the largest natural disasters, but at the end of the day he was flesh and blood like anyone else.

Drift took the proffered rifle and reloaded his pistol, then handed it over along with a couple of spare magazines. 'You sure we shouldn't try to get you back out there?' he asked, nodding towards the door. 'We could get Jenna to see if some of the Europans could come and pick you up. You need treatment.'

'We got nothing on the *Jonah* which can help me,' Apirana growled, threading his thick finger through the trigger guard, 'nor the *Keiko*. Go get this bastard an' then we can all fly off an' see if the Europans'll play nice an' check out my guts.' He scowled as Drift hesitated. '*Go*. I've got this. I'm fucking *Maori*. I might not be able to walk, but I can still fight.'

Drift swallowed, not trusting himself to answer. He nodded soberly, bumped the fist that the big man held out to him, and turned away to follow the tunnel.

The tunnel only went a short distance, perhaps twenty metres, before it took a right turn. Drift followed it and found another tunnel merging from the left, reassuringly empty for now but far from ideal given that it meant Apirana was no longer covering the only way in and out. A short distance on from the junction his way was blocked by another door, this one a high-security model in heavy steel. He paused and activated his comm, wondering if the reception lines would have been run in here; if not, the rock would likely prevent his signal from being picked up by the network in the corridors outside. 'Jenna?'

+*Still here.*+

He sighed in relief. 'Good. I've reached another door. Any tips?'

+*It should be the same access code, from what I can see.*+

Drift double-checked his rifle, took a couple of deep breaths, and punched the code into the small keypad set into the rock on his left. A light flashed green and the door slid aside in two portions, allowing him to leap through with his weapon levelled . . .

. . . into a bedchamber. Or possibly a *boudoir*. Regardless of semantics, it was a room of low-level lighting with thick, luxurious carpet and dominated by a large four-poster bed of dark, polished wood, covered in what looked to be red satin sheets.

The other prominent feature was the chamber's occupant.

She had large, dark brown eyes and high cheekbones on a face which probably didn't quite fit into Drift's criteria for 'beautiful', but for which the term 'pretty' seemed sorely lacking. Her skin was a golden brown not too dissimilar to his own in tone and she would have been an unremarkable, if pleasing sight in most other contexts were it not for one detail: the entire rear of her skull, from the top of her forehead to the nape of her neck, had been either replaced or coated with shiny metal. There was not a hair on her head higher or further back than her eyebrows, which were so dark as to be almost black, and raised high in fear.

She stared at him, wide-eyed, and spoke in a whisper. 'Who are you?'

Drift kept her covered, checking the rest of the room over quickly. There didn't seem to be any shadowy corners, or anything convenient for someone else to be hiding in or under. So far as he could tell there were only the two of them there, although there were two internal doors leading off from the main chamber: regular wood-effect plastic from the look of them, not like the metal airlock he'd just stepped through, or the one facing it on the opposite side of the chamber.

He focused on the girl again, raising the rifle slightly to show he was serious. 'Where's Kelsier?'

The girl didn't speak, but twitched her silvered head in the direction of the airlock on the far side of the room. Drift nodded towards the other doors. 'What're these?'

'Kitchen,' she whispered, another tilt of her head indicating the one to her left. Then she looked to her right. 'Washroom.'

Drift skirted the bed carefully, trying to make sure he kept focused on her while still being aware of the rest of his surroundings, until his hip was nudging the door she'd said was to the kitchen. He scowled at her. 'Don't move.'

She nodded meekly.

He bumped the door open with his hip and spun through, sweeping the rifle's barrel across what did indeed prove to be a small but well-appointed kitchen. He debated opening the drawers to ensure they weren't some sort of facade concealing a hiding place, but decided against it. It was clearly just a damn kitchen, and he didn't have Kelsier pegged as the sort of man who was paranoid enough to build a bolt-hole into a kitchen located in a secret network of tunnels in the middle of a lonely asteroid. You had to draw the line somewhere.

The girl hadn't moved, but he still kept an eye on her as he moved around to check the washroom. Again, everything seemed normal, and there were certainly no hiding places among the shiny tiles and chrome finish. He backed out again and regarded the girl steadily. She looked back at him, her expression hard to read but certainly not hostile.

'What's through there?' he asked, indicating the airlock which was now behind him.

The girl shrugged. 'I don't know. I'm not allowed out of this room.'

Drift nodded slowly. 'What's your name?'

Her voice was the barest whisper this time. 'Emily.'

'Well then, Emily,' Drift said as reassuringly as he could, cautiously taking one hand off his rifle, 'just keep your hands where I can see them. I'm going to take this sheet off to make sure you're not hiding any weapons from me.'

The girl clutched the sheet up to her chest even tighter, if anything. 'But—'

'I just need to know you're not going to shoot me in the back,' Drift told her. 'That's all, I promise.' He didn't wait for her to reply, but grabbed the sheet and pulled.

The girl resisted for a moment, but only a moment; then the fabric slid from between her fingers and Drift yanked the sheets aside to reveal the rest of the bed, empty of anything remotely resembling a weapon unless someone had found a way to make a pillow deadly. It brought into sight Emily's torso, which was slim and toned and had its modesty vaguely protected by underclothes that had certainly been designed for appearance rather than warmth, and also Emily's legs, which were long and shapely.

And made entirely of metal, from the hip joints downwards.

Drift blinked for a second in surprise, then dragged his gaze back up to the girl's face and, inevitably, her shiny scalp. 'What—'

Now her expression changed, anger flashing over her face and turning it almost feral. 'Don't you dare pity me!' She moved suddenly, bringing her legs around and under her into a crouch on the bed. Something else glinted at the nape of her neck: what looked like a metal spinal sheath, running down from the back of her skull.

Drift shook his head slowly. 'I wasn't . . . look, my business isn't with you.' This was all rather more of a headfuck than he'd anticipated. 'It's with Kelsier.'

Emily's expression changed again, the anger fading into a tight alertness. 'Are you going to kill him?'

'Perhaps.'

'Can I watch?'

Drift tried to suppress a grimace. He didn't know what Nicolas Kelsier had done to this girl, but part of his mind was offering suggestions about it that he didn't really want to consider too closely. *Her legs* . . . He shook the images away; whatever had happened here, he had no desire to go in after Kelsier with this girl at his back. The last thing he needed was for an overenthusiastic amateur to see a chance for revenge and get in the way at the wrong moment.

'No,' he told her instead, 'you need to get out of here.' He gestured towards the airlock he'd entered by. 'There's Europan troops taking over this rock right now. Go find them, or head for the hangar bay. Either way, as soon as you see someone yell out that Ichabod Drift sent you.'

'Ichabod Drift?'

He tried a grin. 'Don't wear it out!' She stared at him blankly, and he shrugged mentally. You couldn't win them all. 'Seriously, go on. Oh, and if you take the left fork out there you'll find a big ol' Maori with a gun and a bad temper.' *I hope. So long as Apirana hasn't bled out yet, or lost consciousness or something.* 'So you might want to take the right fork, actually. It'll mean less explaining.'

She studied him for a long moment, dark eyes wide and calculating, then nodded slowly and backed away across the bed, eyes still on him. She pulled a white robe up from somewhere and slipped it around herself, then sidestepped towards the airlock which led to the tunnels beyond. Drift noticed that her feet, which even had individual toes, seemed to be shod in something dark, possibly rubber, for traction.

'Go on,' he said when she hesitated, 'get going.'

Emily didn't reply. She just nodded once, soberly, and activated the door. It slid aside and she stepped through, then turned in a whirl of white and silver and disappeared almost silently. The door hissed shut behind her and Drift was left with just the empty bedchamber.

'Well,' he muttered to himself, 'that wasn't at all weird.' He turned to the next door's keypad and, on the basis that it had worked so far, keyed in the same five-digit access code.

It worked again. The doors slid apart and he stepped through into the centre of Nicolas Kelsier's operation.

It was not, in truth, particularly imposing. It was

about half the size of the *Jonah*'s cargo bay in area, with a few terminal stations scattered about and humming stacks lining the walls. There were also multiple display screens, now showing nothing but static thanks to Jenna rerouting the signal from the asteroid's surveillance cameras, and another security door across the room from where he'd entered. Attached to the wall on his far left was an icon, perhaps two feet high and about half that across: a sleek black rectangle of stone, possibly obsidian, with a lattice of gold lines running across it in geometric shapes. Underneath it, with his back to him and furiously doing something at a terminal, was Nicolas Kelsier.

'What is it?' the old man barked, not turning around.

'*Hola, Señor Kelsier*,' Drift replied, sighting down the barrel of his rifle, '*se acabó*.' He remembered a second too late that Kelsier had never shown much of an aptitude with Spanish and, unwilling to let a dramatic line go unheard, repeated himself in English. 'It's over.'

He saw Kelsier stiffen as he was speaking. Then the old, grey head turned slightly and he saw the gleam of a pale blue eye swivelling towards him. '*Ichabod*. I might have known you would show up to be the little Mexican cherry topping off this shit-storm.'

'It seems you'd forgotten how hard I am to kill,' Drift remarked. 'No, don't turn around.' He kept the rifle pointing at Kelsier and pulled Jenna's drive out of his belt pouch with his free hand, then slotted it casually and quietly into an access port in the nearest terminal.

'I concede, it was rather foolish of me to set a trap for you by expecting you to actually be *on time*,' Kelsier spat. 'It seems you can't even manage a simple delivery job these days.'

'They're big words coming from someone who's having his hideout taken over by a bunch of troops from his former employers, brought here by yours truly,' Drift snorted. 'What the hell were you trying to achieve by nuking an entire fucking *city*, Nicolas? How is that fair payback for being fired?' He paused, aware that the clock was ticking for Apirana, but unable not to ask the next question. 'And what the hell did you do to the girl?'

Kelsier turned, in spite of Drift's instructions to the contrary, seemingly ignoring the rifle trained on him. His expression was flat and shut off, an expression Drift had seen many times. 'The girl? What have you done with her?'

'Never you mind,' Drift retorted. His eyes were drawn again to the icon on the wall. 'That's a circuit cult symbol, isn't it? What happened? You got older and things started to fail? You felt the need to cheat death as long as possible?' Suddenly, the old man's penchant for augmented muscle didn't seem as wholly prosaic as it had initially. 'Took a liking to machines over humanity?'

'Machines are reliable,' Kelsier replied steadily, his rasping voice still holding the weary tone of a teacher with an exceptionally dim student. 'Machines are logical, unlike my former employers. I arranged piracy for them on a grand scale for a decade or more, and they never thought I might decide to cut out the middlemen when it came to my wages? They took issue with it and accused me of corruption, but how can you accuse someone of stealing *from* you what they already stole *for* you? Humans are a vile mess of hypocrisy. If a machine is functioning properly and you tell it what to do in a language it understands, it follows your instructions. Which is more than can be said for the man in front of me.'

'And isn't that just bad luck for you,' Drift snorted. 'Right, chat's over. Put your hands on your head and make for the door, old man. There's a lot of heavily armed people outside who are just *dying* to meet you.'

'And when I tell them that I hired *you* to deliver that bomb? What then?' Kelsier asked, hands still at his sides. 'You can't just kill me; they'll want me alive, to stand trial—'

'Yeah, I wouldn't be too certain about that,' Drift cut him off. 'You committed an act of war, Nicolas. Or terrorism, at the very least. You taught the Europans well. Yeah, they *might* want to interrogate you a bit, but they might just shoot you dead. But then that's them doing it, not me.' He gestured with his rifle. 'Not that I won't, if you give me cause to. C'mon, move.'

'Still, your position would be untenable,' Kelsier mused. 'You're not the sort of man who will sacrifice himself to take down an enemy, you would always rather run and hide and slink away . . .'

'Do I look like I'm slinking?' Drift demanded, hefting his rifle. 'Seriously, you old bastard, I will shoot you in the leg and drag you, if I have to.'

'You'd need evidence of another ship being involved,' Kelsier continued, 'evidence which you wouldn't have.' His pale blue gaze sharpened suddenly. 'Unless your slicer was *falsifying my records*!'

Drift very carefully didn't look back at the drive he'd plugged in. 'Enough speculation, Nicolas. You go see what the Europans will do with you, or I swear to your shiny god I will shoot you and drag you there. Your choice.'

The old man's face twisted into a sneer. 'Your mistake, Ichabod, is that you're happy to use machines for your gain, but you don't *understand* them.' He started to raise his hands towards his head, the fingers of his natural one resting on the back of their mechanical counterpart. 'For example, were you aware that nearly all augmentations are manufactured to the same specifications? Observe . . . or not, in your case.'

He pressed something on the back of his metal hand just as the knuckles were directed forwards, and half of Drift's vision went black.

'What the . . .' Drift automatically reached up to his mechanical eye, an involuntary movement which caused the barrel of his weapon to waver for half a second before he recovered himself. It was half a second too long: Kelsier had grabbed the nearest object – a datapad, judging by the very brief look Drift got at it – and flung it as hard as he could. Drift tried to bat it out of the air, but with his depth perception suddenly gone all he could manage was to flail ineffectually at it and the missile struck him on the temple. He staggered back, the vision in his natural eye fuzzing momentarily from the impact, and pulled the trigger on his rifle with the weapon pointed in Kelsier's general direction.

There were a few *spanging* sounds as rounds struck metal, but whatever he'd hit hadn't inconvenienced the old man any; as he tried to refocus something hard smashed into his jaw from his blind side. There was a moment of shocked numbness before his nerves started screaming at him in white-hot pain, and it was a second or two before he realised that he was on the floor.

'You *stupid* little fuck,' Kelsier hissed in his ear as cold metal fingers clamped around Drift's throat, 'you always have to posture and grandstand, don't you? Lucky for me, really. Please note, as you choke to death, that I didn't start gloating until *after* I'd begun killing you!'

The old man was right. The strength in his fingers was far greater than that possessed by a normal human hand, and Drift could feel his throat being crushed. He pulled at the death grip desperately to no avail and then, with his vision fogging again for a second and probably terminal time, reached up to claw at Kelsier's face. For a moment the old man leaned back as Drift's finger raked at his eyes and the pressure abated, but then Kelsier raised his left hand to protect himself and swat Drift away.

His sight was almost gone now and his heartbeat was pounding in his ears, each thump louder and faster as his brain clamoured for the blood that Kelsier's grip was denying it.

Boom.

Any second now and he would pass out. Then the old man would finish the job of crushing his windpipe, and he would never wake up.

BOOM.

There was something warm and wet on his face. Had the pressure in his head caused a blood vessel to burst in his nose?

No.

Wait.

Owwww . . .

The rush of circulation being restored nearly made him pass out in its own way, but although he still felt like something was crushing his throat, the cold sensation of metal fingers was gone. A second later and his vision returned; first simply brightness, then resolving into lines of lights in the ceiling. His hearing was coming back too, as the thunder of his own heartbeat faded from his ears. There was a buzz of voices now and, approaching from his right, a set of footsteps.

He turned his head weakly, both neck and jaw

protesting the movement, and his left eye found itself looking up at a silhouette. There was no hat or coat, of course, but the familiar shape of a Crusader 920 held loosely in its hands gave the owner's identity away nonetheless.

'You're still alive, then,' Tamara Rourke said, crouching down. She'd removed the helmet of her atmo-suit, and he felt a faint puff of breath as she snorted. 'You're an idiot, you know that?'

'So I've been told,' Drift replied. Or tried to, anyway; his jaw shrieked at him halfway through the first syllable, so he settled for a mewling whimper of pain instead. He wiped at his face gingerly and inspected his fingers. They were smeared with blood.

'Oh get up, you baby,' Rourke told him, without a shred of pity. Drift rolled his head to the left and rather wished he hadn't, because not three feet away was what remained of Nicolas Kelsier's, attached to his rather more intact body. He looked back up at Rourke and pointed at her, then mimed firing a gun with his fingers.

She nodded confirmation. 'Jenna radioed; she seemed to think you and Apirana might have bitten off more than you could chew, so she suggested I look in and told us where the closest entrance to us should be. Quite a little tableau the two of you made when the door opened. It might have been better had I not had to kill him, but . . .' She shrugged. 'I couldn't have him strangling the owner of Agent Rourke's ship, could I?' She looked around, concern painting her features. 'Where *is* A., anyway?'

Drift sat up gingerly and pointed back towards the

door he'd entered by, then left to hopefully indicate the correct tunnel. He mimed a gun again and jabbed himself in the ribs.

'Shit,' Rourke muttered, and looked up at the nearest Europan. 'Get a med team through there and to the left ay-sap! One of my crew is hurt!'

The tone of command had the soldier's hand halfway to her comm before she even knew what was happening. To her credit, she did remember to pause and look over at Lieutenant Hamann for approval, but the Europan officer waved the go-ahead and seconds later a ten-person squad was opening the airlock, taking point for a pair of medics. Drift hoped they wouldn't spend too long gawking at the bedroom before they went and found the big Maori.

'Let's get you up,' Rourke said loudly, offering him her hand. He gripped it and she helped him to his feet, then grabbed him as he wobbled and leaned close to his ear.

'*Did you plant it?*'

He directed his eyes towards where Jenna's drive was still plugged unobtrusively into a terminal. Rourke turned and moved casually towards it, or as casually as one could while stepping over a corpse with a ruined head, and ended up next to the terminal in question looking around as Europan troops bustled through, searching for non-existent threats.

'Well Lieutenant,' Rourke announced loudly, turning away again, 'it looks like you'll need to get your experts in to take a look at all this data.' The slot behind her was empty now, and Drift was sure that only he noticed her fingers fiddling briefly with the pouch at her belt.

Hamann's eyes narrowed, clearly suspecting something. 'I would have thought the GIA would have been interested in the contents of these databanks.'

'I've no doubt we would be,' Rourke responded off-handedly, 'but that's not my remit. *My* team's job was to eliminate the threat of Nicolas Kelsier. I'm sure my superiors would appreciate being informed of anything you find in these databanks via the usual channels, but quite frankly I have neither the resources, the expertise nor the patience to trawl through them myself when one of my team was killed back on Hroza Major and I've had two more injured here today.' She sighed. 'If top brass want to know every figure and detail they can damn well send a tech team out.'

'Amen to *that*,' Hamann grinned, his suspicions apparently allayed by the time-honoured practice of passing the buck. He raised his voice. 'Okay everyone! If it doesn't pose a threat, leave it be! The Captain's mopping up the last of these pirate scum, so let's do a last sweep on the way back to the bay and make sure we haven't missed anything!'

Rourke pulled Drift close as the Europans began to do their last checks. 'You sure it worked?'

Drift just shrugged, then gestured piteously at his jaw. He was fairly sure it was dislocated, and just when he thought the pain couldn't get worse it went and proved him wrong.

'Don't get your hopes up,' Rourke told him, the vaguest hints of a smile playing at the corners of her mouth, 'I rather like you like this.'

The trudge back to the hangar bay was a

thoroughly miserable one for Drift, with every incautious step sending a spike of pain through his face. Finally it seemed his whimpering got more than Rourke could bear, and she pulled him to a halt.

'You've got two choices,' she told him flatly, 'you wait for the Europan medics to finish up with all the urgent cases, which involves a hell of a lot of gunshot wounds including Apirana's, and you keep quiet while you wait . . . or I fix your jaw here and now.'

Drift had never needed to convey alarmed consternation using only his eyebrows before, but now seemed like the perfect time to give it a try.

'It's not like I haven't had medical training,' Rourke sighed. She leaned her Crusader against the wall and flexed her fingers. 'Granted, it was a while ago. And granted, you'd normally get painkillers, but I get the feeling those are going to be in short supply around here. The sooner we get this sorted the better. Ready?'

Drift was still trying to work out how to indicate to the contrary without either speaking or shaking his head when Rourke reached up to his jaw, tightened her grip on it, and—

'*Arrrrrrrgh!*' There was a white-hot moment and his jaw suddenly worked again, at least after a fashion, and he set about testing it out around some blasphemy. '*Jesús, Maria, Madre de Dios!*'

'Careful,' Rourke advised him placidly as he doubled over, clutching his face in renewed pain, 'if you open your mouth too wide it might displace again. And we can't be having that.'

'This is some sort of revenge for me not telling you . . . things, isn't it?' Drift moaned as best he could around near-clenched teeth, falling into step behind her as she picked up her rifle again and continued on towards the hangar bay.

'I don't know what you mean . . .'

The bay itself was alive with action. It had been depressurised to allow the arrival of the Europan frigate's two shuttles and then pressurised again, and now the twin sleek shapes were taking on a mixture of healthy troops, the wounded (of which there were fewer than Drift had feared) and prisoners (of which there were less than he'd expected). He caught a glimpse of white and saw Emily being ushered on board by two troopers, and wondered again exactly what the girl's story was. Still, the Europans would doubtless find out.

'Where's A.?' he asked, worry tugging at his gut.

'Already on board,' Rourke assured him. 'He's been given fairly high priority, apparently; I guess being a GIA operative does have some fringe benefits. Everyone seems to want to keep in our good books.'

'If only Kelsier had known,' Drift snorted, lowering his voice a little, 'maybe we could have avoided this whole mess.'

'Just take a look at this, Ichabod,' Rourke said in the same low tone, gesturing around them at the wounded and, here and there, the bodies of the dead. 'This all happened because you took on a job without consulting the rest of us. Was it worth it?'

Drift took in their surroundings again, feeling the sour taste of bile at the back of his throat, and shook his head wearily. 'No.'

'Well then—'

'I mean, this didn't happen because of me,' Drift

continued, looking down at his partner. '*This* happened because I convinced the rest of you that we could do this. That seven no-hopers in a rust bucket could string together enough bullshit to make this fly.'

For the first time that he could remember, Tamara Rourke looked stunned.

'I'm not saying we should do this sort of thing for *fun*,' Drift added quickly, casting a furtive glance around, 'but c'mon – if I'd suggested a scam like this to you when our lives weren't on the line, what would you have said?'

'I'd have told you that you were insane,' Rourke replied flatly.

'*Exactly!*' Drift beamed, painfully. 'And you'd have been wrong!'

'Just because it worked *this time* doesn't mean it wasn't insane!' Rourke sighed. 'Seriously, Ichabod; I've seen men and women die in front of me today. So have you, for that matter. Are you telling me that doesn't bother you at all?'

'Sure it does,' Drift agreed, 'but it would bother me a hell of a lot *more* if it had been me. Or you, or Jenna, or—'

'That's not what I—'

'I know, but it's what *I* meant.' Drift sighed. 'Look, war is just sending other people to do what you don't want to risk doing yourself, right? These people are soldiers, they've signed up to go to war; we sent them against a terrorist who tried to nuke them. The only bit of information they didn't have is which bunch of luckless sods were duped into carrying the damn bomb in the first place.' He shrugged. 'I can live with that. Don't tell me you can't, Miss GIA Agent.'

'This might shock you, but there was a reason I left the Agency,' Rourke said quietly. 'Even *my* conscience could only take so much.' She sighed. 'Very well. We had limited options, we took a stupid gamble and I guess it sort of worked, for most of us.'

'Mmm,' Drift stepped carefully out of the path of a Europan medical buggy. 'We're not going back for Micah, I take it?'

'The Hrozan authorities have his documents,' Rourke shrugged, 'and I told them to cremate him. I guess they might find his relatives, if he has any. But no, I don't think it would be a good idea for us to go back there.'

'Yeah, I'm thinking we should stay out of any Europan space for a while,' Drift snorted, 'just in case there have been any new messages from the Ministry of Defence. Let them fix Apirana up, arrange to rendezvous with them back at Hroza but just fuck off instead?'

'Makes sense to me,' Rourke nodded, activating her comm. They'd reached the *Jonah*, which looked decidedly sad set against the backdrop of two Europan military shuttles. 'Jia, fancy letting us in?'

+*Sure thing.*+ The entrance ramp hissed and started to lower. +*Jenna came over a couple of minutes ago. Are we taking any troops back out?*+

'No,' Rourke told her, 'oddly enough they seemed to want their own pilots back. Can't imagine why.'

+*Fuck the lot of you.*+

The *Keiko* disconnected from the *Draco* with a palpable shudder and the two craft drifted apart. Jia gently fed power to the manoeuvring rockets once they were a polite distance away and the pilot of the Europan frigate did the same, heading away on a vector to set up an Alcubierre jump back towards the Perun System.

Drift clapped Apirana gently on the shoulder. 'How're you feeling, big man?'

'Rough,' the Maori admitted, rubbing at his side. It wasn't that Europan military medics weren't used to dealing with gunshot wounds, but the bullet had grazed a kidney and the human body still had limits. 'But I'll live.'

'Glad to hear it,' Drift smiled. He watched the stars wheel in front of them as Jia turned their vessel's nose away from the gas giant they'd been orbiting. His right eye was working again, having been reactivated by a Europan medic who had some knowledge of augmentations, and it was a relief to have his full vision back. 'First order of business: to the dead.' He picked up a glass tumbler into which he'd measured a slug of whisky, and raised it to eye level, then paused, considering his words.

'I think it's safe to say that Micah van Schaken was a man we didn't know well. He had his own history of which he never shared much, but we know he had been a part of the Europan Commonwealth's Frontier Defence Unit, and left it for his own reasons.' Now came the hard part. 'I . . . find it hard to speak of the positives one is supposed to at times like these. Micah was not always easy company, and I can't say he spread happiness and light wherever he went. In truth, he was more cynical than even I liked, and had a dark sense of humour. However, we don't know his past and so we won't judge him for how he was in the present. What I can say for him is that he was hired to fight for us, and this he did whenever asked to.'

'And sometimes when he hadn't been,' Rourke put in. Drift glared at her, but the former agent raised her own glass. 'Micah was more than just a grunt with a gun. He was intelligent, and he saw things others didn't.' She swallowed visibly and continued in a voice which, had Drift not known better, he would have thought was slightly choked by emotion. 'The Laughing Man killed him first. That's a compliment to Micah, in its own sick way.'

'He died trying to warn us,' Apirana rumbled, raising a glass of water. 'I've known mercs that would've run for it once they realised they'd walked into an ambush. Micah din't.'

'He never called me for cheating at cards,' Kuai added, 'even when I think he knew.' He looked around at the rest of them. 'What? I don't cheat *you* guys!'

'Don't worry,' Jenna told him, 'we know no one could be as bad as you if they were cheating.'

'See?' Kuai paused, then frowned. 'Hey!'

The young slicer's smile faded as she lifted her own glass. 'I . . . didn't know Micah as well as the rest of you, and hadn't known him for as long. I will say that you always knew where you stood with him. He was one of the most honest people I've ever met; he didn't try to make himself out to be a nicer or better person than he was.'

All eyes turned to Jia. The pilot swivelled around in her chair, picked up her glass and eyed it thoughtfully. She opened her mouth as if to speak, closed it again, then nodded decisively.

'He was great in bed.'

There was a stunned silence for a second before Jia burst into uproarious laughter. 'Your *faces* . . .!'

Kuai looked like he was about to have a fit. 'What . . . *that's not funny!*'

'Do I look like I'm joking?' Jia grinned at him. 'Hell yeah, it's true! We just kept it quiet. Don't mean you don't all look like brain-dead goldfish!'

Drift snorted. 'Well, then: to Micah!' He sank his whisky and waited for the others to do the same. Kuai muttered darkly under his breath in Mandarin and Jenna was still staring at Jia in apparent shock, but they finally followed suit.

'Second order of business: to the living,' Drift continued. 'This has probably been the biggest mess I've been caught up in since I packed in my last career, and it's obvious I made a few bad calls along the way. Micah knew the risks, but it was still my scheme that got him killed; my scheme which saw Jenna trapped in a ship with a bunch of pirates and terrorists; my scheme which got Kuai shot in the leg and Apirana shot in the kidney, and me nearly strangled to death. And as Tamara has pointed out to me already,' he added, nodding towards Rourke, 'it was my call that set this whole circus in motion in the first place. So here we are, with Kelsier no longer a threat and, yeah, the Europans might not be too pleased with us once Rybak reports back and finds out that we tricked her, but there's a lot of galaxy that they don't own.

'What I'm getting around to is that, while I wouldn't want to lose any of you, I'd understand if you might want to jump ship now things have quietened down a bit. Now, I'm not going to be making any major detours in order to drop you off, but what we *do* have, hopefully, is some profits to share out before you make your choice.' He nodded towards Jenna. 'Miss McIlroy?'

Jenna held up the small drive which Drift had plugged into Kelsier's mainframe. Its most immediate use had been to search for and erase any reference to the *Keiko*, the *Jonah* or any of them by name, just in case the Europans had wanted to comb through for data there and then, but it had a backup function as well. 'Moment of truth, folks.'

She inserted it into her terminal's access port and danced her fingers across the interface, then sat back and waited. Drift watched in concern as her lips pursed slightly and her eyebrows lowered.

'Problem?'

'I'm just wondering whether we should collate them all or simply take an account each,' Jenna replied, a slow smile spreading over her face.

'Say what?' Drift found himself standing behind her chair without any memory of crossing the intervening space, but the lines of text on the screen didn't make any immediate sense to him.

'Ladies and gentlemen of the *Keiko*,' Jenna announced grandly, 'Nicolas Kelsier had *several* accounts set up in different places across the galaxy to draw on at his convenience . . . and we have the access codes for all of them.'

Drift blinked. The numbers had suddenly jumped into focus, and they spoke to him in a language he liked very much. He beckoned Rourke over. 'What do you reckon?'

'Hmm.' Tamara Rourke studied the screen for a moment, then reached out a dark, slim finger to tap one of the highest figures. 'I think the Rassvet System. It's Red Star territory, a nice long way from any Europans who might come nosing around. Besides, your Russian needs some work.'

'Right you are.' Drift drew himself up, feeling as though a warm glow was suffusing him. Sure, his jaw hurt like hell and an entire government conglomerate might be interested in hunting him down (well, technically two, if the Federation of African States ever got wind he was still alive), but he was *rich*.

All he had to do was go and get it.

'Pilot!' he declaimed with a flourish. 'To the Rassvet System!'

'Aye, Captain!' Jia shocked him by making a passable attempt at a salute, then spun around in her chair to start programming the nav computer. Apirana grinned and fist-bumped Drift on his way out of the cockpit, with a still-muttering Kuai trailing him like an undersized Chinese shadow. Rourke moved away to take up the co-pilot's seat next to Jia, and Drift was left standing at the back of Jenna's chair.

'So how did your Europan friend like her introduction to the world of galactic espionage?' he asked.

'Sara?' Jenna smiled slightly. 'I think it was all a little . . . hectic for her. She was very eager to get back onto a Europan ship in the end. I think she missed her quiet little surveillance job.'

'I'll bet,' Drift chuckled, then sobered. 'How about you? How's the girl from Franklin Major coping?'

'Franklin *Minor*,' Jenna corrected him absentmindedly. She sighed. 'I'll tell you this, Captain, I never want to have to do something like that again. I mean, spending hours on a shuttle wondering if you're going to be captured and killed or . . . or worse . . . that's not anything I want to live through a second time. Or having to open a hangar bay to a vacuum and kill some men to prevent them from trying to blow their way into a shuttle to come and get me. I'd never killed anyone before today, or yesterday, or whenever it was now. I don't like it.'

'I understand,' Drift replied, his heart sinking. 'So this means you'll be wanting to go your own way once you've got your share of the profits?'

Jenna turned to face him. '*Hell* no!'

Drift frowned, pleased but puzzled. 'But I thought—'

He was cut off by Jenna standing up and jabbing him in the chest. 'It means that next time, we plan this shit *properly*!'

I will start my acknowledgements with an apology. I've portrayed many nationalities and cultures in this depiction of the future, but Apirana Wahawaha the Maori is probably the most notable and detailed, yet the furthest from my own direct experience. Apirana himself was inspired by another Maori character created many years ago by my friend Will, and I am indebted to Will for allowing me to use elements of that creation in my novel. However, even allowing for the centuries between us and the adventures of the *Keiko*, I'm sure I have got things wrong regarding Apirana and his background: terms, language or details of culture. I apologise to any and all of the Maori people should my writing inadvertently offend through inaccuracy or ignorance, and I hope any such flaws may be overlooked (or even better, corrected: you can find me on the internet).

With that out of the way, thanks go first to my

agent Rob Dinsdale without whom this all would have been, if not strictly impossible, at the very least highly improbable. Until he took me on I didn't fully appreciate the level of assistance a good agent provides.

Thanks also go to the Crown Prince of Grimdark, Luke Scull, who put me in touch with Rob in the first place. Projectile weapons and a nuclear bomb, and I'm still nowhere near your bodycount.

Massive thanks to Michael, Emily, and everyone else at Del Rey UK for the fantastic work put into making this book a reality. The feedback, the advice, the awesome cover art . . . all of it. It means a hell of a lot to have people investing so much in stories I made up in my head.

Thanks to Ande for help with the Spanish when Drift decides that one language just isn't enough. Any errors in translation are mine, not his. Thanks to Carrie for pointing out that New Shinjuku was probably a stupid name for a planet (even though I decided to use it anyway). Thanks to Delwyn for letting me know that a Maori accent is not necessarily the same as a New Zealand accent, and providing me with useful links. Legend.

Thanks to my parents for ensuring I grew up in a house full of books, even if they always seemed mildly perplexed at my choice of reading material.

Thanks to Blaise, for being on the other end of a messenger program to bounce ideas off and for being my general writing partner-in-crime. Thanks also to anyone else who read and gave me feedback on any drafts of this novel, at whatever stage.

Thanks to you, the reader of these acknowledgements, for buying this book. Assuming you bought it. If you didn't buy it, but you enjoyed it, maybe consider buying the next one? Cat food and pre-frozen rodents don't grow on trees, you know, and I have mouths to feed.

Finally, and most importantly, thanks to my wife Janine for not being the least bit bothered by my tendency over the last couple of years to disappear upstairs and spend a lot of time inventing worlds, for co-owning our awesome pets, for being supportive without being intrusive, and for generally being amazing.

Also available from Del Rey:

IMPULSE

By Dave Bara

**A remote solar system
A fragile galactic alliance
An interstellar war is on the brink of eruption . . .**

When the Lightship Impulse is attacked without
provocation, Lt. Peter Cochrane, son of the Grand
Admiral, is sent to investigate.

His first deep space mission, this isn't what Peter
has spent three years in training for. Surrounded by
strangers and following secret orders, is he willing
to do what it takes to keep the alliance together?
Even mutiny?

**Book one in *The Lightship Chronicles*, a ground-
breaking new action-adventure space opera from
Dave Bara**

DEL REY

Also available from Del Rey:

THE EMPIRE OF TIME

By David Wingrove

There is only the war.

Otto Behr is a German agent, fighting his Russian counterparts across three millennia, manipulating history for moments in time that can change everything.

Only the remnants of two great nations stand and for Otto, the war is life itself; the last hope for his people.

But in a world where realities shift and memory is never constant, can one man's destiny be the deciding factor in a war between the empires of time?

DEL REY